*I Wished for You*

**AMY HUBERMAN**

PENGUIN

Amy Huberman is an actor and writer. She lives in Dublin with her husband and daughter. Her first novel, *Hello, Heartbreak*, was published in 2009.

PENGUIN

PENGUIN BOOKS

Published by the Penguin Group
Penguin Books Ltd, 80 Strand, London WC2R 0RL, England
Penguin Group (USA) Inc., 375 Hudson Street, New York, New York 10014, USA
Penguin Group (Canada), 90 Eglinton Avenue East, Suite 700, Toronto, Ontario, Canada M4P 2Y3
(a division of Pearson Penguin Canada Inc.)
Penguin Ireland, 25 St Stephen's Green, Dublin 2, Ireland (a division of Penguin Books Ltd)
Penguin Group (Australia), 707 Collins Street, Melbourne, Victoria 3008, Australia
(a division of Pearson Australia Group Pty Ltd)
Penguin Books India Pvt Ltd, 11 Community Centre, Panchsheel Park, New Delhi – 110 017, India
Penguin Group (NZ), 67 Apollo Drive, Rosedale, Auckland 0632, New Zealand
(a division of Pearson New Zealand Ltd)
Penguin Books (South Africa) (Pty) Ltd, Block D, Rosebank Office Park,
181 Jan Smuts Avenue, Parktown North, Gauteng 2193, South Africa

Penguin Books Ltd, Registered Offices: 80 Strand, London WC2R 0RL, England

www.penguin.com

First published by Penguin Ireland 2012
Published in Penguin Books 2013
001

Typeset by Jouve (UK), Milton Keynes
Printed in Great Britain by Clays Ltd, St Ives plc

ISBN: 978-0-141-04914-4

www.greenpenguin.co.uk

ALWAYS LEARNING                    PEARSON

For Brian

Had I the heaven's embroidered cloths,
Enwrought with golden and silver light,
The blue and the dim and the dark cloths
Of night and light and the half-light,
I would spread the cloths under your feet:
But I, being poor, have only my dreams;
I have spread my dreams under your feet;
Tread softly because you tread on my dreams

William Butler Yeats
'He Wishes for the Cloths of Heaven'

*Coronation Street* Battenberg slice in the evenings,' she said, ignoring me. 'Feck it now altogether! How am I going to be able to look at Deirdre's face every night without something sweet to take the edge off it?'

If she was going to fit into that dress in six weeks' time, she was going to have to give up more than her *Coronation Street* Battenberg slice. She was going to have to get her jaw wired and seven-eighths of her stomach removed. Pure and simple. And I wasn't sure there was any nice way of saying that. But when I recommended she try on a bigger size, she looked at me like I was an assassin and told me that if Dolores Mangan from the Tuesday Tulips Golf Society found out she was wearing a sixteen, my life would not be worth living.

Humph. What was left of my life. Because, as I've touched on already, *I was never getting out of here*!

She had always been one of my more . . . 'tricky' clients. The first time she came to me, she wanted me to find her a pair of stiletto runners. That's right: runners with a stiletto heel. The woman is nearly sixty. She'd seen them on Katy Perry at the EMAs and now she wanted them for the ten-kilometre Walk In the Phoenix Park charity luncheon for the Irish Donkey Society or something, because she'd heard that Helen Naughton had ordered an Alexander McQueen shift dress she'd seen on Cheryl Cole and this was the only way she could think to trump her. No: there wasn't much logic to it.

I had to keep telling myself things would get better. That this was only a stop-gap. That my life would not be reduced to stuffing middle-aged women, like sausagemeat, into tubes of turquoise taffeta for ever.

Out of all my clients, Mrs Macnamara was the worst. She was the Moriarty to my Holmes, the criminal mastermind of *fashion* crime. I spent my life trying to outwit her in so many ways, like Holmes himself, *sans* pipe, to ensure justice in the world of style.

Sometimes it had got messy. For her birthday party last year we *might* have ended up in a physical brawl. There *might* have been a number of headlocks involved. And one Chinese burn. *One*. I just couldn't let her go to her own party dressed as a Pussycat Doll. And a Chinese burn was the only way I could get her to drop the leather bra.

She thanked me for it in the end. Only when Nicole Scherzinger ended up 'slated' in the 'Rated or Slated' column of *Starz* the following week. But still. The incident was so bad I developed two new worry lines between my eyebrows that randomly formed the image of a tiny Chinese man when I frowned.

But today was the worst I'd ever seen her. She was choosing a dress for her daughter's wedding and, honestly, it was like having all your teeth pulled out one by one with no anaesthetic when you already had a headache. And two broken arms. And the flu. And your period. And a really bad paper cut.

*And I was already running seriously late!*

'Okay, pretend you're in the church and the bride arrives. Cue uplifting music, cue sopranos heralding the arrival. Blah, blah, blah. Then you see me. Cue Dolores Mangan looking like she might vomit from jealousy. Grace Harte: Is. This. *The*. Outfit?'

I thought *I* was going to vomit. Did that count?

'Mrs Macnamara, I have to say again, I really do think *not* clashing with the bridesmaids is quite important. Seeing as it's your daughter's wedding.'

'Exactly. *My* daughter's wedding. As in, it's my right to look the best. I only have Luleeluleelu's best interest at heart, you know, Grace. She *hates* the limelight so I'm very willing to stand up to the plate and make sure she doesn't get overwhelmed.'

Luleeluleelu? I hope to God that was a pet name. Or I was calling Child Services. Or Lisa, to laugh about it at length.

'Now, if the bridesmaids want to wear a wishy-washy pink then by all means let them. I certainly won't stand in their way. But I am not going to spend the next four weeks in Marbella turning half-caste, only to come home and slither down the aisle in some dishwater-coloured piece of shite. Do you get me, Grace? Well? Do you?'

4

I wanted to say that, no, I didn't get her at all. But I was too queasy, hungry and tired for an argument. And I was partially paralysed down my right side from being scrunched in a ball on the fitting-room floor for far longer than would be deemed safe by any doctor the world over. Or an actor-doctor on *Casualty*, at least.

I nodded numbly.

'Just ask your own mother,' she rambled on. 'I'm sure she made sure she looked her best on your big day.'

Huh?

'Oh, I'm not married,' I said, wondering what made her think that I was, seeing as I had no wedding ring on my finger. Neither had I mentioned a husband, which I think is a pretty important requisite when it comes to being married.

'*You're not married?*' she shrieked.

Christ alive, suddenly she was wailing at me like she'd just seen her entire family shot dead. She seemed to be having palpitations. Balls, I didn't know the twenty-four-hour nurse-line number.

'But you're a very pretty girl,' she said, gasping for breath. 'And, oh, Jesus, didn't you tell me you were, you know . . . turning?'

Turning? Turning what? Turning white from lack of food and air? Turning blue from being forced to sit in a Cambodian jail stress position for so long? Turning against religion in this godless dressing room?

She paused and looked around the fitting room furtively. Really? *Really?* Did she think there was another person in this tiny shoebox we somehow hadn't noticed before now? She closed her eyes, like she was about to implode, then exhaled dramatically. 'Turning . . . *thirty!*'

She said it like I had contracted a terminal illness. Then she sort of withered against the wall and, bless her, she looked all worried and vulnerable and I suddenly wanted to hug her and tell her that it was all going to be okay.

'You're so brave,' she whimpered, after I did end up hugging her and telling her that me turning thirty without being married was really not that big a disaster. We stood there in an awkward embrace as I patted her back while she stroked my hair.

'I mean, I know there's others out there far worse off, like all those people who lost their homes in the floods,' she sniffed, 'but there you are, trucking along like a trooper, as best you can. My Luleeluleeluloopsypop will be married before her twenty-sixth birthday, would you believe? Lucky, *lucky* Luleeluleelu. But I suppose we can't all be that fortunate.'

She cupped my face in her hands, leaned into me and, sounding just as sombre as Humphrey Bogart saying goodbye to Ingrid Bergman in *Casablanca*, said, 'My God, but sometimes life can be very hard.'

I mumbled about us always having Paris, clearly losing all reason.

She looked confused.

Who could blame her?

Though she had my cheeks mushed together quite firmly, I managed to articulate a proper response: 'Well, thank you for your concern, but I do actually have a boyfriend.'

'Oh?' she said, dropping my face. 'Who is he? What does he do? How long have you been together? My Luleeluleelu's fiancé is a financial accountant,' she added smugly.

A financial accountant? Was there any other kind? That was unless I'd missed something and the world of commerce had gone back to bartering farm produce.

'His name is Robbie,' I said, smiling. 'He works for a music promotions company. Oh, and we've been together seven years,' I added, thinking that would shut her up.

It didn't. It only fuelled her fire.

'Seven years!' she squealed.

Jesus, this woman was carrying on worse than I had when I'd found out that CBS was cancelling the original 90210.

'Good God, Grace. Seven years together, turning thirty, and still no ring? That boy is nothing but a time-waster. Do you want me to call him?' she asked, in a frenzy. 'Tell him how devastated you are? Tell him to ship up or shape out? Slap him around a bit? Climb down off the pot? Shit or get off the fence?'

Oh, God, not this again. 'Eh, very kind of you, but I think I'm just going to hang on in there, if that's okay with you?' I said, crossing my fingers in a mock gesture that clearly went over her head.

'Suit yourself,' she huffed. 'It's only your own life you're wasting. Now, back to me. Make. Me. Fabulous!'

I bit my lip and got back to work, smiling to myself. Imagine if Robbie'd been here to hear all that nonsense! My time-wasting no-good boyfriend!

Robbie Cotter was more than just my boyfriend: he was my whole world. We'd been together for seven fun, fantastic years and we'd even just bought our first house together. He was the one person on the whole planet who could lift me and turn me to mush at the same time. (Well, that's not entirely true: Marc Jacobs has the same effect, but Robbie knows about it and he's cool with it.)

No matter what crazy, crap or mundane nonsense goes on in my day, as soon as I turned the key in the lock at home and heard him call, 'Here's my girl!' I knew everything was going to be okay. He could dissipate a bad mood in seconds with one of his infamous 'Robbieisms'. And it wasn't just me he could make laugh: he made everyone laugh. The whole world and its mother were mad about Robbie Cotter, and I knew how lucky I was to be a part of that world.

Now if I could just get everyone to shut up and mind their own business about why we weren't engaged, we really would be laughing.

Finally, *finally*, I got out of there. I'm not saying I was nearly as brave, or that the incarceration was remotely as long, but I felt a little like that Burmese lady Aung San Suu Kyi. (Though I wasn't expecting Bono to honour me at the Mansion House or anything.)

Despite my protestations, Mrs Macnamara ended up choosing an outfit two sizes too small that made her look like a superhero from *Sesame Street*. Some sort of caped sparkly body-con dress with a canary yellow rectangular hat. Ugh, I didn't care any more. It was her funeral/daughter's wedding/*Sesame Street* superhero spin-off. I just needed to get out of there and down to Wicklow ASAP.

Just as I was making my final bolt towards the door, she stopped me in my tracks and peered down her nose at me. 'Grace, I know we don't always see eye to eye in terms of style. I can be a bit fashion-forward at times.'

I bit my lip.

'The thing is, though, in spite of . . . everything, I do think you're a nice girl. So I'm going to give you some advice from the heart. Dump that man. He's wasting your most fertile years, darling. All too soon those cutesy looks of yours will be more Rita Sullivan than Rita Hayworth. So it's time to sell, sell, sell, dear, while anyone's still interested in buying.'

Arrrgh! I was starting to fume.

'Well, let me tell you a little something in return.' I coughed. (I really needed to give up my odd sneaky cigarette.) 'Life is a box of chocolates, Mrs Macnamara, and I can assure you that my Robbie is most certainly not the Turkish Delight, or the coffee one that no one really likes – except my mum.'

That was crap. I should have said he was a secret member of the Avengers or something.

'Well, I have absolutely no idea what you're on about, Grace, but I don't have time to stand here and listen to you prattling on about confectionery.' And with that she turned on her heel and spun out of the swing doors.

Right, well, HA! That showed her!

I think.

## 2

Took me far too long to get home. My legs were still numb and pins-and-needlesy from being squashed into that shoebox for so long. I ran home like a cartoon cowboy with ox-bow-shaped legs, wondering if I had dislocated my hip.

Was possibly being a bit of a hypochondriac as usual. Like last week when I was convinced I'd developed a sixth toe on my right foot. Turned out I had a pebble caught in my sock. 'Ow, ow, ow.' I waddled around the corner and scuttled up to our front door. I still smiled every time I slid the key into the lock.

Our home. *Our home.*

'Christ alive!' I shrieked. Although I should've been used to it by now, considering this happened every time I passed through our hall: Bette Davis jumping out at me.

Not *the* Bette Davis. That would be so weird, considering she'd been dead for twenty-two years. Bette was the cat, a possessed little toe-rag that had come with the house and refused to move out. She quite liked Robbie. She despised me. I was the Joan Crawford to her Bette Davis, and she picked on me mercilessly. That's what we were called at seven Maple Street, Bette and Joan, and the bitter feud between us was even worse than the one between the original pair. 'Euch, Bette, get out of my way or I might just "forget" to leave your food out.'

She slunk over to the coat-stand, not taking her eyes off me for a nano-second, and proceeded to pee into a pair of my shoes.

'That's it, you little slapper!' I growled. 'You can roam the streets for your dinner tonight!'

I pegged it past her and raced up the stairs. I didn't have time for cat-wrestling right now (sessions have been known to last *hours*): I was running seriously late for the rehearsal dinner as it was.

I barrelled through my wardrobe, knowing this was my last chance to wear something fantastic before I was zipped, stitched, buttoned and trussed up into the hell of *Bridesmaid Revisited* tomorrow. For Rebecca Madigan of Newlands Park, Dublin 14 – the bride-to-be and one of my best friends in the whole world, a wonderful person with the biggest heart of anyone I knew, fantastic shiny brown hair, and a talent for singing Chesney Hawkes's 'The One And Only' backwards (seriously – it was amazing) – had absolutely no dress sense. What. So. Ever.

She wore gnome-shaped drop earrings and orange wellies with jeans. Once I even caught her going to the shops in an apron because she said it looked like a cute little dress.

It didn't. It looked like an apron.

Just thinking about her dress sense, I needed to lie down in a dark room and sip some iced water while someone stroked my hair. You see, where Rebecca was into crazy clothes, I was crazy into clothes. I always had been. I could 'speak clothes' before I could speak English, and my earliest memory was of having a canary yellow Babygro with brown polka dots inflicted upon me when I was barely out of the womb. Mum said it was impossible to have memories from such a young age, but I wasn't so sure. I reckoned if it was that traumatizing, it'd stick. I was convinced I'd been such a 'vomity baby' because I was repulsed by my clothes, not because I had colic, as my mother suggested.

I lived and breathed clothes. I adored clothes. If I could have eaten them I would (sometimes I've been known to kiss them, but I make an effort only to do that when I'm on my own). Whenever I couldn't sleep, I counted dresses. When I couldn't concentrate, I looked up net-a-porter.com to clear my head. If I was stressed, I went upstairs and rearranged my shoe-rack. Fashion was my currency, my fresh air, my *joie de vivre*! My 'thing'.

I loved old clothes, new clothes, and everywhere-in-between clothes. They got me charged; they got me excited; they got me wired. Rifling through an uncharted rail of dresses; picking up a display shoe and twirling it in my hand; holding up chandelier earrings to a lobe and admiring myself in a shop mirror. Jesus, it was like a junkie getting a hit. It might actually be an official addiction: if I didn't get my little hits, my skin went all itchy and I started to crave starchy foods. And if I went too long altogether it was like a scene from *Trainspotting*, except with hallucinations of shoes and handbags crawling across the ceiling.

There was nothing in the world that a hit of *Grazia* wouldn't do for me. The girls had often said that if they could eat chocolate while having sex, it would make the whole experience simply mind-blowing. But for me, combing through the Fashion Charts on page seven of *Grazia* while doing the deed might lead to the best orgasm *ever*. I'd yet to convince Robbie, and he seemed a little freaked out by the whole idea, bless him. He didn't really get it. And I was glad about that. I mean if he got *fashion* as much as I did, I'd be a little suspicious. Wouldn't want Lisa saying he had 'a touch of the Des Fergusons'. Des Ferguson was her dad and she was convinced he was gay (in fairness, he gave her cause to think that). Much better for our sex life in general that Robbie was unaware of how hot a trend polka dots were this season.

I simply adored what clothes could do, what they could mean, how they could make you feel. The beauty of different forms and colours, the intrigue they could imbue in the female form, the fun and frivolity they could express of someone's character. I loved all things edgy with a vintage feel. Mixing modern lines with classics. There was no denying I took inspiration from my old-school Hollywood heroines. Robbie said it only ever got a bit odd when I'd quote certain lines to him from the old black-and-whites.

'You fancy a glass of wine with dinner tonight, Gracie?'

'"Gimme a whiskey, ginger ale on the side. And don't be stingy, baby."'

'What? But you don't drink whiskey ever since you puked on your mountains, lakes and rivers lecturer after the freshers' ball in college . . . Oh, right, Greta Garbo.'

I think he finds it quite charming, really.

For someone who'd always wanted to get into fashion when I 'grew up', doing a geography degree at Trinity probably hadn't been the smartest decision. Unless I was thinking of opening a shop that sold an earth-platelets-limestone-rock-formations-inspired clothing line. I'd only put geography on the CAO at the time to annoy my mother. She'd kept harping on at me for being a daydreamer, for having no real focus in life, and for making what she described as 'random choices'. I suppose she was talking about the time I brought my granny to my Debs, or decided to breed and sell carrier pigeons from our garden in Stillorgan. In hindsight, studying geography for four years just to cheese off my mother was probably a little petty.

Doing a post-grad in film was far more up my alley. I had no idea what I was going to do with it, but I loved learning all about my screen idols and being allowed to watch them in action for hours on end. The Jean Harlows, the Bette Davises, the Rita Hayworths, the Elizabeth Taylors, the Audrey Hepburns, the Grace Kellys. The suspense, the drama, the bittersweet heartaches. The fairytale costumes. The beauty of the 'old movies' appreciated as works of art. I often got frowned upon for handing in assignments that weren't exactly 'relevant to the course': I suppose 'Elizabeth Taylor's Amazing 65 Costume Changes in *Cleopatra*' or 'Spencer Tracy and Katharine Hepburn's Fascinating 25-year Secret Romance' were a little out of left field, but I passed anyway.

My sister Tanya had been just as disparaging about film studies as Mum had been about geography. 'Well done, Grace. You now know how to watch movies. A year well spent.'

I suppose my move into styling had been a bit random too. I spotted a styling competition in a copy of *Woman's Way* I was reading at the dentist's. A lady called Maeve from Swords swore she'd let a member of Joe Public style her, she was so desperate to change her image. 'Desperate' was only the tip of the iceberg – brown cord trousers, a turquoise short-sleeved polo neck and a red gingham hair-band with a built-in nylon peroxide fringe. I'd forgotten to vote in the last general election, so this was my belated attempt at doing my civic duty.

Got Maeve from Swords sorted, and it just went from there, really. Now I was working part-time for a fairly bland personal-styling agency, run by a nice, if also a little bland, middle-aged woman called Eleanor Holt.

The height of the excitement thus far had been styling the Ukrainian ambassador's wife for the St Patrick's Day parade. More often than not, however, it was far more banal and routine, like a ladies' luncheon or a charity do, or some 'incredibly fabulous' party the women had been invited to at which they needed to impress everyone else. Women like that lunatic Mrs Macnamara.

I swear to God, those women should give seminars in committed combat, perhaps to professional sports people experiencing a lull in their competitive urge. There were absolutely no lengths to which they would not go to 'look the best', no hemline too short, no earrings too dazzling, no headpiece too feathery. And there was always one person carved out as their rival whom they simply had to out-dress. It was like some sort of Middle-aged Women's Gladiatorial Luncheon-type style-off, and the competition was as fierce as an episode of *America's Next Top Model*, if a touch wrinklier, more feathery and with a substantially higher control-pants-to-contestant ratio.

I worked for Eleanor to tide me over: I'd gone back to college again, this time for something really useful and less 'random'.

Origami.

Yes, ladies and gents, origami was the new post-boom business and economics degree.

Only kidding.

Pig farming. Because, lads and lasses, pig farming was the post-boom 'property portfolio'.

No, sorry, I was just messing. (I had to stop doing that. Perhaps that was why no one really took me seriously and I didn't have a proper job and the only thing I could afford from Asos was hair bobbles.) I'd nearly finished an MA in creative business. I'd thought it was a smart move, trying to anchor my flighty fashion passion with some sort of grounded, useful business acumen.

I wouldn't have said it was the most exciting or interesting thing to sacrifice a year of my life doing. (Once I asked my tutor if business models were girls who only modelled office wear just to see if I could make him laugh. Didn't work. In fact, he didn't break a smile for eight months solid. I've often wondered if that was some sort of record. Or if he had a difficult childhood, like Marilyn Monroe.)

Robbie had been so incredibly supportive when I did eventually decide to go back to college, which was the main thing. Unlike Tanya, who'd just mocked me. 'Creative business? What's that? How to decorate a spreadsheet?'

And Mum said, 'Well, can you not pop off to Kildare Village with the girls at the weekends if you want to get more into fashion?' She couldn't entirely grasp why I'd want to go back and study again after all the study I'd already done. But Mum still wanted me to be a *Blue Peter* presenter, so anything else would fall short of the mark for her. I was still getting rabbit scissors, ribbon and odour-free glue for Christmas.

I'd always been quite 'creative'. Painting the living-room carpet pink aged four because I 'wasn't mad on the brown' had given me that reputation. I suppose. It wasn't that I ever wanted to design clothes, or paint them different colours *per se*, but I had figured out that I wanted to work in fashion, plain and simple. But not in a clichéd *Devil Wears Prada* kind of way. Not that I was ever going to get that opportunity, let's be honest: that only even happens in rom coms and chick-lit novels. And working for Eleanor Holt was certainly nothing like working for Miranda Priestly.

On the whole, business-studies lecturers were not exciting. Neither was business studies full stop. But I figured it was worth it to give myself the tools I needed if I was ever to start up my business, or get ahead in the fashion industry in any serious capacity. What exactly I wanted to do was still One of the Great Mysteries of Life, as Robbie put it.

'Do you think you'd like to be a fashion buyer?' he'd say.

'A boutique owner?'

'A fashion blogger?'

'An accessories designer?'

'A hat maker? How about a hat maker? Who wants to be a milliner?' he'd say, going all Chris Tarranty.

'Hmm, I'm not sure,' I'd say, chewing the inside of my lip while tilting my head and looking up in a very cute Audrey Hepburn kind of way (most people think that's an adorable natural trait but actually it's a look I've been practising and perfecting in front of the mirror since I was a teenager).

'Maybe you could sell trendy garden wear that you could also go dancing in, like if you'd been doing the gardening and had to go straight out in a hurry.'

Jesus! Like I said, if he got it, he'd be gay, right?

I can hardly blame him for being confused, seeing as I didn't really get it myself. I was hoping some unbelievably convenient opportunity would drop on to my lap out of nowhere, or a brilliant fortune-teller would tell me what I needed to do. Or I'd have a light-bulb moment while trying on the most perfect pair of shoes. Something handy and convenient and dramatic, like what happens to confused people in the movies (any day now I was going to watch science programmes on the Discovery Channel to broaden my mind).

But failing all of that, hopefully I'd just 'figure it out'.

Anyway, enough about my not-so-illustrious career. Task in hand. Find a dress! After much twirling and flittering in front of my fairy-light-framed full-length mirror, I finally decided on my old reliable Audrey Hepburn *Breakfast at Tiffany's* LBD Givenchy copy. I'd found it in a charity shop in London yonks ago and the man who ran it tried to convince me it'd been the star's actual dress from the movie. The real McCoy. Ha! I asked him if that was the case why was he only charging twenty-six pounds for it when I was pretty sure the original had fetched nearly half a million at an auction in London. It sort of went against me when he upped the price to thirty-two seventy-five to save face.

'Look, look,' he said, shoving a badly stitched tag on the inside of the dress into my face that read 'Audrey's Dress, Hands Off'. Oh, God love him. Like the labels your mum used to stitch into your knickers when you went off to Irish college – without the 'Hands Off' bit or the cool kids would probably have had her pegged as a bit of a 'spa'.

People always give out about black, saying it's safe and boring. But not so, in my opinion. And especially not if you had a mop of red hair. There wasn't a classier combination in the world, if you asked me. A landscape of inky ebony with a cherry on top. It was my proud collusive ginger nod to Rita Hayworth's *Gilda*. One of my all-time favourites.

I wasn't actually cherry red, although I had toyed with the idea in the past. My mother warned me that if I ever dyed my hair she would chop off my hands, which I always thought was a touch confrontational. I told her to stop watching *Crimes in Thailand* on the Discovery Channel. Plus I'd have to learn how to paint on my favourite pillar-box red Chanel lipstick with my feet and that would just be annoying. A stroke of winged black eyeliner above the lashline would be even trickier.

I sang 'Bette Davis Eyes' as I applied my mascara. 'Aaaah!' I screamed, swiping the mascara wand right across my forehead. Bette Davis was on the bookshelf, staring at me in the mirror.

I pegged it downstairs to my car and spent far too long trying to wedge the suitcase into the boot. Why didn't cars come with shoe-racks, for crying out loud? That way we wouldn't have to consider strapping our groceries and/or other luggage to the roof.

'Selling anything?'

Oh, no! No, no, no! I didn't have time for this now. Ian, our sixty-eight-year-old neighbour, who *always* asked us if were selling anything. What did he think we were – black-market traders?

'What have you got in there?' he asked, peering around the edge of the open boot.

'Shoes, Ian. What size are you?'

'A twelve on my left foot and a seven on my right.'

Oh. I wasn't expecting that. How odd. I looked down at his feet. *Really* odd.

'Er, well, these are a size seven . . .'

'I'll take them!' he piped.

Seconds later he was handing me seven euro twenty-nine and I was handing him a pair of electric blue peep-toes. It was fine. I was bored with them anyway. Plus, it left more room for the damn suitcase. I clicked the boot shut, just about, and sped off in the direction of Wicklow, wondering if I could get Ian to make me an offer for the manky green hoodie Robbie insists on wearing every Sunday.

Or Bette Davis.

He could have her for free.

# 3

'Grace's here!'

'Grace, you're late.'

'I'm so sorry,' I said, as I scooted up the aisle of St Brigid's Church. The priest stood there holding a Bible in one hand, the other, palm facing outwards, raised in the air. I really wanted to run up and give him a high-five. But I was trying to be all 'low-key' on account of being late, so I decided against it.

I unravelled my scarf and loosened the top button of my shirt. Churches always made me feel slightly claustrophobic. I put it down to the time my sister locked me into a confession box so I wouldn't be able to rat on her to Mum that she'd gone down to the local chipper to snog Peter Gunnigle. Four and a half hours I was in there! Tanya ended up with a crick so bad she had to wear a neck brace for a week, which eased the blow a little.

I was finally rescued by the cleaning lady who, as it turns out, was just as traumatized as I was when she eventually found the source of 'Don't think you can get away with this! I'm gonna hunt you down! You are so dead!' She'd been convinced it was the ghost of her husband's ex-wife. Made the whole experience even freakier when she made me swear on my life I wasn't possessed with the spirit of Irene Ennis.

There they all were, lined up around Rebecca and Tony on the altar in a lovely little horseshoe, and I nearly got a lump in my throat seeing them. My God, they were actually getting married tomorrow! I could still see Rebecca in neon green cycling shorts doing Take That routines in my front garden. (Ages ago. *Years* ago. I wasn't friends with a simpleton/excitable courier.)

There was Lisa, grinning at me like a lunatic, her long blonde hair tumbling over the shoulders of her cute little navy tea-dress.

Lisa always looked immaculate. But she was a style slut. She admitted it. She was the Russell Brand of trends: she just couldn't keep it in her pants, her skirts, her jackets, shoes, whatever, and whored herself over more trends than Russell Brand's had hot dinners. Or something. Maybe hot dinner ladies. Anyway, she got bored easily. This month it was Kate Middleton. Next month it might be the Queen herself. But let's hope not because I really don't think solicitors are allowed to wear tiaras.

She had such a broad grin that her cheeks had somehow reduced her normally humungous blue eyes to mere dots at the back of her head, and her face was glazed, like she'd been looking at psychedelic prints for too long. In actual fact, she'd been looking at Killian for too long.

There he was, 'Killian-the-lash', my best mate's new man. I felt a flush of excitement, like I was about to meet a celebrity I'd heard that much about him. Lisa had also resurrected the title 'lash' from 1992, when it was last used, as she felt no modern appellation did him justice. Oooh, he was a hottie all right. Tall and sallow with a cool military haircut, short at the sides and longer on top. He was very Shoreditch: funky black-rimmed glasses, shirt buttoned right up to the neck, skinny jeans with Converse. He could have been a member of the Arctic Monkeys.

I gave her a big wink, two thumbs up in approval, and did a mock-orgasm face for good measure. I should possibly *not* have done that when Killian-the-lash was looking. Along with everyone else. Including the priest. In a church.

Killian-the-lash squirmed and went bright red. And I couldn't blame him. He was already here under duress, the poor love. Whatever about going to the wedding of a bride and groom you'd never met before, being made go to the rehearsal Mass with the entire bridal party, all of whom were complete strangers, was just humiliating. But Lisa had warned him she wouldn't put out for at least another three to four weeks if he didn't come as she was dying to show him off. She drove a hard bargain, that one. But I could tell she was absolutely mad about him, which made me smile.

Poor old Killian. I wondered did he always suffer from high colour, or was he just currently in a state of prolonged, extreme mortification? We'd see if his face went back to normal later on.

Oh, and there was Mel, Rebecca's sister. She had a crazy laugh, said, 'That's gas,' to everything, smelt of radishes and always wore a 'VOTE LABOUR' badge on her lapel. She wasn't into politics, just part of the Anti Too Posh To Push movement. But apart from that she was a lovely girl. Actually, she was laughing right now and there was absolutely *nothing* funny going on. The priest looked rather unnerved.

Then there was Alan, Tony's best man. Alan was a pervert. He hadn't been convicted or anything, but he was a pervert. A legal pervert, if there was such a thing. Actually, there was such a thing. Alan.

Robbie and Tony just laughed at his antics and said he was 'a bit mad'. But having a three-way with two of your mum's best friends while your mum had popped to the shops to get some Jamaican Ginger Cake was more than 'a bit mad'. So was hooking up with grannies on Sex Roulette online.

He winked down at me. Euch. Perv. It annoyed me that he was really good-looking. And he knew it, which was even more annoying. If he could have worn a badge that said, 'I am really good-looking and I get loads of sex. Go me!' he would have done. He really would.

Though they were all very cute – Tony, the groom, Killian-the-(glowing)-lash, Alan-the-perv, and even the priest, Father Neville (are you allowed to say priests are cute? Probably not, but I don't want to be mean and leave him out) – none of them was as cute as Robbie. He was just so edible, with his messy sandy brown hair, and his strong, tall frame in his I'm-a-groomsman-tomorrow-and-I'm-taking-this-very-seriously suit and crisp white shirt. Mmm, mmm, mmm!

I was now acutely aware that I still hadn't eaten, and that Robbie, although a fine specimen of a man, was not actually edible. (Did we get to eat some of the Communion at the rehearsal

Mass? Was that sacrilegious? It was just that I needed to get some carbs into me.)

'Okay, Grace, because you're late, you have to walk up the aisle to us, on your own, the full length of the church, doing your best bridesmaid walk like you've practised,' Robbie called down to me.

Humph! I had not practised . . . not really . . . well, sort of . . . Okay, fine, I'd practised it at home a few times.

'Robbie!' I protested, by which time it was too late, as everyone had already started clapping in support, including Father Neville.

'Come on!' Father Neville cajoled. 'Do it in honour of your dearest friends. For whom your love has brought us all here together tonight.' I could see Killian-the-(now purple)-lash slowly inching backwards towards the side exit. Perhaps a four-week sex ban wasn't so bad.

'And don't rush it either. Take your time,' Robbie ordered. Erm, hello? Why was Robbie now the devil? Must talk to Father Neville later about some sort of mild exorcism.

'Come on!' they all hollered, a bunch of pre-wedding altar bullies.

I started to sweat again. Probably because I caught the edge of a confession box out of the corner of my left eye.

But as I walked up the aisle, staring at Robbie as he smiled down at me, I was completely overwhelmed by one thought and one thought only.

Why *wasn't* it us?

# 4

Wow. I really, really wish I'd invented see-through Blu-Tack. That way I could have been a multi-millionaire like Rebecca's granddad.

Why hadn't I listened in science class? Instead of sketching Oscar dresses inside my homework notebook, could I not have listened to Mr Graves? Even though his voice sounded like air whining out of a balloon. And he had a face like a saggy arse. But, alas, the only thing I managed to pick up was that if you put a Mentos into a bottle of Diet Coke, and shook it up for a bit, the Coke shot twenty-five feet into the air. But no one was willing to give me any money for that.

The Ritz was a vision of sumptuous opulence. It was exactly how I imagined the Beverly Hills Hotel, a.k.a. the Pink Palace, in California where Carole Lombard and Clark Gable used to escape for secret rendezvous while his divorce was coming through. So romantic! (Except for Clark's wife. I grabbed Robbie's hand and thanked God he didn't have a wife.) It was also the place Joe Di-Maggio gave Marilyn Monroe what she described as her 'best Christmas ever' by setting a Christmas tree, a log fire and Champagne on ice in her room as a surprise.

Well, we would be having our best Christmas ever. Normally we did the Twelve Pubs of Christmas and got so drunk we would sneak into Robbie's parents' house and tie his dad up in tinsel while he was sleeping. It was an annual tradition we all loved (Robbie's dad just refused to admit it). But this year was going to be different. It would be the first Christmas in our new home now that we had got all grown-up and bought a house. (Well, sort of. In instalments. Over the next, say, 250 years.) But it was so exciting and we were dying to decorate it like the Griswolds' and, who knew, maybe even tie each other up in tinsel. (Actually, that sounded like a great game.)

I suddenly felt a bit flushed and giddy. I stood up on my tippy-toes and gave Robbie a little kiss, holding on to his big strong arms in case I stumbled with the weight of my cosy fuzzy head.

The giant Christmas tree in the foyer of the Ritz stood over us like a magnificent peaked blanket of twinkling stars. 'Can we get a tree like that for our house?' I said.

'Grace, that tree *is* our house.' He laughed.

Wow. We were just like *The Raccoons*.

'Get a room!' said Rebecca, handing me a keycard for Room 308. Handy.

'This place is incredible,' I gushed.

'I know, right? Thank God for see-through Blu-Tack.'

'So, lads,' said Alan-the-perv, sidling up and looping his arms around Robbie and Tony's shoulders. 'Shall we hit the streets of Enniskerry for Tony's last official night as a single man?'

Jesus, should I call the local Garda station and tell them to drive around the town with a siren and a Tannoy, saying, 'Women of all ages, calmly and quietly retreat to your houses. Lock your doors, shut your blinds, disconnect your phone lines, keep your lights off and put on twenty-seven pairs of pants. We repeat, *twenty-seven pairs of pants!*'

'Thanks, Alan.' Rebecca giggled. 'But I think chaining him naked to the railings of the Irish Countrywomen's Association Dublin Headquarters on his stag was more than enough of a farewell to his bachelor days. Besides, we have our family meal tonight, but you guys go off out.'

No! Don't drag me into this! I didn't want my name to be dirt in Enniskerry. What if I ever wanted to run for mayor here? Rebecca was not a lateral thinker. 'Lock up your daughters!' Tony said.

'Yeah, to my bed with handcuffs,' Alan said.

I snorted my Champagne up my nose. Euch, the visual! Why did he have to give us the visual?

'Well, you boys stay here and have a "respectable" few drinks. I'm borrowing my girls for a while.'

Oh. My. God. The honeymoon suite in the Ritz was ridiculous. I climbed into the giant bath in the middle of the room and folded my legs underneath me, soaking up all the finery, dancing my fingers over the gold taps. Lisa and Rebecca climbed in after me with a bottle of Dom Pérignon and three glasses.

'This bath is bigger than my sitting room,' I cooed.

'This bath is bigger than my apartment,' Lisa trumped.

We clinked our glasses and sat back against the cool white porcelain.

'I cannot believe you're getting married tomorrow,' I said.

'I know. It's so mad!' Rebecca sipped the smooth bubbles from her glass. 'That's why I wanted to pause this moment right here and make a toast to my oldest, bestest friends in the world before tomorrow. Before we're officially grown-up.'

Uh-oh. Lump in my throat.

'No tears!' they warned.

'I know!' God, I hated being 'the crier'. I had to toughen up. There had to be some sort of programme out there in which people pick out all your bad points and use them to criticize you with the promise of making you a stronger person. Actually, that just sounded like an episode of *America's Next Top Model*.

'To be honest, I never thought you were ever going to get over Wilhelm Schreider,' I joked, trying to distract myself from tears. Tyra would have been proud.

'To be honest, I haven't. But I guess you kinda have to move on once your school exchange has imposed an official restraining order against you, and the Bundespolizei need to be notified any time you're travelling through Germany.'

'Hear, hear!' We laughed and clinked our glasses again. 'Bundespolizei!'

'I think I'm going to marry Killian.' Lisa sighed through a Champagne haze.

'Aw, that's sweet. And creepy, since you haven't even slept with him yet.'

'Well, tonight is the night, ladies! Actually, Bec, can we use this room . . . pretty please?'

Daggers.

'I was joking!' I wasn't sure she had been. Lunatic.

'I haven't felt this way since Aidan.' She sighed again.

'Eh, that was only last month, you looper.'

'I know, but I can *really* feel it this time. The connection. I think he does too.'

'What if he's crap in bed?'

'I'll teach him.'

Flashback to Lisa aged eight, setting up a stall outside her house, giving 'kissing lessons' and charging 50p a go. Some might call that Early Signs of Prostitution. Other, more open-minded and generous, people might look on it as healthy entrepreneurship and/or a service to the community.

I still wasn't sure. Mum had put a ban on me playing with her for a week. A whole *week*! That was like years in a child's life. It felt like someone had removed my right arm. Lisa and I did everything together. We got our mums to buy us the same clothes, we wore our hair in the same styles, we fell in and out of love with Blake from *Home and Away* simultaneously. Like I said, everything.

The end of our seven-day sabbatical was marked by a set-up snog with Cathal MacInerny. And she only charged me 25p. Mates rates. Ah, she was the best pimp in town. And she was my best friend.

We'd grown out of the pimping phase, thank God. (And I even managed to find Robbie all on my own, with no money changing hands.)

'So when exactly did you know that Tony was the one for you?' the one-time pimp asked Rebecca, sipping from her crystal Champagne flute. Very pimpin'.

'There was no one defining moment, really.' Rebecca was grinning from ear to ear. 'Although some might say, i.e. Grace, that

"Any man who can still love you when you're covered from head to toe in chicken pox and your face is the size of Terminal Two from getting your wisdom teeth removed is the man for you."'

'Hey, I did not say that! What I actually said was, "Any man who can still love you when you are covered from head to toe in chicken pox and your face is the size of Terminal Two from getting your wisdom teeth out, *and you insist on wearing green-leather dungarees* is the man for you."'

'Do you know what?' she mused. 'I just knew that I never wanted to be apart from him.'

'Awwwww,' we chimed together, my head suddenly feeling all soft and fuzzy from the love trip. And from necking Champagne like it was water.

'Plus,' she added, 'my dad knew.'

'Really?' Lisa asked.

'Yeah, before he died, he said it to me. We were sitting on the bench at the back of the garden watching all the coloured swirls in the summer sky. You know the way they slink and shift right before the sun goes down? Anyway, he said to me, "He's your man, my darling girl. Let him love you."'

My throat swelled to the point where it was literally squeezing the tears out of the backs of my eyes. Oh, Christ, Grace, don't cry! Don't be the one who cried in the bath in the honeymoon suite the night before Rebecca's wedding!

'No tears!' Rebecca warned.

Jesus, I know, I know! I inhaled sharply, trying to dispel them as best I could. 'It's just the opulence in the room making my eyes water. I think I may be allergic to wealth.'

'Bummer.'

'I know. There goes my plan of marrying Rebecca's granddad. Or Roman Abramovich. Or Sir Philip Green. Oh, God, there's just so many men-I-am-never-going-to-marry to choose from.'

We disbanded and arranged to meet in the lobby bar in twenty minutes. Except for Rebecca, who had a pre-wedding dinner planned with her family and her 'outlaws', as she called them.

Tony's family were apparently distantly related to Ned Kelly. Kind of like the way I was sort of related to Vivien Leigh on my mum's side.

Actually, I didn't think that was strictly true, just hoped I was, which didn't make it real. I had to stop doing that.

What was absolute fact, though, was that I was having an exemplary Joan Crawford day. This was the fourth time I'd had to get changed in one day. Fantastic! There was nothing that gave me a greater lift. Apart from hearing about three-legged dogs on those animal programmes finding homes.

Word has it that Joan apparently changed her clothes up to ten times a day. Legend. The most I've ever got to is six. I mean, I could cheat and literally just stand in my room and change my clothes ten times in a row. But that would be fraudulent. No, it has to be far more subtle and cool than that. Six was my top score, and some day I really hoped to be just as prolific a changer as JC, with enough practice and dedication. One of my favourite anecdotes of Joan's clothes-changing predilection was Clark Gable asking her why she was going to see the same play twice.

'You've already seen it,' he said.

'Yes,' she replied, 'but not in this dress.'

Again: legend.

I changed into my Elizabeth Taylor *A Place in the Sun*-inspired sweetheart neckline dress with a fantastic nipped-in waist and puffball skirt that I spotted on a fabulous vintage-clothing website and just had to buy, even if I was meant to be buying mugs and a spaghetti drainer for the new house. The homewares website just happened to default to the vintage-clothing one and there was simply *nothing* I could do about it. (When you type in 'spaghetti' and it leads you to a 1940s spaghetti-strap evening dress, what on earth are you supposed to do? Call the Internet provider to complain? No. You just power on as best you can.)

I slipped into a pair of nude peep-toes and reapplied my fire-engine red lipstick. As I said, this was the last fleeting opportunity

I had to dress like a fashionable human being before being zipped into our gimp-suit bridesmaid dresses tomorrow.

Okay, so the outfits weren't actually gimp-suits, but I'm telling you, they were completely manic/psychotic and, just so you know, in my head they were going to be gimp-suits. Outwardly I would be in a bridesmaid dress. Inwardly I would be in a gimp-suit.

Fact.

Robbie and Killian were sitting at the bar when Lisa and I came downstairs to rejoin them. Killian, as it turned out, was a regular healthy colour when he wasn't suffering from a chronic bout of mortification, and was actually quite sallow with tiny pores. Good for him.

Lisa skipped over and plonked herself on the bar stool beside his, swan diving in and planting a kiss on his cheek. An excited giggle escaped from her mouth and curled its way through the bar.

For the love of God, woman, have I told you nothing? *Every* time! Had my Mae West deportment and etiquette tutorials fallen on deaf ears once again? 'Sexy and coy without giving too much away.' That was the mantra. A little turn of the head, a slow and deliberate flutter of the lashes, then a cheeky but controlled 'Come up and see me some time.' Not batting your lashes like your conjunctivitis drops were irritating your eyes, giggling like you were binned, and projecting 'Come up and see me some time. Or any time. No time like the present. Come up now! Please?'

You see, what was so endearing about Lisa had also been her downfall when it came to romance. Out of Rebecca, her and me, she was always the one who dived in head first, not even checking to see if there was any water to break her fall. She wore her heart on her sleeve; always had. She was a giant human Hallmark Valentine's card. One of those really expensive ones that cost as much as a year's subscription to Sky, complete with flashing lights and a chip that played a hopeless love song on a loop. Although some guys do indeed find this sweet, honest and refreshing, the majority get scared that you may have a casket of ex-boyfriends in your basement that you'd killed after they weren't so keen on getting engaged and/or making you pregnant after four weeks of dating.

You see, that was the problem with getting closer to thirty – men's perceptions of what women wanted. They all just assumed we wanted to get married and impregnated ASAP, like some sort of military deployment when really it came down to people just wanting to be happy. I brushed my hand over Robbie's, knowing how lucky I was. And not only because everything was falling into place and I seemingly had all my ducks aligned, but because I was happy. He handed me my vodka and tonic, having fished out the slice of lemon because I hated lemons. (They were a dangerous fruit. Dealing with any fruit that could make your eyes practically bleed if you got juice in them was a liability.) 'Thanks,' I mouthed.

I knew Lisa was ready to find someone special. She really was. She'd been through the lot. Been the dumper and the dumpee, had her heart broken, kissed a load of eels (I thought frogs were quite cute so I called the no-hopers eels), done long-distance, been single and issued a restraining order (only once, to Derek, who was great at understanding code for computer programs, but wasn't the best when it came to understanding that a break-up didn't mean you could carry on like you were still going out).

But whoever said the course of true love was ever smooth? Or legal?

I just wished that Lisa would hold a bit of herself back so she didn't end up with eight thousand balls in their court and none in her own.

But we are who we are, right? And maybe Killian would turn out to be her Roger Federer and this would turn into the match of her life.

We ordered another round of drinks and all made a solemn promise that no one was allowed to be hung-over in the morning. Even if they were.

Killian and Robbie got on like a house on fire, which made life so much easier. Lisa's last boyfriend, Aidan, had been convinced Robbie was a government spy. I think Aidan had spotted him speaking to a local politician canvassing outside Donnybrook Fair and that had been that. He used to come out with weird stuff, like, 'Oh, you'd know all about the levies on local businesses, wouldn't you, Robbie?'

Needless to say, Robbie wasn't all that keen on Aidan, so when he dumped Lisa and moved to Sweden we opened a nice bottle of Chablis to celebrate. (But obviously we can *never* tell Lisa that. No matter what kind of a spin you put on it, it's always going to sound a bit cruel.)

As it turned out, by complete and utter fluke, Killian and Robbie worked for the same promotions company so it was going to be fantastic for Lisa and me on the double-dating front. We'd tried to orchestrate something similar when we were about twenty-one, by dating two friends we'd met in a bar. However, going out on dates with two Japanese guys who worked in a science lab in Wexford and didn't have a word of English between them wasn't as idyllic and handy as it sounded.

I lie: they were able to say 'Petri dish', 'hand sanitizer', and 'live cultures'. Still, didn't help things hugely.

'Were you involved with the Princess concert in October?' Killian asked Robbie.

'Was I what? After negotiating half the terms of the performance agreements on the Irish leg of the tour, I was the soldier who had to ensure she had enough pink Smarties, pink toilet paper and pink gerbils in her room.'

Aw, I was so proud of him. Organizing huge gigs like that one, knowing everything there was to know about the music business, being able to play the guitar and sing. He could even do a rendition of 'Bohemian Rhapsody' on the spoons if he was really pissed. Not easy to do. Tried it once and ended up calling the twenty-four-hour nurse-line and enquiring about knee replacement ops. Okay, so I was a little drunk and somewhat hysterical – but they didn't need to put a permanent block on my number.

And I was so proud of him for being able to dye gerbils pink with a completely cruelty-free animal dye. And do it *evenly*!

'Yeah, I'd heard she was a tricky one, all right.' Killian laughed. 'Not as bad as Nights of Sound who played the Olympia in September, though. None of them would go on stage until I'd told them how handsome they were in their outfits, and there was no way anyone in the audience was going to be better-looking, and if they were, I'd have them thrown out.'

'Pink gerbils?' Lisa asked, swigging from her glass.

'Don't worry,' Robbie said. 'It's an organic dye that washes out and is "conditioning" apparently.'

I could see the vodkas starting to have a conditioning effect on Lisa. She curled into Killian like a Cheesy Wotsit and stared up at him much like one too.

'You are just the cutest,' she whispered, and nuzzled his neck. He smiled back at her, and then they were snogging. Snogging at the bar! It was only ten thirty.

Mae West, Mae West, Mae West! I projected, closing my eyes and channelling 'in control and coy'.

Robbie murmured, 'Do you have a pain in your tummy, Grace? Do you need to go to the loo?'

'No, I'm meditating,' I muttered back.

'You looked a bit strained. I thought maybe all those dry roasted peanuts were, you know, going to make you need the loo again.'

I looked over at Lisa and Killian snogging the face off each other, totally ignited and consumed by the first flames of fiery passion, and decided to lob the gob myself. If they could do it, we could do it too, right? But I suppose it's not really the right moment for passion when your boyfriend has just asked you if the dry roasted peanuts you've been eating are likely to give you diarrhoea.

Coming up for air, I started giggling.

'What was that about?' he asked, clearly bewildered.

'Nothing. Can I not kiss my man like in the movies?'

'Of course you can, but if you start calling me Rhett Butler, I'm leaving.'

I sneaked a glance at Lisa and Killian. How were they breathing? That girl had asthma. It couldn't have been good for her health. If I had to run and get her inhaler again . . .

'Let's leave these two teenagers at it, shall we?' Robbie said, getting to his feet and extending his arm, Rhett Butler fashion, albeit without the side parting, moustache and dickie bow.

I leaned into him as he curled his arm around me and led me upstairs to our room.

On the way up I thought about Lisa and Killian, smooching like a pair of young horn dogs from *High School Musical*. Had Robbie and I been together so long we'd forgotten how to snog like he was a cheerleader and I was a quarter-back? No, that wasn't right –

Oh, hell, maybe the vodkas were having an effect on me too.

'We have just as much passion as those two, right?' I said, wobbling a bit as I tried to hang my dress in the wardrobe.

'Of course we do, Red,' he said, smacking my bum as he passed.

I looped the hanger onto the pole, feeling immensely proud that I'd managed to accomplish something so skilful. 'D'you remember that time in the stretch limo? I mean, Vanessa Hudgens and Zac Efron downstairs would be far too tame for that!' I scoffed.

He came out of the bathroom, smiled at me, got out his suit for the morning and hung it on the door.

Robbie had been in his job just two months when we'd decided we'd give Jay-Z's limo a proper road test. It was for his own safety, of course. What if he and Beyoncé wanted to get jiggy and there was a safety glitch or something? Company gets sued, Beyoncé ends up in hospital, Robbie gets fired. Disaster. We're just really responsible, accommodating, thoughtful people. And that was why we had sex in the back of Jay-Z's limo while he was inside doing a sound check. End of.

Turns out, though, that when the auto lock on a limo kicks in, any movement within the car sets off the alarm and starts the lights flashing, like at a Manumission rave in Ibiza. Which in turn heralds the arrival of Jay-Z's personal security entourage within 0.5 of a second. They don't tell you that on *Top Gear*.

I still have the emotional scars of talking to all seven foot four of the Brick, Jay-Z's head security man, about why on earth the car would have kicked off like that, as I stood on the side of the street with my jumper on back to front, my shoes on the wrong feet and my bra looped around my neck like a lasso.

I smiled into the bathroom mirror as I washed my face and brushed my hair. We still had that passion. Of course we did. Okay, maybe we no longer felt the need to have a quickie in the back of Jay-Z's car, but that was only because we had our own lovely bed at home now, with the gorgeous Egyptian cotton sheets I'd managed to find on sale in Arnotts with 40 per cent off.

We didn't really need to prove ourselves, did we? After all this time?

Or was that the point?

That was it! I had it! I was going to run a bath! And we were going to have sex in the bath! Woo-hoo! Bath sex!

I watched the water cascade from the shiny gold taps and the foamy bubbles climb up the sides of the bath, like candyfloss. I checked myself in the mirror and adjusted my underwear. Not too shabby for someone nudging thirty. Okay, so I wasn't exactly in *Sunset Boulevard* territory, but it was nice to know I still had it. Who cared if I was turning thirty? Who cared if the rest of the world thought Robbie and I should be getting married? Or having regular sex in Jay-Z's car. Who cared if everything wasn't going to an exact schedule of how life should be – turning thirty, career sorted, marriage, blah, blah, blah!

This was life. Here. Now. This was what we had. Gorgeous Ritz bathfuls of love and passion, and that was none too shabby! And probably none too shabby if you asked Robbie either . . . if he hadn't already fallen asleep.

I stood in the bedroom in the dark, listening to the familiar sound of his breath rising and falling before padding across the soft carpet back into the bathroom. Pulling the plug from beneath the mountain of froth, I sat and watched as the water swirled away.

Crawling into bed beside him, I breathed in the familiar smell. Home away from home. He stirred beside me, taking my arm and looping it over his side until we slotted together like two jigsaw pieces.

'Night,' he whispered, in the darkness.

'Night,' I answered. Our voices were small and hollow, lost in the huge expanse of the room. 'Robbie?'

'Yeah?'

'We are happy, aren't we?'

'What do you mean?'

'Well, it's just I know no one can be in that crazy early-relationship honeymoon period for ever. But, you and me, that's okay, right? We are happy, aren't we?'

The room was so dark and vast, I might have been looking out at a night sky that went on for ever.

He curled his fingers around mine and held them. 'How could you doubt it, my good lady? We were meant to be.'

# 5

I watched the makeup artist poke her brush around the glittering pot of blue eye-shadow, and felt myself break into an all-over sweat. When she'd said blue, she'd really meant *blue*. Not a lovely elegant midnight blue, or a dark, shimmery marine-coloured smoky blue, but *blue* blue.

As in the colour of a Smurf. That's right – Smurf-coloured eye-shadow. Heading straight for my eyelids. If she prodded any more at that pot, she was going to obliterate the whole thing and snap the brush in two. Plumes of Smurfy iridescent dust puffed into the air and I recoiled in terror as she turned the poor violated hairs of the eye brush on me. The arse of some poor squirrel surely hadn't been shorn to execute this heinous crime, had it? In what I was convinced was *deliberate* slow motion, she steadily began her approach. She was getting a kick out of this, the sadistic lunatic! All of a sudden the lovely pop song on the radio sounded like the theme music from *Jaws* . . .

Oh, Christ, she was nearly upon me!

I gripped the edge of my stool so tightly I could feel my fingers start to cramp.

'Stop moving,' she said, through gritted shark-like teeth.

'Sorry,' I said, ducking out of the way as she made another attempt at stabbing my eyes with her squirrel's arse death-wand. Eventually my back was almost pinned against the wall as she made wild lunges at my eyelids.

'Stay still!' she growled, under her breath, the politeness draining from her voice like water from a sieve. Jesus, I was dealing with a sociopath here.

'STAY still,' she repeated.

I couldn't take much more of this. I wasn't even *purposely* trying to duck out of the way. It was just my innate survival instinct kicking in. Same thing happened when Mum tried to wrangle me into the sample-sale crocheted knitwear she buys off grannyfest.com – I've even climbed out of Tanya's old bedroom window and slid down the drainpipe just to get away.

'I can't work like this!' she wailed, throwing her brush onto the table. 'Morgan get me my fan, will you?' she whimpered. Morgan, the hairdresser, was her partner in crime (and when I say crime, oh, boy, do I mean *crime*: what on earth was he doing to Mel's hair? What had Mel's hair ever done to him?).

But now she was doing some sort of fainting thing, like they do in Jane Austen dramas on the BBC, and Morgan was rushing to her with this little battery-run fan-thingie and the whole room had come to a standstill and everyone was looking at me and the fainting Jane Austen makeup lady.

'Grace, do you not like it?' Rebecca asked, her eyes wide and spoony, like those of an abandoned puppy on the M50. I wilted instantly. Then I saw that everyone else was making disappointed eyes at me too, like I was a bold child who'd just defecated in the middle of the room.

Oooh. I shrank back in my seat. What'd I been thinking? This was *Rebecca*'s day. Getting the makeup artist into a WWE-type wrestling lock over the prospect of having to wear blue eyeshadow was possibly a touch self-centred and a move I should really only reserve for Mum because she knows when to tap out. I was a bridesmaid, after all, and it was my job to let them make me up as a clown if they so desired, which, let's be honest, was already well under way.

I looked at Rebecca again, all rigged up like a science experiment, with metal rollers in her hair, towels tucked under her arms and bright pink toe separators wedged onto each foot. If she started worrying, she'd start sweating and then her hair would go fuzzy, the toe separators would pop off, her nail varnish would smudge, the whole day would be ruined and it would be *my fault*.

Breathe.

I needed to rescue the situation.

'Do you know what?' I said enthusiastically. 'I think I'm just nervous, really. I mean, it's so exciting. Isn't it?' The makeup artist rolled her eyes and shot me a knowing look. I don't know what she had to be so smug about: she had her own problems. Big fat sociopathic ones.

Rebecca smiled, looking instantly relieved. 'You know what you need?' she said.

Hmm. An eye-shadow in a nice earthy brown, perhaps?

'I don't know. What?' I said instead.

'Mel,' she called, 'fill her up!'

Out of nowhere Mel the Matrix came at me laughing and saying, 'That's gas,' cranked open my jaw, emptied a bottle of Rescue Remedy down my throat, then snapped my mouth shut again. My entire gullet was now on fire and I found the whole experience traumatizing, not in the least bit 'rescuing'.

'Thanks,' I said, offering a little thumbs-up before everyone snapped back to work, backcombing, hairspraying, face-painting, nail-painting, body-painting (by this I mean fake tanning although, worryingly, I don't think that full-on body art would look altogether out of place on us).

Don't get me wrong. I was so happy for Rebecca. *Really* I was. And I'd have loved to tell you I had my doubts about Tony, that he smelt of Stilton or watched weird Internet porn involving hairy midgets in fancy dress. But the truth was that Tony was brilliant. He was hilarious and smart and *normal* and madly in love with Rebecca.

What it was . . .

Well . . .

Okay, I just hadn't been able to relax at weddings lately. I got all panicky and flustered and sweaty (last month I wore gloves for an *entire* wedding, second day barbecue included, because my hands were sweating so much). And it was down to far more than just the confession boxes I had to see in the churches: it was because all people ever seemed to talk about was:

'It'll be you and Robbie next!'

'We'll all be buying our hats for you and Robbie soon!'

'When is that eejit going to get his skates on and give us another big day out?'

Only last month at my cousin's wedding, Auntie Jean had backed him into a supply closet in the Marriott and threatened to lock him in if he didn't tell her when and where he was planning to propose. Granted it was an extreme case, seeing as Auntie Jean had been a strict teetotaller for forty years before hitting the gin at three p.m. that afternoon. But still.

I mean, don't get me wrong, I knew it was on the cards. *Eventually*. Of course we'd discussed it. But we'd both had so much going on recently – what with me deciding I wanted to go back to college, buying our first house together, and Robbie working every hour that God sent in the hope he'd get a promotion. Although that now seemed about as likely as me warming to the weird sociopathic makeup artist and her crazy blue eye-shadow. Robbie said that his boss was giving automatic pay cuts to anyone who even had the cheek to mention the words 'rise' or 'promotion' in the 'current economic climate'. He went on to tell me about some guy in his office whose wages had been slashed after he was overheard in the staff canteen discussing the promotion on chicken breasts in Tesco that week.

Christ, it was tough out there. And weddings cost money, pure and simple. That was unless you went on that programme where the TV station paid for your entire wedding if you let your future mother-in-law choose every single detail of your big day. Arrrgh! I started to dry-retch even thinking about it. Vera Cotter would have the whole place draped in peach voile and blue geraniums, and instead of a Champagne fountain, we'd have a fountain of holy water flown in straight from Lourdes. Not to mention that I'd be in some hideous mid-calf cream shoulder-padded jacquard 'frock' from Clerys department store. No, thank you! I'd rather live in 'a shroud of sin', as she called it, for the rest of my life than be subjected to that sort of gross inhumanity. Televised to boot. I'd have to move to Fiji.

Everyone seriously needed to back off and leave Robbie and me to live our own life, our own way. We knew what we were doing. Sort of.

No, we did. We did.

It's just the marriage thing had been getting a little too much lately. I mean, absolutely *everybody* seemed to be getting married: Prince William, Drew Barrymore, Lily Allen, Nick Lachey . . . and now, Rebecca.

I shifted in my seat to try and get comfortable but that gallon of Rescue Remedy had given me serious indigestion. Or maybe it had come from the glimpse I'd caught of myself in my brides-maid's dress in the mirror on the back of the door. I wondered if I doused the dresses in Rescue Remedy would it help. Probably not.

Rebecca had seen our dresses on a late night infomercial on the Science Fiction Channel (says so much, really). There were weir-dos out there who thought that cerise pink, ice-skating-inspired occasion wear was a superb idea. Rebecca being Rebecca, she had fallen in love with them instantly, and that, tragically, had been that.

Weirdos and Rebecca. Well, to call Rebecca a weirdo *herself* isn't entirely fair, but I have told her before that she is easily led astray by weirdos. Like that time she got talked into swapping her car for a caravan by some oddball she'd met in Brittas Bay, who'd told her it was blessed. It was blessed, all right – biggest blessed mistake she'd made in a long time. She cursed herself at bus stops for the next year until she'd finally saved up enough money to buy another car. To be fair, she was stoned at the time of the transac-tion. The caravan was now parked in her back garden. She used it as a wardrobe-overflow storage unit and her granny had sold Cornettos out of it one summer to raise money for new church pews. So I guess it hadn't been an out-and-out disaster, then.

The other thing about Rebecca is that she is completely colour-blind (some would say full-on 'blind'). That, mixed with a self-confessed cluelessness about fashion, has made for *a lot* of interesting wardrobe choices along the way. Like today. But although I often wished at times – like right now or, say, at our Debs when all the boys laughed at her for wearing a silver jump-suit with her entire head braided with corn-rows of coloured beads – that she didn't have astigmatism in both eyes, or that she read the odd copy of *In Style* now and then, I also sort of loved that it didn't bother her all that much. Things like that would bring me out in a hairy rash, but they suited Rebecca's quirkiness and made her as lovable as she was.

How was Lisa coping with all this? I sneaked a look at her. Interesting. She was managing to look even more mortified in her get-up than I was, which was unfair because I had the added humiliation of the cerise pink clashing horrifically with my red hair. And when you added the sparkly blue eye-shadow, our sky blue fluffy shawls to protect us from the winter chill, and the orange and pink bouquets, I was coming out less like a brides-maid and more like a character from *Disney On Ice*. I had to keep reminding myself that Rebecca loved us, and wasn't trying to ruin our lives on purpose.

I looked at myself in the glass again, covering my mouth with my hand to muffle any shriek that tried to sneak out. If this shit leaked, my career would be over as quick as you could say Mischa Barton.

Okay, so the chances of this being picked up by TMZ or Joan Rivers's *Fashion Police* were slim enough, but I had Facebook to contend with. What if Eleanor Holt caught a glimpse of me? She'd think I was trying to get fired on purpose.

It's quite a funny thing being a bridesmaid: it's one of the only times in your life that another person dictates what you have to wear (your mum choosing your outfits when you're a kid excluded. I'd got independent quite early on that front. I'd had to as Mum had a rather unhealthy penchant for culottes and lime green). Clothes rarely terrified me, unless I happened upon *Best of the 80s* when flicking through the TV channels. Normally they soothed me. A lot of people like to meditate by putting on a soundtrack of waterfalls and dolphins while they sit cross-legged with their eyes closed. I preferred to open the doors of my wardrobe, sit on the floor and stare at my clothes.

Not today. Today I had the fear. Lots and lots of it. Today I didn't want to sit back and think about what I was going to be wearing. I was like Superman being forced to wear a shroud of kryptonite. But, like I've said, it was Rebecca's big day so I had to grin and bear it. Later this evening I would 'gin and bear it'. And that would help. Lots.

I forced a smile against the crippling power of the kryptonite / ice-skating sparkly number. One last glance at my reflection. The shoes. Christ almighty, the shoes. Well, to be fair, it was a combination of my feet and the shoes. For a relatively petite person, I had large feet. And those flat square pumps were not helping matters. I looked like something from a J. R. R. Tolkien novel, who'd joined the cast of *Hairspray* on Broadway. I had to keep reminding myself that Audrey Hepburn had *size ten feet*.

As soon as my eyes had been Smurfed, I was passed down the factory line to Morgan the Merciless. I had no fight left in me, so I bowed my head in submission and surrendered to the Brush. Out of the corner of my left eye, I caught Lisa grinning conspiratorially at me. I smiled immediately. I could always rely on Lisa for sound judgement. Morgan suddenly left to answer his mobile, and I prayed that he was coming back to scoop the mountain of auburn candyfloss on top of my head into some sort of tragic up-style and that this wasn't me 'done'.

'Nice hair,' Lisa mouthed.

'Nice makeup,' I mouthed back. 'You'd better thank your lucky stars you got Killian into bed last night because he's never going to go near you again.'

'Speak for yourself. I hope you got good use out of your room last night cos it ain't gonna see any action tonight, sista.'

'Yeah,' I answered, and looked away. I didn't want to risk upsetting the bride again.

But as I parted the curtains of fluff that hung in front of my eyes, I could see that Rebecca was taking form nicely. Stunningly, in fact. Her hair was pinned up loosely with a small cluster of fresh freesias sitting in a nest of soft chocolate brown curls. Her Jenny Packham dress was even more divine than I remembered from the day she'd first tried it on for us. It was a present from her dad who had wanted his baby girl to be beautiful on her wedding day and knew what kind of get-up she'd turn up in if left to her own devices. The layers of silk fell magnificently down her tall, lean frame creating a spectacularly beautiful silhouette.

'And now for your "something borrowed",' her mum chirped, fastening a delicate loop of creamy pearls around her neck. They smiled at each other knowingly and a lump caught in my throat as I watched them fold into an emotional embrace.

I caught my breath and steadied my voice: 'Bec, you look . . . amazing.'

'Thanks, Grace!' she said, giving me a big wink. 'It'll be you next!'

# 6

This was my second and three-quarters time as a bridesmaid and by far the most traumatic so far. And that was saying something as, first, we hadn't even walked down the aisle yet and, second, I was including the three-quarters outing when the wedding was aborted on the morning of the ceremony after my cousin Sinéad decided she didn't love her fiancé Ed at all. In fact, she realized, she pretty much despised him and would much rather sleep with lots of random strangers for the foreseeable future, starting with the room-service guy. Mind you, I didn't feel too sorry for poor old Ed, as he was now shacked up with Manseeb, a gay Pakistani arts and crafts trader, who made sequined berets for Cow's Lane market.

As for the other times, well, there was always going to be a certain amount of trauma when it came to my sister Ethyl's wedding (she acts like such an oul' one that I can't help but call Tanya 'Ethyl'. Not surprisingly, she doesn't like it. Which is the only reason I do it). Everything had to be 'just puuuuuurfect' and the colour co-ordination of the outfits had to be in 'mirrored syyyyyyyyyyyyymmetry' with the reception's décor. She annoyed me so much about candelabras and napkins and Naranja roses that she made me want to emigrate, but Mum talked me out of it on the grounds that so much of my life was in Dublin, which, to be fair, she was right about. I decided to stay. (But, for the record, making someone sit down and choose from forty-seven napkins the one that 'makes them feel the most special inside' would break even the strongest character.)

The one up-side of the whole day was that, due to my sister's notions, we all had to wear Vera Wang. I spent most of the day in my own little world, pretending I wasn't at Ethyl and Painful

Peter's wedding but that I was the misunderstood heroine in a wonderful Vera Wang movie. Robbie was confused by all my dramatic, wistful looking-into-the-middle-distance, but I'd just give him a little kiss, then go back to petting my festoons of lovely silk organza, which not only made me smile but made the whole thing seem more bearable.

Lisa grabbed my hand and gave it a squeeze. 'Is your arse chafing yet? Because I have first-degree synthetic-fibre burns on both cheeks.'

'I'll have to sit on an inflatable rubber ring at dinner for sure,' I said, and we both giggled.

The bunches of netting under our dresses were making life a little harder than necessary. The last time my bum had been this chafed was when Tanya had put sheets of tinfoil down my nappy as a toddler because she found my face 'annoying'. Dad said they went through seventeen tubs of Sudocrem that week.

I caught another glimpse of myself in the reflection of the glass church door, and I almost screamed again. Must keep remembering *not* to scream like I did when I saw the finished product before we left the house. I had to lie and tell everyone that I'd seen a ghost, which only served to make matters worse by freaking the shit out of them.

I was just so pleased and relieved that Rebecca looked as stunning as she did. At the end of the day, that was all that really mattered (I was already planning on Photoshopping myself into a fabulous Badgley Mischka bridesmaid number as soon as I got my hands on the pictures). But Rebecca wouldn't need to alter a thing. And it was all thanks to her legend of a Dad, Noel. Her mum had told me the story on the QT. 'What are we going to do, love?' he'd said to her. 'We can't let her walk down the aisle looking like something out of a Hallowe'en catalogue.' (They existed? Amazing! I needed a new pumpkin cutter.) Due to her colour blindness and her 'fashion disability' (she'd once asked me if she was entitled to special treatment from shop assistants because of it), Rebecca had grown up convinced she was adopted because the rest of the family never displayed any overt signs of fashion dyslexia (i.e. when you get the 'nautical' trend mixed up and actually dress like Captain Birdseye from the fish-finger ads). Her sister Mel was a buyer for an *über*-cool boutique in London's Marylebone, her mum was an award-winning interior designer and Noel had won Best Dressed Male at Punchestown in 1995.

Noel decided to make appointments on the sly to look at wedding dresses for Rebecca, and brought Mel along with him to call upon her expertise. The day they saw The Dress, they both instantly *knew* and Mel held her father as he wept, knowing he would never see Rebecca wear it. He knew he was dying long before he told his children. And even longer before he told Rebecca, especially as she'd only just got engaged and he'd never seen his 'baby girl' so happy in her entire life.

And now, even though she was wearing bright green wedges, the rest of her was impeccable and The Dress looked absolutely out of this world on her tall, slender frame. I had never seen her look so beautiful. I was choking up. It had been just three months since Noel had passed away. How were we going to get through this?

'Oi! Ginger! Stop with the tears or I'll make you sit beside Mike Travers at the reception,' Rebecca shouted over.

Jesus! Mike Travers. The very mention of his name had me thinking of police protection. Bad incident in 2002 when I'd had to hide in a cupboard under the stairs at a house party just to get away from him. I sort of fell asleep and the girls ended up calling the missing-persons helpline. It had all got a bit messy. Then their neighbours did a search of the canal to see if I'd been 'chucked in'.

Anyway, the moral of the story is that Mike Travers is a sex pest. And hiding in cupboards that don't have great ventilation when you're drunk can often make you sleepy. And deaf.

The service was so beautiful and I only cried seven times, stopping for discernible stretches of time in between (which was important because Lisa had made a bet with me that I'd be 'an inconsolable snotty mess' for the 'entire thing'). I won a fiver. *Amazing.*

And I only got a slight wobble in my legs, and a mild sweat across my top lip when it was my turn to walk up the aisle, which I was very proud of (I made no direct eye contact with any confession boxes). Although I could have done without catching sight of my own family. There was nothing like seeing your mother scowling at your father, or your sister with her back turned to her husband, to knock the wind out of the moment's romantic sails. Dad nodded awkwardly from the pews while Mum gave one of her best instant-just-add-water smiles. All Tanya could do was roll her eyes at me as she witnessed the *Lord of the Rings/Hairspray* cast members parade past like a circus freak show. I could hardly blame her for that. Besides, it was how Tanya always greeted me: she rolled her eyes to the back of her head, like a pinball machine. Apparently in Tibet they stick out their tongues, so maybe she was just trying to be a bit 'ethnic', rather than displaying her overt dislike of me.

Apart from all that, I remained relatively calm through the proceedings. And when one of the priest's eyebrows caught fire from the unity candle I actually managed to laugh. I had to ask Lisa if she had heard the priest say to me, 'You will be united with Robbie in Christ.' She informed me that he had actually said, 'This is the Body of Christ,' and that she was fairly sure he cared more about the Resurrection than whether or not Robbie and I ever got married. Which I thought was harsh, but possibly a fair point since, apart from yesterday's rehearsal, I didn't know Father Neville at all.

I arched my head around, scanning the crowd for Robbie, and caught him looking at me. I smiled at him and he winked. I loved that. Catching one another's eye across a crowded room when everyone else is oblivious to it. Like two little bulbs on a switchboard that connect and light up a different colour from all the rest.

I couldn't help grinning at his expression. I knew he thought he was channelling, 'The dress isn't as bad as you think,' to me, but what he was actually conveying was, 'The dress *is* as bad as you think but you still look cute.'

Bless him, I could read him like a book (one that I could understand. Not *Ulysses*. Or anything in German).

We spilled out of the church, ready to cover the newly married couple in a shower of rose petals, when we were met unexpectedly with a flurry of white fluffy snowflakes, dancing in the winter-pink sky like flecks of glazed confetti. In the enchanting light of the late afternoon, the sky looked as if it had been drizzled with diamonds, and it was absolutely breathtaking.

'Thanks, Dad,' I heard Rebecca whisper.

Wow. This was amazing. The powdery snowflakes kissed my cheeks as my throat swelled with happiness. Why on earth had I been so petrified?

## 7

So who knew that being dressed like a circus hobbit would make for a terrific day? Sort of reminded me of when Granny insisted on buying my First Communion dress and in a moment of weakness Mum agreed. I ended up dressed like one of those freaky child beauty-pageant queens, but I really enjoyed it because I made seventeen pounds and got a kiss on the cheek from James Murray. (I'm still struggling with the long-term effects, though, needing to sit down for a minute any time I smell hairspray or see a puffball sleeve.)

What was terrific about weddings when your friend was getting married? Well, all your lovely like-minded friends were there. Not at all like Ethyl's wedding, where she only allowed me to invite Lisa and Rebecca and ended up seating us at opposite ends of the marquee so we wouldn't talk. I'm sorry – were we sitting an exam?

Actually, yes, we were: the 'How Amazing Was My Wedding?' exam. I was still made to answer on-the-spot multiple-choice questions seven years on (e.g. 'Rate my wedding favours on a scale of one to ten, ten being the highest and eight the lowest possible score you can give').

The function room was utterly breathtaking, like an enchanted cocoon of winter-wonderland magic. The walls and ceiling were festooned with white organza and spun with loops of twinkling fairy-lights. The candelabra on each table were the most beautiful crystal snowflake hexagons, with tea-lights winking inside the fractured glass. The cake, on a podium beside the top table, was a snow-globe creation, with Rebecca and Tony as two little figurines inside it in their wedding finery. And the fragrance from the clusters of white peonies dotted around the room danced through the air, like invisible circus acts. Was it really bad that I planned to get months – maybe years – of pleasure out of torturing Ethyl with every fabulous detail? Might go against me if she threw herself under an articulated lorry on the N11 and Mum got really pissed off with me.

We all gathered in pockets around the most gorgeous little Christmas trees dotted throughout the room. Dinky Champagne flutes hung from loops on the branches, and when you lifted one off, someone was there instantly to fill it. Oh, it was magical – like *Willy Wonka and the Chocolate Factory* for grown-ups / lushes.

'Isn't this amazing?' Lisa cooed, breathing in her surroundings.

'Out of this world,' I said. 'I just love weddings!' I added, surprising myself. But this really was spectacular and made all the more so by reminiscing about the good old days with good old friends. Unlike a posh tent full of boring fund accountants, who only wanted to talk about guinea fowl and the ISEQ, this bunch was fantastic. All the old crowd from school and college were there, and even Rebecca's cousins whom I hadn't seen since 1998 when we were all going through our tortured teenage phase; I'd gone with them to see David Gray at Slane. (On second thoughts, I wasn't so sure if I was happy or utterly mortified to see them again. But what goes on tour stays on tour, right? There had been a lot of cider drunk, I was still a little raw after 'This Year's Love', all those tents looked the same and I really had thought I was wearing clothes . . .)

'Grace Harte! Always in detention for defacing school property,' Joanne said.

'Hey!' I said. 'Just because I drew an Errol Flynn moustache on a Robbie Williams poster in our form room – he looked so much better! Remember Sister Eileen said I was going to end up a "crack-pot prostitute" if I didn't "buck up"?'

'I remember what she said when you asked her if that was a threat or a promise,' Lisa said.

'How many detentions did you get for "not wearing the correct uniform"?' Lynne asked.

'Making someone wear brown wool for six years is actually

a violation of civil liberties,' I said. '*Brown wool!* God, I think I need to sit down. And I only stitched a lovely ruffled Victorian collar on my shirt *once!*'

'And wore a Philip Treacy-esque hat *once!*' Olivia said.

'And wore sixteen layers of petticoats under your uniform skirt *once!*' Joanne said. 'God, I'll never forget everyone having to pin themselves to the wall just so you could pass by when you were coming down the corridor, your skirt was so wide. But my favourite was when you wore leather gloves for the hockey final in third year.'

'Well, I had to try and do something to spruce up that God-awful gym gear,' I said. 'And the gloves were *so* Grace Kelly.'

'Yeah, I'm just not sure Grace Kelly and the hockey final really go in the same sentence.'

'Yeah,' I said, all the while thinking, *Erm, they so do! Especially if you'd tied a neat Hermès copy scarf around your neck in a sweet little bow.* 'Do you remember Lisa and Joanne getting suspended for sending Mr Kilduff a Valentine's card?' I said.

Everyone burst out laughing.

'What?' Lisa answered. '*He was a hottie!*'

'Erm, he was a fifty-eight-year-old home-economics teacher with a skin condition and no teeth,' Olivia said.

'He had beautiful hair,' Lisa said, under her breath, and downed a mouthful of bubbles.

'Have you managed to get over Mr Kilduff, Lisa?' Judy said, sidling up to our group and joining the conversation.

Judy Traynor, or Judge Judy Traynor as we called her. She'd always been fond of a spot of 'judging' and here she was now in a long black dress looking more like she'd swung by from the Four Courts than ever before. I was surprised Rebecca had even invited her, since we spent a lot of our time marvelling at her shocking Judge Judy comments. ('Oooh, the Ritz, is it?' she had said to Rebecca, the first time she met her after the wedding invitations had gone out. 'Was Dromoland Castle all booked up? I think you need to know someone there, really, don't you?')

'No, still not over Mr Kilduff,' Lisa said, crossing her fingers. 'Any day now, hopefully.'

I braced myself: I could sense Judy's Judgement Pheromone being released into the air.

'Not married, then?' she said, her words drenched in condescension, like she was asking a five-year-old if they were still having problems wetting the bed.

Euch. I decided on the spot that I really disliked Judy Traynor. She was like Simon Cowell only with nicer trousers (a big Reiss fan, apparently) and a better haircut. Still, no matter how good her hair looked, I always imagined her wearing a judge's wig on top of it, which goes quite a way to ruining a good blow-dry.

'No, still not married. Although that would be a touch weird seeing as you asked me the exact same thing last month, and unless I'd run off to Vegas with Mr Kilduff that would be a bit weird, don't you think?' Lisa said. 'And you, of course, are married four years. How would I know that? Because you told me that last month too. So four years and one month now.'

Lisa was smiling all the while so that her obvious dislike would have been imperceptible to a passing stranger. Then she went a bit mental. Maybe the realization that she was wearing a pink Lycra ice-skating outfit in public had just dawned on her. (I had accepted it first thing that morning and fessing up early had helped me no end in coping.)

'Well, Judge Judy . . .'

Uh-oh. Had she really just called her that? *To her face?*

'. . . thank you for your judgements on my marital status. But today's court has been adjourned. Thank you and goodbye.'

And with that she was gone. Holy crap. I plodded after her (when you're wearing canoe-type flats, there is officially no other way of getting around than to plod).

'What was that about?' I hissed.

'What?' she said. 'I'm fed up trying to pretend she's not a twat. Plain and simple. I'm getting too old for that. Nearly thirty, to be exact. Nearly thirty, not married, very honest. It's my new thing.'

'Yeah, but you don't tell someone to her face! We don't call your Mum "Deli Deirdre" to her face! Jesus, I wish you'd warn me when you're trying out new things.'

'Deli Deirdre?'

Balls. That was what Rebecca and I called her. Lisa didn't know. Until now.

'Sorry, yeah. It's just she offers to make everyone sandwiches all the time. Even if she bumps into you on Grafton Street in the middle of the day. It's actually really endearing . . .'

'Deli Deirdre. I like it. And she does love making people a sandwich.'

'She really does, doesn't she?'

We plodded towards the top table as the head waiter tolled the bell for dinner.

'It's just, well, this whole marriage thing, it's everywhere,' Lisa said. 'And everyone has an opinion on it. It's become the new weather as a conversational gambit. It used to be "Oh, nice day today, isn't it? I wonder when it will rain." Now all I hear is, "Nice day for a wedding, isn't it? I wonder when you're going to get married?"'

I laughed, knowing exactly what she meant. 'Maybe they could get that guy on TV3 to swap his weather slot after the news with *The Wedding Forecast*. "In the late afternoon we can expect a shower of weddings in the east of the country, moving to a fair few proposals in the south by the end of the evening." Anyway, don't you be worrying. As you said yourself, you'll be getting hitched to Killian so you're grand.'

She rolled her eyes and poked me in the ribs. 'Christ, I'm bringing feminism back decades! It's not that getting married has to be the be-all and end-all. It's just I'd like to know where I'm going, you know? All the other lemmings seem to be running full throttle and jumping off the cliff with great determination and here I am trying to read the map to find out where all the bloody cliffs are.'

We swigged the remaining Champagne from our glasses and

looked out at the sea of guests swarming and clamouring around the tables.

'Well, if getting married is like a lemming jumping off a cliff, I think I'll plod along as I am, thanks very much.'

We smiled and clinked our empty glasses, only for a waiter to appear magically behind us and refill them again. God, I wished I had one of those at home. But Robbie kept telling me we couldn't afford one. Apparently we needed to get our septic tank sorted, buy a new tumble-drier and make sure we could actually pay our mortgage before even entertaining the idea of a waiter. He was a rock of sense.

'Either way, don't be worrying about what Judge Judy thinks. The only reason she got married so young in the first place was because she was *always* obsessed with getting married.'

'Yeah, maybe . . .'

'Maybe? Who the hell else wears a wedding dress to her Debs? "It was actually purple to start out, but my mum accidentally put it in the wash with bleach so now it's white. It was far too late to start looking for another one,"' I said sweetly, doing my best take-off of Judge Judy. 'My arse! She bought it in Bridal Couture on Nassau Street. Fact. Plus, when everyone else had a corsage tied to their wrist, that lunatic was carrying a bouquet of white roses.'

The dinner and the speeches were just magnificent.

Apart from a few hiccups. The beef was slightly overcooked. Found out why a little later on. Apparently Alan-the-perv was giving the head chef, well, head in the cold room when she was meant to be keeping an eye on *our* meat instead of his. He should have stayed down there because his speech was so embarrassing I thought *my* head was going to overcook I was cringing so much. He tried to make some joke about himself and Tony and a group of lads sowing their wild oats all those years back in Ibiza. Rebecca just rolled her eyes. But when he mentioned the 'twenty-four in twenty-four hours' between the lot of them, Rebecca's mum sort of . . . well, almost . . . actually, definitely started crying.

I tried to smooth over things by making out it was touching to see her getting emotional over the lovely wedding speeches. 'Aw, that's so sweet, isn't it?'

She looked at me like I was drunk (I so wasn't), and cried some more.

Then Rebecca's granny, who has dementia, stood up and, I kid you not, started singing 'All The Single Ladies'. Her cousin who is on medication for an unknown mental illness stood up at the opposite end of the marquee and joined her in a duet. Everyone just sat there in stunned silence until they had finished (and the cousin had wrapped up his ass-shake dance moves). Lo and behold, trust me to be the only person in the room who had come to the conclusion that it was the right moment to break into a round of applause.

So, apart from a few details, the dinner and the rest of the speeches were magnificent. (I was trying to be really positive because I felt a bit bad that Lisa and I had been having a moan about 'the whole getting-married thing', and then I was afraid I had sort of jinxed it a bit. Like the year I told Mum I didn't believe in Santa and the Christmas tree fell on Dad and it took four of our neighbours at least an hour and a half to get him out from under it.)

And finally the wonderful Tony stood up and spoke of his immeasurable love for Rebecca. He said he was often left frustrated with the inadequacies of the English language when it came to describing his wife. 'All of what you are to me, my lover, my friend, my confidante, doesn't quite measure up to all of what you *mean* to me,' he said. 'It always falls short of the mark. There's just too much about you that can't be captured by attributes or labels or qualifications. Or fancy words and flowery language that can never quite get there. The only way I can describe what you mean to me is to know and love you as "my Rebecca".'

Potential tear-fest. Lisa started pinching me, which really didn't help the situation.

Then Rebecca stood up and gave the most touching speech about her love for her new husband and how her father had always known he was the right man for the job in looking after her when he was gone.

'My dad was the first great love of my life. Tony knows I probably won't ever really get over him.' They both smiled and he took her hand, holding it tightly in his. 'I remember one afternoon when we were teenagers, Grace and Lisa were staying over at our house. And, as you all know, our Grace has a slight fondness for old Hollywood movies . . .'

I hoped she wasn't going to regale them with the story of when I was re-enacting that Ginger Rogers and Fred Astaire number on their stairs, tripped and knocked myself out on the knob at the end of the banisters. Her dad had had to bring me to hospital on the back of his scooter because his car was broken down. (I was unaware of all of this at the time obviously, but apparently you transport an unconscious person on a scooter by strapping them to the driver with two large belts.)

'Even though Lisa and I really wanted to watch that world-renowned classic *Suburban Commando* with Hulk Hogan, Grace somehow convinced us to watch *For Whom the Bell Tolls* instead. Best and worst decision we ever made. We all ended up bawling inconsolably on the couch for poor Ingrid Bergman. I'll never forget Dad coming in with a tray of tea and biscuits, and sitting there with us while we dunked our Kimberleys and wailed for Gary Cooper. The last thing my dad ever said to me was based on Gary's parting words from that movie. He handed me a Kimberley Mikado and a tiny bell, and told me to ring it whenever I needed him and he'd be there. "Go on now, love," he said. "Where I'm going now, I have to go on my own. You have to let me go. But it's not goodbye because we'll never be apart."'

There wasn't a dry eye in the house and I thanked God: I didn't want to be the only one sobbing like Barbara Hershey at the end of *Beaches*.

My God, everything was changing so fast. I wanted to be back on the couch at Rebecca's, even for a few moments, where life seemed paused on timeless ease. Now it was stuck on fast forward, throttling full steam ahead and no matter how much we tried to hold on to what we had, we were invariably moving further and further away from where we had begun.

Life.

Birth. Having tinfoil shoved down your nappy. Growing up. Adulthood. Marriage. Children. Ageing. Death. That was it.

Then I came to again and everyone was cheering as the bride and groom cut the cake with a giant sword (their first cinema date was *Crouching Tiger, Hidden Dragon*). I searched for Robbie, somewhere out there in the wall of faces staring ahead. I looked for him to tether me, ground me, like I always did when I felt I was spiralling. We caught each other's eye. He smiled at me. And I smiled back.

Breaking the spell, Rebecca's granny stood up and started singing Drake and Rihanna's 'Take Care'. My God, I needed to download her iTunes account. Everyone laughed. I laughed. At myself.

These were the good times. They really were.

The tables were drawn to the side of the ballroom to make room for a dance floor. And then Rebecca and Tony took their first official dance together to '(Your Love Keeps Lifting Me) Higher And Higher'. I thought the warm fuzzy feeling in my belly was going to end up puffing out of my ears.

Robbie made his way through the crowd, walked straight up to me, took my hand in his, and led me towards the floor. As I watched him ahead of me, it felt like we were moving in slow motion as the world spun and shook around us; the commotion, the music, the dancing. We were moving in our own bubble, where the noise outside was muffled and my mind was still. I slid my arms around him and laid my head against his chest.

'How are you holding up?' he asked, pulling me closer to him.

'It's been a fantastic day, hasn't it? And I think I've done incredibly well lasting this long in a cerise pink ice-skating outfit and blue eye-shadow. Actually, if you're giving out any certificates for being wonderful, I think I'll have one, please.'

'Well, you still manage to look hot.'

'For a circus hobbit maybe.'

'Hey! You're my circus hobbit.'

I smiled and kissed him. Another circus freak whizzed past me. Lisa and Killian. They looked happy. I rested my head against his chest again. 'You get many "Why aren't you two getting married?" yet today?'

'Only about four hundred and twenty-seven. So, you know, not many . . .'

'I wish they'd all just piss off.'

'It's only because we're at a wedding,' he consoled me softly. We stood there holding each other as the crowd swayed to 'You've Lost That Lovin' Feelin''.

'Not the best wedding song this, is it?' he said.

'Not really.' I giggled. I hugged him tight for making me smile. 'We're doing the right thing, aren't we?' I whispered, almost to myself.

'Hey,' he said, dragging my chin up so he could look me in the eye. 'It'll be our time in its own good time. And when it comes, it'll be all the more special because it'll be right for *us*.'

'I know,' I answered, not needing to be convinced. 'I know.'

'The whole wedding thing,' he continued, 'it so often just seems like a race to the post or something. But it's people's lives together, before and after, that's the most important thing.'

I rested my head back on his chest, grateful for his wisdom, but mostly for his heart.

Maybe this was all in my own head. All this pressure from other people to get married. I was probably being over-sensitive about it. Perhaps no one else gave a toss what Robbie and I did with our lives.

Or not.

'Do you know what you need to do, love?'

'Tell me,' I answered numbly, hoping she was going to say, 'Get your drink from the barman pronto so you can rejoin your friends on the dance floor instead of standing here being brayed at by three old donkeys.'

She didn't. Instead she came out with 'Trap him. That's right. Snare him like a rabbit.'

Just when I thought I'd been imagining it all.

I looked at Rebecca's great-aunt Marge, flanked by two of her cronies, like the Destiny's Child of octogenarians. Marge was obviously the Beyoncé of the group, while Netty (Michelle) and Breda (Kelly) stood there posing with their hands on their hips.

I wondered what would happen if I just flicked her face right now. It's sort of frowned upon to do that to someone in their eighties, isn't it?

'If he won't commit, you need to trap him for his own sake. Women have been doing it for years, darling. I cannot believe you *still* don't have a ring on your finger!'

'Well, the thing is that Robbie and I are perfectly happy as we are for now,' I said, wondering why I was justifying my life yet again.

'Hmm, you say that, dear, but I can tell you're trying to convince yourself so as not to lose face.' She dropped her voice. 'I know of someone who went as far as sedating her then boyfriend, a couple of pills into his beef bourguignon, and once he came around she had the engagement ring on her finger, done and dusted. Off she went and got started on planning the wedding.'

'That's awful,' I managed, dumbstruck. 'But what –'

'About the beef? Didn't spoil the taste at all.'

Good to know.

'You could also do the Phantom Pregnancy trick.'

Oh, great. Even Netty, the Michelle of the group, had an opinion and she was meant to be the mute one. 'And then once you have the church and the priest booked, simply tell him that you must have got your months mixed up.'

What was wrong with these people? What was wrong with my life just the way it was? And whatever happened to women's lib? And PS: I did *not* need to be taking life advice from three women who were wearing a collage of brown, navy and orange skirt suits with toffee-coloured tights and nun shoes. Not that people in pink ice-skating outfits should be throwing glass houses. Or however that goes . . .

I looked beyond Destiny's Grannies and smiled at Robbie swinging the bride around the dance floor. I really hoped he didn't give her a nosebleed: she was quite susceptible to them. My shoulders relaxed again. This was all as it should be. We didn't need a priest and a church and 250 people dressed in brown, navy and orange skirt suits to approve what we had. I knew what we had. We knew what we had.

He looked so handsome out there in his tux. I always thought he looked a bit like Owen Wilson, which he quite liked. Although he did make me swear that his nose wasn't as crooked as his, which it wasn't (but it had veered off to the left a bit ever since he'd got smacked in the face with a tennis ball at last year's Wimbledon. There was a bit of a bloodbath afterwards, but the management had given us free Champagne and strawberries by way of an apology, which was lovely).

Owen Wilson with a touch of Gregory Peck. What a perfect combination!

I really did trust this man with my life. And I couldn't imagine how loving anyone but him would feel. It had always been him. Always would be. We'd both known that for a very long time.

I had nothing to worry about. We had all the time in the world.

## 8

For someone who was so happy, and delighted that she'd figured out her whole life on the edge of a dance floor less than an hour previously, I had no idea why I was now bawling with a complete randomer in a cubicle in the Ladies.

Well, it was actually *her* who was crying, but I sort of joined in so she wouldn't feel so self-conscious. But then it was *me* who was really crying, and the randomer with the lovely hair and the makeup smudged all over her face was telling me it was all going to be okay. What a lovely randomer. As far as randomers went, she definitely was one of the nicest ones I'd ever cried with in a toilet cubicle, and I really hoped that we'd become firm friends afterwards, or at the very least keep in touch on Facebook.

'I don't even know why I'm crying,' I wailed, as she held a wad of toilet paper to my nose and made me blow. 'I really didn't mean to start crying. I'm so sorry, I've totally taken the limelight away from your misery . . .'

'It's okay,' she hiccuped. 'To be honest, I don't even know him, so it was possibly a touch over-the-top to start crying when I found out he was married after only just being introduced to him.'

'Well, I don't think so,' I said. 'I mean, who does he think he is, being all married? And why does everyone have to be "Oh, he's married, she's married, let's all get married!"'

'I know! Right!' she answered, her face crumpling again.

'That's the spirit,' I said encouragingly, stroking her hair as she wailed into a fresh wad of toilet tissue.

What the hell was wrong with me? I surveyed my surroundings. 'Cramped' and 'traumatizing' would be two ways to describe them. I wasn't sure my leg was supposed to bend that way, but it had nowhere else to go and, besides, my other foot was resting firmly on top of the sanitary bin. The randomer was curled up on the floor in front of the toilet, and I wondered why cubicle designers didn't allow more room for this type of scenario, seeing as it happened in cubicles every Friday and Saturday night all over the world.

Someone banged on the door.

'Fuck off!' my randomer friend replied. Wow, she was a feisty one. Actually, I think I was starting to go off her already. She was taking up far too much room for this to be in any way an equal partnership of misery. I was also starting to wonder if she was one of those Toilet Cubicle Enablers I'd heard about on the circuit. I mean, why on earth was I crying?

Was it about Rebecca's dad and the gorgeous speech she'd given about him?

Was it that Alan-the-perv had told me my shoes looked like man-sized tissue boxes?

I'd just finished my post-grad in creative business, after a year of studying like a maniac and living like a cretin. Slothing around in tracksuit bottoms, slowly going cross-eyed after hours hunched over massive six-hundred-plus-page books (any book with more than three hundred, the author was just showing off – Tolstoy was a renowned attention-seeker). I was back to wearing normal clothes, reading Mills & Boon and the twitch in my left eye had almost completely corrected itself, which was fantastic. *And* Robbie and I had just bought our first house together. Surely this was a time to be *happy*. I repeat: what was I so upset about?

Why was it that I kept boomeranging from contentment to this unsettling restlessness?

Was it work? Maybe it was. I'd get it sorted soon, I knew I would. I was *not* going to be working for Eleanor Holt and recidivist fashion criminals for ever . . .

Suddenly there was another loud bang on the toilet door.

'Grace? Grace, are you in there?'

'Lisa?'

'Oh, thank God. Robbie was convinced you'd drowned in the fountain out the back.'

Hmm. That was a little dramatic, seeing as I'd only nearly drowned in a fountain *once* before. And it was unfortunate timing that I'd been dared to swim in it when I just so happened to be wearing freakishly absorbent clothing and very heavy clog-type Miu Miu copies.

I opened the door, and stepped over the randomer, who had fallen fast asleep with her head against the loo.

'Who's that?' Lisa asked.

'To be honest, I'm not entirely sure. I think she's with the groom's family. Nice enough girl, but a tad on the moany side.'

'They're giving out the cake,' Lisa said, wiping the mascara from under my eyes and flattening the tuft of taffeta that had bunched up around my backside like a duck's arse.

Aw, I loved Lisa. I also loved cake. Especially a chocolate biscuit cake that was so large it had taken four men to wheel it in on a gurney.

We walked out of the loos and she took my hand, squeezing it tight. I loved her for knowing. And for knowing not to ask.

I felt much better with a wedge of chocolate biscuit cake in my mouth. So much better, in fact, that I now felt really silly for having spent the last forty minutes crying on the floor of the ladies' loos with one foot jammed on top of a sanitary bin.

I barely had time to finish my cake before all our friends spilled onto the dance floor like an army of ants and linked hands to form a large circle around Rebecca and Tony. They were staring at each other, all puppy-eyed, and I nearly melted watching them.

This was brilliant. This was what it was all about. The fun, the love, the friendship. We cheered and whistled as they swung each other about in some mad flamenco routine, and I looked at Robbie and winked.

'You okay?' he mouthed.

'Yes.' And I was. I really was. I always slagged him for the

Spanish-gypsy dancing he resorted to whenever he'd had too much to drink. He seemed to be doing it right now, when no one else on the floor was dancing. He smiled at me, knowing what I was thinking. I could feel the love swelling up again and I clung to it, desperate to keep a firm hold.

All of a sudden, I saw Rebecca clambering up on the stage, bunching her dress around her knees. Everyone started to cheer as she turned her back on us and lifted her bouquet high into the air. I covered my eyes, praying to God she wasn't going to end up in a body sling for her honeymoon. She hated getting an uneven tan.

And when I opened my eyes again, all I could see was a giant bunch of peonies tied with a gorgeous cream organza ribbon hurtling through the air towards me at a million miles an hour. I screamed, and held my hands up to protect my face, not wanting a Wimbledon-style bloodbath, or a nose that veered to the left, like Owen Wilson or Robbie Cotter, and I ended up catching the darn bouquet in the middle of my two hands.

*Ah, for crying out loud! What were the chances?*

The room went quiet. The only thing I could hear was my heart as it exploded into rapid fire in my ears. It was deafening. Everyone just stood there staring at me. Out of the corner of my eye, I could see the randomer from the ladies' toilets. She'd obviously peeled herself from the side of the loo and was now glowering at me, like she wanted to maim me. Yeah, I reckoned it was a safe bet that I wouldn't be getting any Facebook friendship requests. Though I might get a sanitary bin lobbed at my head at any moment. I saw Mum and Dad on opposite sides of the dance floor smiling at me nervously.

What did all these lunatics expect me to do? I stared back at them as they continued to blink at me eagerly.

'Yay?' I offered, in a little voice, not really knowing what else I should be doing under the circumstances. The lunatics took it as their cue to cheer wildly and kick off a spate of wolf-whistling.

I smiled self-consciously, wishing the ground would open up and swallow me whole.

I looked around the room nervously, and right then I saw something that made my heart sink. Robbie caught my eye and, in a flash, I saw it. I saw his face drop.

And there and then I wanted to crawl back into the toilet cubicle and start crying again.

## 9

The great thing about being a lover of old movies is, if you tried really hard, you could put an old-fashioned romantic spin on just about anything. Take our house, for example. In reality it's a bit like the disaster zone from *The Money Pit* and about a two-hundredth of the size, but in my head it's not far off Tara in *Gone With The Wind*.

I liked doing that, Photoshopping reality. Made life far more beautiful to look at, really. Although I have found that it doesn't work so well when it comes to my job. The number of times I've tried to imagine myself as Rosalind Russell in *His Girl Friday* on the cusp of getting my big career break. But no matter how much I squinted I could never seem to make Eleanor Holt look anything like Cary Grant.

Okay, so our Tara was a touch on the small side. And a bit wonky too (the surveyor must just have come from a boozy lunch the day he passed it for a mortgage) – you had to lean backwards out of the upstairs bathroom if you wanted to hang stuff out on the washing line, the oven had sunk into the foundations in the kitchen so we could only use the grill, and part of the ceiling had landed on my head one night. We were in the middle of watching *Alien*, just as a crazy extra-terrestrial was about to burst out of Sigourney Weaver's stomach, and I got such a fright I splashed red wine all over the walls and did a tiny wee in my pants that I never told Robbie about.

But it was *our* house. And to us it was a castle. No more landlords, no more having to share with creepy weirdos who 'sleep-walked' to your underwear drawer and 'accidentally' tried on your knickers, or kept frogs as pets (no one should ever have a frog jump out of a shampoo bottle while in the shower, even if they are cute), or crocheted their own clothes and held religious meetings in your living room. No more paying rent to mean landlords, who told you that having rats in your garden was 'character building', or that lack of hot water would make you grateful 'not to be Eskimos'.

We'd come a long way in seven years of seeing the world from different beds (that makes us sound like swingers, which we *never* were), and sneaking into each other's bedrooms when we still lived at home. Once, I had to hide in a laundry basket on the landing of their house when his parents unexpectedly came home early one night. I was in there for *hours* after Vera Cotter decided it was the perfect time to pack her winter clothes and put them up in the attic. And just when I thought I couldn't take much more, Des Cotter lifted the lid and threw his jocks and socks in on top of my head. As well as confession boxes, I now have quite a fear of laundry baskets.

We'd slept in all sorts of beds in dingy hotels around the world, having gone travelling together. Slept in an old Volkswagen camper-van in the Australian outback. Although I wasn't sure either of us slept that much. (Note to self: the bio-pic of Joanne Lees and Peter Falconio, *Murder in the Outback*, was *not* the film to watch before you set off on such an adventure. And Robbie wouldn't admit it, but I thought he also regretted having watched *A Dingo Stole My Baby*. Even though we didn't have a baby. But still.)

Of course there were the nice beds too. Like when Robbie took me to the Champs-Élysées Plaza in Paris as a surprise for my twenty-fifth birthday. Or when we got bumped up to the presidential suite at our hotel in Bangkok after we came back to our room and one of the male Thai room-service attendants was standing there in my underwear and a dog collar.

I must have *seriously* nice underwear.

Then, of course, there was the first time we ever shared a bed together. The very first night we met.

It's not what it sounds like: I didn't give in that easily. Besides,

I'd just had my stomach pumped and had third-degree burns on my face so it would have been a touch insensitive and self-centred of him if he'd tried it on.

Yes, that was how I met the love of my life. He pelted me in the face with paint bullets until I almost fell unconscious. It was a complete accident, and one he still felt awful about. And he was very gentle normally. He even trapped flies in glass jars and let them out of the window. But the first time we met, he did almost kill me, yes.

I managed to get separated from my group on a paint-balling adventure day out at college and accidentally got mixed up with Robbie's advanced group. Just as I was taking off my mask to look for my team mates, he mistook me for 'the little ginger shit' who'd ambushed him earlier on and unleashed primary-colour hell on me.

I swallowed so much paint the doctors said I 'almost died'. (No one else had any record of them saying this, but that was only because they would have been so traumatized if I had died that their minds had blocked it out.) But I almost did die. I even saw my granddad dressed in a toga (official Heaven uniform) waving at me from the white light. (Again, some members of my family chose to believe this was just the doctor in his scrubs looking into my pupils with his torch-thingie. If that was how they coped, who was I to judge them?)

The force of the paint bullets also removed two layers of my skin, which Tanya said people paid good money to a dermatologist to get done and I was a 'lucky bitch'. I didn't feel like a lucky bitch that night, with a frozen pizza on my face and wafts of coloured gas coming out my mouth every time I burped. But I did feel lucky that my attempted murderer turned out to be the loveliest man I'd ever met. He drove me home from the hospital, sick with guilt, and stayed with me the whole night. Rebecca – I was living with her at the time – asked why I'd let Ted Bundy into the house, which made him melt with mortification. But I stood up for him and said that Ted had killed loads of people while Robbie had only *tried* to kill *one* person. That I knew of.

We chatted for hours about serial killers, like Harold Shipman and Fred and Rose West, which was weird for a first date. Especially since I was wearing a pizza on my face. Around the time we were talking about hiding bodies under concrete slabs, I slipped into a poison-induced coma. And when I woke in the morning, this gorgeous, intriguing, kind man was still there. Fast asleep beside me. He was so handsome, in an old-fashioned, groomed sort of way, and his skin looked so deliciously golden in the early-morning sunshine, it took everything in my power not to touch it. He was divine. And with the sheets wrapped around him like a toga, he reminded me of Richard Burton in *Cleopatra*. And definitely not my granddad in Heaven.

We'd gone from that bed in Rathmines, with Rebecca snoring in the room next to us, to Elvis – Robbie's nickname for our bed, a tribute to the other six-foot king – in *our* Tara, number seven Maple Street.

We were in Heaven. And we were having so much fun doing it up. We'd spend hours in hardware shops, picking out different bits and bobs. The day we set out for Ikea, I got so excited I ended up peaking *way* too soon, and we had to turn around before we even got there because I'd fallen asleep on the M1. The bedroom and bathroom were now completely finished: Robbie had painted them white, and I'd furnished them with fantastic bright rugs, hung gorgeous antique mirrors and fitted fabulously rustic brass door handles and towel rails. It was turning out just as we'd always dreamed. Minus the structural damage and the toilet that, for no apparent reason, would sometimes gush upwards when you flushed. Not ideal if you were feeling sensitive after a curry. The plumber down the road was one of our new best friends – indeed, 'Larry the plumber' had been added to our short-list of favourite children's names. Oh, no, sorry – just Larry.

And definitely minus the cat. I could almost certainly say that

I'd never come across a picture of an evil cat pissing in a shoe when leafing through the pages of *Ideal Home.*

As I said, we inherited her with the house. Along with some doilies and a jar of lemon curd. The lady who used to live here died of old age (although I made the estate agent, the solicitor and the two adjoining neighbours swear on their mothers' lives that she didn't die *in* the house, which they all did, and I even double-checked that none of them were crossing their fingers on the sly). Anyway, it appears that none of her next of kin were too bothered about dividing up the doilies or the lemon curd or the cat. Well, dividing up the cat would have been a touch barbaric, not to mention unnecessary, but no one came to collect her after the papers were signed. The estate agent called the family a few times and left messages, but no one got back to us. I even put her on top of the skip in the hope they'd take it away, but she jumped right back out, the stubborn little shit.

Then one day the old lady's middle-aged son stopped by, with a basket of laundry, to 'say hello to Mammy'.

Christ! Did they forget to put out a death notice? Did someone forget to tell her flippin' son that she'd croaked it? What was I supposed to say? 'Sorry, your mammy's not in because . . . she's dead'?

Turned out her son knew that his mother had passed over. Mammy had, he said, passed over into the soul of the cat.

I. Kid. You. Not.

Most people might get an old fridge or a wardrobe or a kettle when they buy a second-hand house. Us? We got Norman – or Ab-Norman, as I called him – a half-witted forty-five-year-old Cheryl Cole fanatic, who thought his mother was living inside a cat, and called around on a regular basis to visit her and do his laundry (mostly T-shirts with Cheryl Cole's face on them). When I suggested he take his mammy with him, he started crying and saying that this was her home. When I suggested that perhaps he did his washing in his own home, he started crying again and saying it was just like when Simon Cowell kicked Cheryl out of America. And, as we know, I'm not great when people start crying. I always end up crying with them, which is highly unproductive I've discovered.

So, we were stuck with the cat.

Robbie felt sorry for it. But I didn't feel sorry for any cat that jumped out at you from behind doors, or sat in the bathroom and stared at you while you took a shower.

It was the week after the wedding and Robbie and I were mooching around the house not doing very much. There was that distinctive tap on the door: Norman always used the side of a coin to bang on the glass panel. That sound made my heart beat faster – and definitely not in the way it does when I see Balmain's new collection.

'Robbie? Will you let him in?' I called from the bedroom.

'It's your turn!'

'No, it's not!' I panicked. Was it really my turn? Already? Hell I was going to try and lie my way out of this one. 'Remember the last time? He came over and gave out to me for not having his favourite fabric conditioner and sang "Fight For This Love" until I popped out to Spar to get some.'

'Grace, that was last June.'

Damn.

'Fine. Fine. You stay in here and watch TV, Lord Maple, while I go and see to the lunatics. Oh, and you'd better let Bette know her son is here.'

While I shuffled to the door to let the cat's son in, I wondered if our neighbours ever heard us through the walls and thought of calling someone about having us sectioned.

'Norman!' I managed to sound delighted to see him. I found it was the best way to deal with him. If you didn't act happy, he got very panicky and paranoid that we were being mean to his mother and subsequently upped his surprise 'drop-ins'. Then he started referring to me as 'Nadine' and suggesting there had been some sort of falling-out. I just had to remember not to call him 'Ab-Norman' to his face.

'Grace! Well, don't you look just lovely!'

'Oh, Ab? I mean Norman. Stop! You'll make Robbie jealous.'

I loved saying that because it always made him go bright red. On cue, his face filled up, like a tank of crimson petrol. I was convinced Norman was a virgin but Robbie said it was always the odd ones you had to look out for and laid a bet he had seventeen different sex dolls in his basement. We wondered if having sex with a doll qualified as having lost your virginity. Probably not. No matter how lifelike she was or how much 'real Indian hair' she had.

He stood there in his brown cords and navy anorak, blinking at me through his prescription goggles (he'd lost his glasses a few weeks back and was waiting for his new ones to come in).

'Hi, Robbie!' he sang merrily. 'Getting into the Christmas spirit, I see.'

We shot each other a covert 'Huh?'

'The red socks!'

'Oh, yes,' Robbie said. 'Nothing says, "Christmas Time," like red socks!'

Well, actually, nothing says, 'Uh-oh – I Just Ruined The White Wash By Accidentally Throwing In My Cherry Bomb Wrap Dress' like red socks, I thought.

'Hi, Mammy,' Norman chirped, petting Bette's head before plodding into the laundry room with his basket of washing. She peered beyond him, glowering at me, so I just flipped her the birdie.

'Don't be so mean to Norman's mum,' Robbie scolded, under his breath, pulling me down on the couch beside him.

'Ab-Norman's mum is a pain in the ass,' I said, while he poked me in the ribs.

'What was that?' Norman asked, craning his neck around the door.

'Nothing!' we said in unison.

'I don't want to go to work.' I scooped my feet underneath me and snuggled into Robbie on the couch.

'Well, tough luck. You have to. Or how else is Lord Maple going to be able to afford to lounge around the house, casually watching TV, wearing his Christmas socks on a Thursday evening?'

'I wish I had a fun job like you, one that didn't involve having to leave the house on a Thursday evening to go to a Christmas fashion show for the Mums of Transition Year students in a school in Bray.'

'Hey, that doesn't sound so bad.'

'Please!' I scoffed. 'It's going to be hideous. The theme was "Fabulous Forties Fashion", which sounded absolutely fantastic, and I had loads of ideas for it until Eleanor decided to play it safe and interpret it as "fashion for women in their forties". It'll be all slacks and golf jumpers. It's going to be positively Greta Garbage.'

Was it possible to feel quite so deflated and dejected about work? I hadn't felt this way since I'd got paid three pounds an hour to wear a sandwich board that read 'Men's ties, 4 for 3 offer inside today'. My first foray into the fashion industry, aged sixteen.

Things hadn't picked up much.

'I hate seeing you like this,' Robbie said, drawing me in for a hug. 'If it makes you feel any better, Princess made me brush those pink gerbils with a sparkly pink brush until their fur puffed out like little balls of cotton wool.' I laughed, despite myself. 'Aw, that's so lovely. It does make me feel better. Thank you.'

'Welcome.'

'I still don't want to go to work, though.'

We sat and watched a few minutes of the match on TV. 'Oooh! GOAL!' I roared.

'That was a try. This is rugby, not football. Best to check with me first the next time. Especially if we're in public.'

I dug him in the ribs. 'Hey, you know what I think would make me feel better?'

'No, what?'

'A pink gerbil.'

Humph. Bette would probably eat it anyway. God, I really didn't want to go to work.

'Grace? Robbie?' Norman called. 'Have you any Vanish Power Stain Remover for my sheets? I've had an awful kidney infection for the past few weeks and it's made me a bit leaky at night.'

I was up and out the door in less than three seconds.

Walking up the school driveway, I braced myself for everything this night *wasn't* going to be. The only assignment Eleanor Holt had given me in recent months that I had even been remotely excited about. It didn't matter that the bigger picture wasn't quite so glamorous – a fashion show of mums in a school in Bray trying to raise money to build a climbing wall next to the hockey pitch.

It was going to be a veritable feast of 1940s screen glamour and I was going to be in my element! Clothing inspired by the greats: Ava Gardner, Katharine Hepburn, Lauren Bacall, Marlene Dietrich. I was going to do a photo shoot with each of the mums in the style of Rita Hayworth's 1944 movie poster *Cover Girl* for a donation that would go straight to the climbing-wall fund. And on the catwalk: moonlit spotlighting, dark contrasting shadows, piano music, cocktails, Hitchcock.

Unfortunately the only 'hitching' going on when I got there was a wall of cheap polyester being hoisted over a procession of flesh-coloured control underwear. My heart sank to the bottom of my vintage lace-up Oxford knitted-ankle boots. It was an assembly line of badly dressed forty-somethings in some sort of fashion *faux pas* factory.

'Grace!' Eleanor called. 'Just in time! Susan Barnwell wants to practise her walk for you.'

'Sure,' I responded, with about as much fortitude as a tea-saturated digestive biscuit.

I sat back as Susan Barnwell trotted along the line of polyester, like a Schnauzer at Crufts. The onlookers clapped their encouragement.

Congratulations, Susan Barnwell: Best in Show.

The fashion show went as planned: safe and underwhelming. The audience shifted uncomfortably in their seats in a bloat of *ennui*. They came, they sat, they handed over their money and the school was well under way to getting its climbing wall. They would go home to their beds, not to lie under their ceilings and quietly review the images they'd seen earlier in the evening, laid out like a constellation of stars. No, those images would already have been lost, too bland and uninspiring to stand out from the already grey backdrop.

The women had been lovely and I cursed Eleanor for letting them down. And myself for not pushing her harder. I knew they'd wanted more from tonight. More excitement, more adventure, something a little daring, something fun, something *different*. I could see it in their eyes, which were buzzing about like tiny fairies trapped in lidded glass jars.

'Well, Grace, that was fun,' Susan Barnwell said, standing beside me as I folded up the stacks of beige slacks.

No, it wasn't fun. It was average. Why did things have to be average when they could be fun and exciting and adventurous and fulfilling?

'Yes, it was, wasn't it?' I answered, seeing the fairy flitting behind her eyes. Dying to get out, dying to stretch, dying to do something outside the everyday. Susan had wanted to do the 1940s screen fashion as much as I had. We had come up with all sorts of ideas for dresses and hats and she, a seamstress who'd recently been made redundant, had been ignited with the excitement of the challenge. Carole Wallis was going to make the hats and Tess Maguire, a part-time hairdresser, was going to re-create the hairstyles.

Until Eleanor had flounced in, like the dictator of the fashion show regime, and stamped out any creativity whatsoever, deeming it all far too complicated and difficult.

'I could have made that Judy Garland number from *Meet Me In St Louis* in no time,' Susan said softly. I could hear the disappointment in her voice.

'I know,' I said sadly, replacing the stack of tan sandals in their respective shoeboxes. So bored with looking at the same old scenery, I wondered if my eyes would stop focusing. I hadn't the heart to remind Susan that *Meet Me in St Louis* was set in 1904, so Judy's get-up might have stood out a tad.

'You know, that's still the film I watch when I'm feeling a bit down in the dumps. It's my guilty secret when David's out of the house and all the kids are in school and everything is still for a bit. Silly really, but . . . it makes me smile.'

It's not silly. It's *not* silly!

> 'Meet me in St Louis, Louis,
> Meet me at the fair . . .'

I smiled and joined her as she softly sang,

> 'Don't tell me the lights are shining
> Any place but there,
> We will dance the Hoochee Koochee,
> I will be your tootsie-wootsie,
> If you will meet me in St Louis, Louis,
> Meet me at the fair.'

I wanted to take Susan there. Meet her at the fair. Take them all there! Why not? Why shouldn't we? Why shouldn't we go there?

When I turned to smile at her, Susan was already walking away. Heading home to clock on to the same routine.

I could feel it gurgling in the pit of my stomach again. The desire to help women discover something else about themselves.

Feel good about themselves. Let the world see they weren't just the housewife clearing up after the kids. The bank worker chained to the desk crunching numbers. The grandmother who'd long forgotten her own dreams for the sake of the ones she loved.

Why couldn't Eleanor see that all they were looking for was a bit of escapism? Escape the rat run. Relationship worries. Money problems. Life chasing off with their plans in its jaws; never really catching up with it.

Wasn't that what we were all looking for?

I was toying with the idea of becoming an alcoholic but the thought of slipping into an unkempt mess was sort of putting me off the notion. Although, come to think of it, Joan Crawford used to have her flasks of vodka covered with material to match her outfits. I liked the sound of that. I'd stop in Hickeys on the way home from work.

'So this woman called me today, asking for you,' Eleanor had said. 'Said she knows you've an eye for vintage and wants to go Jane Russell for her Christmas party.'

Sweet Jesus. I'd had to clutch on to the rack of hideous sequined rainbow-coloured dresses in Eleanor's office for support. And I normally only ever touch them if it's an extreme emergency. Was I hearing correctly? I'd lifted my *Anna Christie*/Greta Garbo-inspired beret up over my left ear. 'Jane Russell? Really?'

'Yes, really,' Eleanor had puffed impatiently. 'It'll be your last client before the holidays. Can you do it?'

Could I! *Miracle on Grafton Street*! This was fantastic – someone wanted me to dress them like a screen siren from the Hollywood Golden Era. I had felt like breaking into a song, hugging Eleanor, wrapping her in tinsel and screaming, 'I believe! I believe! It's silly but I believe!'

That was until I met said lady and believed in becoming an alcoholic instead. Albeit a stylish one with a hip flask that matched my shoes.

'So I'm thinking Jane Russell in *Gentlemen Marry Brunettes*. A leopard-print figure-hugging dress with a slit up the leg?'

Holy Mother of God! This woman was sixty-eight if she was a day, just shy of five foot and had a tight crop of grey curls.

'Do you not think we should go for something a little more . . . understated?'

Her face dropped to around where her boobs were hanging in an ill-fitting bra. 'Okay,' she whispered despondently, shaking her head. 'It's just . . .' she hesitated '. . . my husband always had a bit of a thing for her. He used to tell me I reminded him of her when we first met. I know it sounds silly, but I just wanted to make the effort for him this Christmas – we'll be fifty years married on Christmas Eve. Show him that we aren't two old bats that are over the hill completely.'

Oh, Jesus. Now I felt utterly awful.

It was heartbreaking, but beautiful, and it was exactly why I wanted to do what I wanted to do. Whatever that was. But I sort of knew it had to do with making people feel a certain way with how they dressed. It was just a bit of a pain that there wasn't a college course in it specifically and why I'd had to do my post-grad in something else, in the hope I'd get there in the end. But I wasn't going to think about that now. Or for the whole of Christmas, I'd decided. I had just finished studying and it was Christmas and I would hopefully figure out my career path sooner rather than later.

For now I had a sixty-eight-year-old romantic with an ill-fitting bra and notions of leopard print on my hands. And, by God, I was going to help her.

'Why don't we do something from *Gentlemen Prefer Blondes*? I have the perfect outfit that I know will look drop-dead gorgeous on you and have your husband's eyes popping out of his head!'

We headed off shopping and I was thrilled to piece together the ingredients of that fabulous black halter-neck pantsuit and black-and-white check swing coat that Jane Russell had rocked in the movie. Obviously I was never going to source a coat with the exact yellow lining, so we brought the look together with a bright yellow scarf instead.

'Fantastic!' she said breathlessly, taking in her reflection as she stood in front of the mirror back in Eleanor's office. 'Thank you so much, Grace. This is going to be the best Christmas present ever.'

I was so moved by the undeniable glint in her eye that I was suddenly at a loss as to how to answer her. How amazing, after all those years, that the spark was still there.

'I'm going to phone him on the way home,' she giggled conspiratorially, 'and let him know that he'd better forget about an early night. Jane always said that life only begins after nine.'

Would Robbie and I be like that when we were sixty-eight, I wondered, staring at the elaborate train set in the Christmas window of Brown Thomas. I took the last drag from my cigarette and exhaled slowly as the train circled the snow scene. Little figurines dotted the landscape, singing, smiling, holding hands, and in the middle I caught the faint trace of my own reflection staring back at me from the glass.

And it caught me completely off guard. Just in that fleeting moment, I thought it was a stranger until I flicked my hair and mirrored my own image.

Getting Robbie's Christmas present into the house without him seeing it was no mean feat, seeing he was already home when I got back. Was he not meant to be working at a concert in the Olympia? As soon as I put my key in the lock and heard his voice, I slammed the door shut again and ran around the side of the house.

Shit. That was not a well-thought-out plan. Now he'd either think he was being robbed or that I had been kidnapped on the doorstep. Neither of which was wholly conducive to the furtive operation of sneaking in his present and hiding it under the stairs. What was an even worse plan was that I was now half-way up the trellis on the side wall of our house with his new guitar strapped over my shoulder.

'Grace . . . Grace?'

Damn. Okay, keep cool.

'Oh, hi there,' I said casually, poking my head around the side of the chimney. 'I really think it's about time we got our gutters weeded.'

And, apparently, that was what *not* to say if you didn't want your boyfriend thinking you were having a nervous breakdown when he found you on the roof at nine thirty on a Tuesday night. In December. I climbed down, leaving the guitar on the flat lip of the roof. Lucky it was a fine night.

'Robbie, I'm fine. Really.'

'Really?'

'Really.' I was quite enjoying the *giant* pot of tea and the plate of Party Rings he'd laid out for me. They only came out in serious emergencies. Like when my sister had printed out a PowerPoint of what was wrong with my life, or when Robbie had promised to put the immersion on but forgotten or, worst of all, when I was outbid on something I *really* wanted on eBay. A plate of Party Rings was the big guns.

I felt bad that he thought I was having a nervous breakdown when really I was only trying to hide his Christmas present. I knew he was going to absolutely love it and I really didn't want to spoil the surprise. Even though he was such a music obsessive, he'd never learned to play the guitar and it had always been a big regret. So I'd bought him the most fantastic Gibson model and organized lessons for him with some old hippie on Baggot Street who was meant to be amazing.

I knew he thought I'd got him a new dressing-gown to match the new towels in the bathroom after I'd kept saying, 'D'you know what I think you'd love?' and he'd kept saying, 'Erm, no, I hadn't really thought how much I'd love a new dressing-gown to match the new towels in the bathroom.' Poor Robbie. I was so mean to him sometimes.

And here he was, force-feeding me Party Rings. *Big Fat Liars and Their Feeders*. Could have been a new Channel 4 documentary.

'I hate seeing you so frustrated with work,' he said, looking at me with his big green eyes. Jesus, and tonight was the first night in ages I actually felt okay about work.

I smiled at him. He was so kind.

I leaned in beside him on the couch as we stared at our Christmas tree. And I tried something I'd never tried before: to fit three Party Rings into my mouth in one go.

It worked!

This was lovely. Just us two. On the couch. In our own home. Comfortable enough to wedge an uncomfortable amount of food into my gob, which invariably made me drool down both sides of my face, and know he would still love me anyway.

'Do you think you have enough fairy-lights on that Christmas tree?' he asked, surveying the scene of Our First Proper Official Tree. Of course, we'd had other trees before this one (well, our first was technically just a branch we'd hacked off my parents' tree and put in a vase on our kitchen table because it was all that would fit in our apartment). But this was Our First Proper Official Tree because this was Our First Proper Official Home. So it was a Proper Official Big Deal.

'Really? You think we could do with some more? I've already tripped the main fuse twice, but I guess I could wedge a few more in between the top branches.'

'Grace, I'm kidding. The angel alone is like a football-pitch floodlight in a dress.'

'That's because she is.' I smiled, thinking of Lisa handing me the cerise pink plug-in glittery fairy that you could 'totally put on a shelf or somewhere once Christmas is over'. It scared Robbie slightly (only because his weird uncle collects tiny thumb-sized dolls on the Internet. But I've told him, 'Robbie, you can't hate all dolls because your uncle is really creepy'). Anyway, when I told him Lisa had given it to us as a little guardian angel to watch over us in our new house, he thought it was really sweet. Lisa was always sweet. And pink and glittery and glowing. That's why I loved the angel: it reminded me of her.

'If you put any more lights on that tree you'd be able to see it from New York,' he said, 'which might be a good thing, actually, as we're off there in a few days.'

He sipped his tea nonchalantly.

I stared at him blankly. God love him. And he thought *I* was stressed about work? They really had been overworking him lately, hadn't they? So many concerts he had to take care of. So many difficult artists he had to look after. Only the night before he'd gone back to our old apartment by mistake after work. The new tenants had nearly died of fright when he'd walked into the living room and they'd all stood there for 'a good seven to ten minutes', screaming at each other 'like schoolgirls' (Robbie included). He was mortified. More so for screaming like a school-girl than barging into an apartment he no longer lived in. He asked me if I reckoned they were all going to say how 'particu-larly effeminate' he was when they relayed the story to their friends. I lied and told him I reckoned Vinnie Jones would have done the same thing under similar circumstances (he quite often uses him as a benchmark for toughness after seeing *X-Men*).

But let's call a spade a spade: they were totally going to refer to him as the six-foot, sandy-haired Carly Rae Jepsen.

So now he was getting Ikea mixed up with New York. Okay, I knew we were excited about finally making the trip out there, but thinking we were off to New York instead of a Swedish dis-count furnishing chain was a touch worrying. I was definitely going to make him have an early night tonight. Or force-feed him Party Rings. Actually, I might see if he could stuff five into his mouth at the same time.

'Robbie, we're going to *IKEA*' – I shouted the name for extra clarity – 'tomorrow, not New York.' (I whispered that bit.) 'But it's sweet you're getting as excited about coffee-tables as I am.'

'No, I don't think we'll make it. Not with a flight to New York to catch.'

Oh, Jesus. The new tenants whacked him over the head with a golf club, thinking he was an intruder, and now he was *concussed*.

'Okay, Robbie, what's my name and how many fingers am I holding up? I don't want to alarm you, but I think you may have sustained a brain injury.' I was annoyed that I had a Party Ring wedged on each finger, which might have detracted from the seriousness of the situation and might also have been 'too colourful' to his light-sensitive post-concussed eyes.

He laughed and sat back into the couch. 'Come here, you daft thing,' he said, extending his arm and curling me into him. 'We may have to leave the coffee-table for another day. Because we really are off to New York in a few days so you'd better head upstairs and start sorting your clothes.'

I stared at him cross-eyed and totally dumbfounded.

'Happy Christmas, baby,' he whispered, kissing my lips.

Later that night, after all the excitement and the clothes-sorting and the impromptu sex under the Christmas tree (blindingly bright and very prickly – in no major rush to do it again), and after Robbie had *finally* fallen asleep, I climbed up onto the roof to get his guitar.

The sky looked absolutely breathtaking from up there. Like a giant infinity pool of deep midnight ink, splattered with flecks of bright twinkling dots. The frost along the roofs of all the other houses glistened under the brilliance of the moon's glow, making everything shimmer in the stillness. I sat for a moment, enchanted.

New York. *New York!* Honestly, I had to pinch myself.

I'd never ever been before, and Robbie always knew how bursting I was to go. I'd watched all the movies: *Breakfast At Tiffany's, Miracle on 34th Street, Annie Hall, Home Alone 2, Maid in Manhattan* (I was going to leave out *Maid in Manhattan* as it's a bit embarrassing but, actually, it serves to highlight the point: not *even* Jennifer Lopez's appalling performance as a chambermaid with an annoying voice could put me off wanting to visit the Big Apple). But New York. New York! One of the fashion Meccas of the world. Home of Michael Kors, Marc Jacobs, Zac Posen, Kate Spade, Diane Von Furstenberg, the Met Ball, Carrie Bradshaw. A cocktail of fun, ingenuity, style and creativity with a cherry (well, an apple) on top!

I wanted a drink! I wanted a bite! Maybe this was exactly what I needed right now. Maybe that was all that had been unsettling me lately. Maybe all I really needed was to be inspired. To be ignited and challenged by something new and exciting.

Ha! Eleanor Holt wouldn't know what hit her when I got back.

I unzipped the guitar from its case and started to plink quietly at the strings, playing the only song I'd ever learned to play – 'True Love', the honeymoon song from *High Society*, with Bing Crosby and my namesake Grace Kelly. I sang it softly to myself as I thought of Robbie, his incredible thoughtfulness and generosity. And our home. And New York.

And our glittery pink fairy.

And as I sat there staring out into the infinite night sky, being slowly enfolded in the cold December air, I couldn't help but feel lit up from inside. *This* was what I'd always wanted, I thought, as I sat on our roof.

Our house. Our own life together, as we wanted it.

Here at last.

## 11

Visiting my sister made me think of *The Fighter*. Probably because it involved two siblings of a mental family meeting up and an inevitable row.

Oh, and also, my mum, like the mum in *The Fighter*, once had a bit of a mullet (very upsetting, can't actually talk about it too much). She said it was just because the hair on the back of her head grew faster than on the top and the sides. Likely story, Mum. Likely story.

I liked to think I was Mark Wahlberg, in my prime, and Tanya was Christian Bale, the has-been. But, of course, she saw it the other way round.

Her doorbell sounded like the bell ringing for round one. Well, I didn't care how heated this got: there was no way I was wearing a gum shield with this amazing vintage Biba number.

God, I'd have loved a whiskey chaser right about now.

Uh-oh. Maybe I was Christian Bale after all. Shit. I was starting to get seriously worried about my cravings for daytime tipples (at least I had the Joan Crawford hip-flask thing nailed if I did decide to go down that route).

I'd already learned the hard way that getting sloshed before visiting Tanya could backfire on your ass in a major way. Case in point: the last time I tried the numbed-by-alcohol technique before calling over to her, she stripped me at the front door and hurled me into an ice-cold bath. It was not a pleasant episode. Made even more unpleasant by Painful Peter coming home from work and barging into the bathroom to use the loo after Tanya had failed to inform him I was in the tub stark naked.

He'd already unzipped. There was a lot of nudity. A lot of

thrashing about. A lot of screaming. It was not pretty. Actually, much like Mum's mullet, I don't think I can talk about it any more.

Don't get me wrong: I did love Tanya. It wasn't like I had a real dislike of her in the same way I had of Great-aunt Nuala on my mum's side who'd always insisted on telling me that my red hair was a sign of a 'brain-defected' recessive gene passed down from her great-great-grandmother's lineage.

No, I did love Tanya. Just in bite-sized chunks (bites of the tiniest living mammal on earth, which I believed was the Kitti's hog-nosed bat of Thailand. So, I loved her in tiny hog-nosed bat-sized chunks).

It was just that, well, Tanya could be a tad on the overbearing side sometimes. She hadn't always been that way. Okay, yes, she'd always been . . . how should I put it? Assertive? Like that time when we were kids and she kept insisting that the way I wore my hair in a low ponytail did not suit me. And when I wouldn't listen to her she'd shaved the bottom half of my head so I'd have to find an alternative way to wear it. Or that time she locked Mum and Dad out of the house and made them sit on the porch for an entire night 'until you've sorted out your differences'.

So, she'd always been feisty. But she was definitely getting worse in her old age. I knew she was stressed out, trying to juggle her high-flying legal career with chasing around after two small children, but I wished she'd take me up on my suggestion of the Prozac Milkshakes. I'd even bought her a top-of-the-range smoothie-maker and some delicious banana shake mix, so now all she needed was the hard stuff and she was away. (Oh, God, maybe I really was the Christian Bale sibling.)

Today was going to be a particularly brutal visit. I knew that. The interrogations. The mind games. Tanya's dogged determination to extract information. I just had to remember to stay strong. I'd learned quite a lot of resistance techniques from watching *Good Morning, Vietnam* over and over.

Today was going to be considerably worse because of the trip to New York.

The reason?

Tanya was possessed. Pure and simple. The possessed ring-leader of a terrifying group called the Wedding Cult. An unsavoury underground operation that targeted innocent unmarried people and attempted to perform black magic and wedding sorcery on them. Other members included my mother, the vast majority of my friends, most of my work colleagues and, evidently, quite a lot of random strangers.

And now I had the spine-chilling task of calling over to the Cult Headquarters to borrow luggage for my trip. Good God, why did we have to throw out our own suitcases in the move? Sure, the hinges hadn't worked any more and the zips were all broken, but three rounds of clingfilm and they would've been safe as houses.

Me, Robbie, Christmas time, New York. It could only mean one thing to the possessed ring-leader of the Wedding Cult: that Robbie was about to propose.

I'd received the obligatory wink-wink nudge-nudge dig-in-the-ribs reaction when I'd told everyone we were off to New York for a few days.

'That'll be an extra exciting Christmas for us all, won't it, Grace?' Mum had wink-winked.

'Why's that, Mum?' I'd asked, playing dumb. 'You can't honestly be getting *that* excited about slippers that heat up and smell of lavender when you put them in the microwave, surely.' I had wanted to get her a haircut or some extensions for the rest of her hair, but that was a side issue.

I finally talked her down off the wedding ledge and back onto safer mother *terra firma*: turkey and potatoes. She warned me to get my turkey now and put it in the freezer as we were getting back just a few days before Christmas Day and all I'd be left with would be 'a few tough cocks'. She didn't get it when I told her that didn't sound so bad. She said wasn't this supposed to be our first Christmas dinner together as a couple in our first home and wouldn't Robbie be disappointed if all I served him on the day was 'a dried-out cock'?

She had a point. I don't think he'd be into that.

And then even Auntie Joan rang me and told me that I needed to book myself in for a manicure before I headed off: there was simply nothing worse than a brand new shiny rock on a hand with raggedy cuticles.

Christ alive. I could be off to Gaza on my holidays for all I cared, just so long as I was getting away from the Cult for a few days (Robbie did say it was very crass of me to call those flotillas to Palestine a 'Dead Sea Cruise').

I was seriously going to have to start wearing a sandwich board with big print on it that read, 'Getting married is not the be-all and end-all of my life so please stop asking.' Or handing out flyers. Or taking out an ad at the back of the *Irish Times*. All substantial inconveniences. And there really was nothing flattering or fashion forward about sandwich boards.

Thank God all Lisa had said was, 'Get me some trackie bottoms from Abercrombie, would you?'

Thank God for Lisa.

Thank God for Robbie.

'You do know what everyone's thinking, don't you?'

'Yes, I do,' he said. 'But we can't stop living our lives because we're too afraid of what other people will be thinking. You and I know why we're going to New York. Because we've both worked damn hard over the last year and, more importantly, because I'm so proud of you that you are now the very sexy owner of a master's degree.'

Exactly.

I rang Tanya's doorbell again. It was very unlike her not to answer on the first ring. In fact, normally she'd be standing out on the road already, peacocking about and gearing up for me.

Suddenly the door was pulled open. I was reefed in off the street and whipped inside before you could say 'Katie Taylor'.

'Sorry, I was spying on my neighbours' kid from the attic window. I'm convinced he's pissing on my azaleas. And stop calling me Ethyl. You know I hate it.'

'I haven't said a word,' I told her.

'Yes, but I know you will, so don't.'

Great. She was in top form obviously. This should be fun. I hoped the kid who was pissing on her azaleas knew what he was getting himself into.

She sashayed back up the hall, waving her hand for me to follow her.

'Peter's working late and I've sent the kids to bed early so here's what's going to happen.' She plonked me down on her mustard plush-velvet couch.

'You've sent the kids to bed?' I interjected. 'It's only five thirty!'

'They're not good with numbers, they'll never know. I told them it was actually eleven p.m. and way past their bedtime.'

Poor Eoin and Milly – being conned left, right and centre. Only last week Tanya had told them that if they didn't eat their broccoli they were getting alligator brains for dessert.

I had categorically never seen that technique on *Supernanny*.

'So, we're going to open a bottle of Sauvignon and you're going to sit there and tell me *everything*. I want details. How he's been acting lately. Weird? Manic? Nervous?' she fired off, clicking her fingers in rapid succession. 'Has his breathing got shallower? Has he been mumbling his words? Sweating profusely? Waking in the night shouting "She's the One!"? Been extra nice to you even when you're being a bitch?'

'He's been doing that shouting in the middle of the night thing ever since we met,' I lied. 'And, Ethyl, I'm never a bitch.'

She arched her left eyebrow and went into the kitchen. Her infamous archy left eyebrow. It was her signature look. Used to convey any one of the following things:

1. Are you kidding me?
2. Take a good hard look at yourself.
3. Do you think I came down in the last shower?
4. Get your f@*!ing feet off my f@*!ing coffee-table.

In this instance it was a combination of 1, 2 and 3. Oh, and 4.

I swiped my feet off the coffee-table and plopped them onto the floor.

She came back into the living room with two beautiful Waterford crystal glasses filled to the brim with deep golden pools of chilled wine.

'Tanya,' I started, trying to muster up a cache of inner strength, 'I know you're dying for Robbie and me to get married but, I have to tell you, it's not going to happen just yet.'

'Rubbish.'

'Really, it's *not*,' I stressed, placing my drink on the coffee-table. Nothing like putting your drink down during a conversation to highlight a point or denote an important shift in an argument.

She stared at my glass incredulously. I placed a coaster under it and she visibly calmed.

'Do you *not* want to get married or something?' she asked, in a tone that suggested I was simple-minded.

'No, it's not that. I'm just so fed up of everyone *obsessing* over it. Tanya, honestly, it's none of anyone else's business,' I said, my voice rising. If I'd had another drink in my hand, I'd have put it down too. 'Not to mention the fact that it places undue pressure on Robbie's and my relationship and makes out that it's all essentially worthless if we don't get married ASAP!'

'But what are you waiting for?' she asked, as though it was as simple as putting milk in your tea, or tying your shoelaces. Not that I'm saying it wasn't simple. But – oh, now I was flustered – *it wasn't the point*!

'Grace, I'm just scared it's all going to pass you by! I don't see what your problem is. For crying out loud, even Kate Middleton's got there before you!'

'I don't have a problem!' I suddenly exploded. 'That is the whole problem! We don't have an issue with our love life. It's everybody else who does! And, PS, I hadn't realized I was in a sodding race with Kate Middleton to get to the altar!'

'Christ, Grace!' Tanya grumbled, lighting a cigarette and folding herself back into the corner of the couch. 'There you go again about your "love life". Getting married is *real life*. It's what people do. Just ask Kate.'

WTF? 'Just ask Kate.' That's right. Note to self: call St James's Palace and Just Ask Kate.

'What on earth difference does it make to you, Tanya?' I asked bluntly. 'Honestly, what the hell difference does it make to your life?'

She sucked on her cigarette and paused for thought before letting the spirals of smoke escape from her pursed lips. She'd always possessed that air of cool ascendancy. Ever since she was a child. And I always thought it made her features look slightly harsher than Nature had intended. There was no doubting that she was a striking woman: tall and slender with dark blonde hair, green almond-shaped eyes, high cheekbones and an angular nose. And although I was smaller, with auburn hair, brown eyes, wider lips, a button nose and exceptionally large feet, we still, oddly, looked quite alike. You could tell we were sisters definitely. But then she'd look at you with one of those blunt, austere expressions, and I'd swear she could have been adopted. How Brad and Ange of my mum and dad to have blended the adopted with the biological when it came to kids.

'Grace, just do everyone a favour and get on with it. For God's sake, you're nearly thirty. Kate got in there at twenty-nine,' she said concisely, tapping her cigarette into the marble ashtray she'd dragged all the way home from a work trip in Singapore because it matched her flipping coasters.

What on earth was the sudden obsession with Kate Middleton? Although sometimes I did feel like I had just as many people scrutinizing my wedding plans as she'd had.

'Plus,' Tanya said, 'Mum has block-booked three months next summer to get skinny, find an outfit, and have that grey tooth at the front whitened. So just go with it, will you? Get married and get going on your career path. Hopefully, Robbie will propose early in the week so you can spend the rest of your trip trying on wedding dresses and stuff. My advice to you is to check out some décor stuff while you're over there because (a) it's cheaper and (b) no one else here will have it so they'll all be *über*-impressed.'

'Tanya, I'm actually going to scream,' I said, flipping up onto my feet. I could feel my cheeks burning with indignation. But just as I was about to launch into a tirade before I stormed off, we were interrupted by a loud scream, followed by a suitcase thudding down the stairs at high speed.

'Shit. I thought I'd fooled them.' Tanya sighed, stubbing out her cigarette and getting to her feet.

I headed out to the hall to see what all the commotion was about, while Tanya trailed languorously behind me. Eoin was standing at the top of the stairs in his pyjamas, laughing his head off. Brilliant – he'd thrown the suitcase down the stairs and now all I had to do was pick it up and get the hell out of there before I spontaneously combusted with anger. People have told me that's not physically possible. But I did not want to be the 'No way? Really?' case. 'Flames. Actual flames,' they would say. 'Pity, because she was wearing the most fabulous 1960s Biba shift dress with pearl detailing at the neckline.' I could practically feel a knot of lit coal smouldering in the pit of my stomach. I flipped the handle of the suitcase up and started wheeling it furiously towards the front door. 'Goodbye!' I said. 'Thanks for the case and the lecture.' I whipped the front door open and marched down her driveway towards my car.

'Grace, wait!' she called after me. I flipped her the finger and kept walking.

'Grace, hang on. I think one of my children is in that suitcase.' I turned to her and shot her one of her own famous freaky arched-eyebrow looks. Then, as sure as eggs were eggs, the suitcase came to life and out popped Milly, like the scene from *Alien*. Thank God I wasn't holding a glass of red wine or it would have gone everywhere.

''Bye, Auntie Grace!' she shouted, amid squeals of laughter, running back up the driveway at full throttle. I would have laughed but I was still trying to look utterly aggrieved for Tanya.

'Have fun, Waity Gracie!' Tanya called, all chipper, as if the last twenty minutes hadn't happened.

'Waity Gracie'? Euch! The *cheek*! She probably only wanted me to get married so she could have her Pippa Middleton moment!

I looked at the three of them standing on the porch, waving at me.

Humph!

I turned on my heel and began to walk away, dragging the child-bearing suitcase behind me.

''Bye, Auntie Grace!' Eoin and Milly caterwauled, into the early-evening air.

'Have fun on your holidays,' Milly said then. 'We're so excited you and Uncle Robbie are getting married!'

## 12

**Code Tanya. CODE TANYA.**

Lisa texted back immediately: **Message received. Glass of Sauvignon poured and waiting. Over.**

I was at Lisa's in less than eight minutes. I still had the suitcase in my hand. Wasn't sure why I hadn't just left it in the car. And now I was drinking a glass of Sauvignon Blanc like I'd just come from a ten-day pilgrimage in the desert and it was an ice-cold pint of water.

'Is it wrong that I pray for my sister to emigrate?'

'Like we said, we only pray she'll move to Singapore, one flight. We're not being unreasonable by hoping for somewhere *very* far away like New Zealand, two flights.'

'True. Okay. Maybe I'm not such a bad person. And I do like her sometimes. Like last month when she had tonsillitis and couldn't talk.'

'Or when Milly put her phone in the dishwasher and she couldn't call you.'

'Yeah. I *really* liked her then. Oh, Leese,' I sighed, sinking onto her couch under the weight of all this expectation, 'why are my family so odd?'

'I'm not the one to ask. My mother's going out with a twenty-six-year-old who plays for Shamrock Rovers, and my brother is a vegan who refuses to wear shoes. I don't have to elaborate on my father.'

Lisa's parents had separated years previously and nothing would persuade her that her dad, Des, wasn't gay. So what if we'd caught him coming out of the George one night? Or the fact that he wore his chinos rolled up with loafers and no socks? I reckon he's just 'trendy'.

We laid our heads on the back of the sofa and looked up to the David Beckham poster on the ceiling for inspiration. Of course we were far too old for David Beckham posters but it was sort of 'post-modern irony'. (Lisa called it that. Didn't have a clue what 'post-modern irony' was but it sounded far cooler than 'cos we still fancy him lots').

'Has Killian met David yet?' I asked, studying his beautiful torso.

'Not yet. His flat is so much handier. He didn't buy an apartment in an industrial estate off the exit to the N4 like some of us. I told him I had a picture of David on my ceiling and he said, "Cool. You're a Michelangelo fan, then? I like the Sistine Chapel touch but with a picture of David on the ceiling instead. Very post-modern irony."'

Jesus, what was with all this 'post-modern irony'? What was wrong with *modern* irony? Was everyone already rushing past that? I was going to start saying I was 'retro ironic', and that my 1950s puffball skirt and my constant quoting of Grace Kelly movies was 'very vintage ironic'. I imagined her slipping on a pair of her delicate calfskin Hermès gloves and fixing the bow in her demi-chignon and instantly relaxed. In a very 'retro-ironic' sort of way.

'I just hope he doesn't stop having sex with me when he realizes I'm a Philistine and would prefer to worship an ex-Premiership footballer over the work of a sixteenth-century artist,' she continued, 'because the sex is a-*mazing*.'

'Brilliant.'

'Kinda reminds me of you and Robbie – at it like rabbits all the time! I haven't had that in *ages*. Aidan had such a low sex drive. He was so freaked out when I tried to spice things up by buying a whip in Ann Summers that I had to lie and tell him I'd just taken up dressage and he should chill the hell out. Ha! I'd like to see Zara Phillips doing the circuit with a pink sparkly leather tasselled crop that miaowed when you used it. Or maybe he just didn't fancy me. Or maybe he was a bit Des Ferguson.

'Anyway, me and Killian are joining you in the Rabbit Club. Not that we want to swing with you guys or anything. But you know what I mean.' She grinned and I couldn't help smiling. I was delighted for her.

The Rabbit Club? Jesus, I seriously needed to renew my membership on that one. Did guinea pigs have less sex than rabbits? Maybe we were guinea pigs now.

There had just been so much going on lately, what with work and study and the move. And then Robbie had had that sinus infection.

'Can't believe those other two rabbits have gone and deserted us too. The cheek!' she scoffed, referring, of course, to Rebecca and Tony's year-long sabbatical. The one they had sprung on us just days before they'd taken off. They'd said they didn't want it to overshadow the wedding so they'd kept it to themselves until it was over. I still couldn't believe they were gone. A year! A full year! Off to travel the world, the lucky sods. I would have loved to go with them. But apparently you can't go along on someone else's honeymoon.

'Hey,' she asked, tearing her eyes away from David for a moment, 'were you okay at the wedding? You know, in the loos?'

'Oh, God, yes,' I answered triumphantly. 'I've discovered that the reason I was crying was because I've never been to New York.'

Silence.

'Really?' she said tentatively.

When I said nothing, she said, 'Right.'

'What?' I said.

'Nothing. It's just I've never been to the Caribbean but I don't think I've ever cried in the toilets at any of my friends' weddings about it.'

'Well, that's because you want to go to the Caribbean on holiday because it looks lovely and you hope you'll come back looking like Rihanna, which is weird because you're blonde with seriously pale skin.'

'Hmm. Well, I admit, I have cried in many toilets about not

looking like Rihanna. Even cried through "We Fell In Love In A Hopeless Place" on the dance floor in Pink a few months back. But that was a mixture of not looking like Rihanna and Aidan not wanting to have sex with me, and perhaps he wasn't having sex with me because I didn't look like Rihanna. Maybe I could get corn-rows or a perm or something. What was my point again?'

'Point is, New York for me is about so much more than a holiday. It's – I don't know, finding something that's missing. Leese, I really need to find out what I want.'

'You need to find out what you want?' she asked, looking worried.

'Yes. With work. It's like I'm stuck in a shit car that keeps stalling at the lights whenever they've turned green and it's time to go.'

'Okay.' She sighed. 'Well, then, I'm really glad you're going. And that's all it was?'

'Yes, Leese. Honestly, that's all.' But I couldn't stop myself looking away from her when I said it.

'Okay, Grace,' she said.

We both knew there was something else that wasn't being said, but I honestly didn't have a clue what it was, and I was pretty sure she didn't either. We sat in the silence as my mind jumped, like bad reception on a TV screen.

I was relieved when she decided that now wasn't the time to go probing.

'You know my dad was talking about getting the angel wings tattoo across his shoulders, like Becks,' she said, resting her head back on the sofa and looking up at St David.

'Trendy!' I cooed.

'What? Grace! For a hot young footballer that looks like an Adonis and is married to an *über*-cool fashion designer it's trendy. For a pot-bellied sixty-three-year-old life assurance broker who insists on wearing wife-beaters with cardigans, it's gay.'

Maybe.

That was all it was, I rumbled on in my head, still having the argument with myself while Lisa sat silently in a Beckham trance, contemplating her father's sexual orientation.

New York. That was why I'd been sad that time. I'd never been to New York.

And now I was going.

See?

Sorted.

## 13

There was something about air stewardesses that made me want to be Gok Wan. Or, at the very least, have my own styling programme on Channel 4 with spin-off books and a column in one of the monthlies. Although I would never make people strip to their underwear in a hall of mirrors and then, when they were bawling and utterly traumatized, tell them I had the very thing to make them feel better – a gorgeous dress. I didn't care how pretty that pink floral tea-dress was, that was just mean! Sort of like kicking a child, then giving them a lollipop to cheer them up. Why not just give them the lollipop?

That was telly for you: if you can't track the progress someone has made from crying in their pants to smiling and walking around in a full outfit, you haven't successfully made a show about clothes.

'Grace, why are you wearing sunglasses on the plane?'

'I'm being Gok Wan,' I whispered to Robbie, in my best English accent. I was very 'method' when it came to these things. A bit like Daniel Day-Lewis. But I didn't like to brag or go on about it or anything. I was quite humble about my craft. We both were.

'Gok Wan wears prescription glasses, not sunnies. Plus I think you're wearing three-D glasses. Did you take them from the top of the *Avatar Home Experience* box set?'

Shit. Yes. Yes, I did. I was wondering why I was getting a migraine.

'Sssh,' I said. 'I'm working.'

I continued to study the air stewardesses. I'd never make them strip down to their smalls as I'd be too afraid they'd be wearing matching green synthetic underwear with '*Fáilte go hÉireann*' printed on the bum. Then they'd be crying, I'd be crying, and no amount of pink floral tea-dresses would ease the trauma. No, I'd opt for the softer approach of burning their bright green outfits and creepy silk neckties, using a wallpaper Strimmer to hack down the fifteen layers of fake tan from their skin, hew off their crispy hairspray dome buns with a scythe, then take them shopping. We'd even stop off for tea along the way and I'd order some of those cute cupcakes with all the multi-coloured sprinkles on top, just so they knew I was on their side.

I smiled as one of them walked past me, and I wondered if she'd be up for a quickie in the loo. (A quickie *makeover* obviously!) We could get the whole plane involved, and she could walk up and down the aisles afterwards, posing like she was on a runway, and then the good people aboard flight EI 113 to New York JFK would cheer and applaud and my work here would be done. Bow. Encore. Bow. Exit to the rear of the plane.

Or I could just watch one of the in-flight movies.

I flicked through the selection. Not the best. Chipmunks, tourists being kidnapped, warring brides. I simply didn't want to subject myself to the combat, the fighting, the savagery, the bloodshed. Okay, so *Bride Wars* was labelled 'romantic comedy', but I just wasn't taking that risk. I mean, brides warring? Actually *warring*? I couldn't believe it wasn't rated '18'.

Maybe I'd annoy Robbie instead: make him try to guess the prices of the duty-free stuff in the in-flight shopping magazine again. That was fun. For me. He said for him it was like having the hairs on his chest slowly plucked out one by one and then stuck back on with an acid-glue mix (he has an over-active imagination, that boy). But, like he also said, this was my holiday. Well, our holiday, but my Christmas present so, you know, I could do what I liked.

He was fast asleep. Boo. I prodded him. Nothing. Dead to the world.

I looked at him for a few moments, tracing the outline of his face with my eyes. No one ever looked particularly sexy while sleeping on public transport, did they? What with the head dangling and the mouth wide open and all that.

Still, I couldn't wipe the grin off my face whenever I looked at him.

New York!

*New York!* Yes, so bloody brilliant I just had to name it twice! (I kept doing that: I asked the air stewardess how long the flight to New York New York was. And the Passport Control guy. 'Where will you be travelling to today?' 'New York, New York.' And then I hugged him. Which, as it turned out, was frowned upon. Robbie wasn't happy when we were taken to a separate room and they brought in the sniffer dogs to look for narcotics in my suitcase. I told him to be grateful they didn't get out the latex gloves.)

But what an absolutely amazing present. And so generous and thoughtful too. I suddenly felt like one of those Cadbury's Creme Eggs that get splatted in the ads. All gooey and mushy and drippy.

My head melted on his shoulder and I smiled to myself. I was one lucky lady.

When we finally arrived in New York, I thought I was going to pass out with the excitement. Even the airport was cool, which was unprecedented progress, as usually airports were like massive holding pens of misery with the only redeeming features being magazines, lip glosses and giant bars of chocolate.

All those crying people. I usually joined the group hug, and even though I was only trying to be nice, I'd invariably get told to fuck off.

I did, however, start to panic a bit when the immigration guy took an *age* to check my passport details. I'd managed to slip through intelligence in Dublin airport, but just my luck to be called for a random check in New York. There was no way they'd actually have it on file, would they? I started to sweat. I hadn't been to the United States since my 'little incident'. What if he wouldn't let me through? Good God, I was so close to the Big Apple I could almost taste it, and the thought of not getting in was enough to make me salivate. (Actually, maybe I was just starving. I'd missed the in-flight meal because I was telling the man on the other side of me that it was possible to dye a gerbil pink safely. I'd waved the stewardess away with her plastic tray of plastic chicken while miming the very specific 'shampoo technique'.)

Just as I was about to tell the immigration man that the time I *nearly* got arrested in Newport Beach on my J1 for *nearly* 'borrowing' a cop scooter to go and get more beers was a case of complete mistaken identity (it wasn't, actually, but 'Todd' at Passport Control did not need to know otherwise), he let me through.

Phew. Thank God I didn't blurt out about the 'flashing' on Rodeo Drive either.

We headed outside and hailed – wait for it – a yellow cab! Okay, I know it's essentially just a taxi. In yellow. But it meant we were actually here! I held my tongue and made a concerted effort not to shout, 'I'm in a yellow cab!' in case we were kicked out of said yellow cab and had to wait around for another (in yellow. A yellow cab. So I would look forward to that should it happen).

I put my 3D glasses on and tried to look all cool and cavalier and New York.

I was here! I was finally here. I took Robbie's hand and squeezed it. 'Thank you,' I said, as we sped off towards the heart of the Big Apple.

New York was everything I'd ever hoped it would be, and more. The shops, the cafés, the bars, the whole vibe: it was electric. We queued for cupcakes in Magnolia, ate pancakes in Pastis, went for cocktails in the Gansevoort. And I spent every other waking minute poring over all the delicious finery in the fantastic boutiques on Elizabeth Street in SoHo. I couldn't afford any of it, of course. That was primarily down to the fact that I'd blown my entire shopping budget on a beautiful 1950s cream lace day dress and vintage pair of silver pumps on the first day.

I was in Heaven.

We even took a trip to the Brooklyn Museum Costume Collection at the Metropolitan Museum of Art. An awe-inspiring collection of over 62,000 pieces of vintage, avant-garde contemporary and eclectic clothes, bags, shoes, hats and accessories amassed from famous designers, fashion icons, movie stars and wealthy New York socialites over the past hundred years. But best of all was visiting a travelling archive of Paramount's most prolific and famous costume designer, Edith Head, and drinking in the plethora of her original drawings of exquisite costumes for all her favourite starlets: Barbara Stanwyck, Bette Davis, Ingrid Bergman, Elizabeth Taylor, Audrey Hepburn and, of course, Grace Kelly.

It was truly incredible. I felt like Charlie with his golden ticket in Willy Wonka's chocolate factory. Maybe I'd be good and wouldn't take the 1940s Swarovski-crystal-studded peep-toes – though it seemed like I could just reach out and pick them up and they were practically begging to come home with me. Then perhaps they'd take me into a small room and tell me that, for being so honest and virtuous, I could have the whole museum. Although, I was pretty sure they expected you just *not* to steal them in the first place, and that I should avoid flirting with a third potential arrest on American soil.

This was exactly what I'd dreamed of – that I'd get charged and fired up about fashion, then go home and get stuck in. What I was going to get stuck into was another matter but thinking about it too hard would have ruined the moment and burst my beautifully inflated shiny bubble.

I just wanted to think about how lovely this was. Just me and Robbie in New York, hanging out together and having a ball. It was such a treat to be able to spend the whole day together. It'd been so long since we could do that, what with his work, my studies and the move. Not that I needed reminding, but I loved how happy I felt when I was with him, without even trying. And my tummy was nicely toned again from all the laughing we'd done, particularly when 'Joseph' from the live nativity crib in Times Square made him come up and be the donkey in front of two thousand onlookers.

Just me and Robbie, away from all the nosy pains-in-the-ass

back home. Who were probably all glued to their phones waiting for 'the call'. Bringing them into the loo with them, sealing them inside clear plastic bags so they could take them into the shower, looping them through chains to wear around their necks so they'd never have to put them down, going to bed with the phone wedged to their ear and held in place by a tight-fitting sweatband. Well, they were all just going to have to deal with it because we were *not* getting engaged.

Okay, I have a small confession to make: I thought we might be getting engaged.

Christ!

I'd only started to get suspicious earlier in the day. Right about when I'd tried on my fifteenth pair of shoes of the day, after we'd happened upon the most adorable hub of boutiques just off Bleecker Street.

Robbie was as patient as any male of the species could ever be expected to be. He sat and made very convincing 'Oooh' sounds whenever I came out of a changing room, and he tried his best not to slip into an unconscious state whenever I was ankle deep in a Shoe Trying-on Session (in the past, these have been known to last in excess of two hours and have necessitated refuelling at regular intervals).

Which sort of set off a few alarm bells. Robbie was never, ever so patient.

*Ever.*

Normally after that long he'd look like he was being electrocuted, fingernails clawing into his seat, mouth gurning, eyes rolling. It was quite uncanny, really. And that was what sort of got me worried. He was sitting there, smiling at me, and being a bit too 'homosexual' in his interest in puffball skirts. And it got me thinking of when Tony took Rebecca away to Italy to propose. She got really bad mosquito bites on her bum on her first day and ended up not being able to walk/sit down/do anything. By her own admission, she turned into a flea-bitten Antichrist, who just wanted to lie in a ball on the bathroom tiles, eat ice-cream (double cooling effect) and cry. And although Tony really should have considered ending their relationship, rather than proposing, he asked her to be his wife while they lay there on the bathroom floor and he spoon-fed her a hazelnut Cornetto. (He had actually planned to propose beside the Trevi Fountain but since his girlfriend had a blistered bum he had no opportunity to reach the heights of his romantic potential.)

And now here was Robbie grinning at me inanely when really he should have been starting a row with me for taking so long.

'Would you look at that? We've been in here two and a half hours!' I said, in a really loud voice like our local pharmacist's when he asked really inappropriate questions in a packed shop – 'Do you need any thrush cream? There's a special offer on for October!' – when all you'd gone in for was nail-varnish remover.

'Wow, you sound like Pharmacy Man,' he said.

Ah! It'd worked! But that was not the point of the operation. I tried it again in the hope he might get pissed off with me and demand that we leave soon. 'We've been here for simply *hours*!' I said.

'Take your time,' he said placidly.

Holy shite!

I tried again. 'I think I may be here *days*!' I bellowed. 'We may need to go straight from here to the airport.'

The shop assistant popped her head around the rack. 'Sorry, you wouldn't mind keeping the noise down, would you?'

'Yes, of course,' I whispered.

Robbie smiled. 'Don't worry, take your time. Enjoy yourself.'

Oh. My. God. See what I mean?

OK, so either Robbie was the new Des Ferguson, or I was getting proposed to in New York.

## 14

From behind my enormous skinny frappuccino with the extra frothy whippy blobs, and the swirly caramel gooey bits and the giant reindeer stirrer, I studied Robbie intently. Same inane grin on his face: check. Same unshakeable patience while I drank my coffee *really slowly*: check. Same unmistakable feeling that he was going to propose: check.

A carousel of familiar figures churned around my head: my mother, my sister, Mrs Macnamara from the fitting room, Rebecca's great-aunt Marge, all chanting the same mantra: 'You're nearly thirty, it's time. What are you waiting for? What is *he* waiting for? You don't want to be on the shelf, surely. Everybody else is getting married; it's the natural next step. You're nearly thirty, what are you waiting for? *What are you waiting for?* WHAT ARE YOU WAITING FOR?'

'*Shut up!*' I suddenly exploded.

'Grace?' Robbie was startled.

'Hi there, you,' I said to him, smiling, hoping he'd simply say hi back and ignore that I'd just shouted, 'Shut up!' in the middle of a busy café for no apparent reason.

'Was that your inner voice telling you to go to Marc Jacobs again?'

'Yes.' I nodded guiltily.

We headed off down 49th Street to look at the Christmas tree in the Rockefeller Center, and I kept sneaking looks at him out of the corner of my eye. Was that a bulge I could see in his front jeans pocket? Christ, it was. And, no, not that kind of a bulge. If he had that kind of bulge in one of his front pockets, it would make him highly unsymmetrical; almost unsightly. And Robbie didn't have that problem at all: he was lovely and symmetrical.

The bulge was more of a box-shaped bulge. Yes, there was definitely a box-shaped bulge in there!

'Grace?'

I whipped my eyes away.

'Grace, were you just staring at my crotch?'

'Maybe. I'm a woman . . . with needs,' I answered, cringing slightly on the inside.

'You okay, Red?' he said, tucking me under his arm as we kept walking.

'Yes. I'm fine. Are you okay?'

'Yeah, great. I did have something to ask you, though.'

*Holy mother of shite!*

My heart thumped manically in my chest and suddenly I thought I was going to throw up my frothychinoyolky. Here? He was going to ask me to marry him here? We weren't even at the Christmas tree yet and there was a homeless man taking a piss up against a wall right beside me.

'Grace Harte, will you . . .' Jesus Christ, I was going to faint '. . . will you do me the honour . . .' Actually, puke first, followed by fainting, slipping and landing in my own puke. Here it comes . . . *Here it comes!*

'. . . of trying on that Victoria Secrets underwear you bought today when we get back to the hotel? I myself am a man with needs.'

Oh.

I could feel the blood return to my head, and the banging in my chest start to subside.

I was going to have to stop this. Maybe I was wrong. Maybe this wasn't going to happen now. Good God, maybe I was slowly being broken down and brainwashed by the Wedding Cult. I mentally gave myself two sharp slaps across the face and splashed myself with a glass of cold water. *Grace, just relax and enjoy your trip to New York*, I counselled. *Do not go to the dark side. No matter how much the Wedding Cult tries to suck you in, do not go there!*

'You got yourself a deal,' I answered, forcing a big grin.

I seriously needed to cop on. If I kept acting so odd, Robbie would never bring me back to New York. He'd think the place made me 'unhealthily excitable', like the vintage clothes fair I went to last month in the Berkeley Court Hotel where I ended up having to take a suck off someone's inhaler. And I didn't even have asthma. Robbie reckoned there had to be some sort of sedative that girls could take before they went to the sales or shoe shopping: he was convinced all the adrenalin and the near fainting weren't good for our long-term health.

I really was going to have to behave a bit more normally or he would be too afraid to bring me back to New York, and that would not be good.

Only yesterday I started screaming and holding on to a wall for support when I saw Robbie bending down on one knee. I'd thought he was about to pop the question then too, but he was picking chewing gum off his shoe. I had to pass the whole thing off as my shock at seeing a sign for '50% off' in the window of Marc Jacobs over his left shoulder.

*Get a grip, Grace!*

We arrived at the Rockefeller Center and cooed at the giant Christmas tree with all the other excited tourists. Some bearded man from Michigan told me it had been cut down from his very own backyard, and there was still a family of squirrels living in it; he was convinced that Christmas squirrels could be the new Christmas elves and he could make millions on the whole thing. I was convinced that the man had a problem discerning reality from Disney movies. But as I was a bit like that with rom-coms, I gave him a sympathetic smile. I liked the sound of Christmas squirrels and felt slightly annoyed that I hadn't come up with the idea myself. But I felt like that, too, about see-through Blu-Tack and red-soled shoes and electricity and stuff, so I had to let it go.

After the Rockefeller Center, we headed over towards Central Park to try our hands at some ice-skating. (Well, our feet, really. There was no way I was doing any handstands on the rink, I don't care what rumours of scouts from *Dancing on Ice* being there were going round.) I hadn't done it since Mum had tied biscuit-tin lids to my feet and sent me off on the frozen lake in Bushy Park near our house. Chances were, though, that this bunch was going to be a little more on top of things and have *real* ice skates. Although I do have to say that a little part of me wanted to get dressed up in the full-on ice-skating leotard regalia. But, obviously, that was a daft notion. Because it was too cold.

We queued for half an hour to pay and get our boots. 'We'd better get our skates on before it starts snowing,' I said, trying hard not to be openly chuffed with my hilarious gag.

'You're on thin ice with jokes like that,' Robbie answered. A few flakes had started to drift down from the heavens, making the rink look like a magical Christmas card come to life.

This was amazing. Ice-skating in Central Park at Christmas time. Could it get any better?

Well, yes, it could have got a whole lot better if I'd been able to skate. It didn't feel quite so magical when I was gripping the fence beside the ice with one of the instructors telling me to move off, that this area was for the under-fours only. Christ, they were far more competitive than the Bushy Parkers.

Shit. I'd never get on *Dancing on Ice* if I kept hanging out with these 'losers' (it's probably bad to call four-year-olds losers, isn't it? Especially when you're twenty-nine).

I looked out on to the rink and wondered if I just launched myself out there and really believed in myself, could I manage a little circular move with a hint of a pirouette thrown in? I unhooked my hands and pushed myself forward, telling myself I could do this, that it couldn't be that hard. There was a pensioner out there who should have been on a zimmer frame and was doing backward zigzags, for crying out loud.

And there I was, going for it, really trying. Sweet Jesus, the *Dancing on Ice* people better not be taking a coffee break right now! This. Was. My. Moment.

I managed to take out the last three children in a line from a school group and everyone screamed so loudly they put the temporary siren on that normally only gets used in emergencies. I scuttled back to the fence, where I was met by a little four-year-old with pigtails, who looked at me with big, sympathetic eyes and said, 'Next time, honey, next time.'

'Come on, Grace! I got ya!' Robbie had sidled up beside me.

I told him he should go on and leave me behind. That he should just *go* and do what he needed to do.

'Grace, we're in an ice rink, not a war movie,' he said, shaking his head while he watched my legs slowly but steadily adopt the splits. Really needed to stop quoting *For Whom the Bell Tolls* when I felt under siege.

'Come on, take my hand and I'll bring you around.'

How on earth had he got so good at this ice-skating lark? Had he heard about the scouts too and been practising on the sly? I linked my arm in his as we moved off, leaving the toddler 'losers' behind.

'When did you get so good at this?' I asked, as I watched my feet scramble around like those of a newborn deer.

After a while we sort of got the hang of it, but I was still terrified of falling and that mad backward zigzagging granddad slicing my fingers off with his boots. I looked up at Robbie and smiled. A snowflake had landed on one of his eyelashes and his nose was all red and shiny from the cold.

Hey, hang on a minute there, sunshine! What was he doing? We'd only just mastered standing up straight and moving forward! Why was he suddenly doing some sort of Torvill and Dean move? I knew it! He'd been secretly practising, probably on biscuit-tin lids in Bushy Park.

What was he planning on doing if he got picked? Upping and leaving for the States for a few months to do shoulder lifts with Mario Lopez?

'Grace, will you . . .'

Oh, Jesus.

Oh, Christ!

This was it. This *actually* was it.

I suddenly felt all hot and sweaty even though I was freezing. I pulled at my scarf, feeling overcome with a sense of claustrophobia, and gasped sharply at the crisp evening air. The ice rink seemed to shrink and it felt like everyone's eyes were on us as I stood there looking down at Robbie on one knee.

Oh, Jesus, everyone's eyes *were* actually on us, courtesy of the giant flat-screen TV with the live videolink at the top of the rink. We'd been watching the random shots of different tourists waving and saying, 'Happy holidays,' into the camera earlier. And we'd laughed at the two Japanese tourists who'd managed to do the Macarena on skates and the American Eminem wannabe who'd rapped, 'To all my homies from London, Paris, New York and Tokyo – Santa's not comin' cos he's hanging with his ho', yo.' But then he'd got kicked out and barred on account of all the crying four-year-olds.

And now the zoom-in camera was fixed on us. I could hear everyone's skates suddenly crunching to a halt on the ice.

Silence. Silence and expectation. Two things I'm not a fan of. Unless it's a shop assistant about to tell you that they do in fact have those shoes in your size, on sale.

I blinked like a simpleton at my own image up on the twenty-foot-square television screen and couldn't help thinking I looked like Ralph Wiggum from *The Simpsons*: bug-eyed, gormless, confused. I couldn't see Robbie's face. Everything had started to blur now, like I was looking through fogged-up glass. I couldn't remember the last time I'd taken a breath.

Oh, Jesus!

*Oh, Jesus!*

And then, on cue, the Giuliana Rancic-type lady, dressed in a pink fluffy snowsuit, who had been compèring the whole live feed suddenly came on the microphone. 'Oh my gosh, my little holiday gnomes, what do we have here?' I felt the shiver of excitement spread through the 'holiday gnomes' like a bad case of herpes.

*Oh, Christ!*

Out of nowhere, something rushed up through me. Looking to escape, searching for a gap in the dam to explode from. I pulled at my scarf again. Everything felt so tight. So hot.

All of a sudden I felt like I was leaving my own body, and my voice sounded like someone else's as it suddenly burst out of me.

'*No. No. No,*' I shouted. '*I don't want to marry you!* I DON'T WANT TO MARRY YOU!'

## 15

In that instant, my whole world changed for ever. Everything was moving like I was under water. I couldn't speak. Couldn't breathe. Couldn't walk properly.

That might have had something to do with the fact that I was still wearing my skates.

Robbie had somehow managed to change back into his runners. But I couldn't co-ordinate such a complex task as that when my whole world was falling apart around me.

Faces floated past me. All with the same expression. Those two Japanese tourists certainly weren't doing their happy little Macarena dance any more, I can tell you. No, now they were staring at me, agog, as if I'd just told them Hello Kitty wasn't real.

'Robbie!' I glugged, desperate to find my voice as I watched him stride away from me. More shocked faces swarmed past, like mass shoals of consternation in my disturbing underwater world. *Jesus*. It was worse than Costner's *Waterworld*. That was just how bad my waterworld was.

'Robbie!' I tried again. Every step I took was like trying to swim upstream as I watched even more distance flood between us.

All of a sudden the Giuliana Rancic lady was closing in on me, like a shark. 'Sweetheart, you all right? Hey, you wanna come back in there and tell everyone why you said no? You could be, like, a celebrity if you wanted.'

Aaaargh! Get out of my way, crazy fluffy pink shark-lady with your microphone! Robbie was shrinking further and further from my view. I couldn't let him go! I was panicking, gasping for air. I grabbed the microphone and shouted, '*I'm sorry, Robbie! Robbie, please! I'm sorry!*'

Silence.

Then the microphone made that awful high-pitched interference sound just to ensure that every single person in the whole of New York City was now looking at us.

What the hell was I doing?

I could see Robbie stopping in his tracks. And then slowly turning towards me. I couldn't see his face. I couldn't see his face! It was blurred and out of focus and I wanted to run to it and touch it and feel it cupped in my palms and kiss it. Kiss his eyes, kiss his nose, kiss his lips, and tell him I was so, so, so sorry.

'This is better than an episode of *The Hills*,' I heard someone say beside me. 'You think he's gonna come back? Will we cancel our lunch at Tao?'

Oh, Jesus! Was this actually happening? *Was this actually happening?* I felt as though I was about to have a full-blown panic attack. A few moments ago, I was skating around an ice rink with Robbie on our holiday in New York, another moment in our life together, another memory to share and treasure and keep for only us, and now it was like everything had dissolved, the plug had been pulled and my entire world was disappearing down the plughole. Then he turned away again and started fading from view. Like a mirage on the surface of a dried-up puddle.

I clacked down the path after him as best I could in the skates, my ankles screaming with discomfort, hoping to God I wasn't about to be arrested for larceny on top of everything else.

'Robbie!' I cried feebly, more as a comfort to myself than a call to him.

Eventually I caught up with him (quietly accepting that my ankles might indeed need to be in orthopaedic braces for a considerable time).

'Robbie,' I pleaded. He ignored me and kept walking. I had to settle for clopping awkwardly behind him, and I appreciated his decency in allowing me do so.

We got to the hotel and headed silently to our room. Not *too* silently, mind you. Skates on a tiled hotel foyer go quite a way to shattering the peace and quiet. I could feel every set of eyes on me as we walked the green mile.

He pushed the button for the lift. We waited. And then it arrived, the ping as the doors opened sounding like a death knell.

I saw his face for the first time in the lift. Under the harsh lighting where there was nowhere to hide.

My stomach heaved at the sight of his raw, exposed hurt, and it was like watching my heart flat-line before my very eyes.

'Robbie,' I whispered, reaching out to touch his hand, 'I didn't mean it.'

He flinched and his hand recoiled from me. 'Yes, you did.'

I clung to the rail inside the lift, as the doors stretched open, and watched him leave. This couldn't be happening. My head reeled as I gasped for breath and tried to fight the panic burgeoning through me. I was losing him.

*I was losing him!*

'We need the defibrillator, stat!' Sweet Jesus, Grace, this was no time to be quoting *ER*.

By now I could feel the hot tears race down my face.

'Robbie, please,' I wept, chasing him into our room, 'can we talk? Can we just sit here and talk about it?'

'No,' he barked, turning to face me now, his eyes hollow with hurt, humiliation, anger and loss. 'We will not sit here and pick over the bones so you can try and make sense of it for your own head. Believe me, more than enough has already been said.'

'But – but –' I stammered, my words like distress signals '– I didn't mean it!'

'Yes, you did mean it, Grace. I was looking in your eyes and I know what I saw there. I will never, ever forget it.'

*Oh, God!*

'I'm obviously not the man for you. I really thought I was. I really thought we were . . .'

*Oh, Jesus, Jesus . . .*

'Please, Robbie,' I sobbed, 'please don't say that. Let's just forget it ever happened.'

I wanted to run and put my arms around him, hold him, comfort him.

'I can't. Grace, I will never, ever forget it.' He looked at me from his sorrowful eyes. 'And I love you too much to let you waste your best years on someone you don't truly love.'

Under the weight of my own despair, I crumpled to the floor like a fallen house of cards. How was this happening? *How*?

I tried to think clearly, to say something that would make sense, that would stop this madness, but grasping at solid thoughts was like trying to grab wisps of smoke.

'I'm going home,' he said softly. 'You should stay here and get the use of the hotel. I think it will be good for you. Figure things out for yourself.'

And there he went again: putting me before himself as he always did.

On the floor, I wept silently as I watched him pack his bag. Everything inside me was screaming as my body lay in a paralysed heap. I watched him fold his shirts, his trousers, his T-shirts. Close the wardrobe. Zip his bag. Like a displaced scene from a movie I'd never seen.

'Well, Grace . . .' he whispered, the threat of tears in his unsteady voice.

*Oh, God, don't cry. Don't cry, baby. If you cry I will never, ever be able to move from here.*

'I suppose . . . well . . .' he coughed, clearing his throat and meeting my eyes briefly '. . . goodbye.'

I watched him as he left, the door clicking shut softly behind him.

Silence.

Everything was still.

Everything was numb.

My eyes dropped from the back of the door to a T-shirt he'd

missed on the floor. I watched my hand slowly reaching for it and lifting it automatically to my face. I inhaled the smell of him deep into my lungs. My heart recoiled with the sting. I buried my head in it and cried and cried until I was too exhausted to cry any more.

He was gone.

## 16

A few hours later, I shuffled out of bed and put my clothes on over my pyjamas, like one of those scary people that hung around newsagents in Smithfield. It was only three p.m. How was it only three p.m.? And that was after I had gone back to bed and cried for *hours*. This was officially the longest, shittiest day of my life. And it was only three p.m.

I stared at the ice skates beside the bed. Haunting the room like ghosts.

Coffee. I needed to get out of here and get a coffee: one of those frothy ones that was like a three-course meal in one. And a reindeer stirrer to decorate the darkness.

I made my way down to Reception and headed for the Starbucks on the corner. But before I got to the big revolving doors at the front of the hotel, I was stopped in my tracks by the concierge. 'Honey, a little housekeeping, er, HR matter I want to sort of clear up with you.'

Uh-oh. Had they caught me fleecing an abandoned trolley of those cute little shampoos on their CCTV? You are *technically* allowed to do that, right?

'Your shampoos are lovely,' I offered, trying to offset him with a touch of flattery.

He looked confused. 'Oh, no. Was Beatrice hounding you about our guest questionnaire? She was, wasn't she?'

Who the flip was Beatrice when she was at home?

'Beatrice?' he said, almost reading my mind. 'Our new junior receptionist? I swear to God I find her actually stalking our guests, following them into toilets, barracking them when they're just about to tuck into their main course, chasing them into elevators . . . Her first day, I said, "Beatrice, if you have nothing to do you can always ask a guest politely if they would be so kind as to fill out a questionnaire." And now that's all she does. That is literally *all* she does. Please don't tell me she asked you about the shampoos while you were actually *in* the shower.'

Oh, God, I wanted that coffee. *Now.* With seven reindeer-stirrer things.

'No one has asked me about filling out a questionnaire,' I said, almost hurt. If this Beatrice one was stalking everyone else, why hadn't I been stalked? Or at least followed into a toilet and mildly harassed?

'Okay. It's just that, well . . .' He started to flap, and I could see a flurry of sweat patches bloom across his forehead. He stood there puffing and pouting and I wondered if I had ever met a more camp concierge-type person before in my entire life. His Poirot-style moustache was a little out there, especially considering he was only about twenty-five, but I guess it was some sort of brave New York style statement.

Tanya used to have one of those before she discovered Immac. But I really don't think hers was any New York fashion statement. Just unfortunate hormone distribution.

I did like his quirky pink bow-tie and I was just about to ask him where he'd got his black skinny jeans and cute pumps when he interrupted me again: 'Thing is, sweetie, we know Mr Robbie Cotter checked out of here in a hurry earlier today, and . . . Well, how do I put this?'

My stomach dived at the mention of his name and I thought I was going to vomit all over him. But I held it because he looked so darned fashionable and I didn't want him to have to go and change his outfit on my account.

He paused for thought and stroked his 'tache. 'Okay, I'm just gonna come right out and say it! He's left. You look upset. *And* you're about to go out in public in pyjamas and slippers.'

He'd obviously never been to Dublin. I buttoned my jacket defensively.

'So . . . okay here we go. We were wondering if you'd caught him with that whore who cleans the rooms up on the fifth floor. We've had a lot of wives calling here threatening to sue us if we don't get rid of her but, by golly, she can shine a brass knob, so to speak. Sorry, was that inconsiderate? So basically, honey, will you be filing some sort of law suit against us?'

He stood there with his head cocked to the side, waiting for an answer.

'Oh, no, not at all,' I answered.

He smiled and mimed, 'Phew,' raising the back of his hand to his forehead.

'No, Robbie went home because I told him I didn't want to marry him in the middle of the ice rink in Central Park.'

Silence.

'Oh. My. *Gaaaad* . . .' he said, recoiling and fanning his face with his beautifully manicured hands. 'Hug?'

'Yes, please,' I answered.

So we stood there hugging in the foyer. It felt nice, if a little weird. And then I started crying again, drizzling streams of black mascara all over his gorgeous white Tom Ford blouse. (It was definitely more of a blouse than a shirt. I was jealous of it, actually.)

'You can tell Beatrice that the crying facilities are outstanding,' I wailed, as the camp concierge with the Poirot/Tanya-style moustache shushed me softly and patted me gently on the back.

Half an hour later I was back in the foyer in a red dress (no pyjamas underneath) and a pair of skyscraper red heels (not hotel slippers).

Big step.

I had managed to stop crying and was momentarily not thinking about throwing myself out of one of the top-floor windows.

Major step. (They didn't open all the way anyway: you could only squeeze one leg out and then you'd get stuck and graze your entire shin when you tried to drag it back in again. And, for the record, I definitely did not try it.)

I had even gathered myself enough to wash off the car-tyre mascara tracks skidding down my face.

Ridiculously commendable step. In fact, with all these marked improvements to make me more acceptable to high society, I was starting to feel a little like Eliza Doolittle in *My Fair Lady*.

And now I was waiting for Andy. The incredibly camp concierge, a.k.a. my new BFF. The one who'd offered me a lie-down on his 'psychiatric retail-therapy couch'.

Which basically meant kicking the shit out of our credit cards in a series of ass-kicking fabulous boutiques around SoHo. He said I should go and blow a whole lot of cash now that I wasn't going to be saving for a wedding.

Which made me sob uncontrollably. But he did offer the ultimate sacrifice and wipe the snot away with the sleeve of the Tom Ford blouse, which more than made up for it. Then he told me to go upstairs and put on an outfit that would stop my tears.

So I did. And now here I was. Numb, exhausted, hollow and tortured. But dressed for the world like Marilyn Monroe in a fab frock and a fake smile. (Just needed to get some plasters for my shin . . . )

Andy told his boss that he had to go home because he had his period. Odd. Maybe it was a gay-rights thing in New York and gay men were entitled to time-of-the-month equality as well as civil marriages.

God, Ireland was so backward. I knew for a fact that Ian Nochton, Lisa's gay friend from college, *never* had his 'period'. Neither did her dad. But perhaps he'd already been through the menopause by the time he'd decided he was gay.

None of this made sense. I seriously needed either straight alcohol or peep-toes in a size eight ASAP to start seeing things a little clearer.

The next two hours were like a crazy E trip. A hazy swirl of fantastic texture and colour and excitement. Shop after shop of tantalizing clothes, shoes, handbags, coats, hats. We touched them, we felt them, we tried them on. It was a surreal distraction.

Like a carousel ride that spun me into a wonderful place where the real world couldn't touch me as long as I stayed on board.

And then all of a sudden the real world slammed on the brakes and pressed the eject button.

'Okay, ma'am, that will be seven hundred and eighty-nine dollars and ninety-nine cents.'

Wow. Nearly eight hundred dollars later, I was sitting on a bench in Greenwich Village, with a bag full of clothes, a cup of mulled wine, and a man who was not my boyfriend of seven years.

I watched the world from my perch, like an awkward extra on a movie set, completely surplus to requirements and disconnected from everything around me. It all looked very well oiled: people bustling past us, going about their daily lives. Normal.

Yet nothing was normal.

And I hadn't a clue where I really was or what was going on.

'So I take it you like your clothes, then,' Andy said, inhaling on his extra-slim menthol cigarette while I dragged on a trusty Marlboro. I smiled automatically. 'Retail therapy, eh? Christ, though, I'm not sure my health insurance is going to cover this one.'

'Yeah, but it's great, though, right? Like a little hit off a morphine drip.'

'True that,' I said, like someone off *The Wire*. God, I was such a spa, trying extra hard to fit in with my new American buddy.

'Trouble is, when it eventually wears off, you realize how royally fucked you really are,' he said.

I sucked on my cigarette again, pretending not to hear him, and imagined instead that I was Marlene Dietrich, standing tall in my own Paramount Pictures movie, cigarette in hand, gazing back at the world with detached apathy.

'Gotta serious thing for the golden oldies, dontcha?' he said, almost reading my mind.

I smiled, suddenly feeling exposed.

'Everything you picked up today had some reference to an old film or Hollywood starlet. Were we born in the wrong decade, Miss Grace?'

'Probably,' I said. The cold December air suddenly whipped around us and I took a sip of my warm mulled wine. 'I suppose it's something I've always been into.'

'I know,' he said. 'I just love them too. Particularly the musicals. They're my religion. I don't think I could actually marry a man who was not of the Church of Camp Musicals. We could have our service on the stage at the Gershwin.'

Ha! I liked Andy.

'Although Fred Astaire is my all-time favourite non-gay gay icon so, you know, go figure.'

Maybe it was because he was a relative stranger, because he didn't really know me or anything about my life back at home, but I found myself telling him something I had never told anyone before in my entire life.

'It's always been my escape. For as long as I can remember,' I said. 'Whenever my parents were having a fight, I'd go up to my room, close the door, put on one of the oldies and get lost in a world I didn't belong to. One full of romance and glamour and drama that was a million miles away from the stale, dull monotony of my own. Where the heroines were powerful and beautiful and elegant, and held the promise of far happier endings than any I knew of.'

I closed my eyes as the words drifted out of my mouth and flitted, like snowflakes, through the air before finally settling softly on the bench around me. And in that moment, I felt both stunned and calmed. On that park bench with that stranger I'd shared a secret I'd always known but had never admitted, even to myself. The truth of my life.

## 17

A couple of hours later, another costume change, two swift gins and a family-sized portion of room-service macaroni and cheese, and I was back in the foyer of the hotel, waiting for Andy to take me out on 'A Night I Would Never Forget'.

I liked Andy. He was like my accomplice in a runaway movie, one in which the more we disguised ourselves in dress-up the further away we got. He was sort of the Tony Curtis to my Jack Lemmon.

Bless him, he'd sung *Cabaret* songs with me all the way back to the hotel so we wouldn't have to talk about what was really going on in my life. (He had started out with a few hits from *Seven Brides for Seven Brothers*, but considering the day I'd had, and after I'd burst out crying again, he'd moved on swiftly to *Cabaret*.)

I stood there in the lobby, in one of my newly procured 1950s prom-style dresses, and waited for my *Some Like It Hot* co-star to pull me aboard the train to Escapism again. And I prayed for him to come soon, so I wouldn't have the unbearable company of my own thoughts for too long. Not that they were making any sense.

None of this was making any sense.

'There you are, sweetie!' he suddenly cooed from the doorway, sashaying across Reception and offering me his arm, a vision of Errol Flynn. Maybe it was the 'tache. Maybe it was just me wanting to keep fleeing, this time to run away with Robin Hood. Maybe it was the exhaustion.

'Don't you look like a cupcake?' he purred, sounding less like Errol and more like a New York queen.

*Cupcake!* Oooh. Not good. Too much pastel?

'You look divine!' he said.

Phew. It was a term of endearment: I didn't actually *look* like a cupcake. Good to know. I was in a fragile state as it was: I did not need to go out in New York City with my new friend Andy looking like a souped-up bun.

'Are we off, honey?' he asked, stroking my hair just like my mum does when she's trying to get me to eat broccoli.

'Andy, I'm really not sure this is such a great idea. I mean, I really do think I have more tears in me tonight, and what if I start crying in front of all your friends?'

'Cupcake, you don't worry your gorgeous little head about that, you hear me? They're always crying anyway so you're not going to be on your own. Carly is *always* in tears. She gets weepy after eating carbs. It's the guilt. She has no self-control. Then there's Ben. He's weaning himself off anti-depressants so he's always in floods. Tiffany's cat's gone missing, we think it's been run over, and only today I saw the pair of D-and-G boots I bought last week for full price on sale with fifty per cent off. So, you know, there's a *lot* of misery floating about.'

Brilliant. I was so pleased.

We met the Misery Convention in a nauseatingly trendy bar on the Upper East Side. Waitresses in silver lamé bikinis whizzed around on roller-blades, while others danced provocatively inside huge glass cages. Now, that was definitely going to push me to the brink of a big crying session. I'd spent the previous hour eating an entire vat of macaroni and cheese. (I'm not exaggerating: room service brought up an industrial-sized kitchen pot of it, with a large wooden spoon, after I'd rung downstairs and started whimpering into the phone about 'stodgy carbs' and it being a life or death situation.)

Maybe this Andy character was actually a sadistic little shite, not the 'runaway buddy' I'd previously thought. I sneaked a sideways glance at him. He was stroking his 'tache. In a very sadistic way.

'Andy! Andy! Andy!' a group called, like a coop of excitable chickens. 'Over here!'

The next few minutes were filled with a lot of screaming,

hugging, kissing and, oddly enough, crotch-grabbing (I hoped they didn't expect me to join in. I didn't know them well enough yet). I stood back awkwardly, hands splayed protectively down below, surveying the rest.

Well, that was definitely Carly, with the mascara stains on her cheeks, clutching the empty bread basket. And I presumed that was Tiffany with the 'Have You Seen My Pussy?' T-shirt. And was that Ben? He seemed too jolly. Perhaps he was back on the meds.

'Hey, Andy! Is this Irish?' Tiffany had spotted me over Andy's left shoulder. 'Shut the hell up! She has freakin' red hair! I thought that was a myth or somethin', like how they say the Canadians have sex with bears!'

They say that?

She dropped Andy mid-air and made her way over to me. She stood in front of me staring, then started stroking my hair, broccoli-style.

'It ain't true about leprechauns too, is it? A friend of mine is four foot nine, but she calls herself a dwarf. Isn't that politically incorrect, or somethin'?'

I shrugged. Where did you begin with that one?

'Shut the hell up!'

Jesus, I hadn't even said anything. Then she punches me on my left shoulder and I stand there wobbling, trying to regain my balance.

'So, your man gets down on one knee in Central Park today and you shout at the top of your lungs that you don't wanna marry him? Christ, I thought I had problems,' she said. And added, 'I can't find my pussy.'

I signalled to the bikini on roller-blades and ordered a double vodka on the rocks with a shot of Sambuca.

An hour in and a few double vodkas later, I was delighted Andy had talked me into going out. We'd already decided he was coming over to stay with me next Christmas. But I'd have to remember to warn Mum as she gets into an awful flap about how many extra potatoes to put on when there's a guest coming. The Misery

Brigade wasn't so miserable after all, and just for the record, Tiffany had had her cat for fifteen years. Fifteen years! Multiplied by cat years that was, like, a *million*, so I could totally see why she was so upset. I just wished she wouldn't keep talking about how she used to 'stroke my pussy every night' until she fell asleep, as it was sort of making me nauseous.

And Carly. Poor Carly. She didn't just hate carbs because they made her put on weight: she'd walked in on her mum in bed with their neighbour while she was eating a foot-long sub. She had association issues, which I thought was absolutely fair enough.

I still couldn't figure Ben out. I wasn't quite sure why he kept laughing at everything. Especially when Carly said her dad had moved out and still lived in a hotel.

But all in all they were a great bunch. Later in the night, we had so much fun sitting around the grand piano singing Whitney Houston's complete nineties repertoire. Who knew Andy's song catalogue exceeded the big camp musicals? I was so proud of him and his lovely moustache.

See? That wasn't so bad! It was positive and uplifting and, you know, maybe I could just come and live here with my new friends and keep playing dress-up and . . . and . . .

It was only when a bloke in a red T-shirt sidled up beside me and offered to buy me a drink that the world didn't look quite so 'I'm Every Woman' any more.

'Oh, no, thank you. I have a boyfriend.'

'No, you don't. Your friends just told me you're single.'

Holy Christ.

It hit me like a tonne of bricks. Hearing him say those words. Suddenly the room closed in on me, like someone had pressed a zoom button on a video camera.

I was single.

I was *single*? That didn't sound right. It didn't make sense. I was so used to saying I had a boyfriend.

My stomach took a dive and I suddenly thought I was going to be sick. Seven years with Robbie. *Seven years!* And it was over?

*What* the hell had happened today? I stood up in a panic, looking for somewhere to run to – a door to escape through.

I could feel the pit in my stomach deepening. I looked around me, at Andy and the rest of them singing at the top of their lungs and swaying in time with the music.

What had I been thinking? I wasn't some character in a runaway movie where I could keep changing my outfit as a disguise and just keep on running. No. The crazy train had run out of steam and it was time to get off.

And the only place I was going was home. First thing in the morning.

Home to face the music.

## 18

'What are you looking at?' I asked the cat, as she sat on top of the bookshelf staring at me. Why did she always have to sit so high up? It was unnerving.

'Yes, I know you liked him better. But he's gone. So we're just going to have to try to get along, okay?'

I surveyed the room. It looked so naked and bald. I'd never realized Robbie had so much stuff. I'd also never realized he was the one buying the good CDs. And now all I was left with was *Smash Hits Volume 7* and the soundtrack to *Good Luck Chuck*. They stared at me from across the room, exposed and mortified.

Everything else seemed so new. New paint on the walls. New couch. New rug. New mug on a new coaster. All the old familiar stuff was gone. And already I ached for it.

He'd moved everything out, including himself, by the time I'd got home. And here I was. In the house we'd always dreamed of. In our first proper home. Suddenly on my own. Without him.

With a cat I hated.

It felt like a Lego house that had been picked apart and fleeced of all the good bits. And my favourite bit was most definitely missing: the Lego man with the sandy hair and the friendly smile.

'Bette, you do realize we're going to be known as "the spinster and the cat in number seven" by our neighbours from now on, don't you? I know it's not your fault exactly, but if I was ever going to go down the spinster-and-her-cat route, I would at least have had a nice white fluffy Persian one that liked me.'

I shuffled into the kitchen to make a cup of coffee before they arrived. I needed all the strength I could get. I'd already downed a share-size bag of Tangfastics in the hope I'd slip off into some sort of sugar coma in which I looked conscious but my mind had switched off entirely. That way I wouldn't have to hear them go on about how I'd ruined my life.

Well, not Lisa. Lisa would never say that. But what would she say? I didn't even know what to say myself.

I flicked the switch on the kettle and waited for the water to boil. It was only then that I noticed the note pinned to the fridge. The photo of the two of us on the doorstep on our first day in number seven, grinning like fools, had been taken down and replaced with a Post-it: *I'll be back for the rest of my stuff during the week.*

I could feel the pinch in my heart and the familiar lump swelling in my throat. I leaned my forehead against the cold metal surface of the fridge.

Half an hour later, they were there. Staring at me. Bette was on the shelf, still staring at me too. Three sets of eyes blinking at me expectantly.

What?

What did they want me to say?

'Do you like the colour of the walls?' I asked meekly. 'It's Cappuccino Froth.'

Silence.

'I think it looks good with the –'

'Fuck the froth!' Tanya said, so loudly that I jumped in my seat and had a sudden urge to run to the loo and do a wee.

'Fine, you're more into creams. Each to their own.'

'Grace, stop this! We can go on with this charade all night. I can see that the rug is burgundy, that the shelves are white and that the coasters match the rug. But that still doesn't change the fact that you've made a huge mistake and you need to get Robbie back.'

Lisa made an 'Eeeeek!' face behind her back.

I'd known this was going to happen. I hadn't even wanted Tanya to come over but, as usual, I hadn't had much choice in the matter. The last time I'd told her I didn't want her calling in, I'd turned off all the lights and hidden behind the couch so she'd think I was out. But the mentaller climbed up the trellis out the back and got in through the upstairs window. When she found me hiding behind the couch, she crouched down beside me and told me in no uncertain terms that I'd be wise not to try to fool her like that again.

My sister did not take no for an answer. And was also, quite clearly, a monster Chuck Norris fan.

'Tanya, I know you mean well, but, really, I can't do this right now,' I said, hoping she wasn't going to respond by whipping me into a headlock and forcing me to dial Robbie's number so that I could tell him I'd marry him at the earliest possible convenience.

She narrowed her eyes and scanned me up and down. 'Fine,' she snapped.

Phew.

'You have twenty-four hours to retract your decision. Or I'm going to do it for you.'

Oh, God.

'Right, so you're going to get back with Robbie for me, are you? I'm not sure you can actually do that past the age of eight!' I huffed.

'Have you even thought about Mum in all of this?' she said, ignoring me. 'She'll be devastated. *And* I've already helped her pick a hat for the wedding – a beautiful turquoise one with a parrot plumage that rises above it like a halo.' (Good God almighty, if there was one reason *never* to get married, Tanya had just identified it.) 'You can't do this to us, Grace!'

'Well, I'm so sorry this whole thing has been such an inconvenience to you both. Please tell Mum that if she can't find the receipt for the hat, I'll give her the money. It's the least I can do.' (Or ceremoniously set fire to it at no extra charge.)

'Twenty-four hours,' she barked again, before standing up, turning on her heel and storming out of the house.

'Oh, my God, I think I just wet my pants,' Lisa whispered.

'She's so scary, isn't she?' I whispered back.

'Totally.'

We sat there, shell-shocked and exhausted.

'Grace, why is your cat staring at us like that?'

'She hates me.'

'Okay.'

'Why are we still whispering?' I asked.

'I'm afraid your sister's going to come back. Or that the cat's going to jump on my head.'

'Yeah. Me too.'

I plodded over to the CD player and hit play and repeat on Daniel Bedingfield 'If You're Not The One' and started singing along again. It was a routine I'd got into since I'd come in last night and I was at a bit of a loss as to what exactly I should do next.

Seemed the most logical thing, really. I'd seen all the break-up movies. I'd read *Bridget Jones*.

'Grace, no. Uh-uh. I refuse to let you do this,' Lisa protested, marching over and hitting stop.

'What have you got against Daniel?'

'I have nothing against Daniel. Actually, I quite like him. I saw him being interviewed on T4 once and he came across as very down to earth. But what I am against is you turning into some bad break-up cliché.'

'What do you mean?' I asked, stuffing an entire finger of Twix into my mouth and washing it down with some red wine.

'This!' She waved her hand in front of me. 'First of all, that is not your friend,' she counselled, taking my remaining Twix finger and trying to feed it to Bette.

'Oi!' I remonstrated. The last thing I needed was to capitulate in front of Bette and have her thinking I was on her side. I had big plans for Hating Her Even More as my new hobby to fill the deep ravine my crumbled relationship had left behind. Plans for us to become real-life Bette and Joan reincarnations from *Whatever Happened to Baby Jane?*, spending hours on end acting out revenge tactics against each other . . .

Oh, God. Was I really planning to make a hobby out of hating my cat to fill my time? Yes, I believe I was.

But that was good, no? It was at least original. Not at all 'break-up cliché'.

'Remember what happened to Ellen from college when she broke up with Ronan back in '05?'

Oh, God, yes, I did. I nodded solemnly, the all-too-pertinent image flashing in my mind.

'They say it was the KitKat Chunky that did it.'

'Apt.' This was great, I thought, as Bette licked the Twix. Maybe she'd get really fat. I was winning already. Ha-ha!

'Now, arms up,' Lisa instructed, with unnerving authority. I looked at her blankly and gave her my 'Huh?' Elvis lip.

'I'm not going to tell you again,' she said sternly.

Flippin' heck! Had Lisa been hanging out with my sister on the sly? Or was everybody into Chuck Norris now? Was it being repeated on Dave or something?

I put my arms up and she whipped my hoodie off over my head. What the –? Next she reefed my tracksuit bottoms down so they sat in a crumpled heap around my ankles as I stood there in a skimpy pair of knickers.

I Elvis-lipped her again. Why was she picking on me?

'I'm not going to let you sit there and mope around in Robbie's clothes and eat chocolate and drink red wine. Actually, I am going to let you drink red wine, but only if I drink it with you. Now get your glass. We're going up to the roof.'

Oh, yay! I loved the roof! The roof was where we solved all the world's problems.

But it was also where I went to dissect the world with Robbie. And now he wasn't there. And I was in flesh-coloured pants, with tracksuit bottoms around my ankles, on a chocolate ban.

'Okay, but can I please put some clothes on first?'

It was freezing cold up there, but the magic of the view was worth it. We sat huddled in our coats under a blanket with hot-water bottles under our bums, and looked out at the twinkling lights of Dublin Bay. The stars and the moon outshone them all, hanging in limbo in the dark expanse of the night sky.

I thought about Tanya, my family. About how I couldn't even feel the heaviness in my gut that usually accompanied my thoughts of them.

Everything was numb. Frozen. I looked out at the frost blanketing the houses and the trees and the roads, and I thought that maybe everybody else out there felt this way too. That perhaps I wasn't on my own. I exhaled and watched my breath on the clear air. And momentarily I felt thankful that at least deep down, on the inside, I was still continuing to function. Even while frozen.

'Do you want to talk about it?' Lisa asked gently.

I flicked at the zipper on my coat absentmindedly. 'I don't know what to say,' I answered honestly.

'Okay. Well . . . do you feel . . . okay?'

'That's the worst part, Leese. I don't know what to feel. I really don't know.'

'Okay. Well, we don't have to figure that out right now.'

'Thanks,' I mumbled.

We let the silence speak for us as we sat and listened to it spin our own thoughts.

'So, I have to ask,' she said, after a while. 'You really shouted, "I don't want to marry you!" to Robbie in the middle of Central Park?'

I watched the frost glimmer along the tops of the roofs in front of us, reminding me of the ice rink. Reminding me of everything. Deep down, under all the layers of frost, I could feel a dull pang echoing in my heart. Like a doctor was tapping away at a part of me that was under anaesthetic.

*Can you feel that?* I heard a voice say in my head. *Can you?* It was Robbie's voice.

*I can*, I answered silently, *but I don't know what it is.*

'At the top of my lungs,' I said to Lisa.

She bit her lip and I couldn't tell if she was about to laugh or cry.

'Oh, Leese . . .' I started, which prompted her to laugh nervously. I nudged her playfully, relieved that she'd just punctured the awful swell of tension and sadness. 'What am I like, Leese? After I'd said it, everything just stopped. I could actually hear the people skidding to a halt around us. All these eyes staring at me in disbelief. And Robbie down there on bended knee, frozen to the spot.'

'Jesus!' Lisa said.

'That's what everyone at the ice rink started saying. I could even hear some kid behind me whimpering, "Mom, why did she say that to the man? It's so mean."'

I looked at Lisa and we started laughing. And I laughed and laughed until the laughs turned to heart-wrenching sobs and she sat there and hugged me so tightly that I thought I would break.

'The worst thing was, *he wasn't even proposing*! He was just doing some silly ice-skating move!'

It was true. He hadn't been about to propose to me.

'Oh, Grace.' She sighed, the sadness in her voice as deep as mine.

'Lisa, I've never seen him look so hurt in my whole life. It was horrific. Utterly horrific.' My voice shook.

She put her arm around me, and I folded into her shoulder.

'I don't even know where it came from. It shocked me as much as it shocked him.'

'And then what happened?'

'He said it was obviously how I really felt about him, and he didn't want to be around me. The weird thing was, I didn't even fight it. I mean I did. But then I just let him walk away . . .'

We swigged from our glasses, and I let the cool liquid trickle over the lump wedged in my throat. We sat there for a few moments, looking out into the night, letting our heads tick over in the silence.

'So what now?' she asked softly.

'I don't know,' I said. 'I really don't know.' I laid my head on her shoulder again as the words floated up into the night sky and hung there in the endless space between the moon, the stars and the lonely Lego roof of the crumbling house of our own crumbled dreams.

## 19

Gloria Swanson stood on her head every day to release tension. It wasn't really working for me. Actually, it was making me even more stressed. I could see Robbie's trainers under the bed, staring at me like abandoned puppies in a dogs' shelter advert. His lonely iPod dock. The stack of travel books we'd collected from our trip around the world. I closed my eyes, trying to shut them out, only for a deluge of images of Thailand, China, Australia to come flooding into my mind. Cycling around Hong Kong on a tandem, exploring vineyards outside Sydney, spooned in a hammock on a beach in Phuket.

I flipped back onto my feet and wobbled to the bathroom. Gloria Swanson was full of shit. Not only was I now on the verge of tears, I was also dizzy and had Jedward hair.

Euch. The Real World.

I knew I'd have to come down off that roof eventually and face it. And now here it was. Laughing at me like a circus clown. Cruel, goading and unrelenting. Well, I just had to stick my fingers in my ears and say, 'Nananananananananana . . .'

Some would call that childishness. Under the circumstances, I was calling it bravery.

I had made a pact with myself that I wasn't going to mope. That I just had to get on with it: get up, get dressed and go to work. As normal. Even though nothing about any of this was remotely normal. I was going to put on my Janet Leigh-inspired cream and red polka-dot dress from *Bye Bye Birdie* and just get on with it. I quoted Ann-Margret about picking up the fragments of my shattered dreams and sighed into the mirror, before mooching back into the bedroom and getting dressed.

Honest to God, I had had no intention of turning into a

slob – inhaling Twixes around the clock, drinking cans of cider mid-morning, dressing in pyjamas and shouting at Jeremy Kyle that all relationships were doomed, and who needed a man anyway? Okay, so I'd slipped into a mini-rut of singing Daniel Bedingfield, but that was where I was drawing the line (and the only witness to that had been Lisa, and I had made her swear on her Louboutins that if she told anyone I would have them. Even though she was three sizes smaller. But I could totally cut a hole in the top and let my toes hang out over the edge).

Now I had decided I just needed to get on with it. I didn't want any more attention. I couldn't bear it. I had ended it with Robbie and it was *my* cross to bear.

I clung to the wall for support. Hearing those words in my head caught me off-guard every time, throwing my head into a spin, as if I was trapped on an unrelenting fairground waltzer. I. Had. Ended. It. With. Robbie.

Oh, God.

And then it would pass.

And I would be okay.

Work would help me through. It would be a good distraction. I wasn't meant to be back in until after the Christmas holidays, but I phoned Eleanor and told her I was coming in to work during Christmas week.

Ladies would come to me, asking me to dress them for their parties and their drinks nights. And I would smile and do my best and they would leave. And then I would go home and pretend to pay attention to the news and to care about all the bad things that were going on in other people's lives. I would undress and hang up my clothes and wash my face and go to bed and stare at the ceiling until it was time to get up and do it all over again.

And I would keep doing this until I knew what else I should be doing. Or what exactly I should be feeling. Or just how to 'be' again. When I didn't feel like such an intruder in my own thoughts, my own home, my own skin.

Well, that was the plan.

Wasn't exactly working out, unfortunately. For that plan to succeed, it would have needed a degree of compliance on my part. But when I got into the office, instead of going along with the Real World, all I could seem to muster was growing frustration at the minutiae of my day. And it was slowly gaining momentum. Like molten lava hurtling up towards the rim of a volcano. I was a human Vesuvius waiting to happen.

And it was ignited by neon jelly shoes.

'I'm sorry, Mrs Caffrey, I just don't think neon jelly shoes work with a navy plaid skirt suit.'

'But I saw Blake Lively wearing them on dailymail.co.uk. They're very on-trend you know, Grace.'

*On trend for someone twenty-five years younger than you with legs eleven and a golden tan.* I didn't say it, but it gurgled inside me like bubbling magma.

*NEON JELLY SHOES.*

Breathe. Breathe. Do not collect all the neon jelly shoes you can find and fire them at Mrs Caffrey.

'Grace, get me into that sequined red dress and looking fabulous for the opening night of the panto. If I don't get into *Dublin Social* magazine I'm firing you.'

*Not before I fire you – out of the third-floor window, you old bag. Are you sure you're not in the panto? As the evil queen?*

'No problem, Mrs Ward,' I answered calmly.

But it was Nuala O'Brien who proved to be the final straw that broke the camel's volcano. So to speak. Ah, Nuala . . . Nuala, Nuala, Nuala . . .

'So, I'm thinking a green satin jumpsuit and red wedges. Very Cheryl Cole meets Christmas.'

Perhaps it was Mud singing 'It'll Be Lonely This Christmas' on the changing-room Tannoy. Perhaps it was the fact that no self-respecting fifty-four-year-old, size sixteen woman should be wearing a green satin jumpsuit. With the added crime against Christmas of red wedges. Perhaps it was the sudden realization that no amount of distraction could help disguise the fact that the bottom had just fallen out of my world. Or that for the first Christmas in eight years I was going to be on my own. Standing on my head in an empty house without a clue how to cook the turkey in my freezer or what in the world was going to become of me.

But just then something snapped.

'Nuala O'Brien . . . YOU ARE NOT CHERYL COLE!'

Poor old Nuala O'Brien got such a fright, she shouted right back at me, 'I don't care! *I want to wear a green satin jumpsuit so you are going to go and get it for me. Now!*'

I don't remember much else, but I do have vague memories of my hand, a fistful of pins and her bum. In that order.

I'm not saying I'm proud.

'Grace, seeing as you got fired, we will not be paying you for your services today.'

Eleanor. My entirely underwhelming boss, in her entirely underwhelming office, kitted out with an entirely underwhelming selection of sample clothes and shoes.

'What?' I said. 'But I quit. I didn't get fired!'

'"Technically" you quit, but only because you jumped in and shouted, "I quit," just as I was telling you you were fired.'

'Ah,' I quipped, 'but I got there first.'

She rolled her eyes to indicate what a child I was being, which, let's be honest, I was. But all bets were off at this stage and, God-damn it, I needed that cash for my quarter-life-crisis Louboutins. 'Let's call it quits at half the pay,' I suggested generously.

'Grace, you used a client's bum as a pin cushion – I can't be seen to endorse that sort of behaviour.'

'But she deserved it!'

'I don't care! Her bum looks like something from a police report on a nail bombing now. She showed me. Very unpleasant.'

I folded my arms and huffed. I knew she was right, but I'd gone too far to back out now. Oh, for crying out loud, why was I bothering? It had been a part-time job to earn some extra cash while I was at college. It wasn't the end of the world. In fact, it was probably a *good* thing! College was over now: time to get out there and explore my career.

I still wasn't entirely sure what my career entailed, but I was pretty sure it didn't involve spending eight hours trying to convince a fifty-four-year-old woman that she couldn't wear a satin jumpsuit to a charity ball, no matter how many days she'd been off the carbs, and ending up getting so frustrated that I had no alternative but to stab her in the bum with a fistful of tailoring pins.

In my defence, the pins were *teeny weeny*, and she'd been telling me all about the 'amazing acupuncture' she'd had for her gout, so she should have been well able to handle it. *And*, for the record, any woman who has gout in the first place *should not be wearing a satin jumpsuit*!

'Look, Grace, I heard you've had a bit of a rough time of it lately. Perhaps it's best you concentrate on your personal life for a while.'

Humph! The cheek! Was this woman insinuating that I was acting a touch *oddly*? I was only *fantasizing* about emptying her handbag and shoving it over her head. I wasn't actually going to do it.

'Fine. I'm gone. But if you won't pay me, I'm going to leave with these. Ha!' I started grabbing fistfuls of scrawny metal dry-cleaning hangers off the clothes racks. What was I doing? I grabbed so many that I was struggling to grip them all, and one by one they plinked to the floor.

Eleanor looked at me with increasing concern and, really, I couldn't blame her.

'Well,' I said, trying to regain my composure and straightening as best I could, considering I had an incredibly uncomfortable amount of hangers stuffed under each arm, 'nice working with you, Eleanor. I'll be off.' And away I went, a trail of metal hangers in my wake.

## 20

Right. So this was certainly *not* the intended follow-on plan. Destroying my relationship, and ending up living on my own in the love nest we'd made together, was definitely not meant to be followed up with me quitting my job.

Oh, boy.

Was I having a quarter-life crisis or something? Hang on, if it was a quarter-life crisis, that meant I'd have to live to be 120. Shit, I was really going to have to get another job soon or I was going to be *very* bored.

I hadn't anticipated that I'd find turning thirty so traumatizing. I'd never really cared about birthdays or getting older. Although, having said that, I do remember locking myself in my room and hiding under my bed when I turned thirteen. But I'd put the whole thing down to my left boob having had a growth spurt all of its own, a giant spot on my chin, and the fact that Johnny Depp had not written back to me.

Tanya had to climb on top of the conservatory so she could get in through my bedroom window and drag me out by my ankles from under the bed. Come to think of it, she'd been perfecting that deft little move for quite some time now. Only last month, she reefed me out from under Milly's bed where I'd been hiding to avoid another lecture on my personal life and/or on trans-fats (she has a big thing about trans-fats – hates the things and can get highly irate if she catches me scoffing Hunky Dorys).

So, what was it? Was I like a man on the cusp of turning fifty or something? Just with more hair and a cuter wardrobe? I should have just had a haircut or a tattoo, not quit my job. Or at the very least bought some wildly expensive shoes that I couldn't afford.

Although really, now that I had no discernible source of income, it probably wasn't the best time to be thinking about gold Louboutins. Perhaps I could steal them. Yes, brilliant idea! I don't usually steal things, but you're sort of allowed to do those things when you're having a quarter-life crisis, aren't you? I mean, when else are you going to do it? *Plus* if I became a kleptomaniac or a criminal, then at least everyone would have something else to talk about other than me and Robbie breaking up. It all made perfect sense. Yahoo! Free shoes!

Hang on. On second thoughts, finding another job might be a bit tricky with a criminal record, no matter how adorable my new shoes were. And if I went to prison, they would take my gold Louboutins off me and beat me with them until I shaved my head or joined a gang. Crap.

No job. No Louboutins. Could this day get any worse? Yes, it could. I think I'd just figured out that I was, in fact, on the cusp of thirty, too old for a quarter-life crisis.

Balls.

I got back to the house, threw my remaining two hangers on the ground and closed the door behind me, grateful to be able to shut the world out with just one giant plank. Then I did something that people only ever do in the movies: I slid down the length of the door until I'd reached the floor in a hunched heap. Resting my head on the cool wood behind me, I stared down the narrow hallway. It suddenly seemed so bare. Not for want of furnishing: the beautiful mosaic mirror hung on the wall; the little table nestled into the corner with the retro telephone sitting on it; the plaited rug stretched out on the floor. But it was all so flat. So grey. There was no voice. No greeting. No 'Here's my girl!' ringing out from the kitchen.

I shook my head to dispel the thought. Feck this, anyway. I could sit here and start whumbling to the insipid walls, mirror and rug or I could get up and do something else that wasn't so pathetic. ('Whumbling' was something I'd invented: a mix between whining and mumbling when no one could decipher what you were saying and it served no real purpose. So you know,

143

even though I was sad, and far too old for a quarter-life crisis, I was very clever altogether.)

I dragged myself to my feet and plodded into the sitting room, throwing my keys on to the coffee-table. They landed with a clunk that hit the walls and echoed back in a hollow reverberation. Ugh. It was far too quiet. I flicked on the telly: people shiteing on about the state of our jobs and the economy. Not exactly what I needed to hear right now. I switched it off and sat in the deafening silence.

Okay, time to call someone. Bridge the racket of my thoughts and the eerie stillness of the house with some actual conversation.

Lisa.

Oh, I forgot. Lisa was having dinner with her grandparents. Her granddad had had grommets put in his ears and the operation had gone very well so they were celebrating with a beef casserole. They liked to put on a celebratory meal a *lot* apparently. Especially when it came to matters involving their health. Only last week her granny had celebrated the successful removal of a cataract from her left eye with a roast goose.

Rebecca.

I couldn't call Rebecca: she was still on honeymoon. God, what was Rebecca going to say? I couldn't think about that now.

Eleanor.

Maybe I'd call Eleanor and see if she felt any guilt at all about firing my ass when I'd just broken up with my boyfriend *and* it was nearly Christmas *and* Lisa's granddad had had a scary grommets operation and Rebecca was still away on honeymoon. Although, to be fair to Eleanor, she probably didn't even know who Lisa and Rebecca were. But she had to know it was nearly Christmas. Unless she'd been so busy firing people and being an all-round Mean Person that she hadn't noticed.

Tanya.

Not a snowball's chance in Hell. She'd have me sectioned. She'd actually have me sectioned. I was already on what she called 'psych watch'. Imagine what she'd do if I told her I'd quit my job! Tranquillizer guns, shackles, solitary confinement: the whole shebang. And I didn't want to go to a mental institution tonight. I *really* wasn't in the mood.

I just wanted to talk to someone. Maybe if I called up and asked to speak to Milly and talked to her about the Sylvanian Families. Nothing wrong with that. I liked the Sylvanian Families, with their cute little accessories and their adorable little outfits and their lovely little faces. Hmm . . .

Mum.

No, I couldn't face Mum. Her phone would be off anyway because she'd be in Mass offering up novenas for myself and Robbie. Or the latest one: getting all her golf friends together to light 'hope candles' in the church foyer. Sounded like great *craic*. She said she wasn't bringing her hat back just yet as ten of them from the club had gone up with their lighters yesterday and that, right there, was a whole lot of hope.

Sounded more like a fire hazard to me. All that starched plaid and noxious 'mature-lady' perfume huddled together around lighter fuel. Asking for trouble.

Although I did have Mum to thank for infiltrating Tanya's 'Operation Reconnect'. I kid you not. Mum found a book in her downstairs loo entitled *Tapping Phone Lines for Dummies*. Even Mum found that a bit unnerving.

'She thinks she's Mata Hari now!' Mum had said. 'I told her to back off a bit and leave you both to work it out on your own. Because you will, won't you, Grace? You will work it out?'

Dad.

How about calling Dad?

No. Dad was the one person I couldn't talk to about any of this.

I stared at my phone idly and tossed it onto the couch absent-mindedly. It was met with an unappreciative miaow. Bette.

'Go to Hell, Bette,' I said, in the most Oscar-winning Joan Crawford performance of all time.

She appeared from behind a cushion and stood there with her

back arched, picking at the couch cover noisily with extended claws, like the psychopath she was. She looked over at me.

'What?' I asked her. Nothing. Maybe Bette and I could have a chat, get to know each other.

'Hey, Bette, how about we put the past behind us, eh? Start trying to get along. Say, have you ever caught a mouse?'

She responded by miming a miaow.

Super, the cat wasn't even arsed miaowing properly now. She plopped down to the floor and disappeared up the stairs, probably finding a new hiding place to terrorize me from, come bedtime.

I wasn't going to go up there anyway. It was too quiet, too empty.

Too lonely.

I wondered where he was. What he was thinking about all of this. I sighed.

There had been no contact. And I was still numb.

I sat on the couch and reached out as if to touch him. My fingers felt nothing but the empty space beside me. I folded into it, wanting desperately to fill it, and pulled the throw over me. I still couldn't bring myself to go upstairs. I'd stay down here another night.

I closed my eyes as the clock on the wall ticked louder and louder, while the tears came silently, as they always did.

## 21

This breaking-up-with-someone lark was definitely not all it was cracked up to be. I'd bought loads of magazines that kept telling me how lucky I was to get this fresh start in my life, that 'he' obviously was not the guy for me. And I should think of all the fresh adventures that now lay ahead of me.

The only adventure I'd been on so far was a trip out to Carrickmines Industrial Estate to pick up some clear plastic tubs from Homebase to put the rest of Robbie's stuff in.

They also said I'd feel relieved, free, excited.

But the only thing I felt was profound sadness.

I spent my days watching old movies and reading books. Some days I'd dress up in my fifties-style outfits and sit on the roof pretending I was Joan Crawford. Smoking seductively and eyeballing the world like I was just as bold and just as confident when really I felt about as formidable as a dandelion in a gale-force wind. I'd watch, in my mind's eye, all the fluffy little umbrellas dancing away from me as I tried desperately to grab at them.

To be honest, I'd never felt quite so lost and unsure of myself in my life.

The fact that it was Christmas probably wasn't helping. Normally I loved Christmas, but this year it felt tacky and annoying – like a stage-school performer who was trying too hard. Everywhere I looked people were smiling and laughing, being nauseatingly festive. Maybe there was some grinch colony I could retreat to until the 'magic of the season' had passed. Only yesterday four little kids had called to the door singing Christmas carols but all I wanted to do was whip off their stupid little Santa hats and set fire to them. And then there were the carollers on Grafton Street, being all jolly and shaking their collection boxes at the passers-by to raise money to send to orphans in Lapland or the like, and I just wanted to throw my coffee in their faces.

I didn't even have the heart to turn on the Christmas-tree lights at home. But I didn't have the heart to take them down either, so I'd just sit and stare at the tree. It stood in the corner of the room like the ghost of my Christmases past, haunting me, all the little trinkets and decorations we'd amassed over the years dangling sadly. In the kitchen I'd set up some sort of unhealthy homage to my now broken relationship by making a little altar of Christmas cards addressed to myself and Robbie, wishing us every happiness in our new home.

I felt like a crab in a shell that didn't fit. It was too big for me. And all I wanted to do was crawl into another that felt more familiar.

And now I had Christmas dinner at Mum and Dad's to contend with. At first I'd declined the offer, telling Mum I already had plans for the day. When she asked me what they were, I informed her that I was going to sit in my silk dressing-gown and drink brandy for the day, like Elizabeth Taylor had done when Richard Burton died. She told me not to be so ridiculous, that Robbie hadn't died, that I had dumped him, and if I came over she promised not to clamp my head and force Brussels sprouts into my mouth. Which I thought was actually a fair enough exchange.

In the end, she convinced me to come over on Christmas Eve so she could 'mind' me. I think it was also to ensure I wasn't going to take my turkey from the freezer, saw it in half and defrost it in the microwave. Funny, I could have sworn Rachel Allen did a piece on that in her *Handy 30 Minute Meals Special*. Oh, no, sorry, I'm mistaken. That was actually on *Extreme Drunk Chef* on the Food Network.

I warned Mum that I was still going to be in my dressing-gown, brandishing a glass of brandy, the entire time. And she said that was fine, she was used to it. That was how Granny went down to Spar these days.

So now there I was. Dad nodded at me awkwardly when I arrived, not really knowing what to say. Which was good, because I didn't know what to say either. Then he sort of patted my arm clumsily, and all I could think was how uncomfortable he looked in the paper hat he'd got out of a cracker.

'I said to Mum, "This'll cheer her up."' He laughed nervously, pointing to his green crown.

'It did. Thanks, Dad.' I smiled.

See? That's all you needed. A cracker hat. It was the new Prozac for cool kids.

Mum was in the kitchen washing a colander of carrots. Organized as ever, so she wouldn't have to do the veg in the morning.

'Do you want me to peel them for you, Mum?'

'Oh, Grace, that would be terrific. You've always been amazing at peeling carrots.'

Bless. Mum's strategy for upping your confidence was to praise even the most menial tasks. She'd always done it. Like when I'd failed Irish in my mocks: instead of getting angry, she reminded me how good I was at folding socks. And now, when I'd essentially destroyed my life, I was the Master Carrot Peeler. It was sweet, I guess, because underneath it all, I knew she was deeply disappointed.

'Mum, I'm sorry,' I said awkwardly, standing over the bin, watching the carrot peel fall away.

'You don't have to apologize to me, Grace,' she said gently.

'I know, it's just, well, Tanya said you'd bought a hat and –'

'Oh, for crying out loud. A hat is a hat. Mind you, it is a particularly nice hat that did wonders for my wrinkles by more or less hiding my entire face. But, love, your happiness is far more important to me than any hat. Don't mind Tanya – you know what she's like.'

She busied herself with the turkey, grateful to have another distraction so the conversation wouldn't descend into a blub-fest.

'Thank you,' I said.

We stood there in silence, but I knew she was dying to say

more. She was desperate not to leave it there but unsure how to articulate what she wanted to say. Then it came.

'Oh, Gracie, what happened? I just don't understand . . . You loved Robbie so much – the two of you were mad about each other. It doesn't make sense . . .' On she went. She spoke in a rush, desperate to make use of the small window she had.

I concentrated on the carrot I had in my hand. By the time she paused for breath, it was a tiny orange stub. 'Mum, please, I can't . . . It just . . .' I trailed off, feeling lost as I looked at her, like I'd mislaid all my thoughts and didn't know where to find them. I wished she could understand. I wished *I* could understand – that I knew what to do or how to feel. That I didn't feel so unsteady and adrift.

It was far from a gesture of absolution, but she did what mums did best: she hugged me. And I clung to her and her disappointment, because I felt it so much too.

'How about we move you on to the potatoes, eh?' She smiled, taking the carrot stub from my hand.

'Probably for the best,' I said.

Granny was sitting out on the stairs in a silk dressing-gown much like my own, a sherry glass balanced between two gnarled fingers. 'Good morning, Grace.'

'Morning, Granny,' I said, even though it was nine p.m.

Poor Granny had had dementia for over ten years. She had rare flashes of lucidity, but she spent most of her time in a dream world. Like she'd rewritten the script of her life and climbed into her new role as if it were a second skin.

For a few fleeting moments every other week, she'd remember who she was and that Granddad was dead. Her childhood sweetheart. Her best friend. Her soul-mate. The grief nearly crushed her every time. Soon after, she'd be gone again, back into her bubble where there was no grief and no reality. No pain. No loss.

Tonight I envied her that.

*Can I visit you there?* I thought, as I swirled the brandy around my glass. *Just for a little while?*

'Grace, what on earth do you get the man who has everything for Christmas?'

I wasn't sure who she was married to this week.

'I mean, Harry from One Direction has it all! Their promotion company sends them so much stuff . . .'

Wow. I'd heard he was into the older lady, but Granny was breaking new boundaries altogether. Perhaps she should have gone for Wayne Rooney instead.

I joined Dad in the living room after Mum had prised the sherry glass out of Granny's hand, got her dressed and brought her to Midnight Mass.

We watched a programme about the origin of cranberry sauce in silence. European cranberry sauce was bitter, unlike the American one. Fascinating.

'Gracie . . . are you okay?' Dad asked finally.

'Yeah. I'm fine,' I said, letting him off the hook. My father was never one for heart-to-hearts. I suppose it just always felt duplicitous for him to be that honest.

'I thought you two had something.'

'Dad, please.'

'I just don't want you to be afraid of committing because . . .' He trailed off like a radio station dipping in and out of signal.

We stared at the cranberries being squashed, each one exploding under the building pressure. 'Grace, life isn't perfect sometimes. But you have to let yourself love and be loved or it's nothing but existing just because you happen to be here,' he said, speaking about relationships with more conviction than I'd ever heard from him before.

'For someone with that insight into love, Dad, you seem awfully alone.'

I saw the words sting him like a swarm of angry wasps I'd just released from a jar. And I was sure I felt the pain more for watching it happen. I cursed myself for my unnecessary cruelty. I'd never punished him for what had happened. I'd never wanted to.

'Dad, I'm sorry . . .' I said. Why could I never get on his wavelength properly?

'It's okay, Grace. I'm sorry too.'

The next morning I was woken by the dulcet tones of the Normandy D-Day beach invasion. Dad's favourite film to watch on Christmas morning, *Saving Private Ryan*. Said it helped him feel grateful.

He'd obviously jammed the volume button on the remote again and now the clatter of American soldiers getting shot was on surround sound throughout the house. Merry Christmas, one and all!

Time to get up, I supposed. And 'give thanks' that we weren't in the Second World War.

But when I got downstairs I discovered it wasn't Private Ryan but Private Tanya bursting through the front door and launching an assault on the house with her two screaming children. Perfect Peter was looking like he was thinking of deserting the front line. But he knew he'd only get shot for treason so persevered through the trenches.

I necked a neat brandy and thought of Blanche DuBois in *A Streetcar Named Desire*. She had a fantastic knack of being able to blend fantasy and reality like a fine cocktail and, good God, I needed to muster up some of what she had if I was to come out of this alive. I eyed Tanya from the bottom of my empty tumbler and remembered what her rough brother-in-law Stanley said to Blanche, how he tried to destroy her illusions, told her that making the place smell sweet and covering the bare bulb with a paper lantern didn't make it a palace and her the Queen of the Nile. I raised my glass to Blanche who believed in imagination.

'What was that, love?' Mum asked, as she whipped past me with a handful of turkey giblets. 'You want to stick paper lanterns over the light-bulbs? Sweetheart, there's already enough decorations on the tree and that sounds more like a fire hazard to me than anything else.'

Ooops, hadn't realized I was talking out loud. No wonder the kids were steering well clear. Milly looked adorable in a red velvet dress with a set of reindeer antlers on her head, while Eoin was dressed as a snail.

'Don't ask.' Tanya groaned, rolling her eyes. 'He has an obsession with snails at the moment. He likes to rub the slime everywhere and other times he just pops them into his mouth and swallows them whole. He wanted to be a snail in his nativity play this year so we got him that costume online. He hasn't taken it off since.'

'Ah, yes,' I mused. 'The Holy Snail of Bethlehem. All too often overlooked, if you ask me.'

'Well, what are you dressed up as? Miss Princess Christmastime-slash-Bedtime 1947?'

I wasn't even going to dignify that with an answer. I was channelling Blanche today in my pink chiffon robe with flared sleeves and appliqué floral detailing. So what? Technically it wasn't a dress, but technically I was dressed, and that was more than I'd thought would be possible for today. And it was meant to be 1951, to be exact. *A Streetcar Named Desire*, 1951. Twelve Oscar nominations. Four wins. Thank. You. Very. Much.

I was actually wearing a glorified bathrobe. But I was wearing a beautiful mock sapphire tiara with it, which dressed it up beautifully. And I was definitely *not* going mental, even though it was Christmas. I didn't know where Robbie was or who he was with; I was unemployed; and I was carrying a cat under my arm.

Oh, yes, the cat. In my addled state I had decided that if I dragged the little witch along my family would say, 'Let's not talk to the weirdo with the ugly cat,' even though they knew exactly who I was and they all really liked the cat. It had been a bit of a palaver, getting a cat carrier on Christmas Eve, but amazingly easy to get her ladyship into it for the drive over to my parents.

She looked at it as if to say, 'At last, my carriage awaits.' Once she'd got to Mum and Dad's she'd turned into another cat, serene and compliant – more Olivia de Havilland than Bette Davis, hostilities apparently suspended for the holidays. What a pro.

But going back to me going mental – the point was that, even though I was in a bathrobe with a tiara on my head, a cat under my arm and three whiskey chasers under my belt on Christmas Day, I was most definitely not going crazy. Which was wonderful news.

And what exactly had Tanya come dressed as? A trussed-up turkey? Aw. How festive.

I looked at her sitting stiffly in her 'sensible' clobber and instinctively wanted to untie her ponytail, pop open the top three buttons on her insipid grey blouse and loop a vibrant silk scarf around her neck. And I don't know what I wanted to do to those Godawful trousers. Burn them? I'd have to take them off her first, I supposed, or she'd start complaining again. Perhaps I could cut them up and use the scraps to mop up all that snail slime she kept harping on about. Did she not know how sexy she could be if she just *tried*?

'What did Santa bring you, Milly?' I asked, picking her up and giving her a big squeeze. Oh, there was simply nothing that a big delicious hug from a niece or nephew couldn't fix. The uncomplicated innocence and unconditional love of it all.

'A vibrator like Mummy's!' she said.

What the –? I nearly dropped the poor child on her head. I had to bite my tongue to stop myself bursting out laughing. It didn't work: I burst out laughing.

'Milly!' Tanya said. 'We talked about this earlier. You got a Laughing Elmo from Santa!'

'But, Mummy, it shakes when you press the button like your toy!' she said, giggling with me, not understanding the joke but loving the attention.

Peter was so red and swollen with embarrassment, I thought he was about to pop. Mum pretended she hadn't heard what was going on and busied herself wiping the snot from Eoin's nose instead.

The whole thing had gone over Dad's head. 'Is that the electric lemon squeezer we got you for your birthday last year, Tanya?'

Oh. My. God.

*Gold!*

I started shaking with repressed convulsions. Tanya shot me her Death Stare but I was too far gone for that.

And then Peter turned and faced the wall. It was, like, if he couldn't see us, it wasn't happening, and he just stood there staring at the wall two inches in front of his face. I wanted to ask him did he like Mum's wallpaper, but I thought he might start crying so I picked on Tanya instead.

'Did Santa give you a toy, Tanya? You're such a lucky girl! Milly, does Mummy like rabbits?'

'Em, I think so!' she said, slipping from my lap to the floor where she started hopping around the TV room. 'Daddy, look! I'm a rabbit! I'm a rabbit!'

Peter started to inch further away until he was nearly out of the room.

'*Grace!*' Tanya growled.

'Okay, okay! Game over!' I surrendered, holding my hands up. 'Jeez, no need to throw your "toys" out of the cot.'

'*Grace!*'

'Right, everyone,' Mum said, coming back into the room. 'Before we open the presents we'll be sitting down to Christmas burgers because Eoin has dragged the turkey down off the counter onto the floor, covered it in glitter and shoved toilet paper up its arse.'

'What? Mum! *Eoin!*' I scolded, as he ran past me with his finger up his nose.

'What on earth is a Christmas Burger?' Tanya said, folding her arms like an insolent child.

'As I said, Tanya, it's a burger you eat on Christmas Day when your child has dragged the turkey onto the floor, covered it in glitter and stuffed toilet paper up its hole and you have nothing else to eat. Now, go and get the burgers from the freezer in the shed before Eoin finds them and flushes them down the toilet.'

Wow. I'd never heard Mum say 'hole' before. I think I liked it.

Actually, the Christmas Burgers didn't work out too bad in the end. Mum made the stuffing into nice patties and we had cranberry sauce with them instead of tomato ketchup. And all in all it would have tasted okay if I'd had the stomach for any of it.

It wasn't that I felt sick. I just felt removed from it all. Like Ebenezer Scrooge looking in on Christmas Day from the outside, albeit a weird Christmas Day, with burgers instead of a turkey and a child dressed up as a snail. The last time I'd felt so flat at Christmas was when Brenda Howlett tied my shoelaces to the radiator in Irish class, stole my Poochy pencil case and told me there was no Santa. That had been a bleak one. Somehow, this one felt even bleaker.

Then we all brought our presents in to open them around the table. Peter handed Tanya a beautifully wrapped parcel with a red bow, and I asked him if it was a set of AA batteries. It turned out, however, to be the most gorgeous pair of pearl drop earrings.

'Wow, Peter, they're fab!' I said. 'Tanya, hold them up to your ears!'

'Not now,' she answered brusquely, snapping the box closed again. 'They're lovely, Peter. Mind you, I haven't a clue when I'm ever going to get to wear them, but thank you all the same,' she said, without so much as looking at him. 'Who's next?'

Poor Peter looked how I had when Brenda Howlett had broken the news back in '86. The disappointment. Jesus, Tanya could be a right Ice Queen sometimes. I felt like keeping the cashmere jumper I'd bought her for myself, just to stick up for Peter. And as a by-the-by reward for my staunch loyalty, I would net myself a lovely vintage rose cashmere sweater in the process. It was definitely the right thing to do.

Dad gave Mum her present, a new espresso machine, and

Mum gave him the car mats he'd asked for. She pecked him on the cheek briefly and he patted her arm awkwardly.

Then Mum handed me my present and sat there while I opened it.

The post-holder. Oh, God, the post-holder. Robbie and I had always joked about getting a proper post-holder when we had a proper house like proper grown-ups.

'I'd already bought it, Grace, and then the lady in the shop said she'd only take it back in exchange for store credit, and sure what else would I be buying in that shop? It's only full of paperweights and weird compasses and telescopes and . . .'

I started crying.

And after a few minutes of everyone just sitting there staring at me, Eoin joined in too. 'Where's Uncle Robbie?' He started bawling, 'I want Uncle Robbie!' which prompted me to cry even louder.

'Oh! Oh! I have a joke!' Dad piped, trying desperately to rescue the situation. I watched him unfurl a piece of paper that had been rolled up inside his cracker.

'Why was Santa's little helper feeling depressed? Because he had low *elf*-esteem!'

Then Granny stood up and started singing 'That's What Makes You Beautiful' at the top of her lungs.

Eoin and I looked at her in bewilderment, and both started bawling again.

Then my tiara fell off into my uneaten Christmas pudding and the cat shat all over my pink chiffon bathrobe with the flared sleeves and floral appliqué. Clearly, the truce was over.

Happy bloody Christmas.

## 22

Robbie was calling to the house.

Robbie was coming here. *Here*.

I hadn't seen him since he'd left our hotel room in New York. That image of him walking away from me as I lay paralysed on the floor in my ice skates and the door clicking shut behind him played on a loop in my mind, like a projector reel malfunctioning. It had been more than four weeks ago. The longest hiatus in the seven years I'd known him.

He had called my phone the night before and left a message. I couldn't answer when I saw his name flash up. I just froze to the spot, stopped breathing, and lost all use of my extremities. The only time that had ever happened before was when I checked the price tags of the Victoria Beckham dresses in Brown Thomas.

I listened to his voicemail over and over until it finally deleted itself from overuse. 'This message has been deleted,' the voicemail lady said.

'Screw you, voicemail lady! That was an important message!' (That I had listened to thirty-five times. And had a grand sum of thirteen perfectly audible words.)

'Hi, Grace. I'll be over tomorrow evening to collect some things. Thanks, 'bye.' And that had been it. It had taken me thirty-five goes to digest it. Process his voice. Understand why Robbie, my Robbie, was calling over tomorrow evening to collect the last remaining evidence of the life we'd once shared.

Like a funeral director coming to take away the remains for burial.

I sat at the top of the stairs smoking from my three-in-one, dinner-length, theatre-length and opera-length Cabriole cigarette holder. There was no funeral-length so I adjusted it to theatre-length and waited for my cue.

· The doorbell rang. And there it was. I took one long last drag before the curtain finally went down on the closing scene of this tragic two-hander.

I thought of Rick and Ilsa's reunion scene in *Casablanca* as I pulled myself off the top step and trod down the stairs in a trance to open the door.

'Hi.'

'Hi,' I replied.

We stood staring at each other, our gaze a sort of lifeline, reminding us of what we had been to each other, what we had shared for seven long years, and how we had now ended up here. It was really good to see him.

'Come in, come in,' I said, almost forgetting my cue.

I registered the hurt flash in his eyes as I invited him into his own house, and it stung more than he could possibly have imagined.

The initial relief and excitement I'd felt at seeing him subsided, to be replaced by the realization that he didn't belong here any more. Now he was a visitor. In his own safe place. And I felt as though I would drown in the sadness of it.

He walked down the hallway, his steps creating a dull echo on the floor that I had never heard before. Maybe I'd just never noticed it. I stared at his feet as they walked away and disappeared into the sitting room.

'Would you like some tea?' I said, like we hadn't spent seven years waking up in each other's arms.

'That would be lovely,' he answered, like we hadn't planned an entire life together.

As I stood over the kettle, I imagined my own version of the famous moment from *Casablanca*:

Robbie: 'How long did we have together, sweetheart?'
Grace: 'I never counted how long.'

Robbie: 'Well, I counted every moment. But it's the ending I remember most. The grand finale with the guy left looking like an idiot because he's just had his *insides* punched in.'

It went something like that, I thought, as the steam billowed in front of my eyes.

I came back into the sitting room, brandishing two cups of tea: two superfluous props in an unfamiliar scene we didn't have the lines for.

'Em. I'll leave it here, shall I?' I said, placing it on the coffee-table. The place where he'd put his mug down every morning while getting ready to go to work. Fixing his tie. Flicking through Sky News. Calling up the stairs to ask me what I fancied for dinner that night.

'You look lovely,' he said softly, and I could hear the longing in his voice. In that moment I ached for him. I wanted to forget every single awful second of the past month and kiss him and hold him to me, like a delicate glass ball, and mind him and never ever hurt him again for as long as I lived.

'Look, I don't want to drag this out, so I'll just collect my stuff and let you get back to your evening.'

And suddenly the stranger was back and the delicate little ball tumbled out of my hands and I watched it shatter into a million shards.

'Yes, of course.'

And that was it. There were no pleasantries. No dissection of what had happened and what had gone wrong. Just a silent acceptance of something neither of us understood. I followed him upstairs silently. No laughter bouncing off the walls. No chatter looping us like accomplices in this big bad world. Just two strangers clearing up the messy leftovers of what had been a great dinner party.

'We should discuss what to do with the house. If we want to buy each other out, sell it entirely . . .'

'Yes,' I answered, already feeling the indigestion.

'I'll take the rest of my things now anyway.'

'Yes,' I repeated, on a dull auto-pilot.

I sat on the top step and waited for him to finish what he had come to do, like a doctor concluding a botched operation. I couldn't look. I couldn't see him clear away what might have been.

I lit a cigarette and prayed for it to be over soon as the guilt engulfed me, like a thick fog. I could hear him in our bedroom, opening drawers and filling a suitcase on the bed. The last of his books, CDs, clothes, pictures. Him, me, us. Going, going, gone. I wiped away the tears that crept down my face.

'That's everything, I think,' he said sadly.

I looked at him, his tall, strong frame, his sandy, unkempt hair, his doleful hooded eyes. And I wanted to hold him, touch him, feel him against me and plead with him to stay.

'Okay.' I nodded, overwhelmed by grief, and shocked at feeling anything that wasn't the perpetual numbness.

What had I expected? That this would be *easy*? That somehow the world would be set to rights? That I would go on protected by this prolonged desensitized confusion?

I stood up to let him pass and he dropped the bag on the floor and suddenly pulled me close to him. We hugged each other for an eternity and I wept in his arms without making a move or a sound, apologizing inwardly for every shake and sigh I felt of his.

Eventually, he pulled away, running his hands through his hair, and I could feel the distance fall between us again.

'Well, goodbye, Grace,' he whispered, without any trace of cruelty or spite, because that was just not the type of person he was.

''Bye,' I heard myself say.

All of a sudden the bag moved and I could hear a rustling from inside it.

Bette.

Jesus, the cat was so desperate to leave with Robbie she had jumped into it. Thanks for shitting on my parade, Bette. Jump the sinking ship, why don't you? 'Men and cats first – let this old dame sink here on her own!'

'You can't come with me, I'm afraid, Bette,' he said, lifting her out and placing her on the landing. 'Too much going on where I'm staying.'

What? What was going on where he was staying? Who was he staying with? Was there a girl there? A girl who was allergic to cat hair and wanted to marry him immediately and have his babies because he was handsome and funny and caring and kind and they would sail off into the sunset together with a bald cat that he had ordered on the Internet because he was so kind and caring and funny?

'Where are you staying? Is there a woman who is allergic –'

'I'd better get going. Look after yourself.'

'Em, yes. You too.'

He bent down to zip up the bag again, knocking a small black box out of the side pocket as he did. We watched it tumble to the floor, roll awkwardly to my foot and then stop dead.

My chest constricted and I could hear Robbie's sharp intake of breath.

Holy shit.

A ring.

*An engagement ring!*

I could only see the box. I couldn't see the ring. But it felt like this box and the ring inside were mocking me. I bent down to pick it up in a slow-motion trance.

'Grace –'

'I thought . . . I thought in New York . . . you weren't going to propose?' I said quietly.

I looked up. His eyes were fixed on me with a resigned sadness.

'Grace, I thought you knew I was always going to propose.'

Silence. A long, torturous silence.

I could feel his words slowly crushing me as I gasped for breath.

'Oh, God, Robbie . . . I'm . . . I didn't . . .'

'Grace. Please,' he said softly. 'It's okay. I can't bear to see you like this. I just want you to be happy.'

I stared at the small black velvet box cupped in my hands.

'I thought I was,' I said, the words seeming to leave me of their own accord.

I could see them stinging him, one by one, and I wanted to run over, whip them back and hide them from him.

But they were out. *It* was already out. Whatever it was, it was out and raw and exposed, and no amount of kicking the dirt back over could cover it up.

I wanted to. I wanted to take the pain away for both of us. But I couldn't.

'I wasn't going to ask you to be my wife in front of a thousand strangers in a New York ice rink. I knew you'd hate that. I knew you were sick of everyone looking at you and waiting and watching and judging and, quite frankly, it wasn't about anyone else. I wanted to do it here. In our home. On our roof. Under all the stars you'd ever wished on. Where no one was looking and no one else mattered. Where it was about us. Just you and me. Which is all I've ever wanted.'

He stared at me searchingly, then rubbed his hands over his tired face as if to wake himself up from this nightmare.

'And I wouldn't have asked for an answer there and then. I knew because of everything else you'd want time to digest it, live with it a while until you were ready to own it.'

'I'm sorry, Robbie,' I said blankly. 'I'm so sorry . . .'

'I'm going to go. Even though I want to try to understand this, I can't stand here and watch you stumble and trawl through the reasons you don't want to be with me. Because when you do, and when everything I thought I knew has been stripped back and laid bare, the same fact will still remain. You don't want to marry me.'

I let his words go straight through me, like poison. I stood there as they took me over entirely, until I felt I wasn't in control of any of it.

I could feel the last light and life of what we had been drain from my body. I stumbled back towards the wall and held on to it for support as I watched him pass me, walk slowly down the stairs, open the door and disappear.

I turned the box over in my hand and contemplated the dying ember of what we'd been. Me and Robbie. Our life together. Then I opened it frantically, desperate for one last glimpse before it went out entirely.

The ring. The most beautiful ring I had ever seen in my life. The one I'd always dreamed of. A perfect Asscher-cut art-deco diamond ring.

I stared at it blankly, then snapped the box shut.

And with that the last glow was gone and everything went black.

# 23

I sat at the top of the stairs in the dark, the only light coming from the end of my theatre-length Cabriole cigarette holder. And Bette's eyes, boring up at me from the bottom step.

'You fool,' I could hear her say. 'He was the best thing about you two. And now he's gone.'

'Screw you, Bette,' I said. 'I will not die a miserable old spinster. Or turn into Jill Lawlor. How dare you!'

'Yes, you will, you so will!' I heard her say. I really could hear her say it – all with one 'judgy' look. (Either that or she was saying, 'Will you please let me outside to the garden or I'm going to shit all over the carpet?')

'I won't. *I won't!*' I said, feverishly inhaling from my cigarette.

The doorbell went.

*Robbie!*

'He's back, Bette! He's come back!'

I hoisted myself up and promptly stumbled down the first few steps, my legs giving way under me. Gosh, how long had I been sitting there, I wondered, as I scarpered to the front door, moving as fast as my numb legs could carry me. Robbie had come back. He was back. He was back!

'*Robbie!*' I shouted, swinging the door open and throwing myself at him.

It wasn't him. It was Lisa, who was tiny and I totally crushed her, and now we were lying on the pavement, like half-mashed double-hit road-kill.

Bette ran out and squealed as she jumped over us and pegged it down the road. It was all very scary.

And I think I broke Lisa's glasses.

'I'm sorry. I'm so sorry. I'm just so confused,' I babbled.

'Okay. It's okay.'

'How are you?'

'I'm fine, I'm fine.'

'Okay, good. How was your day?'

'It was fine.'

'Good.'

'Grace?'

'Yes?'

'Can you get off me, please?'

'Yes.'

We got up and went inside to get some Sellotape for her glasses.

'I'll buy you a new pair. When I get a job. I'm so sorry. You can have mine in the meantime. They have no prescription. And they are sunglasses, but that's all I have . . .'

My lower lip started to wobble like a four-year-old's. Shit! Now, on top of everything else, I was massively regressing. This was not good. I grabbed hold of it to stop the shaking.

'Grace? Are you . . . okay?'

'What do you mean, I'll be the next Jill Lawlor?' I exploded.

'What the f –?'

'Oh, God, I'm so sorry,' I said, still clenching my lip.

'Who the hell is Jill Lawlor?'

'Oh, Jesus, Lisa!' I howled, dropping to my knees and holding the little black velvet ring box up to her.

'Fuck. You are confused. Grace, I love you and I think you're a wonderful person, but, I can't . . . eh . . . marry you. Sorry.'

'I don't want to marry you either,' I said, in the same dramatic howl, still on bended knee in the kitchen, still brandishing the ring box in her face.

'Okay, Crazy. Intervention time,' she said, picking me up off the floor and marching me to the couch in the sitting room. 'We need to get you a strong coffee with a shot of brandy in it. You stay here and breathe.'

'Okay. I will. I'll breathe.'

I sat on the couch, still holding the little box in my hands, breathing.

'Why wouldn't you want to marry me, Lisa?' I whimpered after a while, as she navigated her way around the kitchen. 'I might be the most horrible person in the world, but underneath it, I'm lovely, really.'

'For Christ's sake,' I heard her mutter.

Poor Lisa. I knew I was being a complete spasmo. (I hadn't used that word since the mid-eighties. I was definitely regressing.)

'You could at least have said you'd think about it.'

'Right!' she said. 'Here's your stiff drink. You have no coffee. Or brandy. So you're having tea with a splash of wine.'

'That is so gross,' I scoffed, knocking it back in one. (It wasn't actually too bad, although I think a nice Riesling might have worked better than Sauvignon Blanc.)

'Okay, what on earth is going on? And who the hell is Jill Lawlor?'

'Eh, hello?' I said. 'Jill Lawlor!'

Nothing.

I mimed a blow-job.

'Ah! Jill *Lawlor*! You won't. You won't be the next Jill Lawlor.'

'Why not?'

'Because you can't write.'

That was the *only* reason? Shit.

Jill Lawlor was this lovely girl two years ahead of me, Lisa and Rebecca in school. She'd broken up with her fiancé a few years back, thinking that life had more to offer than what she already had.

It hadn't.

She's now a recluse who writes filthy novels and sells them on a dodgy website from a one-bedroom flat in Singapore. She's also six stone heavier, wears duvet covers with slits for her head and arms and reportedly 'smells of sex even though she doesn't get any' (although this is unconfirmed). Her ex-fiancé went on to marry a UN ambassador who was also an ex-Miss France and he

167

recently won the Business Philanthropy Award for helping raise awareness of the plight of underprivileged children in South America. And apparently one of his own children is so cute she's the face of a new advertising campaign for pull-up nappies.

On the plus side, I heard somewhere that one of Jill's books is being made into a porno movie.

'Grace, what's with the engagement ring? Please don't tell me you're going to ask the Edge to marry you again.'

'What? No. Christ, will you ever leave me alone about that? That was *years* ago. And I was so drunk that I completely gave up drink. For three weeks.'

'Seriously, the Edge. I honestly think you would fall in love with me if you just *tried*. When have you ever been a quitter, huh? Huh?'

'Oh, God, stop. *Stop!*' I said, laughing. 'I think I need another tea and wine.'

And then I cried. And cried and cried. And Lisa apologized. And I told her it really was nothing to do with the Edge, but thanks all the same, she was very kind.

'Robbie called over to pick up the rest of his things. Everything is gone now. I was kind of in this place for a while where none of it seemed real because he was still sort of here. But he's gone now, Leese. There's nothing left. He's really gone.'

'Oh, Grace,' she said, putting her arm around me. 'I'm so sorry.'

'This fell out of his bag before he left,' I said, handing her the ring box.

She stared at it in stunned silence. 'You are shitting me? But I thought he said he wasn't going to propose in New York . . .'

'No, he wasn't . . .' I said, the words catching in my throat. Ah, shite, there went the lip again.

'Oh, Jesus,' she said in a panic (was the lip that bad?).

'Did you know? Did he just call you?' I said. 'How did you know to come over? How did you know what had happened? Does he hate me? Does he really hate me?'

'No, he didn't. No, he doesn't. I mean, I don't know. No, I mean, I was calling over to tell you something.'

'Oh, fuck. Are you getting married? Lisa, I'm so sorry. I've totally ruined your moment.'

'What? Grace, no! I've been seeing Killian two months!' she said. She looked at me and then said, in a teeny-tiny voice, 'That really would be too soon, wouldn't it?' when she really meant, 'That is not too soon. I would have married him last week if it had been at all legal/if I could just get him to agree.'

'What were you coming over to tell me, then?' I asked, suddenly worried.

'Nothing.'

I knew she was lying.

'Nothing! I was coming over to tell you that you needed a bath.'

What? I so didn't. Plus how the hell would she have known that? Shit, did her smartphone have a sniff app or something? I hope my mum doesn't download that and ring me when I'm skulling wine and telling her it's carrot juice. Or Tanya call me when I'm eating Chickatees and I tell her I'm eating some 'crunchy quinoa'.

Anyway, I did *not* need a bath. I knew that because I'd had a three-and-a-half-hour Blueberry Bliss bubble bath that afternoon because I'd had absolutely nothing else to do.

'How long do you think you need before you stop crying?' she asked.

Was I crying? Oh! So I was . . . would you look at that?

'Grace!'

Oooh. Tough love. Brilliant. I seriously needed some of that.

'Em, would half an hour be okay?' I asked hopefully.

'Yes. That's fine,' she agreed strictly but fairly. 'You will stop crying at eight twenty-five.'

I nodded.

'How long will you need for the clean-up?'

'The clean-up?' I asked.

'Yes, the clean-up. Your mascara is currently running down your cleavage and you have dried snot on your top lip.'

'Em, an extra three minutes?'

'Yes. Fine. You will have stopped crying and look more sightly at eight twenty-eight. Now go up and have your bath. When you get back down I will have cooked dinner and come up with a plan.'

I cried until eight twenty-five, then washed my face and neck and got into a tracksuit. Which was what normal people did when they felt sad/their boyfriend had just moved out/they had no life, and I really did want to be a bit more normal about everything.

I realized that things really weren't great, and that I was lost. Very, very lost. And I was hoping to find some clarity and perspective in this velour two-piece like a normal person. (I really didn't approve, however, so I put on a cute little twenties pillbox hat and a string of pearls too.)

'That's my girl!' Lisa cooed, as I came down the stairs. 'Well, sort of . . .'

'Lisa, I am lost and sad,' I said, 'owning' my feelings like they tell you to do on *Oprah*.

'Yes, yes, I know you are. And I'm glad you're owning your feelings,' she replied, like one of the 'supportive friends', who are good, and not one of the 'enablers', who are bad. 'That is why I have a plan for us!' She clapped. 'Sit down here and drink this [tea and wine] and eat this [Weetabix].' Euch, Weetabix. It was eight twenty-eight, for crying out loud! (Or not *crying* out loud, because it was eight twenty-eight and I was now on a ban.)

'All you have is Weetabix because you refuse to buy anything but pearls and pillbox hats at the moment.'

Hum. She had a point, I thought, adjusting the birdcage netting over my eyes.

'What's your plan?' I asked, intrigued. 'Get a new job? Sell the house? Take up Biking yoga.'

'Bikram yoga. You're getting your spinning and your yoga confused.'

'Sorry, always doing that,' I answered. I *never* did that because I never did either. What on earth was spinning? Did you pay twenty quid to go into a room and spin around with other people until you vomited up your dinner from vertigo and subsequently lost weight?

'No, the grand plan is, we are going to . . . the Wish Factory!'

'What – now?' I said, confused and shocked, yet somehow liking the sound of the Wish Factory infinitely better than 'You will sell your home at a loss of 35 per cent of its purchase value and live in rented accommodation in a housing project in the North Inner City with a host of recovering unemployed junkies.'

Hmm. The Wish Factory? What was it?

'When you were in the bath, I Googled "lost, sad, confused, pathetic, Ireland" and the Wish Factory came up.'

Silence.

'I'm sorry, I probably shouldn't have told you the "pathetic" bit.'

''S okay,' I said. 'It's true.'

'So we're going to the Ring of Kerry!' she chirped, trying to plaster over the 'pathetic' crack and 'move forward'. Another helpful *Oprah* pointer.

Okay, so we were going to Kerry. Why Kerry? The Ring of Kerry? The *Cult* Ring of Kerry, more like.

To find out what I really wanted, she said.

I told her I was pretty sure what I wanted wasn't in Kerry, but she said that wasn't the point.

I asked her was kissing the Blarney Stone a part of it all, and that I wasn't exactly sure I wanted to as I'd heard Mum's friend Rita from the Rathmichael Church Choir got a cold sore from doing that. I also wasn't mad on the idea of being hung upside down by the ankles and kissing a slab of rock backwards. Was that how people in Kerry found Jesus?

Lisa said that you didn't kiss the Blarney Stone to find Jesus, and they didn't hang you upside down from your ankles, you sort of just slid in backwards, and that she was pretty sure you couldn't get herpes from a block of limestone. Oh, and that Blarney was in Cork, not Kerry.

'Fine. So why exactly are we off to Kerry? And are you sure it's not a cult? I am very vulnerable right now and if we ended up in a cult, I know I would absolutely, most definitely join.'

'No. We're going because I read that it's meant to be fantastic if you're feeling a bit lost in life. You go and have chats and do these fantastic cleansing rituals.'

'Oooh! Do they use Eve Lom?' I asked hopefully. 'I bet they do if it's a posh place. There's apparently a whole ritual involved with a muslin cloth and hot water.'

'Grace! You don't get on a train for four hours to go to Kerry to wash your face with a fancy towel and a bucket of hot water in the hope it will give you spiritual enlightenment!'

'Oh.' That was a bit silly of me, I have to admit.

'No, the Wish Factory is about helping you find what you really, *really* want – and then you wish for it and that changes your life. It said on the website that it can really help you sort out your head. There was this super testimonial by a woman from Leitrim whose husband ran off with the nanny and she went down to this place and it really helped her get her life back on track.'

'Well?' I asked expectantly. 'Did she get her husband back? Did she find some wonderful toy-boy with a yacht in the South of France to take his place?'

'No, erm, well . . .' she made a coughing noise in the hope I wouldn't hear the next bit '. . . she sort of became a nun.'

I inhaled sharply. Oh, I'd very much heard the Next Bit.

'That is *not* going to happen to you!' she stressed. 'There was another lady from Tuam who was severely depressed and went on to open her own glitter factory.'

'Now I like the sound of that! A glitter factory. How lovely. Has that been used up already now, though? Would I have to wish for something else?'

'Grace, do you really want to open your own glitter factory?'

'Sort of . . .' I trailed off.

'Wow. You really are in a fog, aren't you?' she said, lifting up my net veil to force-feed me some more mushy Weetabix. Jesus, this was a *foie gras*-type carry-on.

'Leese, why are you coming? You're as happy as a pig in shite!'

'Because you're my best mate and you're in trouble. And I'm going to help you,' she said, dusting the crumbs off her fingers. 'Plus,' she said, her voice dropping to a whisper, 'if it is a cult, I'll be there to make sure you don't come home all Tom Cruise.'

'Are you going to wish for Killian to marry you?' I said, with a wink. '"Dear cult-type people of Kerry who have all our bank details, I wish to marry my sexy boyfriend who is incredibly lovely and great in the scratcher!"'

'And to find Louboutins in my size in the January sales!' she said, forcing a smile.

Was she okay? She was okay, right? I knew she and Killian were more than okay.

'Oooh! Can I have that one too?' I said. 'Or have you bagsed it now? How does it work? Shit. Actually, I have no money so you can keep it. Good luck. Enjoy them. I, on the other hand, will be selling the remainder of my shoes to our weird neighbour to buy more Weetabix, tea and wine.'

We headed out to the sitting room to watch a documentary about a woman in India who was born half tree, half human. I sat there looking at Sholina with her branchy arms and thought it really could be a lot worse.

'Can we not just Google "Chicken Soup for the Soul" and jot down the main points from Wikipedia? I mean, are we really going to go down to Kerry to this Wish Factory?'

'Yes. And no. Yes to Kerry. No to Wikipedia. Rebecca tried that once, and all that happened was she got sidetracked and ended up scribbling down a lovely new recipe for chicken noodle soup from the *Afternoon Show* website. Good for a lovely lunch, yes. Figuring out why she'd spent four years studying science when she wanted to be a Montessori teacher, no.'

'*Feel the Fear and Do It Anyway*?'

'Yes, that might help you turn the light off when Bette's about,' she said.

'Nah . . . I think I just need tranquillizers for that.'

'For you or her?'

'Me. Or her, maybe. Actually, both, I reckon. What about *The Power of Now*? Apparently that comes with a CD you can chant to.'

'No, Killian finds it unsexy. I actually tried it a few weeks ago and when I got really relaxed during sex I got a bit carried away and started chanting, "Life is now! There was never a time when your life was not now, nor will there ever be."'

'Jesus!'

'No, Eckhart Tolle, the guy who wrote *The Power of Now*.'

'No, I mean *Jesus*!'

'Oh, right. Yeah. I know. You can see why I gave it up.'

'Yes, I can.'

Why was Lisa reading *The Power of Now*? Very unlike her. And now demanding that we head off to Kerry to join a cult-factory-type-yoke-thing. And this was coming from the girl who once said, and I quote, 'Dr Phil needs a kick up his soul-searching hole.' Shocking. (He *so* doesn't. He's so lovely, and I want him to sit on a tall stool beside me and sort out my life/be my friend.)

'You really like him, don't you, Leese?'

'Jesus? Yeah, he seemed like a good guy.'

I poked her in the ribs. The one shining light in the middle of all of this relationship blackout was that Lisa was really falling for Killian.

I watched her as she looped her hair around her fingers with a faraway misty look. We called it the *Days of Our Lives* Look of Love. And she had it.

'Leese, please don't not gush about him on account of me and Robbie. This is an exciting time for you.'

'Thanks, Grace.' She smiled coyly, her eyes dancing, like two ravers on Mission Beach. 'I know I fall for guys so easily, but this is *different*. I can just feel it. And I think he feels it too.'

'I know I'm on a ban, but you never said anything about *happy* tears. These are happy tears!' I said, before I was made to eat more soggy cereal or packed off to an additional dream factory in Donegal.

'Thanks, Grace,' she said softly, taking my hand, and I held it as the tears plinked off my chin.

'Poor branchy-arm lady,' I said, feeling so sorry for Sholina. At least I could turn the taps to run my Blueberry Bliss bubble bath and zip up my own tracksuit. Both incredibly fulfilling.

Christ, who was I kidding? If we did go down to this place in Kerry I was going to have to wish for a lot more to do with my hands.

'Maybe she should try that new velvet body moisturizer from Boots. I've heard it's amazing.'

'I think her problems stem from more than dry skin,' Lisa said, in the voice of Meredith Grey. She always did that when she spoke 'medical'. 'Good God, Grace, I cannot wait to get you down to Kerry.'

I sighed, the crack in my resolve starting to widen further. 'Can we not go off and just do what Julia Roberts did? Get a tan while travelling around India eating shit-loads of carbs?'

'Grace!'

Was worth a try. Anyway, if I couldn't afford new shoes or that cute pansy print tea-dress I saw in George's Street Arcade, I *definitely* couldn't afford to swan around the world eating pizza. I was good at economics like that.

'Fine,' I said. 'Let's do it. Let's go to Kerry to this Wish Factory.'

'We already are. I've booked it. If it were up to you to make a decision on it, the entire cult would have been locked up in jail for fraud and larceny by the time we finally made it down there.'

Harsh. But possibly more than accurate.

Wow. Lisa was my very own Dr Phil. I needed to get her a tall stool. Maybe I could get one from Westlife at a knock-off rate now they'd broken up. They must have had so many stools just lying around.

'And before you say anything, it isn't a cult and they're not going to fleece our bank accounts,' she said.

''Kay,' I said. (My bank account was empty anyway. And maybe this cult thing would be kind of exciting and I could get into private investigation. I could be the new Donal MacIntyre. In a hot dress. And bare feet. Because I'd had to sell off all my shoes to buy Weetabix.)

'Before we head down to the Wish Factory, I really think you should read the book *Eat That Frog!*'

No way! Was she reading my mind? 'Lisa, I do not need to read a book about being more adventurous in what I eat. I just really need to do a big supermarket shop. The Weetabix thing was just –'

'*Eat That Frog!* is Amazon's top-selling book on procrastination.'

Oh.

God, was I really that bad, I wondered, flicking through the channels again until my thumb went numb with repetitive strain. Yes, perhaps I was.

'Lisa, I know, I don't know . . . It's sort of . . . God, I hate feeling unsure,' I said. 'It's just . . . I feel . . .'

'What? It's just you feel what?' she said, turning to me. We both knew we were talking about Robbie now.

'I feel . . . I feel I should be doing this,' I said. 'I know I've broken his heart. I think I've broken my own, but somehow it feels like the only thing I can do right now.'

Lisa slumped back on the couch. 'Wow. For a minute there I was sort of hoping you'd say it was all a mistake and my two best friends were madly in love after all.'

'I wish,' I whispered, catching the lump in my throat, 'I wish I could.'

# 24

There were a few things about not being in a relationship that I was going to have to get used to in the mornings.

1. No tea and toast in bed. Every morning I used to get tea and toast in bed as Robbie was up before me. He would bring it up on a tray with a little 'thought for the day' on a Post-it. Something like 'Today is Indian Goat Appreciation Day: you, my lady, are one sexy goat.'
2. No warm showers. Every morning he'd put the warm water on for me, and my bathrobe on the heated towel rail so it was nice and toasty for me when I got out. I kept forgetting to put the damn water on so every morning was like a re-enactment of the shower scene from *Psycho*, but with freezing water instead of a large kitchen knife. One day, our weird shoe-collecting neighbour even called to the door to ask was I okay as he'd heard all the screaming, or was it just that I'd found a new boyfriend and 'Is he really that good?' Wink wink. Oh, and did I have any shoes I didn't need any more?
3. No relaxing showers. Not only were my showers now a Janet Leigh-inspired scream-fest: they were also terrifying. Bette (channelling Norman Bates) would stare at me from behind the shower curtain until I was done, probably because I hadn't fed her or let her out or done something equally 'non-pet-friendly'. And I couldn't close the door to keep her out because the wood was warped on the floor that Robbie was going to fix before I ended our relationship and broke his heart.

And this was all before nine a.m.

But I was being positive and decisive now that Lisa and I had had that big chat about me being a terrible decision-maker, and I was determined to get organized and be all Kris Jenner about things, and definitely not write lists about how crap things were. (Points 1 to 3 above were only to provide a little insight into my new life and I *definitely* did not write them down in a journal-type ring-binder entitled 'My Shit New Life', along with ninety-seven other points and observations. Just to be clear.)

And I know you're thinking, Kim Kardashian's mum is an overbearing bossy boots with far too much plastic surgery who should never be allowed to leave the house wearing those leopard-print leggings in public again and why would I like to be like her? Well, you know, you've got to admire her get-up-and-go spirit. So I was off to Spar to print my new Personal Shopper business cards to hand out to different shops in the hope I could earn some money to buy some non-cereal food types/glittery peep-toes/new net tutu to go under a few of my dresses/a new lavatory cistern.

I was in my I-mean-business ensemble, which, to quote Momma Jenner, I was 'going to totally kick ass' in. It consisted of my Katharine Hepburn *Philadelphia Story* long, tiered, high-waisted check skirt and crisp white blouse with matching check necktie and a pair of black patent Mary Janes. There was absolutely no way I was not getting employed wearing this outfit.

'"Why, Mike, it's almost poetry,"' I said, looking at myself in the mirror at the hall door, quoting Katharine from the film. I smiled at myself 1940s style (there's a knack, you know) with my hand on my hip and my mouth cocked to one side, and tried to disperse the feeling that, under all this frill and chintz, something was missing. The smile wasn't reaching my eyes. But come on, it was seventy-one years old.

I redid the bow on my necktie and looked up again. There. Was that better? I thought so . . .

This was it! I was 'bringing it' Kardashian/Hepburn style! Try and hold me back world: I'm a-comin'! Yeeeehaaaw! Okay, so I got kicked out of my first Spar. I'm not proud. But I did stick up for myself, in a very loud way, and for that I am a tiny bit proud. Although, they do these really good Cajun chicken wraps and it's now slightly annoying that I won't be allowed back in there any time soon.

There I was, printing off my business cards like a proper oul' Kris Jenner, and over pops the manager and goes, 'Not today, love. We're not having this again.'

'Pardon?' I said, half a Cajun chicken wrap wedged politely between my teeth.

'No, we have to shut this down now,' he said, switching off the card printer. 'We've been getting awful grief from the police for "collusion".'

'Collusion with what?' I said, between chews of my delicious wrap.

'You know.'

'No,' I said. 'I don't.'

'You know . . .' he said, gesturing to my frilly tiered skirt and puffy-sleeved *slightly* sheer blouse '. . . printing up cards for your "business".'

Blank face.

'Your . . . "business"?' he repeated.

I shook my head. Not a clue.

'Street Walker? Joy Girl? Human Trampoline? Lady of the Night? Peanut Butter Legs . . . ?'

I clapped my hand to my mouth (which was hard, with a half a Cajun chicken wrap hanging out of it). 'Peanut Butter Legs?' I said.

'Easily spread. I know you're probably one of the high-class ones, and I'm not saying your "olde worlde" fetish costume isn't fetching but –'

And then I sort of shouted and smudged the rest of my Cajun chicken wrap into his display of *Tatlers*, which took a lot of cour-age, really, because those wraps truly are delicious, plus Reese

Witherspoon was on the front of the magazine and I really like her. And then there was a mild tussle. And then I got kicked out.

This was not the start of the new life I had hoped for.

But I was determined to battle on. Yes, the temptation was to run home and draw myself a three-hour-long Blueberry Bliss bath, but I really did have to start expanding my interests a bit. (Were you allowed to say 'taking a bath' in the hobbies section of your CV? I hoped so.)

The next Spar was lovely, despite the lady behind the counter asking me if I was on my way to a fancy-dress party, and wasn't that lovely? However, she didn't call me a prostitute, which really was lovely. And I left with two hundred printed business cards. And a Wham bar.

My first few ports of call didn't exactly go swimmingly. I went into shop after shop handing out my card to a bunch of unappreciative grunters.

'We're not looking for anyone now, I'm afraid.'

'We're actually not hiring until 2017.' (Goddamn European debt crisis! I needed a new cistern for my toilet – I couldn't run out of the room like Eamonn Coghlan every time I flushed the loo until 2017.)

'Leave your card with us and we might take a look at it some time.'

Humph! She could at least have waited until I'd left the shop before she mushed her chewing gum into it and slam-dunked it into the bin.

For God's sake, they were glittery. My cards were glittery! And I was dressed like Katharine Hepburn and had the attitude of Kris Jenner. Good God, people, this shit was gold!

Just then I saw a sign in a shop window: 'Personal Shopping Assistant needed'. Thank you! Oh, God, thank you! Finally! Woo-hoo! In your face, slam-dunking Kobe Bryant lady!

'Hello, I'm here about the personal shopping assistant position?' I gushed, as enthusiastic as a performing circus squirrel. (I've seen them: they're excitable little fellas.)

The girl looked at me apathetically and blew a large bubble

from the gum she was chewing. I stared as it swelled and popped, closing my eyes as a gust of air faffed into my face.

Okay, this was not ideal. I was effectively asking a sixteen-year-old in a tracksuit, chewing Watermelon and Cola Hubba Bubba, to please employ me. But, like I said, I needed shoes and cisterns and a life and things.

I did *not* want to be the worst case study at the Wish Factory when we went down. The one that was talked about for years. The one that was met with 'Wowee,' and 'Sweet Jesus, of course I remember her! How could you *not*?' whenever it came up in the future.

'I just *adore* fashion. This little number, you ask?' gesturing at my outfit.

She shook her head. Well, no, I suppose she hadn't asked, but, sheesh, Watermelon Tracksuit Child Employee, throw me a frickin' bone here!

'Why, I had it fashioned by a tailor in Savile Row. I like gowns that are "tight enough to show I'm a woman and loose enough to show I'm a lady" – Mae West.' I winked.

'What's not the Mae West?' she said.

Okay, breathe. She seemed unaware that Mae West was actually a person and not just random rhyming slang.

'Hopefully you'll be able to see from my résumé that I have an awful lot of experience in the fashion and retail fields, and I would just love to work here as your personal shopper!'

'Really?'

'Yes!'

'Okay . . . Well, the position is to figure out the shape and running gait of the customers' feet so they can get the runner that's best suited to them. You need to look out for bunions and corns, and if they have athlete's foot or really bad fungal nail infections you can't let them try them on. Oh, and also you can't wear that freaky outfit. You'll have to wear one of these track –'

I was running before she could finish. I couldn't have digested the entire 'tracksuit' word without screaming in her face.

'Oh, Christ!' I wailed, racing down the middle of Henry Street, like a distressed damsel in a Victor Fleming remake. 'This is Hell!'

'Sorry, love? You wouldn't mind keeping it down, would you? There's a child asleep in that buggy,' a lady said, pointing at her pram as I beat the stone building at the intersection of Mary Street, like I was Vivien Leigh and it was Clark Gable's chest.

'Oh, I'm terribly sorry,' I said quietly, wiping my nose.

And off I plodded, my heart and my resolve sunk all the way down into my cute black patent Mary Janes.

Even though I was trying my best, I was pretty sure I was still wailing. But I think it was a really, really low wail that perhaps only a barn owl could hear – if a barn owl happened to be hanging around Henry Street. But when I walked into a coffee shop to console myself with a large cappuccino and the lovely chocolate-dipped raisins I'd bought in a newsagent, the manager thought I was drunk and asked me to leave.

Maybe it was because it was so bloody cold outside, but my jaw had sort of frozen, and I was still kind of wailing, and there was a good chance I had snot on my upper lip so I could see where he was coming from. I just nodded and headed back outside, walking at a forty-five-degree angle into the wind, which was now howling down the street and up my skirt. Not sure why I had come out with bare legs – so distracted thinking about my new life as an entrepreneur and the Kardashian empire that I had forgotten I was in Dublin not LA – I cursed Kris Jenner for having such a massive business empire. And 2.4 million followers on Twitter. And a book on the bestseller list. And probably never having to wear tights.

Why was everything so much easier for the Kardashians? *Why?*

'I want to be in the bath!' I said to myself, as the rain started to beat against my face. 'This is pointless. I may as well just give in, go down to the Wish Factory with my wrinkly bath skin, and declare I'm the biggest loser of them all.'

'Are you talking to me?' The man at the bus stop I had paused at looked bewildered. And a bit scared.

'No, sorry,' I muttered, and kept going.

'There's the girl who had it all,' they'd say, 'a lovely guy and a lovely new house with great prospects for work, but she could never get out of the bath to do something about it and now all she does is walk the streets of Dublin with mascara and snot running down her face onto her silly *Philadelphia Story* outfit.'

'Oh, I'm sorry, were you talking to me?' a lovely lady laden with grocery bags asked me on the street. Jesus Christ, I was nearly thirty years old. Had I not yet comprehended the mechanics of the human brain? That I could in fact hear my own thoughts without having to say them out loud?

'Are you lost?' she asked.

Man, she had no idea.

She looked like she was in a bit of a hurry so I really didn't want to slow her down with the answer: 'Sweet God, yes. I have no idea what direction to take in life.' If she didn't get home and put those spuds on soon, she wouldn't be having dinner till at least nine!

The weather seemed to be getting worse, and just as I was contemplating crawling into a recycling bin for shelter, I caught myself and decided that that was a new all-time low I could possibly do without. I forged on instead, the tiers of my skirt flapping like flags at the top of a pole in a storm. Tiers of a clown, I thought.

Not entirely sure where I was headed, I ducked down a side alley, thinking it might offer some protection from the elements. Turned out my theory on aerodynamics was way off. It was a wind tunnel. I battled along it, half wailing, half crying in utter frustration.

'Why? Why?' I roared, all the resolve I had felt this morning being whipped from me and carried off with the wind. 'I just wish things were different. *I wish things were different!*'

All of a sudden a gust quite literally swept me off my feet and whooshed me backwards. I stumbled around helplessly, still wailing pathetically as it took hold of me again, threw me up against a window and pinned me there.

Sweet Jesus! This was like that lady on the Biography Channel who had been suspended in mid-air, clinging to an uprooted tree, for an hour and a half during a tornado in Thailand!

Okay, this was nothing like that, but my skirt was rather annoyingly being blown up over my knickers and they were really dodgy ones that said in cartoon letters 'Supergirl! Pow!' on the bum. It was sort of ruining my Katharine Hepburn look.

I continued to sob pitifully as the wind held me pressed against the window. My nose was mushed into the glass, my cheeks were squeaking noisily against it, and with all the rain and tears and snot there was a distinct lack of Supergirl! Pow! resolve, whatever my bum might have suggested.

What the hell was going on? How had my life turned from Supergirl to Supershit as quickly as you could say, 'Ridiculous knickers'? Why was I out here in a storm on my own with no job, no boyfriend, no goals . . . and with my skirt around my chin?

Why? *Why? WHY?*

Ooooh – nice shop!

Right there, in the middle of my incredibly loud and snotty meltdown, pinned to a pane of glass, I was stopped in my tracks by what lay on the other side of the window.

## 25

All of a sudden the wind abated and my skirt fell down covering my cartoon knickers. Which I was quite relieved about: there was a man in the office window over the street and I thought he'd been taking photos of the whole sorry incident on his phone. I couldn't be sure but I was almost sure. Like when I knew Lance from 'N Sync was gay before anyone else did.

I stepped back and adjusted my skirt as if nothing out of the ordinary had happened and he hadn't just witnessed a grown woman dressed as a forties movie star wailing in the street with her skirt over her head in a pair of blue and yellow Supergirl pants, her stash of business cards now whipping around her, like she was a contestant in the Dome on *Crystal Maze*. 'Will you start the fans, please!' I could hear in my head, as I leaped about like a lunatic, grabbing at the air around me.

I glanced over the street and saw the frame of a tall, broad-shouldered man recede from the window into the dark shadows of his office. I only caught a glimpse of the side of his face before he'd disappeared.

Humph. Why did good-looking men have to be such weirdo creep-fests? Bet he was friends with Rebecca and Tony's best man Alan-the-perv. Bet they were in there together right now, laughing their pervert laughs (there is such a thing you know: apparently Ashley Cole and Sandra Bullock's ex-husband have one) and compiling their *Annual of Semi-naked Pictures of Unsuspecting Women* 2012.

Even though I couldn't tell if he was still looking at me or not, I flipped him the one-fingered salute anyway and turned away. Then I stepped back to take in the window in its full glory.

A beautiful duck-egg-blue hand-painted wooden window frame hugging delicate panes of bevelled glass. Over it hung a white-painted shop sign that read 'Best Wishes . . . Verity Vintage xx' in a swirly, dream-like script.

*Cute!*

Where was this place? How had I never come across it before? It looked utterly magical, like part of the set of Tim Burton's *Alice in Wonderland*, poking out and twinkling at me right in the middle of Dublin's grey urban sprawl.

I moved closer to peer inside again. Oooh, this really was like *Alice Through the Looking Glass*! Except it was now *Supergirl Pants in the Window*. Because the glass was bevelled and warped, all I could see inside was a kaleidoscope of wondrous colour. But if I squinted really closely, I could just about make out dresses. And shoes . . . and bags . . . and hats . . . and jewellery . . . all moving around like a carousel of delight!

I inhaled sharply. It looked *incredible*! Like no vintage shop I had ever seen in my entire life. I was so dumbfounded I was momentarily frozen to the spot. Then I collected myself enough to head for the door.

It was locked.

Shit. How could it be locked? Just when I'd found it! This really *was* like *Alice in Wonderland*!

I searched frantically around the doorframe: I needed a key to open that door so I could get inside that magical little world, far, far away from the tracksuit child with talk of fungal nail infections, the *Crystal Maze* with my knickers on show, the creepy sex pest in the window over the street, my broken cistern, my dull, grey, lonely new life . . .

I lifted up the 'Welcome' mat at the door and patted around for the Goddamn key. I was starting to feel panicky. I *needed* to get in there. It looked perfect. It looked like me. It looked like an idyllic little world I could escape to just to get away from it all for five minutes . . .

'May I help you?'

I jumped and screamed all at once, rambling and spluttering at the lady who had just peeled back the door. Suddenly I was channelling Alice: "'If I had a world of my own, everything would be nonsense. Nothing would be what it is because everything would be what it isn't. And contrary-wise: what it is it wouldn't be and what it wouldn't be it would. You see?"'

'No, not really. Just looks to me like you're looking for a key to get into my shop when the door is locked. And that is kind of rude. Quoting *Alice in Wonderland*. Strange. And you're looking for a key to open a door? How apt. I suppose you're off to a tea party while you're at it?' she said, in a languorous drawl, blowing the smoke from her long Cabriole cigarette holder into perfect loops that floated through the air then dispersed like tiny whispers.

Christ. I was transfixed by my apparent flash of insanity; by this strange vision in front of me; and by the fact she knew the quote.

*She knew!*

No one *ever* knows my quotes. Normally they just make me sit down and eat a digestive in case I'm 'having a sugar low' (I do get them, to be fair).

Christ, I was having a serious episode of the *Alices* and had just tried to get into a random locked shop. Wow. Hadn't done that in a while, twenty-two years to be precise. Last time was when I was seven. Mum and Dad were having the mother and father of all rows (apt) and I just walked out of the house, got the bus to Stillorgan and tried to break into Nimble Fingers toyshop 'to have a play'.

I can barely remember what the garda who brought me home referred to as 'the incident'. What I do remember was officially being the most popular kid in my school for an entire week because I'd 'sort of got arrested'. And Georgia Cox, two years ahead of me, didn't threaten to flush my head down the loo for a whole month. That's when you know you're cool.

I blinked back at the lady standing in front of me, eyeing me like a prize goat at a fair. That, or a criminal she might call the police to deal with.

What was going on here? It was the strangest thing . . . but she looked like me! Well, she looked like me if I'd been on the beer for thirty years solid and never thought to apply any moisturizer. She must have been in her late seventies at the very least. Early eighties, even. It was more how she was dressed, in that to-die-for outfit, smoking from her Cabriole cigarette holder, than any physical parallels *per se*. I studied her in wonderment: despite her advanced years, she was still incredibly beautiful with an old Hollywood glamour she wore like a perfectly tailored gown.

With her fabulous brown velvet skirt suit and charming little turban hat, with the single white peacock feather splaying from it like a fountain, she reminded me of Gloria Swanson in *Sunset Boulevard*. Albeit a little older, but with the same poise, style and grace.

She was mesmerizing. Her impassive expression gave nothing away, yet her deep-set navy blue eyes sparkled at me from their hollowed sockets, like two large brilliant-cut sapphires. She radiated authority, which unsettled as much as intrigued me.

'Who are you?' she asked, leaning on the doorframe blowing smoke rings at me.

I bit my lip and thought for a second. If this woman was as fabulous as I was almost sure she was – in the way I'd been sure Lance from 'N Sync was gay – she would be looking for something clever and considered. I racked my brains, trying to remember the book, trying to remember the film, trying to remember the quote. Come on, it had been my *favourite*!

Standing there toking on her long, perfectly poised cigarette she looked just like Absalom, the enigmatic hookah-smoking caterpillar. In a far cuter outfit. And less 'furry'.

'"I can't explain myself, I'm afraid,"' I suddenly piped, '"because I am not myself!"'

*Good God! How true was that!*

She stared at me inscrutably, drinking me in and savouring the taste, like a rich wine. I twitched and hopped from one foot to the other. She narrowed her eyes and took another drag.

Uh-oh. Maybe she was going to spit me out like a cheap cava. Maybe I should have just answered, 'Hello, I'm Grace Harte, and I'm very sorry I tried to find the key to open your shop door, but I've had a very shit day. But now that you've opened it, would you be terribly offended if I came in and, I don't know . . . had a little snoop?' instead of quoting ridiculous Lewis Carroll lines like some idiot let out of a lunatic asylum.

'Well,' she purred, her face suddenly cracking into a fleeting smile. '"Curiouser and curiouser . . ."'

I inhaled sharply. It had worked! She knew the quote. Of *course* she knew the quote!

She turned from the door and beckoned me to follow her. I scurried in behind her, terrified of missing my golden opportunity. *I was in!*

I shut the door behind me. Goodbye, cruel world!

'I can never figure out which of them is my favourite,' she said, in a thick New York accent. Oooh, she was from New York! How exotic! How exciting!

*Alice in Wonderland*? Hands down the 1933 one, I thought. By far the strangest.

'You'd have to go with the original, I suppose,' she said, almost reading my thoughts. 'It has an oddness that intrigues me. A bit like yourself.'

You ain't wrong there, sister!

'Plus, if I went with another, old Coops would be terribly cross with me,' she said, looking skywards.

'Coops?' I said.

'Gary Cooper,' she answered matter-of-factly, sitting down in a large mahogany chair and stubbing out her cigarette in a dainty purple crystal ashtray.

'Oh, yes.' I laughed conspiratorially. 'He'd be very cross with me too.'

She shot me a baffled look.

'Well?' she said. 'Are we going to have some tea or not? We can't have a play in Wonderland without a tea party, now, can we?'

'No,' I answered, smiling broadly. 'I suppose we can't.'

She disappeared into a little nook behind a wardrobe to where I figured there was a kitchen. And while she was gone, I took my opportunity to savour what really *was* Wonderland.

This place was breathtaking, like an old curiosity shop, a beautiful forties movie set and a cavern of vintage delights all whipped together. Was I dreaming? Perhaps this was a dream. Had I slipped into a hallucinogenic mirage as some survival mechanism from the elements outside? I turned as I heard the wind and rain beating against the window.

Irish weather. I told myself to remember to wish for a visa to Australia when I went down to the freaks in Kerry with Lisa. Okay, two virtual slaps across the face: I was not Alice in Wonderland who had slipped into a magical parallel world while asleep. I was Grace, from Dublin, with no job, a broken relationship (and toilet), and a cat with behavioural problems.

Oooh . . . perhaps I was already dead and this was my Heaven? Hmm. I wasn't sure I deserved a Heaven this good. No one deserved a Heaven this good when, say, they had broken the heart of the nicest guy in the world in front of hundreds of people in an ice rink in New York or something.

I could hear the far-off whistle of a kettle coming to the boil as I gazed around, mesmerized. At first the place seemed small but the more I looked the more it seemed to stretch into infinity. Dresses, blouses, skirts and tops all displayed on beautiful padded silk hangers. Old white-painted wardrobes with the doors pulled apart to reveal rack upon rack of delicate shoes. Antique dressmaking mannequins draped in loops of creamy pearls and sparkling crystals in a rainbow of colours. An array of hats, fedoras, boaters, pillboxes, sitting proudly across the framed mirror of the most beautiful handcrafted dressing-table. The drawers were filled with twinkling rhinestone brooches and ornate clip-on earrings, folded velvet gloves and bright multi-coloured silk scarves. Wooden bookcases hugged the walls, lined with threadbare tomes and ledgers, photo frames, crystal jars and pots. Every spare inch and nook was taken up with some secret from the past.

It was more like a boudoir in an enchanted castle than a shop hidden down an alleyway.

'Here we go . . .' she said, almost purring with insouciance, placing the tea set down on a silver tray table beside her chair. A charming tea set comprising a large, ornate bone china teapot sitting on a gold pot-warmer, flared cups with fine gold edging, a cake plate, tiny sugar bowl and matching spoon, all hand-painted with an Olde English rose design.

If I'd had that tea set I wouldn't have needed a life at all. I would happily have sat at home and drunk tea, watching *Murder, She Wrote*, perhaps. Actually, no. Then I'd have had to use the loo a lot, and it didn't really work. So, on second thoughts, I *definitely* still needed to get a life . . .

She looked at me reproachfully.

'Sorry,' I said. 'I'm soaking your carpet.' I looked down at the soft blue and cream Tabriz Persian rug.

'It's not that, sweethawt. It's just that you're making some sort of weird noise.'

Oh, so I was. I appeared to still be crying. Except there were no tears: I was just standing there 'wa-waaing', like a dying engine.

'Sorry about that. I've been doing it for the past two and a half hours or so and I sort of got into a routine.'

'I see,' she said, like it was a normal enough thing to do, which was very nice of her, I must say, because most people would think it was just plain odd.

'Are you sad?' she said matter-of-factly, pouring the tea.

'I am, actually,' I said, surprised at my own frankness.

She nodded knowingly and I instantly liked her and wanted to be her friend. Which was weird, really, because, as I said, she was about eighty. I didn't have many eighty-year-old friends. In fact I didn't have any. I was pally with a woman called Janine whom I used to work with and she was a good bit older than me. A full eighteen months, perhaps. So this was brand new territory.

I turned to my (fingers crossed) granny friend and stared at her. 'How have I never seen this shop before?' I said. 'Are you only just open?'

'No, sugar, not at all. I've been here for twenty-six years.'

'But I've never even heard of . . .' I stammered '. . . or seen . . .'

'You have to literally trip over me,' she said pointedly. 'That's how I like it. You don't see me coming and then, before you know it, you're lying on your tushie not knowing why your world is upside down.' She smiled to herself and I saw the memory of a private joke flee across her face.

'I don't advertise,' she continued, 'and I warn my customers not to tell other people about this place. I don't want strangers in here pawing over my babies unless they have a genuine appreciation for what is in here. Which most of them *don't*.'

I assumed she was referring to the stock. A woman in India had had twins at seventy, but that had been very unusual and I was fairly sure I would have heard if it had happened in Dublin as well.

'All of this stuff is my baby,' she said, gazing around her lovingly, 'and I won't give any of it up unless I know it will be truly loved and respected.'

Wow. I was touched by her solicitude. And delighted she didn't have twins. It was rare in this day and age on both counts. But then again, so were treasure troves like this run by eighty-year-old granny-type people.

'I love it,' I said, clapping, unable to contain my enthusiasm for another second. I knew she was a cool customer but this was *far* too exciting.

'Why?' she asked suddenly, studying me with her discerning

eyes. I studied her back. She looked like a doll. A strange doll set apart from all the cutesy plastic clones. A curious doll, sitting in the middle of a captivating dolls' house, frozen and lost in time.

'Why do I love it?' I repeated, biding my time. I looked around me, feeling a tingle. 'Well, because I can tell that I've just stumbled upon something very special,' I answered honestly. 'There's something so fascinating about what's in here that it makes me want to be a part of it.'

She remained poised for a moment or two, not breaking eye contact for a second. 'Good answer.'

Yes! She was *so* going to be my granny friend. We could watch *A Prayer at Bedtime* and eat custard creams together.

'Right, Alice, take your clothes off,' she ordered, clasping her hands together.

Uh-oh! New granny friend was turning out to be a crazed lesbian sex attacker. This was *not* the plan. I'd sort of thought the plan would include bonding over clothes and that maybe, just maybe, I could try on the gold net ballgown hanging up there and she could clap while I twirled around and quoted Grace Kelly movies.

'Off! Off!' she urged.

Good God. This was the stuff of *horror* movies!

'Your fingers are going all blue like the people in *CSI*.'

*CSI*? Oh, dear Lord! Why was she so interested in *CSI*? What was wrong with *A Prayer at Bedtime*?

'You'll get pneumonia if you stay in those wet clothes. Not on my watch. Debbie Reynolds took a whole month to dry out after *Singin' in the Rain*, and had a cold for a whole year. Never again, I said.'

Phew. She was less of a crazed lesbian sex attacker and more of a kind, caring old lady. Common mix-up. One of the old ladies at my granny's bingo club *always* reminded me of Grandma Death from *Donnie Darko*.

'Erm, that's very kind. Thank you . . . ?' I mumbled, searching for her name.

'Verity,' she said.

'Verity! From the sign!'

'Yes. Verity from the sign. Why don't you choose something else to wear while I dry off your clothes? Pick something out and slip behind that dressing screen there.'

I was on my feet at 'choose'. 'How about this little number?' I said.

She smiled. 'I'd hardly call it little.'

We gazed at the giant blush pink satin ballgown with the puff sleeves and beautiful double bow on the front V of the boned corset. It was so big and elaborate I could barely hold it up with both my hands.

'That hoop skirt is made from *actual* metal rods,' she said. 'Deborah Kerr had to wear foam rubber pads on her hips just so she could do the "Shall We Dance?" number in *The King and I*. I was sort of thinking you could get into a trouser suit or something. But if you think you can handle it, by all means . . .'

Woo-hoo! Permission granted!

'Gosh, it is just like it, isn't it?' I said, thinking of Deborah swooshing around in the king's arms as I raced behind the dressing screen and started to clamber into the gown.

'Would you like more tea?' Verity called, from her perch.

'Oh, yes, please, Verity!' I said, manoeuvring myself behind the screen. Good God, this was a monster. I had never before been in a dress the same width as a 46A bus, and it was quite an experience.

As soon as she clapped eyes on me, her expression changed to utter shock.

'Why, you . . . it . . . you look just like –'

'What?' I said. 'Who?'

'No one, it's . . . eh . . . nothing,' she said, collecting herself as she gathered my damp clothes from the top of the screen and turned for the kitchen.

'It's just been a while . . .' she muttered, as she walked away.

I followed her to the archway at the edge of the wardrobe that led to the kitchen. The 46A couldn't fit through, so I waited there for her.

What was it with this lady? I wondered, watching her peel off her evening gloves to hang up my clothes.

Why had her door been locked?

Why did she not want anyone knowing about her shop?

How was she managing to make a business out of it?

She pinned my things carefully on a wooden clothes frame and placed it in front of her incredibly fabulous baby pink and chrome retro stove. Oooh. That really was very lovely. It made me want to whip right in there and start baking a roulade. And I'd never even made a roulade. In fact, I wasn't entirely sure what a roulade was!

And the cute little white porcelain stand-alone bath in the corner, with the gold taps and legs, beside the stand with the old candlestick telephone.

'I've never seen a bath in the kitchen before,' I said.

'Yes, well, how else can I keep an eye on my scones when I want to take one?'

Made perfect sense to me. I'd be in the same quandary with my roulade. 'I can see Doris Day in that bath – polka-dot frilly bath hat on, talking on the phone to Rock Hudson in *Pillow Talk*.' I sighed dreamily.

'Oh, yes, Rocky was a favourite with the ladies, all right. I knew he preferred to bat for the other side long before anyone else seemed to notice . . .'

'Me too! I mean, me too with Lance from 'N Sync!'

She looked at me quizzically. Her nest of white hair was reflected in the large bubble chrome clock behind her head. Gosh, I could have sat in that bath all day and stared at the beautiful old clock and not cared for once that time was ticking away from me with every little tock.

'So what's your fascination with all of this, then?' Verity said, looking at me intently.

'I've just always really loved baths,' I cooed. 'Could sit in them for –'

'No, no, sweethawt,' she said, waving her hands out towards the shop, 'with this world. Old movie stars, old movie clothes . . .'

'I dunno,' I said. 'Just always liked them, I guess.'

She took me in and I shrank self-consciously. She had a peculiar ability to make you feel she was leafing through your mind as if it were the pages of a magazine. This was her world, her era. I didn't *really* belong to it, only wore it like a cloak I'd stolen because I coveted it so much, then simply professed it as my own.

Would she think I was a fraud? I hoped not. But I suddenly felt like one of those weird Peter André lookalikes in *Starz* standing beside the Real McCoy.

'What are you running from?' she said bluntly.

'Running from? Wha –? N-nothing . . .'

'Then why are you here? On a Tuesday evening? Dressed like Tracy Lord in *The Philadelphia Story* and running through the streets in the rain with nowhere to go?'

'I, er . . .'

'What's *your* story?'

'I, em . . . I don't have one.'

'Nonsense.'

'I don't, really.'

'Will no one be wondering where you are? It's getting late and it's now dark out there. And yet here you are, lost in my world, happier, it would seem, than out there in your own.'

Humph. I searched my mind to find a retort. Who did this woman think she was? Just because I liked it here it didn't mean I didn't like my own life. Or my own story.

Actually, yes, I *did* have my own story.

'Well, Verity, not that it's any of your business, but I'm sort of going through a transitional period right now.'

'And you like to play dress-up so you don't even look like yourself any more and you won't have to look at your true reflection?'

'Yes. I mean no!' I said. 'I just . . . like it, that's all. And, for your information, I did have someone who would worry about me and where I was. And I did have a life, actually, full of love and excitement and fun and adventure. But now I just have a cat that hates me. And pees in my shoes when I spend too much time in my house. So, *ha!*'

Shit. That was so not a *ha!* moment. I really did need to get better at that. I fixed the bow on the massive ballgown self-consciously, suddenly feeling terribly exposed. And silly. Like a little girl caught playing dress-up in her mother's clothes. I did not want to be friends with this granny lady and watch *A Prayer at Bedtime* and eat custard creams. I took it all back!

I stood there indignantly as she studied me. Euch, why did she do that?

'*Ha!*' Jesus, there I went again. But I couldn't help it – the anger in my stomach was suddenly making me brave. 'You talk about me hiding myself in another world. What about you? You sit in here with the door locked, telling your customers not to breathe a word of this place. How are you even running a business? What are *you* so afraid of?' I gasped at my nerve, reeling at the over-familiarity.

Shit. Was that too much? The words were out before I'd had a chance to think about what I was saying. It wasn't like me, but she had provoked me.

There was a crushing silence, and then she snapped, 'None of your Goddamn business.'

'Fine!' I said. 'Fine! I'm out of here. *Ha!*'

The *ha!* would have worked this time if I hadn't forgotten that I was still wedged in the archway in the stupid dress.

'Sorry . . . I am going now . . . but I seem to be stuck.'

'Yes,' she said icily. Then she gave a little shudder and said, 'Good God, I used to be so like you.'

'Stop it!' I said. 'Stop saying that! You don't even know me!'

'Oh, but I do. I *do*.'

'You *don't*,' I said, feeling hot tears running down my face. With the force of my anger I somehow managed to free myself from the archway. I turned on my heel and ran for the door.

'That's it, keep on running, Alice! Keep on running down that rabbit hole!' she called after me, as I escaped and ran for my life.

## 26

I had been more than a little dubious about the Wish Factory malarkey. Would we have to wear hairnets and white coats and those awful plastic sanitary gloves? Would we all just stand there in an assembly line, clocking off for wees after a long, arduous eight-hour shift of 'wish making'?

Lisa had managed to rope us into the weirdest of things over the years. Like selling Ugg-type booties for dogs and cats one Christmas door to door. Or attending a rally in town for fishermen on the Blasket Islands. Or making kites for National Kite Day 2003.

Seriously, I didn't know where she found that stuff. Or how I always managed to get dragged into it. Rebecca was lucky she was away. She still had a scar under her chin from when a kite stick snapped in her face.

Poor Bec. She'd spent an hour calling me from a payphone in the middle of a monsoon in Thailand last week after Lisa had told her about the break-up. I knew it was unrealistic I'd keep it from her for a whole year, but I really didn't want her to be worrying about me. Anyway, she ended up with so much water in her ear after the call that she had to get it professionally syringed. And when she said 'professionally', she really meant by a child in scrubs in a beach hut. So I told her to text me from now on.

A postcard arrived from her this morning. A picture of two little kids on a beach looking out at the sea arm in arm. '*I may not be here, but I'm always here,*' it said, which made me cry for just under an hour. And then I laughed when I read her little note on the other side: **Although I may never be able to actually hear ever again, I love you, Bec xx**.

Well, as it turned out, I was now *dying* to go to the Wish Factory.

Anything to get away from the feral wildness that was unfolding downstairs. Seriously, I had to remember to ask Mum if Tanya had actually been raised by a pack of wolves in her formative years before Dad and she came across her in a forest and courageously adopted her. For all my parents' foibles, that would have been awfully noble of them. But I bet they never gave her anti-tetanus and anti-rabies shots before taking her home. Would explain so much.

'*Grace!*' she called, from the foot of the stairs. Gosh, that really did sound like a wolf cry. Honestly, I was going to hunt for her birth certificate next time I was home.

'*GRACE!*'

'What? For crying out loud [like a wolf], what is your problem?' I stood at the top of the stairs, arms folded in protest.

'That man is putting a wash on and telling me his mother is that *cat*!'

'My mum!' Ab-Norman suddenly yelled, poking his head around Tanya's. 'She's being mean to my mum!'

Bette shrieked, jumped over my head and bolted down the stairs.

You *see*?

You see why I wanted to get out of there and high-tail it to the Wish Factory as quick as the speed of light? Even if it meant wearing hairnets and asking permission to do a wee?

I turned on my heel, rolled my eyes and thought that a woman raised by wolves should understand above anyone else how someone's cat was now their mother. All of a sudden, my feet were whipped from under me and I was pulled down the stairs, bumping and thudding with each step.

'Tanya!' I shouted aggressively. 'What are you –'

'Listen to me!' she said, pinning down my arms and legs so I couldn't move.

'Tanya, you can't pull someone down the stairs like that when they're over the age of eight. Please don't tell me you do that to your interns at work. I'm not a kid any more! I'm almost thirty, for Christ's sake! And I shouldn't have carpet burns on my bum! Unless I was having amazing sex with . . . a floor guy!'

'Exactly!' she harrumphed. 'You're nearly thirty! What the fuck are you doing running away to join a circus?'

'Guys! Please!' Norman implored. 'You're upsetting my mum with all this shouting!'

'Sorry, Norman!' we chorused.

'I'm not joining a circus,' I whispered.

'What the fuck is "a floor guy"?' she snapped back, under her breath.

'I dunno. A guy who likes doing it on the floor, I guess.'

'Grace, cop the fuck on. You're not going to run away with the circus – you can't even juggle mandarins,' she wheezed, in exasperation. 'You're coming with me to see Ms Walshe.'

What the f –?

'Mandarins? How do you know? [Bet I could.] And Ms Walshe? Our school career-guidance counsellor?'

'Yes!' She clapped, thinking she was finally getting through to me.

'Okay, Psycho Pants. First, I'm not joining a circus, I'm going to a "facilitating programme" down the country to help me figure a few things out.' I totally made up 'facilitating programme'. On the spot. Amazing. Couldn't tell her it was a Wish Factory, or she'd have nailed me to that step in a modern-day crucifixion-intervention-type thing. But 'facilitating programme' was genius. I'd have taken a bow if I wasn't pinned to the stairs by my thirty-six-year-old sister against my will.

'And second, if you must know, Ms Walshe's advice to me when I was filling out my CAO? "Possibly join a circus, Grace."'

'Shit,' she said, sounding miffed. 'Well, perhaps if you hadn't insisted on dressing like some sort of freak show, she might have advised you to become an accountant or something and we wouldn't be having this problem.'

'We are not having any kind of problem,' I said, finally wrestling her off me and scuttling back up the stairs, with, I'm pretty sure, my French knickers on full show seeing as the lining of my skirt was now knotted in my lovely pearl hairclip after that rather unwelcome skirmish.

Okay, so we were having a teeny-tiny little problem. But it was *nothing* to do with Tanya – as usual. And I really wished she'd just sod off and mind her own business.

To be honest, I was still a bit rattled after my trip to Wonderland the other day. The shop . . . Verity . . . the chat . . . It had crawled into the pit of my stomach and nestled there, like a knot of indigestion.

Perhaps it was because I'd left in a panic in that massive pink ballgown. How was I going to get it back to her? I really didn't want to have to go there again.

Maybe I'd post it to her. But then I'd have to pay for haulage, it was so bloody colossal. I'd looked like a right clown, even for me, when I'd stopped for cigarettes on the way home. Guy at the till asked me was I playing a fairy in the Gaiety panto and could I get him Twink's autograph.

Doorbell.

Phew! Taxi! Lisa! Freedom!

I grabbed my overnight bag, put on my cherry-red beret, fastened the amethyst brooch at the front of my cropped wool jacket and made for the front door. I ran down the hall, words flying past me like bullets as I ducked and dived.

'Lunatic . . .'

'New. Age. Bullshit . . .'

'Thirty . . .'

'Grow. Up . . .'

'Mandarins . . .'

'You're out of fabric conditioner . . .'

That last bit was Norman. Didn't have time to tell him it was under the sink in the kitchen before I slammed the door and raced to the getaway car, like Alec Guinness in *The Ladykillers*.

'Sweet Jesus, man, put the foot down!' I shrieked, *potentially* over-dramatically, to the taxi driver.

Lisa understood perfectly: 'Tanya in there?'

I nodded.

'Put the foot down. This is life or death. Pretend to be Daniel Craig as Bond. You could totally pull that off, you horny sexpot.'

Jesus, Lisa was intimate with her taxi drivers.

Oh! We weren't in a taxi! Killian was driving!

'Hi,' I said, leaning in. 'Thanks for giving us a lift.'

'No probs,' he answered casually, doing a U-turn with one hand and hitting sixty k.p.h. in less than three seconds. Fuck me. We were looking at the new Bond. And I knew exactly who to call for any future bank heists.

'If you guys get abducted down here I don't want to be racked with guilt that I didn't even drop Lisa to the station,' he joked. She tousled his hair and he grabbed her hand, mock biting it as she burst into a shower of giggles. My God, they were really nuts about each other.

I sat in the back, watching them, feeling further adrift from anywhere I'd ever been before but knowing exactly where I wanted to get to.

Before we got out of the car, I thanked the new Bond and shuffled about nervously before finally striking up the courage to ask him what had been swimming around my head for days, just to satisfy my curiosity. 'Where's Robbie staying, do you know?'

'He's with Alan.'

Jesus Christ! Alan-the-perv! My worst suspicions confirmed!

I suddenly felt nauseous. I knew it was none of my business, but I just needed to know that he wasn't involved in mass orgies and live Internet streams of strip poker. You know, the normal things that cross your mind when you break up with someone.

'Hey, I was really sorry to hear about you guys,' he added, with an apologetic smile.

'Yeah, well, whatever.' I shrugged, trying to sound cavalier in the face of the mass orgies and live strip poker streams. 'Shit happens.'

'Erm, okay,' he answered awkwardly. 'Well, enjoy your trip.'

Bond and his new leading lady continued to snog the face off each other in the car while I dragged my wheelie-bag in a huff towards the ticket office.

We clambered aboard our train and I promptly turned to Lisa and bagsed the top bunk.

'Okay, Marilyn. This is not *Some Like It Hot*. This is the thirteen oh-five to Killarney. With a change at Mallow. There are no bunks. There is no steam engine. No carriage where you can mix up a dry martini. Your seat is beside that old lady with the hairy chin and the egg sandwiches.'

'Oh,' I said, wondering where on earth I was going to store my hatbox. I'd brought a fabulous vintage plum fedora in case we were allowed to dress up our hairnets. I hadn't been on a train in quite some time. Not since myself and Tanya had been sent as punishment down to our cousins in Wexford. Mum and Dad had disguised it as 'a treat'. We knew better. Nobody is forced to spend time with people who hide under the bed and eat frog-spawn as a treat.

To be honest, there had been no bunks on that train either, but I had had hopes for this one. Slight, foolish, wispy hopes.

'"Story of my life. I always end up getting the fuzzy end of the lollipop,"' I sighed, in my best Marilyn voice, while wedging myself into seat A47, trying not to get egg mayonnaise on the arse of my 1940s wartime-silhouette grey skirt suit as I shuffled past the old dear. Most apt outfit I could find, considering we were being conscripted to some barracks down the country to do battle with an unquestionable despotic cult leader.

But, you know, in a good way.

I was sort of looking forward to it. There was only so long I could replace the buttons on all my clothes as a distraction, watch *Family Fortunes* reruns, ditto.

The train journey, when you were not Marilyn Monroe in *Some Like It Hot*, was, as expected, a bit shit. Most eventful thing was making a Jenga-type game out of the crusts of the old lady's egg sandwiches. We bonded, me and the granny. Which was strange as

I was officially off grannies after my run-in with crazy Verity. And I was sort of avoiding my own granny because she was still on at me about getting tickets to One Direction in the O2 next year.

Lisa had a far more comfortable journey and even fell asleep on the shoulder of a bony, conservative businessman in a suit. She got a great kip but had to apologize to him for drooling down the lapel of his pale grey jacket when she woke up.

I think she was just exhausted after the Trauma. She was hovering over the scummy train loo, jeans around her ankles, when the automatic door defaulted and slid open. The trolley lady was passing and a good-looking stranger was waiting to use the toilet. She screamed. Not knowing what to do next, she asked the woman if she sold Tayto. She didn't. The good-looking stranger laughed. Lisa didn't.

Poor mite.

We finally got to Killarney and waited for our pick-up at the station as instructed. When a perfectly normal red Nissan Primera pulled up, I was so relieved we hadn't been bundled into the back of a white Hiace van and sedated with chloroform that I started to relax a little.

Our driver nodded at us, then hit play on his mixed tape. For the next twenty minutes we were subjected to a compilation of Sophie B. Hawkins's 'Damn I Wish I Was Your Lover', Go West's 'King Of Wishful Thinking', Dusty Springfield's 'Wishin' And Hopin'', and 'Wishing Well' by Terence Trent D'Arby. I couldn't quite figure out if I found it terribly sweet or utterly terrifying. Perhaps a little of both.

All I knew was that whenever Lisa and I tried to work out how Cheryl Cole had ever thought that teaming shearling boots with a pink body-con halter-neck dress on the front of *Closer* magazine was a good idea, the driver turned up the volume. It was clearly meant to get us in the mood for all this wishing we were about to do down at Wish HQ.

We arrived at the Wish Factory after the initial brainwashing operation in the car and I suddenly relaxed. The 'factory' was a gorgeous log cabin set in the middle of a beautifully manicured garden in a small forest. All of a sudden I wished I was seven again so I could play with my Sylvanian Family Forest Friends, and then I wondered should I go and tell one of the invigilators, or whatever they were called, that I'd just had my first wish.

I decided against it when we were deposited in a waiting room labelled 'First Timers'. It should have been called the 'Mortification Room' as it was essentially a holding pen of, well, mortified people. My sense of reprieve slowly drained from me and my self-consciousness increased. I went puce red and started sweating. What, in God's name, were we doing here?

Well, at least there were others who were thinking exactly the same thing. A gathering of lost souls who were suddenly coming to the realization that they probably should have bought *Man's Search for Meaning* on Amazon instead of signing up to this place. We smiled at one another awkwardly, then apologized for our very existence by staring at the floor and praying for it to open and swallow us whole. Then, just when the atmosphere in the room became almost unbearable, in burst a troupe of 'non-first timers', brandishing dream-catchers and singing 'Wishing On A Star' with interpretive dance moves, like a crazed version of the final mask scene in *Shall We Dance* with Ginger Rogers and Fred Astaire.

I must have looked horrified when one of the performers picked me out and led me into the centre of the room and circled me, a tiny baby buffalo in the middle of a pride of lions, all the while singing into my face and dancing at me.

All the non-first timers clapped and joined in while the first timers stood there aghast, wanting to cry /escape/call the police. I searched for Lisa amid the farrago only to find her, to my sheer horror, clapping and swaying, singing along about wishing on rainbows and stars and other weirdos who dreamed things.

, I screamed. But the singing troupe just thought I was hitting the high notes of the song and clapped encouragingly.

And just when I really wished somebody *would* sedate me with chloroform, in rocked Fred Astaire himself, the Daddy Mac of the all-singing, all-dancing League of Lunatics, dressed like a cross between a Lakota Sioux chief, in a full eagle-feather war-bonnet, and Father Declan from St Mary's Church on Booterstown Avenue, in a floor-length gold vestment belted at the waist.

Bloody hell.

He shimmied over to me in a disturbing side shuffle until he was mere inches from me. His eagle feathers were tickling my nose so much as he zigzagged his head to the music, I thought I might have sneezed into his face if I wasn't already devoting all my strength and concentration into not defecating in public. I hadn't been so scared since I'd read that neon was coming back in for the summer.

As everyone held the last note of the song, I sensed the finale of the ritual and held my breath in terrified anticipation.

And then it came: Fred West (formerly known as Fred Astaire), still holding the final note, suddenly signalled the closing of the ceremony by raising his giant dream-catcher hoop-yoke up over his head before crashing it down over mine in an explosion of feathers, bells, crystal and netting.

And just as I thought he was *finally* done with me, he leaned in slowly, winked, pointed his finger and purred, in a nauseating pseudo-American accent, 'I'm a-wishing on you, baby, yes, I am.'

Boom.

Done.

Cue fevered applause. Cue ostentatious self-satisfied bowing from Fred West. Cue my face turning a dangerous shade of purple.

Cue the non-first timers all jumping in the air and high-fiving each other like an over-zealous college fraternity.

Cue the first timers all reaching for their phones and presumably switching on their iPhone locaters to aid the police investigation.

My eyes darted to Lisa – I was unable to move my head under the weight of the shock and humiliation, and the dream-catcher lassoed around my neck. As she looked back at me with a smile breaking on her pretty little face, and her hands clasped under her chin in jubilation, I mouthed to her the string of threats and expletives that I reserve for very, *very* special occasions.

## 27

After she'd listened to an outburst from me that would have made even John McEnroe blush, Lisa eventually calmed me down and in no uncertain terms told me how ridiculous, childish and ungrateful I was being. Then she issued me with a bribe of seven Party Rings from a packet she had stashed in her wheelie-bag in case the place turned out to be a bit 'religious' and they made us fast.

'I like Party Rings. Especially the pink ones,' I said, munching away. I might have been a lot of things, but childish was *not* one of them.

Lisa rolled her eyes and removed the dream-catcher from around my neck.

'Sorry, Leese, I just hated being singled out like that. The whole thing sort of reminded me of when –'

'You were picked out in school and made to stand on a table in the middle of the classroom for having ginger pubes?'

'Exactly. Except I didn't even know what pubes were back then. I thought they were just talking about me having red hair again so I told them that, yes, I did have ginger pubes and, what's more, I brushed them a hundred times every night before going to bed.'

Lisa puffed her cheeks out as though she was trying to contain a laugh.

'It's not funny!' I said. 'Tanya tried to dip-dye my hair in black poster paint, she was so embarrassed. *She* was so embarrassed! Ha!'

'Because you're worth it,' Lisa purred, in her best L'Oréal voice.

I giggled and popped the last Party Ring into my mouth. 'I'm sorry for being ungrateful. This is a super present. And so thoughtful.'

She grinned, and just as I was about to tell her she looked like the Cheshire Cat, I reconsidered on the grounds that someone who was renowned for hating cats should not tell the people they loved that they looked like a cat.

'And when I gave you that really shit birthday present of a portable neon blow-up bath that time,' I continued, 'you had the decency to act grateful.'

'Exactly.'

We had all been led to our sleeping chambers, 'where dreams are made', according to Fred Astaire/West, who, as it turned out, was actually called StarDust.

My hole. Bet he was actually called Fintan Murphy. Anyway, I wanted to tell StarDust that that was possibly the creepiest thing I had ever heard from a man dressed in a feathered hat and gold dress, but Lisa was in earshot and I was doing my best to appear 'grateful'.

A golden wand had been left on the pillow on our bunk beds, and just as I was about to say, 'You have to be kidding me?' I exclaimed instead, 'Oh, my God, I've always wanted one of these!' Which, to be fair, was partly true.

Fintan instructed us to leave our bags, collect our wands and meet them downstairs at the Wishing Well to 'begin the process'. I quickly logged onto Facebook on my phone so I could enter a status update and leave some clues just in case this was all about to get a bit Fred and Rose, when a photo popped up on my screen.

*Robbie Cotter was tagged in Claudia Varian's album.*

Jesus.

A picture of Robbie and some girl. Her arm around him. Both smiling into the camera.

I thought I was going to be sick.

Who the fuck was Claudia Varian? And why did Claudia Varian look like Jennifer Garner? And why was Robbie being tagged in photos? Robbie never used Facebook! I had forgotten he was even on it.

I dropped my phone onto my bed as if it was a hot coal. I grabbed my wand and ran out of the room, flailing it like a mad-woman and *wishing* to Jesus I had *not* just seen that picture.

We all reconvened at the Wishing Well, a circular room decor-ated to look like the inside of a well, with the ceiling painted like the underneath of a well's hood and dotted with fairy-lights, like a constellation of twinkling stars. A giant wooden pail hung from the middle of the ceiling on a large rope with a pulley wheel.

Lisa and I scuttled to the wall, where most of the other first-timers seemed to be hiding out, and burrowed down into our star-shaped cushions.

It all looked wonderful, and if I hadn't felt so uncomfortable, I might even have let out a little 'ooooh'.

I looked around the room, which contained about twenty-five people holding wands and squatting on their hunkers with expressions that ranged from sheer delight to confusion to out-and-out terror. It was like my school nativity play – without a weird Irish teacher dressed up as a donkey.

As we waited for our first class to kick off, I thought that if this were a secret Scientology gathering, maybe John Travolta or Kirstie Alley would pop their head in, and just, you know, say hi. That would be great! I was such a fan of *Look Who's Talking*.

'All rise to give thanks to the Wishes that have gone past,' Star-Dust bellowed, as he jetéd, like the head dancer in *The Nutcracker*, into the well room in a cyclone of feathers, wands and gold tassels.

We all stood to attention and I sneaked a sideways glance at the lady standing to the left of me and wondered if it were at all possible that she was Kirstie Alley in a really good disguise. It would have to be really, *really* good as the lady was about four foot tall and looked twenty. But maybe Kirstie had been doing a lot of microdermabrasion. Celebs could do anything nowadays with all their money.

I looked at her again. She was wearing train-tracks and had bad skin. Would anyone go out of their way to get acne and have painful, extensive orthodontic work to avoid getting recognized at a Scientology gathering in Kerry?

Hmm, maybe Killarney was too far to attract the heavy hitters. Pity. I would have liked to have met Kirstie.

'Good, good, my little Star Gazers. Now hold your wands up to the sky and start thinking about your heart's greatest wishes. Close your eyes and wish. Wish. Wish. *Wiiiiisssh!*'

The non-first timers broke into a quiet hum of 'Wishin' And Hopin'' by Dusty Springfield as they sprinkled little stars over us. (I knew for a *fact* you could get tubs of those in Eason's so Star-Dust wouldn't convince me they were celestial dust particles from a meteorite shower or something.)

It was so hard not to laugh! Was everyone else closing their eyes and actually doing this? I sneaked a surreptitious glance out of the corner of my eye. Yes, they were! Even tiny Kirstie Alley with the bad teeth and problem skin. Even Lisa.

Her too! I swear to God, if I found her watching *Top Gun* one more time, I would know it was less about the 'Take My Breath Away' sequence and more about the couch-jumping alien wrangler.

Suddenly StarDust's creepy gaze was on me and I scrunched my eyes closed and started wishing.

'Now, my lovely Star Gazers, I want each and every one of you to tell the room what your wish is and then place your wand in the wooden pail for the stars above to listen to you and attempt to process your wish.'

Sweet Jesus.

Tell the room?

What about the theory that if you told someone what you wished for it wouldn't come true?

'Come on, don't be shy! You over there, be brave, dare to wish, dare to dream.'

I had to keep thinking of the time I'd seen a kitten getting squished on the N7 so I wouldn't laugh.

First up was a tall, skinny man, with sad, saucery eyes, who placed his wand nervously in the pail and said, 'I wish my family would understand me.'

I hear ya, sister/tall, skinny, sad-eyed man, I thought. Good wish. Excellent wish. I gave him a small clap (which I soon discovered was frowned upon. Those non-first timers were scary. And no glittery buckets of stars could have convinced me otherwise).

Next up was a short middle-aged lady who reached up to the pail, plopped her wand inside and proclaimed that she wished she could go back to college to study psychology.

Hmm. I had serious doubts they would let her in if they'd found out she'd willingly paid hard-earned cash to spend a weekend with this bunch. Surely universities had standards about such things.

Next up was a young man in his twenties who placed his wand in the bucket and professed that he wished he could tell someone he was bisexual.

I was pretty sure he just did: twenty-five strangers with wands and a man dressed as an Indian chief.

Suddenly StarDust was pointing at me and beckoning me to the centre of the room.

I looked from right to left.

Me?

'Go,' Lisa whispered, giving me an encouraging nod.

Shit. I was up! *I was up!* I peppered my way through the crowd until I was at the hanging pail. I looked out at a blanket of expectant faces, their eyes all blinking at me in earnest support. I coughed, clearing my throat. Okey dokey . . .

I sang a verse from one of my favourite songs, 'I Wish'. Granted it wasn't wishing for world peace but being taller and becoming a baller and getting a rabbit, a bat and an impala . . . Okay, it was a bit obscure for this lot, but I thought it was inspiring.

Ta-da!

Silence.

More earnest blinking. I laughed at my little song. But no one else did. Except Lisa, despite herself.

What? I'd thought they liked the singing thing.

StarDust looked like he wanted to knock me out with one perfectly executed *pas de bourrée*. The non-first timers looked at me with as much disdain as my own mother had when I'd told her I didn't want to join the Irish Countrywomen's Association to learn how to make brown bread and loop curtains.

'Ehm . . .' I laughed nervously. 'Okay . . .'

Come on, Grace, think of something! Something worthwhile. Something meaningful. What was it I wanted?

'Well, I sometimes wish that not all vintage clothes had a dry-clean-only tag. Very annoying. And that I could get shoes to fit me properly. I have very large feet and sometimes my big toe can hurt in badly made shoes.'

Silence.

I placed my wand in the pail and listened as it thunked to the bottom. What? It was true! I did wish for those things sometimes.

'Out!' StarDust boomed. 'Out of my class!'

Hey! Having big feet wasn't easy. And the cost of dry-cleaning? Well, let me tell you . . .

'*Out!*'

Oops.

'Can I take my wand?'

'No.'

'Okay.'

I scuttled out of the door with my tail between my legs, Lisa scurrying behind me.

We were sent to our sleeping chamber to 'reflect' on what we'd done and to 'consider taking this seriously', and just as I was about to tell them all to go and take a long walk off a short pier, I remembered Lisa, how lovely she'd been about her neon bath, and swallowed it.

'Sorry, Leese,' I said, as she lay on the top bunk above me. She really did deserve the top bunk after I'd been so silly. 'I was trying, it's just . . . I don't *know* what I want. There. I've said it. I don't know. I wish I knew that I was bisexual and wanted to study psychology, but I don't.'

'That's okay,' she said, munching a Party Ring and passing the hip-flask of whiskey down to me. She was such a clever packer. I always brought the wrong stuff. Like now – a thesaurus and an ink-removing pen. Party Rings and whiskey were far smarter. I sighed heavily at my own ineptitude.

'What was your wish going to be?' I said. 'You're so happy with Killian. And you like your job.'

'I – I –' she stammered '– I just wanted to support you, really.'

'Aw,' I said, downing some whiskey. 'Tell me more about Killian.'

She flipped around and hung her head over the edge of her mattress, a massive grin stretching across her face. 'Okay, well, he's so clever. Do you know? He told me that oil from oranges is flammable.'

'No way!'

'I know! And he's just so lovely, Grace – he cut out these Lidl coupons from the paper the other day because he knew I was collecting them to win ceramic pots.'

'Aw, you love pots!'

'I do! I really do! And, Grace, he is unbelievable in bed. Unbelievable! Honestly, we cannot keep our hands off each other.'

I smiled, remembering a time when I'd had that in my life. It was indeed amazing. And I was so happy for Lisa. She deserved it so much.

'Do you think you'd like to go on a date soon?'

I could feel my stomach physically lurch. 'The Dating Scene'. It sounded like a Wes Craven horror movie.

Christ. It had been so long.

My last two forays before getting together with Robbie had been, first, with a guy who had a framed picture of his mum and dad over his bed and sucked stones while watching telly. The other oddball had told me – after one date – that he needed to have sex immediately 'to correct a potentially debilitating disc problem' in his spine and would I be kind enough to 'facilitate' him?

I was not looking forward to going back out there. Had the rules changed? How long did one wait now before one 'did it'? Like with normal people, not those with potentially debilitating disc problems. Were you still able to wait four months when you were almost thirty?

Poor Robbie nearly had to be sedated when I eventually told him I was ready. Good God, I'd been watching far too much *Seventh Heaven*.

Were pubes totally out now too? I'd read somewhere that they were. Shit, was I going to have to get a Hollyhead?

No, that wasn't what it was called . . . a Hollywood!

'You could have wished for a date,' Lisa suggested helpfully.

Hmm. I wasn't sure I wanted one.

I puffed up the pillow under my head and thought of a midnight stroll on the beach with Ewan McGregor and my new Hollywood.

Perhaps I did.

And then we did what Lisa and I did best: we choreographed old Madonna songs and I wished Rebecca was there and that things didn't have to change so much. Were you still allowed to choreograph Madonna songs when you were married? I hoped so. Rebecca had a great way with 'Crazy For You'.

Then some Wish Prefect knocked on our door and told us to keep it down and get into our beds. I didn't normally take instruction from grown adults in unicorn-printed onesies, but I decided to make an exception now, seeing as I was already sort of in trouble.

'Night, Leese,' I whispered, in the darkness. 'I'm so happy you're happy.'

'Yep,' she answered. 'Sleep well.'

'I will. Lisa?'

'Yeah?'

'I think I'm going to get a Hollywood.'

'Okay.'

'Night.'

'Night.'

I searched for my phone to switch it off, vowing to myself I wasn't going to look at Facebook again. One new message from Tanya: 'CTBS campaign starts today. Cut The Bullshit. This new-age dreaming is for wasters. You and that fabric-conditioner chap need to be certified.'

I turned it off and stared down the barrel of the darkness, praying for it to pull the trigger and let me sleep.

The next morning, after a bowl of Lucky Charms, we were told to snap the wishbones that had been left out for us and proceed to our next class. Back in the Wishing Well room we were instructed to lie down on the yoga mats, stare at the stars in private meditation and think about what we really wanted.

Phew.

This was more like it. No wands, no singing, no feathery weirdos, no public declarations.

The Wish Facilitator seemed the most normal person I'd seen down there. She just sat cross-legged on her mat and smiled at us warmly.

'I want you to really relax now, everyone. Just lie back and block out the noise. Block it all out so you can hear yourself. Your voice. What is it saying? What is it wishing for?'

I lay on the mat and took in the fairy-lights, letting them blur and crystallize as I squinted them in and out of focus. I thought about camping in Rosslare with my family. I thought of the row Mum and Dad were having, carried on the wind up the beach to where Tanya and I sat looking at the night sky, searching for Polaris. I thought of me and Robbie sitting on the roof, looking up at the moon, feeling the universe was ours, as we toasted our first night in our new home.

And then I thought of Grace Kelly's wedding dress and how

the tiny seed pearls had twinkled like stars in the abundant undulations of beautiful rose-point lace.

I thought about lots of things. Old and new. Good and bad. Some happy and some, well, not so happy. And I let them play out in my mind's eye, like the reel in an old movie projector. But that was like every good movie, wasn't it? You had your comedy, your tragedy, your regrets, your atonements and always, always, your hope for a happy ending.

I thought about Verity, and what she had said about me trying to escape from my own world. I could see little red Dorothy shoes running and running and running as the reel spun faster and faster. The shoes suddenly drained of colour and now they were running through old black-and-white footage. I could see Verity watching me as I ran. She sat on a *chaise longue* on the set of *Casablanca*, fixing a loop of pearls around Ingrid Bergman's neck. It was Laszlo's line, but it was her that stood up and looked me square in the eye as she told me that *if* I was trying to run away from myself I would never succeed. She took a drag from her long, slim cigarette and let the curls of smoke slip from her red lips.

'*Cut!*' the director roared, as the clapper-board crashed down.

I bolted upright as the meditation instructor clanged the bell to signal the end of the class.

'You okay?' Lisa asked, pulling me to my feet.

'Yeah, fine. I think I just . . . yeah. You?' I stumbled, trying to gather myself.

'Well, did you wish?' she questioned, looping my arm.

'Erm, I think I did. Did you?'

She had a distant look in her eyes as she smiled at me. 'I wished Miss Psychology hadn't eaten so much fibre. She was clearly asleep and farted her way through the whole class.'

'Oh, Jesus.'

'I know.'

'Lisa?'

'Yeah?'

'Did I fart?'

'I don't think so.'

'Phew.'

We were herded into our next class before I'd had time to collect my thoughts. They were escaping from me, like little butterflies through a net as I swooped to catch them.

That was the first time I had dreamed in ages. I wanted to savour it, commit it to some kind of meaning before it had slipped away entirely. It was the very first time I had dreamed since New York. For the past six weeks, whenever I laid my head on my pillow, all that crept in was a thick, heavy fog that wrestled with sleeplessness until it was time to get up again.

That had been the first dream. Or was it even a dream? I didn't think I'd fallen asleep. But perhaps neither had Miss Psychology with the high-fibre diet.

Whoa. *Whoa!* What the hell was going on in here? This was like some sort of creepy eighties porno set. Leopard-print rugs. Mirrors. Heart-shaped cushions. Candles. What was more, I was pretty sure that 'Touch Me (I Want Your Body)' by Samantha Fox was playing on the stereo.

*Creeeepy!*

I looked at Lisa. She seemed unconcerned. In fact, she was singing along.

Jesus.

Could we not just go back into the room with the stars for another snooze, please?

Fintan StarDust slithered in dressed in a new floor-length robe, this time a red satin dressing-gown. Holy shit! Mum and Dad would *kill* me if I ended up in a sleazy eighties porno movie! Honestly, when she saw me rewinding the sexy bit in *Dirty Dancing*, she'd told me she'd ground me for a week. And that was only last November!

'Okay, my little Star Gazers, welcome to the Big O,' he purred, folding onto the leopard-print rug.

The Big – *Oh My Fucking God!*

I must have been doing one of my famous silent screams, because Lisa took my hand and told me to relax. I only ever did them when I got a particularly bad shock, like when the girl behind the counter suddenly told you that your Favourite Foundation of All Time has been discontinued. Or when you handed a male cashier a tampon instead of your reward card because you've had a really, really long day and you're really, really tired.

'Relax,' Lisa counselled. 'Bet he's talking about Oprah. Bet we're getting her latest copy of *O* so we can sit down and read the inspirational bits about eating fruit and changing our lives together.'

I nodded, unconvinced.

'Take your seats, beautiful ones,' StarDust ordered. 'Under your heart cushions, you will each find a mirror. I ask you all to keep an open mind. Only when your mind is open can you be truly honest with yourself. Then, and only then, can your wishes come true.'

We picked up our mirrors slowly and sat down on the heart cushions. I gave him a dubious look and he gave me a condescending smirk.

'Now, lovelies, our elders have often let it be known that one of the times we are truly ourselves is during the act itself –'

Oh, no! No! *No!*

'– be it solo or a joined effort, so to speak. That's right, when we achieve the oh-yes.'

Oh, no!

'The Big O!'

Arrrgh! He was *not* talking about *Oprah* magazine!

'So now I invite you, with your mirrors, to take a closer look at "your tools", to help you to get to know yourself.'

Holy shitballs! Where had this come from? One minute it's all fairy-lights and wands and the next a creepy man in a red satin bathrobe is asking us to look at our bits in a hand mirror in a room full of strangers!

I bet they were filming this! I bet they were going to put it on the Internet and, yes, we'd be a massive YouTube hit but we'd all have to subsequently leave the country and live on a small under-populated island off Sweden and get extensive plastic surgery so no one would recognize us.

I must have been doing my silent scream again because Lisa took my hand.

No, no! Not another 'try and be grateful and get into this'. I couldn't. I had nothing left.

She leaned into me, looked me square in the eye and growled, 'Let's get the fuck out of here.'

The next few minutes were like a scene from *The Great Escape* with Lisa and me in the lead roles as Steve McQueen (me) and James Garner (Lisa).

We ran to our room to grab our bags. 'Quickly Squadron Leader!' I said. I told her I could feel something coming right behind us – *just like in the movie!* – as I threw all my stuff into my suitcase and slammed it shut.

'Huh?' Lisa asked. Hmm, she was a shit James Garner. I might consider recasting.

I was right! All of a sudden StarDust appeared at the door, brandishing a wand and a hand mirror, and Lisa screamed, '*RUUUUUUN!*' so we ran out of the front door, through the forest and up to the roadside where we collapsed with laughter and exhaustion.

A few minutes later we managed to hitch a lift from a passing farmer on a Massey Ferguson tractor who said he'd drop us into Killarney station. We climbed up onto the back of his trailer and I was told to hold his goat if I wanted a lift. I'd hold any man's goat if it meant I didn't have to pull down my pants and stare at my 'tools' in a hand mirror.

'Sorry, Grace,' Lisa puffed, still out of breath. 'What a crock of shite.'

'Don't be silly. It was . . . an experience.'

'Waste of time.' She sighed, patting the top of the goat's head.

'I dunno about that,' I contested. 'We choreographed all of "Dress You Up", and at least half of "Holiday".'

'Yeah. We did.'

'And you know? I don't think it was entirely a waste of time.'

'Really? Why? Apart from Madonna.'

'Well, despite myself, I think I might have figured something out in that meditation class.'

'No way!' she retorted, stunned. 'What?'

'I dunno, it's a bit weird, but maybe the wish thing came through a bit and, to be honest, I never thought I'd say this –'

'What? *What?*'

'I think I've changed my mind. It sort of all made sense and I think I've decided I'd like to go back to R –?'

'*Roh* . . .' Lisa was making a weird O-shaped mouth, like someone in a church choir. '*Roh* . . .' she went again, leadingly. What was she doing?

'*Ruuu* . . .' I corrected. '*Ruuu* . . . I'd like to go back to *run* Verity's shop! Lisa, I think I made a "Job Wish". Or something . . .'

She blinked at me furiously, trying to make sense of what I'd said. 'Who's Verity?' she asked eventually.

'Who's Verity?' the farmer asked, turning his head around.

And then the goat shat on Lisa's shoe.

## 28

When I got home I was so excited about my brand-new wish-related plan that I said hello to Bette and even attempted to pat her head. It was difficult because she was swiping her claws at me but I persisted. 'There, there, nice cat.'

I think confusion stopped her running to the shoe-rack and pissing in my peep-toes. I was so super-positive about the wish I had come up with at the Wish Factory that nothing could dampen my day. Maybe my shoes, but not my day! (Actually, if Bette pissed in my crystal-studded pumps, I was going to have to put her down.)

I wasn't sure what I was going to do exactly, what my *modus operandi* was or what I would say to Verity. Or what she would think of it. There would have to be a few ground rules, like 'No Being Mean' and 'No Being Judgy'. Here's hoping she wasn't sore about me running off in her 1940s original metal-hooped ballgown. People could be touchy about that sort of thing and you had to be careful.

But I had to try. I just *had* to try. Imagine I got to run *that* shop!

I had never run a shop before. I had never really run anything. Except a stall in my bedroom in '86 where I sold used birthday cards and old soap at a discounted rate to family members. I could put that in the shop's remit. I just knew Verity was a soap lady.

Oh, God, I just *had* to try! This was the first thing I'd felt really excited about in so long.

The bell went and, without too much thought, I skipped to the door and swung it open.

Tanya. Bugger!

'Tanya, Tanya, Tanya!' I said, enveloping her in a hug. 'You are

223

just the loveliest thing, aren't you? And Eoin and Milly! My favourite nephew and niece!' I leaned down to squeeze them both.

She looked so shocked I thought she was going to pass out, but she came to quickly, like the trooper she was. She was just great, wasn't she?

'Do come in, do come in,' I said, skipping down the hall like Julie Andrews.

'What the fuck is your problem?' she said, looking at me like I was a vest top from H&M. (Tanya shopped exclusively in Brown Thomas. She abhorred H&M vest tops. Called them 'the vermin of the high street'. Sometimes I hid them in her laundry basket to terrorize her, like when kids put spiders under a sibling's pillow.)

Milly handed me a drawing of a squashed hedgehog on the side of the road and Eoin gave me a soggy tissue dripping in snot.

Delightful, I thought, doing a little twirl. I was going to pin them both to the notice-board.

'Children, sit down and watch cartoons,' Tanya said. 'I have important things to discuss with your aunt. If you come in and interrupt us you will be eating cabbage for a week.' With that she fish-hooked my neck and reefed me into the kitchen.

See? What was not to like? She was *adorable*, my sister.

'Okay, enough. This is nonsense. You're freaking me out. What was Lisa thinking bringing you to a cult bullshit workshop? She should have known better. You are so impressionable. You always have been.'

'No, I haven't, you daft ninny,' I said merrily, smiling inanely. Be positive, Grace!

'You bought a dead goldfish off Ted Langan because he told you it'd come back to life, like Jesus.'

'I'd been reading a lot of *Bible Stories for Kids* at the time,' I said quietly. 'I was intrigued . . .'

'Did they "get" you? Have they hypnotized you? What's with all this Mary Poppins shit?'

'Tanya, look, it wasn't a cult. It was just a money-making scam where they wanted us to look at our vaginas in hand mirrors. But it's fine. We had some quiet meditation time down there and, you know, I think I might have figured –'

'What?' she screeched. I wished she wouldn't as it was having an awfully adverse effect on my positivity. Although I should have known better. You did not mention the word 'vagina' around Tanya. She cannot discuss either of her labours, or the first few days of either of her children's lives as they were far too vagina-y.

'Grace, I'm worried about you. What the hell is going on? You've just been drifting since before Christmas –'

'I know, I know, but I have a plan now. I know what I'm doing and it's going to be great.'

'Oh, thank God.' She sighed, plopping down on a chair at the kitchen table. 'Robbie. You've called Robbie. You're going to get married.'

Euch. It was like a punch in the solar plexus. The image of the engagement ring flashed in my head, mocking my new-found positivity.

'No,' I said, shaking my head. 'No, Tanya. It's nothing to do with Robbie.' I looked her dead in the eye. 'I want to run a shop. I'm going to see if I can run a shop!'

Silence.

Milly had poked her head around the kitchen door. 'Mummy, can we –'

'*Cabbage!*' Tanya said, not even looking at her. She scuttled off.

Shit. By the look of things I'd be eating cabbage for a year. I smiled tentatively.

'Jesus! Mum asked me if I thought you'd like to make rolls in the deli in Spar because apparently they were looking for someone but I told her no.'

'Tanya, listen. I won't be making rolls –'

'Did you go back to study an MA on top of your degree so you could put coleslaw in a bap?'

I'd love a coleslaw bap right now. 'No, no, listen to me. It's a *clothes* shop. A *vintage* clothes shop.'

She rolled her eyes.

'Oh, look, I shouldn't even be telling you this because I don't know if I'll be doing it . . .'

'What do you mean?'

Uh-oh. Should have lied about that one.

'I'm sorry, did you ask for tea?'

'No, I didn't,' she said. 'You don't even know if you'll be doing it? So another pipe-dream? Another fairy tale, is it?'

'No!' I said, angry with her for diluting my excitement and raining on my parade, like she always did.

'Grace, you're thirty in less than two months. Thirty!'

'Aarrrgh! I bloody know how old I am!'

'Look at Rebecca! She got married and is getting on with her life like a normal person. Here's you, faffing about the house all day, playing dress-up and looking at your vagina in a hand mirror!'

That's gas. Tanya said 'vagina'. That was massive. I'd have to tell Mum and Dad. They'd find it so funny. Either that or they wouldn't know what I was talking about and Dad'd suggest I try online dating again.

'Look, I know that turning thirty is a big deal. That's why I'm taking stock, deciding what I really want.'

'"What I really want". For crying out loud, Grace, can you hear yourself? You lot all watch far too much of *The Kardashians*. You all need to go and "find yourselves". Ha! Well, what you'll end up finding is that it's all passed you by.'

'I've never even seen one episode,' I said.

'Did you see Kourtney's black dress she wore to her birthday party?' she said, suddenly all girlie.

'I know!' I squealed. 'A-*maaazing*! But then again she can pull off anything –'

She shot me down with her victorious archy eyebrow.

Shit. Walked straight into that one.

'You're just afraid.' She sighed. God, I hated when she did that.

Like she had me all sewn up. Like the debate was already won. Like hers was always the only possible conclusion.

'What? I'm afraid of what exactly?'

Hmm. This would be good. Afraid to admit I'd done the wrong course? Afraid to admit that going back to college had been a complete waste of time? Afraid to admit this figure-hugging calf-length velvet number wasn't very Julie Andrews (admittedly it wasn't. I had been in such a tizzy of excitement when I'd got home that I'd managed to get today's dress code *all* wrong).

She picked at the nail varnish on her French manicure. 'Afraid to admit that perhaps what you actually want is a husband and some kids and a half-fulfilling way to earn a living. But you're scared of admitting it and sinking to the lowly level of the rest of us. You want the dream job and the dream romance and the dream life all played out to the sound of a fabulous orchestral MGM theme song. That's not real life, Grace.'

I watched as she picked and splintered the polish onto her lap.

'There isn't anything else for you. And I mean that in the nicest way possible.'

I could feel the anger gurgle in the pit of my stomach. 'Do you? Do you really, Tanya?' I spat.

I was a *grown woman*: how long was this going to go on for? Until I bowed in submission and just accepted a mediocre life? Go to school, go to college, meet a guy, date a guy, get a job, get engaged, get a house, get married, have kids; tick, tick, tick, tick, tick! Then what? *Then* what? Then perhaps join Tanya on the bench, next to Mum, and we could all sit there like three not-so-wise monkeys and gaze out on the rest of the world longingly as it continued to strive for something better.

'Do I what?' she said.

'Do you really mean that in the nicest way possible? Or are you so caught up in your own regrets you refuse to allow me to think it could be different?'

The words were out before I could even think of holding them back. And I stood in shock as they rang in my ears, like an ill-timed cluster-bomb of pent-up aggression.

I looked at Tanya, her obvious hurt piercing me. She *never* emoted. Not even when her favourite pink Ralph Lauren cashmere cardigan balled in the dry-cleaner's. For the first time since we were children, I thought she might cry. Her eyes were wide and glassy, her mouth open, no sound coming out.

'Tanya, I'm sorry. That was so incredibly out of line.'

My words sounded muffled, like the shell-shock silence after a bomb had dropped.

'I'm sure my drab little life could never be glamorous enough for you, but there's no need to belittle me.'

Her words sounded warped and muffled too, as if we were both under water. I wished I was: then I could feel weightless, float to the surface and not feel like I was sinking with the weight of my own heart. Tears swelled in my eyes. This was not the conversation I wanted us to be having. Ever.

'I'm sorry, Tanya. I just got defensive because you always seem to get so aggressive. I don't think your life is crappy. It just sometimes seems that you think that. All I'm saying is that I want the chance to become the woman I'd like to be, however silly and crazy and new age that may seem. But I promise not to use a hand mirror to look at my vagina for answers.'

A fleeting smile crossed her eyes. But it might also have been repulsion. I couldn't be sure.

'Right, so,' she said, steeling herself. 'And who is she when she's at home?'

'I don't know – someone strong, self-possessed. Like Grace Kelly or something. Just, you know . . . strong.'

'But you come from strong women. Mum is strong, I'm strong – Jesus, we both have to be.'

The tears were coming now and I couldn't stop them. 'But that's exactly it – I don't want to be strong like that.'

'Strong like what?'

'I don't want to just persevere, Tanya, to endure. I want to be fulfilled and happy and stand by my own convictions, and I don't think that should be an unthinkable thing to ask for.'

'Yeah, well, good luck with that,' she muttered, shaking her head. I could see her winding her vulnerability back in, like a fisherman reeling in a deficient catch before anyone else could see it. 'And, for the record, I didn't see Robbie Cotter standing in the way of you achieving any of that.'

I sank into a chair. This was draining every last bit of energy from my body. It was like digging up the grave every time and forcing me to stand there and look into it.

I swallowed hard, trying to be as measured as my sister.

'Tanya, I love you.'

'Oh, please, for the love of God, don't. You know I can't stand that shite –'

'*Stop it,*' I shouted in frustration. 'Just let me tell you this.'

She looked at me, stunned.

'Shut up and listen. You are an amazing woman. I know you're not as happy as you'd like to be, but you never complain because you're a great wife and a great mother. Apart from the cabbage threats.'

'If I don't, they run rings around me, you know.'

I smiled, stalling for a breath, hovering over my next words. 'I do admire Mum, despite everything that, well . . . that went on. But I could never do it that way, Tanya.'

'But Robbie would have never let that happen . . .'

'You have to let Robbie go,' I said firmly. 'I have.'

She looked at me sadly, and I felt every inch of her disappointment mirrored in my own.

'Some people need all their ducks in a row,' I continued, 'so they can sit back and look at them, all in a neat line, for the rest of their life. I don't feel that. I just want to have a good life. Whatever that involves. And however unconventional you think it is.'

I swallowed the lump in my throat. 'Tanya, I know we've never talked about this before, but maybe the reason you haven't got to where you want to be lies in the past – in how Mum and Dad were and are. But maybe also you could be happy with Peter. I think that your life has the potential to be fantastic.'

I could see her shoulders sagging. This was taking just as much out of her as it was me.

'I don't feel ready to talk about this stuff, Grace. But I do hear what you're saying. I'm going to get the kids and go home now, okay?'

I nodded. 'Are we . . . okay?'

She looked at me plaintively and gave me a weak smile. 'You're my little sister. Of course we're okay.'

## 29

The shop door was locked. I'd known it would be. I stared at the dusty 'Closed' sign hanging askew through the glass, and knocked again.

Nothing.

Was she in there? I squinted through the bevelled panels, but couldn't make out any shapes or movement. Perhaps she was in the bath. Waiting for her scones to brown.

I sat on the window ledge and waited. Well, it was more like half squatted in a slight perch because, I have discovered, it is near impossible to sit on a window ledge in a 1940s metal-hoop-skirted ballgown with a bustle and twelve layers of netting.

It was the only way I could transport the dress back to the shop: I had to wear it and get one of those wheelchair-accessible cabs. It didn't fit into any of my 'bags for life', even the extra large ones for the 'big shops'. So I'd had to get into it, pull the stays as tight as I could so it was reasonably snug, and throw a cloak over it. Even for me, this was pushing it a little. There were more panto jibes. As soon as I got out of the cab, someone asked me if I had found my sheep yet, and I even got egged by a swarm of schoolboys on their lunch break.

But I was undeterred: this was just how committed I was. And I would wait for hours if that was what it took.

Oh, God, I was bored. How long had I been there? I was going to die of boredom. I was starving and cold and my bum was numb from the metal rods . . .

Four minutes. Whoa, Grace, that was not good. I needed to remind myself never to go on a pilgrimage to Knock. Or work in a science lab that took years to discover cures for diseases.

I sighed. How long was this going to take? The net curtain on the window over the street twitched and I could see the frame of a tall man hovering behind it.

It was the sleazy man, peering at me again! I leaned forward, straining my eyes to get a closer look at him, but he had moved away. I'm sure he thought it was great fun to perv on the lady in the oversized Little Bo Peep outfit who'd had her knickers on show only last week.

I flipped the net curtain the birdie again. Just in case he was still looking. Just in case he thought he could mess with the lady in fancy dress who had had her skirt up over her head. People can be so strange, I thought, adjusting my ballgown.

Seven more days passed (three minutes), when I whipped my eyes down to the 'Welcome' mat where I could hear a faint scratching noise. A small envelope was being shunted out from behind the door. I plopped down off the ledge and sashayed over. I would have jumped and run, but you have to moderate your movements when you're wearing a 1940s metal-hoop-skirted ballgown with a bustle and twelve layers of netting.

A gold-embossed envelope with 'Alice' scrawled on the front poked out from under the door.

Hmm. Curiouser and curiouser.

I opened it, holding my breath. Please don't say, 'Remove my dress immediately and go home in your crappy flesh-coloured granny pants, you silly girl' (not that Verity would have known that I'd just put on a wash and was running low on the pants front).

Oh, *please*, don't let her say that!

*Alice. I see you have returned in my dress. It is a special one you know and I'm glad to have it back. If you can manage not to run away for five minutes, you can come in and have another crack at the tea party if you so desire.*

*Best Wishes*
*Vintage Verity*

I folded the note back inside the envelope. Okay, so I wouldn't be getting the 114 home in my flesh-coloured granny pants. That was good. But what now?

She was intriguing. That made it all the more magical, I thought, as I turned the door knob and stepped inside.

And there she was. Standing in front of the art-deco-style full-length mirror, a scone in one hand (I *knew* it!) and an emerald drop earring in the other.

She turned to me, eyeing me intently, trying to process me again, calculate me, figure me out. I attempted my Marlene Dietrich enigmatic face, and raised one eyebrow languorously, hoping it would shield me from her forensic scrutiny.

'Are you going to be sick, Alice?' she asked, raising an eyebrow of her own. Fine. So my enigmatic face needed work. No biggie.

'Well . . .' I started nervously '. . . here's your dress back. I got egged. Sorry. Most of it went on my face and into my mouth, though. I thought I was going to vomit for a while but I'm okay now. But I'll still leave you a fifty for the dry-cleaning 'cause there's a bit on this sleeve right here . . .'

She kept her eyes on me, the same impenetrable gaze. 'Uh-huh,' she said, in her sing-song drawl.

Oh, she was so fantastic! Like a *bona fide* heroine that had just rocked up on the back of Errol Flynn's horse outside a saloon (albeit in a grey woollen two-piece and in need of a hip replacement).

'Do you like these earrings?' she purred, holding the dangling emerald up to her face.

'I do. They look just like Liz Taylor's!'

'You know your stuff, Alice, I'll give you that.' She turned to the mirror to study the earring next to her face and mumbled to herself, 'Clearly they're a mock-up. There was no way she could have given me the real ones. Richard would have *murdered* her . . .'

What was she saying? That Liz Taylor gave her a mock-up set because Richard Burton would have murdered her if she'd given

Verity the real ones? Ah, yes. My granny comes out with all sorts of mad stuff too. Only last week, while pruning her azaleas, she tried to convince me she was a trained spy and could hide in a Ryanair carry-on wheelie-bag.

'Verity,' I said, steeling myself. Come on, Grace, it was now or never! No time like the present! Do what you came here to do! Out with it!

'Yes?' she said, looking at me over her shoulder in the mirror.

'Uh, I, er . . .' Jesus, come on, Grace! Get on with it! I could see Tanya in my mind's eye, shaking her head. Robbie walking away from me in Central Park. Eleanor Holt firing my ass. My empty, still house. My empty, still heart. While all the while I was running, running, running through the quicksand of all the disappointments. I closed my eyes and fisted my hands.

Grab it! Grab something. Stop sinking! Stop chasing! Grab on to something. Grab it now!

'I want to run your shop!' I said suddenly, the words exploding out of me, like a fireworks display.

There!

Phew.

I cleared my throat, trying to dispel the deathly silence that had now fallen on the room. I fidgeted with my hair. I coughed again. God, I sounded like one of the consumptives in *Angela's Ashes*. I fixed the bow on the front of my dress.

'I'm sorry?' she said finally, after a fourteen-hour-long impasse. (Okay, fifteen seconds is possibly a fair guess.)

'Yes, well, I sort of had a big think after our little . . . Ahem, ahem . . .' (God, Grace, stop coughing! Verity would not let someone work in her shop if she thought they had consumption. She was ancient. She knew all about consumption.)

'Our . . . tête-à-tête?' she said.

'Yes, that. The very thing . . . You see, I went to this Wish Factory place that was very strange altogether and they even tried to get us to look at our – Oh, you don't need to know that part . . . But I did this meditation class and, well, all these things came into

234

my head without me even trying, really, and then it made me think that maybe I had wished for them you see . . . for, you know, clarity. And then on the tractor home with the goat that shat on Lisa's foot, it suddenly hit me. This is what I want to do! I want to run your shop!'

'Riiiight,' she said. 'But this is my shop.'

'Oh, I know. Exactly. I mean *help* you run it. There's just so much possibility here! This place could be a gold mine if you wanted it to be, but it's all just locked away, hidden . . .' I trailed off. The last thing I wanted was to come across as condescending. 'That is, I'd love to help you if you wanted me to. If . . . if you'd let me . . . ?'

'No,' she said brusquely, turning back to face her own reflection. 'I don't want you to.'

Oh.

Okay.

I could feel my heart tumble to my boots, like a free-falling lift.

Looked like I'd be making coleslaw baps after all. Perhaps it wouldn't be so bad. And maybe Bette and I would make friends and by the time I'd finally got out of the fog of my own head, and every eligible man in Ireland was taken, Norman would marry me. And we could put on our wash-loads together and save electricity.

See? Every cloud had a silver lining. And, you know, I could get my Hollywood wax done and maybe Norman was a man for the tidy bikini line . . .

Oh, Jesus. I felt a bit sick at that thought. I could taste the egg repeating on me.

My lower lip started to wobble. And then, all of a sudden, Verity's relentless gaze was on me once again, like a giant flood-lit magnifying lens.

I flicked her my insouciant eyebrow, trying anything I could to shield myself from the glare by attempting to look aloof and unconcerned.

Ha! I thought. I will marry Norman and make coleslaw rolls and save electricity, thank you very much! So there!

(Was it working?)

'If you really want a Dietrich eyebrow, you'll have to shave off your own and draw a thin semi-circle higher up your forehead.'

(That'd be a no, then.)

How did she do that? How did she *know* what I was thinking?

The corners of her mouth curled slightly and I could see her enjoying a memory. 'Marly always said she had sacrificed two eyebrows for a movie career.' She lifted her piercing sapphire eyes to me. 'They can look good with a veiled cloche hat, you know.'

She plucked a small hat off a mannequin and placed it on my head.

'Gosh, that looks just like the one she wore in *Shanghai Express*!' I piped.

'Shall I get the razor? Whip those brows right off? We can have you looking like Marlene in no time, if that's what you really want.'

I blanched, knowing all too well where she was going with this. 'Well, who are you trying to be, then?' I scoffed defensively, indicating her amazing two-piece grey woollen suit and yellow silk neck-tie, her white spun silk hair looped into an immaculate bun on the top of her head. And her casual scone-holding.

'No one,' she answered frankly. 'This *is* me. These are my clothes. From the time in my life I was happiest. There. Simple as that. I'm not trying to *be* anyone.'

I felt my resolve drain away. I didn't know what I was talking about. Of course I didn't. I didn't really know this world at all. It was just pretend for me. The whole bloody lot of it. Why would *she* need *my* help?

I shuffled uncomfortably, feeling stupid and unearthed and frustrated all over again. So much for my stupid bloody wish and the stupid bloody Wish Factory. I wanted to turn and make a run for it, sit at home, put on *The Scarlet Empress* and mime all the words. *So what if I wanted that?*

I flinched, unsure of my next move. If I ran, she was right.

Verity *was* right. I did keep running. Running from one disguise to another.

I steeled myself, looking her straight in the eye. Why was it exactly that I was here?

Suddenly it was as if I was having an out-of-body experience. I saw myself standing in the middle of this strange yet familiar world in a huge pink ballgown. With an arched eyebrow. Well, here goes nothing, I thought, staring at myself.

I heard the words pour out of my mouth. I felt cut off from them, as if the usual me was on mute and my lines were being dubbed.

'I . . . I have always dressed up. Always watched old movies. Because it's always been my escape. The old films had no parallels to my own world – the arguing, the resentment, the bitterness, the disappointment. They were exciting, glamorous, full of mystery and enchantment. And by simply turning up the volume, I could block out all the noise.'

She looked at me, absorbing my words calmly, like she already knew.

But how could she? I'd never said those things to a living soul. Even myself.

'It's all very well and good to play dress-up, my dear,' she said carefully. 'Everyone loves to indulge. To dream. To embellish. To accessorize. But so long as you know who you are when the costume comes off . . .'

Jesus! (Not Jesus as that's who I thought I was when the costume came off. But just, *Jesus*!)

'You really don't want to think about the possibility of me coming on board to help you with the shop?' I said one last time, thinking I had absolutely nothing left to lose. 'I've just done an MA in creative business and I really think, you know, with some clever consideration, we could make a strong business out of this.'

'No!' she said, interrupting me. '"It's all about the money now!"'

I very nearly burst into the Jessie J song, but I knew that was absolutely not going to help matters, so I sang it in my head instead.

'All you Celtic Tiger Leopards, you'll never change your spots. It's not all about chintz and glitter and greed. It's about quality and appreciation. And that should mean something,' she said, turning away. 'All these social climbers coming in and cawing at my things like avaricious magpies. Just wanting more, more, more. With no respect or real consideration.'

'I agree,' I started. 'I do. But it was you who was just telling me I had to live in the real world. I'd love to sit at home all day in the amazing Valentino dress I found at a fair in Dun Laoghaire last June and appreciate the true art of Hepburn, but I also have to pay my bills and be accountable. And I think I might be getting psoriasis from only eating cereal because I can't really afford to buy anything else. See my elbow there? Actually, no, it's okay, you probably don't need to see it. Psoriasis is really not the point.'

'Oh, good, I'm glad. 'Twould be a shame if the point of all "this",' she said, indicating my dress, her shop, her world, 'was a flaky skin condition.'

'What is the point of all of *this*, then?' I challenged, squaring up to her, wanting a tiny bit of honesty from her in exchange for having bared my own soul.

'None of your Goddamn business,' she said.

She'd said that last time we met. 'You can't just keep saying that, Verity,' I said, well aware I was in serious danger of overstepping both the mark and my welcome. 'You keep telling me all I do is run. But it seems to me all you do is hide. You hide out in here, locked away in the past because you're convinced you were happier then. Convinced also that no one else will understand. Why don't you give someone the benefit of knowing what you know? Sure the finished effect may be a little different, but that's not to say the principles behind the tailoring aren't the same.'

She blinked back at me and, behind her impervious glare, I could almost detect shock.

'From what I can see here, you lived in a very exciting world with some pretty amazing things. But they're all just props on a stage when the curtain's dropped and the players have gone home, if no one is allowed to breathe some life into them.'

She held my gaze, her navy blue eyes smouldering from across the room. Who was this woman? Why was she here, in Dublin, with the most explosive arsenal of vintage wares I had ever seen in my life?

'I know you say you were happiest then. But there's not a lot you can do about that now,' I said gently. 'If that was Verity then, who is Verity *now*?'

The moment was broken by a sharp rap on the window. We looked to the door, almost in slow motion. The knob twisted. Nothing. It was locked. Like it always was. Another knock.

I looked back to Verity.

'Well, then,' she said, 'are you going to stand around here all day with egg on your face or are you going to show me what you've actually got?'

Holy shit! Really?

*Really!*

My heart started hammering wildly in my chest. I looked to her again for confirmation. She nodded blithely, shrugging her shoulders and taking a seat in her large leather armchair. The 'casting couch' (well, hopefully not – I mean Verity was lovely and all but she really wasn't my type).

Mother of God, this felt like the biggest audition of my life.

I inched over to the door and unlocked it, hoping to God it was someone looking for a dress and not just the postman. I knew my stuff, but there was honestly only so much I could do with a postman.

It wasn't the postman.

Phew.

A diminutive lady in her late thirties dressed in jeans and a parka jacket stood outside.

'Hi,' she said, in a small voice. 'Is this . . . Oh, I thought this was a – a dress shop?'

239

'It is.'

'I'm – I'm not looking for fancy dress,' she said apologetically.

Okay. I *seriously* needed to get out of this dress.

'No, no,' I assured her, terrified she'd go away and take my golden opportunity with her. 'You've come to the right place. It's a vintage clothes shop.'

I opened the door wider so she could see in, knowing that when she did, she couldn't help but be hypnotized.

'Wow!' she cooed. 'It's amazing! I'd heard it was, but this . . .'

'Come in!' I said, looking to Verity nervously. She was surveying us like she was savouring a familiar scene from a movie she hadn't seen in a while.

I let the customer explore the shop, discovering what was in there and letting her process it for herself first. Pushy shop assistants were the nadir of retail, in my opinion.

'Do you have any idea what you're looking for?' I asked, taking my cue when she eventually stalled and eyed me for some help. 'Do you need something for a particular occasion or is it just for a little treat you think you might deserve?'

'Em, well, it's for my anniversary. Ten years. I can't believe it's that long,' she said, trying a smile. 'We . . . Well, he's booked a really nice restaurant and I think maybe we'll be staying in a fancy hotel in town. I don't normally dress up. I don't want to make a statement as such – I don't want to look showy . . . but I want to look . . . special.'

I surveyed her furtively. Simple clothing. Plain colours. Flat shoes. No jewellery except a simple gold wedding band. This was a woman who would feel like a fraud in anything ostentatious. I unhooked a simple cream shift with a sleeve to the elbow and a soft cowl neck. It was stunning in its simplicity and I knew it would be perfect.

She gasped as she touched it.

'Maybe this would be a nice subtle throwback to your wedding day, without making too much of a statement, of course,' I said.

She nodded enthusiastically, swallowing her emotion, and it

was then I saw that there was more to this story than she was divulging.

'I don't know why I'm telling you this but . . . we – we've had a tough few years. It's been both our fault, really. It's beyond placing blame now. I just want him to remember me before it all got derailed.'

I nodded, feeling a sudden rush of emotion. The back of my throat felt strained as I tried to swallow back the tears. 'Why don't you try it on?' I coughed, clearing my throat.

'Do you think it would suit me?' she asked hopefully.

'Shit, yes!' I said.

Oops. 'Sorry,' I said. 'Just got a little excited for you.'

She took the dress and went behind the screen to change.

I didn't look back at Verity once. There was no middle ground here. I was either in or I was out and my job wasn't done yet. I could feel her silent presence behind me as we waited. Come on, dress, work! It had to. I just knew it!

When the lady finally stepped out from behind the screen, I could practically see the excitement pulsating from her. She looked exquisite. She looked like herself, but confident, radiant, full of promise.

'What do you think?' she said.

'What do *you* think?' I turned her to face the mirror.

The way she smiled at herself made my day, and I was insanely close to asking her if I could come along to the dinner, maybe hide in the kitchen to see how things were going. But I was *almost* certain that would scare her off, so I didn't.

'It's perfect.' She beamed. 'I'll take it!'

'No! Marilyn! You can't!' Verity bellowed from behind me.

What in the name of –? Had she gone nuts again? And who the hell was Marilyn? Monroe? Oh, merciful hour, she wasn't going to start on about Liz Taylor and Richard Burton again, was she?

'You can't take it!'

I thought the lady was about to start crying with the disappointment, followed closely by me. We both blinked at Verity, wondering what the last ten minutes had been about if she wasn't allowed to take the blessed thing.

'You can borrow it,' Verity said, after she'd caught her breath. 'My things aren't for sale. I'm sorry, they're too valuable. You may rent the dress, if that's what you wish. But you have to bring it back.'

I looked at the lady. She nodded, delighted.

After she'd left and the door had clicked shut behind her, I looked at Verity. Well? I thought impatiently. What was it to be?

She sat in her armchair, silently rearranging a case of earrings.

'When a woman like that walks into a shop like this, she's usually looking for more than just clothes. There's always a story, and you have to be the right person to hear it.' Was I the right person? Was I?

'Welcome to "Best Wishes", Alice,' she said, lifting her eyes to me.

Sweet Jesus! Really?

*Yes!* Oh, my God, I did it! *I did it!*

'Erm, Verity?' I said. 'It's actually Grace. My name is Grace.'

'Well, Grace,' she said, smiling for the first time since I'd met her, 'it's nice to finally meet you.'

I couldn't remember the last time I'd felt so happy. So light. So giddy. So charged.

How wonderful to taste a steak when all you'd been living on was empty, unsatisfying calories. Verity and Best Wishes were like the finest cut of *filet mignon*, drizzled with a perfect rich red wine *jus*, offered to me, while I read the September issue of *Vogue*, by Antony Worrall Thompson (but only if he hadn't nicked it from Tesco). It beat cereal any day of the week.

This was fantastic, I thought, as I skipped out of the shop, just fantastic. I had a job. A *real* job. I was like the Pinocchio of the employment world, the master of my own dance.

I clocked the netted window on the other side of the street and bounded straight over to it. I wasn't sure why but all of a sudden I found myself banging on the glass and shouting, 'Ha, you perverted Perv Man, I have a job! Perv on that!' before skipping down the cobbled road, like Pinocchio himself, the strings finally cut.

I wanted to tell Mum and Dad. Tell Tanya. Tell them I wasn't going to feel so lost and sad and confused any more. And, most importantly, to believe it myself.

'Lisa?' I said, into the phone. 'You by any chance free to meet me in, say, the next forty-five to sixty seconds for a mojito?'

'I thought you'd never ask,' she said.

We met in the foyer of the Shelbourne, the place we reserved for when one of us was feeling particularly pleased with ourselves. (Except last time Lisa took a complete liberty and arranged a meeting when she had finally completed level three of Angry Birds on the medium difficulty setting on her iPhone. Personally,

I think that was more of a gin-and-tonic-in-O'Donoghue's occasion.)

'I wish Rebecca was here,' Lisa said, when she saw me.

'That's how I like to be greeted, all right,' I answered, 'by someone wishing I was someone else.'

She smiled. 'You know what I mean.'

I did. Rebecca always met us here too. And she always had one too many cosmos and tried to play Kelly Clarkson on the piano in the Lord Mayor's Lounge. She loved a bit of Kelly Clarkson. The businessmen in their Boss suits discussing the Dow Jones usually didn't. But that was what made it entertaining.

'I miss her,' Lisa said dolefully. 'Everyone is gone, it seems. Rebecca and Tony. Ro –' She caught herself mid-word and looked at me.

'Lisa,' I implored, 'please don't . . .'

'No, no,' she backtracked, 'I was talking about Robbie Williams. He's gone from Take That again. He can never make up his mind, that one. I wasn't talking about . . . you know. So get over yourself,' she said, and linked my arm.

'Hey. Have you heard anything about Robbie seeing a girl who sort of looks like Jennifer Garner? Just out of interest . . .'

'Come on, there's no way he's seeing someone who looks like anyone if he's living with Alan-the-perv! There'd be a *million* girls coming and go – Oh, Jesus. I didn't mean that. Maybe he is seeing the Jennifer Garner woman. Oh, Jesus. I didn't mean that either!'

'It's okay.' I shrugged, ignoring the high-pitched horror scream inside my head. 'None of my business anyway.'

'Nice outfit,' she said, attempting to sidestep the elephant in the room that was so large she was sure to dislocate her hip.

'Isn't it? Isn't it honestly one of the most fantastic things you've ever seen in your entire life?'

'Well, Machu Picchu was pretty fantastic . . .'

'Yeah, it was, wasn't it?'

'And Phuket. I liked Phuket a lot.'

'Hmm.' I considered. 'I see where you're going here, all right.'

'But don't get me wrong, that outfit is lovely . . .'

'It is a bit lovely, isn't it?' I agreed, beaming.

I was about to leave the shop in the pink ballgown again when Verity stopped me and told me it was about time I gave her Debbie's dress back.

'The film wasn't called *The King and Grace*, you know, kid,' she said, unzipping me there and then with the dexterity of a professional dresser, one who knew the complexity of the hooks and eyes, the intricate corsetry. But she did it without so much as stalling, like it was the native language of her hands and she was speaking it fluently.

'Don't get your shoes caught in the netting. You don't want to give yourself a "Debbie Scar" when you fall flat on your chin,' she said, holding the metal hoops while I stepped from it gingerly.

I narrowed my eyes at her. Debbie Reynolds? Hmm. I'd have to get used to all this crazy talk if I was going to be working with her. I suppose it was more entertaining than Gran's story of the time she hid in a tumble-drier for three days.

She let me take a tidy little pink tea-dress and a cropped woollen blazer to go home in.

'Have the hat,' she said, referring to the Marlene Dietrich-style one I'd tried on earlier. 'You've earned it. Just remember to bring them back. I need them all back.'

'"Glamour is what I sell. It's my stock in trade,"' I said, tipping my hat and winking at her, knowing she'd appreciate the words of the great star.

And then I left, finding it impossible not to have seen the sadness and reminiscence in her eyes, like a match that'd flared briefly and gone out.

'So why are we here?' Lisa said, tamping down the fresh mint in the glass with her straw. 'Did Bette get run over?'

'Nah.' I sighed. 'I wish. But on that subject, speaking of wishes – I know we thought it was a load of old nonsense but, Leese, it came true! My wish came true!'

'No way!' she said. 'You've . . . *grown?*'

Huh?

'Huh?' I said, baffled.

'You said you wanted to be a bit taller? And a baller?'

'Oh, no! God, no! I have not grown. And I am also not a pro basketball player either. The other one, the *real* wish.'

'Oh!' she said. 'The shop!'

'Yes!'

'No!'

'Yes!'

'Oh, Grace, that is so fantastic! I'm so proud of you.' She hugged me for an age. Clutching me to her like a life-jacket. And I could feel her vulnerability, like a sheet of sugar glass in my arms. Something wasn't right.

'You okay, Leese?'

She nodded.

'So, then, what about your wish?' I asked, trying to change the subject if she didn't want to talk about it. 'Has it come true? What you wished for?'

She lifted her dark brown eyes to me and shook her head silently. 'The opposite, actually,' she said. 'Oh, God, Grace, something's wrong.'

'What? What?' I said in a panic. 'Is it Killian? Is it work? Did the television-licence man call? You told me you were going to pay it and they've heard all the excuses and *none* of them work!'

'No. God, no. Killian is great. And work. And I did pay the licence fee. It's me. I think there might be something . . . wrong with me.'

I could feel the blood drain from my face. 'Well, we all know that,' I said, wanting it to go away. She couldn't be saying this. There could *not* be something wrong with Lisa. This only happened in movies. Bad, shit, horrible ones.

'Grace,' she said, 'I've been having pains. Sort of like period pains but worse. At first I thought it was that Lego tree I swallowed as a child finally dislodging from my gut.' She laughed nervously.

'You swallowed a Lego tree?'

'Yep. My brother was annoying me and I didn't want him to have it, so I swallowed it. I'm convinced it's still trapped in my small intestine.'

'But it wasn't the Lego tree?'

'No. At first they weren't sure what it was. I got a load of tests done and they thought it might be endometriosis . . .'

'But it wasn't?' I said, my nerves piquing through my body.

'No, it wasn't. I mean, Grace, they still don't know for sure, and I have to go back for more tests, but they have warned me . . .'

'Warned you what?' I said, spitting out the words like they were indigestible pips.

'That it might . . . Grace, it might be cancer.'

Suddenly there was no air in the room, her words slowly slinking around my neck and choking me until I couldn't breathe.

No. No. No!

'Hey, I know it's going to be okay,' she said, taking my hand and smiling.

Why was she the one comforting *me*? I needed to comfort *her*. Promise her everything was going to be okay. Tell her she was going to be all right.

But I couldn't speak.

I chased around my head for the right words but they eluded me, slipping through my fingers and scarpering before I could grab a proper hold of them.

At least she'd come to me. At least she'd told someone.

'Bec knows,' she said, circling the rim of her cocktail glass with her finger, 'but I told her not to worry, that I was going to be okay. She asked me why the two of us had decided to have major life crises as soon as she buggered off out of the country.' She smiled valiantly, but her big eyes gave the game away as they swam with uncertainty.

Bec knew. She'd already told Bec and Bec wasn't even here. As childish and selfish as I knew it was, I couldn't help the flare of jealousy I felt.

She'd gone to Rebecca first.

I sat there quietly, digesting it all. And the fact that if I had to choose between Rebecca and me, I'd probably choose her too.

Perhaps our friendship had become a little unbalanced lately. Lisa was always coming to my rescue, armed with love, support, advice. And Sauvignon Blanc. And I just soaked it all up. Like it was a divine right rather than a privilege.

Now that we were getting older, hitting thirty, shedding our skins of naïve youth, there were going to be times when the real world would try to kick the shit out of us. We had to be ready for it. Ready to fight back. And, my God, it was better to go out there with your own little army gathered around you than stand and fight all on your own.

'Lisa.' I grabbed her hands in mine and held them as tight as I could, trying to transfer every shred of strength I had in me to her. 'It's going to be okay. I promise this is going to be okay.'

## 31

Working at Best Wishes could not have come at a better time. If I'd had to sit at home and contemplate my life, my lost love and my best friend possibly having cancer, I might well have gone and shaved my head. I'm not sure why exactly but Britney Spears did that when she felt overwhelmed and now, for the first time ever, I could relate to her. I couldn't when she wore those velour tracksuits, or that red PVC catsuit in her 'Oops I Did It Again' video. But now? Now I could.

If Lisa lost her hair, I'd decided I'd shave my head as well 'in cahoots'. (Maybe that wasn't the correct term, but you'll have to forgive me: did I mention that my friend might have cancer?)

There were a million hats in the shop we could wear while it was growing back, I thought, as I picked through a new consignment. Where was Verity getting this stuff? If we were going into business together, she really was going to have to stop being so vague about where she got her supplies and saying things like 'Oh, they're just from a few old contacts . . .'

I'd told Lisa I was going to be by her side for all of it, and that was exactly what I was going to do, starting with her MRI scan.

At the hospital, they told me I wasn't allowed to squeeze into the scanner beside her so I had to get off it.

'This isn't Funderland,' they said.

'Well, certainly not with that attitude,' Lisa said.

I even heard one of the nurses ask the other if she thought I was a simpleton, which was massively unfair. I'd made a promise, that was all.

I watched from outside as she was slowly pushed into the narrow, claustrophobic tunnel. How on earth had I thought I was ever going to squeeze in there too? Even if I was to 'bunk down really low'. Sitting outside the ominous contraption, I read *Jane Eyre* aloud to her as best I could over the noisy drone of the machinery. Her favourite.

The weight in my heart pulled at my lungs.

'Hey, if you're not careful, you're going to fall right in there and I'll be hauling your tushie all the way back from 1942.'

'Oh, sorry,' I said, coming out of my trance and springing out of the large cardboard box in the middle of the shop floor.

'What's on your mind, kid?'

'Oh, you know, nothing. The European bailout and stuff.'

I didn't want to tell Verity about Lisa. She already knew enough of my woes. The crazy-ass family that had forced me into a life of escapism. The cat that wanted to kill me. The fact that I had had a very recent relationship breakdown. And that I was afraid to flush the loo in my own upstairs bathroom. That was enough baggage for now, I figured. I'd only been there two weeks.

'What, oh, what are the ECB going to do?' I said, shaking my head and rifling through the clothes.

'You thinking about that boy of yours?'

There she went again. She was like a dog with a bone, or 'Elizabeth Taylor with the Hope Diamond', as she liked to put it.

'Mario Draghi? Well, yes, actually. I mean, what is he going to do about Greece?'

'Grace!'

'*Greece!*' I said, playing dumb. That woman was obsessed with quizzing me about my love life. Or lack thereof.

In fairness, I was relieved she hadn't passed out on the floor and called for the paddles because – shock, horror – I had 'no prospective suitors on the horizon' at the age of – shock, horror again – almost thirty. It was such a pleasant change. But it didn't mean she wasn't digging around any opportunity she got. I put it down to her sharing my love affair with the Golden Era of movies and old-fashioned romance.

I lifted a gorgeous plum fedora out of the box and placed it on my head in an attempt to divert the questioning. 'Where did you get this beauty?'

She narrowed her eyes and looked at the hat, like a bull studying a matador's cape.

'I don't care what you do with that load of old cobble,' she said. 'You can put it in the skip for all I care.'

'What? Verity? But it's amazing!' I said, and went back to the box of goodies that had just been delivered by the postman. I pulled out another hat. 'Look, this one is the absolute ringer for Molly Keats's hat in *The Whistling Wind*!' I put it on for good measure and did a little twirl around the coat rail. '"My, my, my, will you look who just came back into town, all spruced up in his silver grey Cadillac. Why it's the same Goddamn fool who rode out of here on horseback with my own heart slung over his meat-neck shoulder!"'

'Ha!' she said. 'Looks better on you than it did on her. Strange-shaped head, that one. To go with her strange everything else. And "Goddamn fool" . . . Well, you can say that again,' she added, under her breath.

I looked at her quizzically. She had never spoken in any way disparagingly about any of her 'darlings'. What on earth did she have against Molly Keats?

'I always loved Molly Keats!' I said. 'She was so beautiful and funny, and . . .'

Well, holy Jesus, had I just raised the red flag! And this bull was charging straight for me!

'Funny?' she snorted. 'Only thing funny about her was that face after twenty years of plastic surgery. Only time you'll see me going under the knife will be for my autopsy and that ain't no word of a lie. Only talent that girl had was spinning people's lives around like a dreidel at a Hanukkah party. If she had her career all over, she'd land nothing but a part in *Jersey Shore*. Or a sex tape. Now, that would be perfect casting. Bette Davis said the only leading man Joan Crawford never slept with at MGM was Lassie. Well, Bette sure as hell never came across Molly Keats!'

Whoa. Whoa! *Whoa!*

Hold up just a second. I could not believe what I was hearing. Verity watched *Jersey Shore*? Really?

'Molly "Snooki" Keats,' she huffed, sitting back down in her armchair.

Wow. Touchy subject obviously. (But *Jersey Shore*? *Really*?)

'So what happened to your boy, then?' she asked, trying to divert attention back to me, though anger still swam in her voice. 'Did he get "Mollycoddled", as I like to call it?'

'What's that?' I was nearly afraid to ask.

'It's when some stuck-up lady tramp nestles into your relation-ship like a virus until she's eventually brought your man down.' She rolled her eyes in fury. 'That was the only story Hedda Hop-per chose to write about for a week, even when Ava Gardner ran away to the Copacabana Palace Hotel to get away from Old Blue Eyes.'

Wowsa. She was still livid! Did they really have gossip columns back in the day? Gas. I mean sure, I got annoyed when Ashley Cole did the dirt on Cheryl, but I can't imagine I'm going to lose too much sleep over it in fifty-five years' time.

'So did he? Did he get Mollycoddled, then?' she said.

'Well, no,' I answered. 'I sort of ended it, really.'

'You fell in love with another boy?'

'No. I just . . . Well, we . . . Anyway . . . No.'

I really did not want to be diving into all this with the gusto of Michael Phelps in that Head and Shoulders advert. What was the point? I had enough to be worrying about and I really needed to get all this floor stock sorted into either 'eras' or 'occasions', I couldn't decide which. Should it be separated into 1930s, 1940s, 1950s or 'Black Tie', 'Formal', 'Tea Party', 'Wedding', 'Smart', 'Casual'? I *loved* the haphazard way it was currently all jumbled together: it was like opening the lid on a child's box of higgledy-piggledy magical toys. But there was no order to it and it might be a bit off-putting if you were a customer new to the game. It just didn't look businesslike. And that was what we were attempting to make this, after all – a business. It excited me as much as it terrified me.

I'd gone to the lectures, read the notes, had countless cappuccinos in the college cafeteria, nodded along in a charade of comprehension in the tutorials, as if I was Steve Jobs himself. And then completed the exams like Ferris Bueller. But I'd passed. And now here I was: 'in business'.

Gulp.

How exactly were we going to make a business out of this? I'd come to understand that there was no way on earth Verity was actually going to sell anything. I hadn't read *Trump: The Art of the Deal* from cover to cover. (Are you kidding me? I'd read *Grazia* from cover to cover during the lecture. One is boring, the other is not; I did the maths on that one, even though I was studying business – but that's me, multi-tasker *extraordinaire*.) So I never *actually* read it, but I'm pretty sure 'not selling anything' is a less than ideal way to start the old commerce ball rolling.

After much discussion Donald Trump over there, in the fabulous olive green trouser suit but without the comb-over, decided she could live with a rentals system, explaining that she could not part permanently with *any* of her stock. She was like a territorial black swan, squawking furiously around her brood of cygnets. And that was one bird I did not want to have a run-in with!

I suggested buying in some cheaper vintage stock that we could perhaps sell in conjunction with the rentals, but she warned me that under no circumstances was she ever going to preside over any 'ersatz attempts at tawdry substitution for the real deal'. (I got the gist of that, although I was definitely going to have to look up 'ersatz' in the dictionary when I got home.)

She also said she would do it only if the clothes would 'help someone discover something wonderful in themselves', and if we made money off the back of it, then so be it.

This was not the business model I took to my mortgage broker when I informed him of my new employment, all the while begging him not to send me back to live with my parents because I was already a few months in arrears: I would 'surely die within days'. Jim Manahan thinks I'm a bit of a drama queen. But I can tell you now that when someone casually calibrates the variables on changing around your mortgage terms, I personally do not consider it unthinkable that one might grab said mortgage broker's tie and start screaming like Mia Farrow in *Rosemary's Baby*.

Verity had started leaving the door unlocked, which was major progress. Even if her own personal circumspection was still very much under lock and key. Okay. I knew I'd rattled it somewhat. Like a trespasser with a coat hanger. But it would take time. She'd spent the last twenty years hiding in the shadows of her old life. There were so many things I didn't know. Like what a Jewish woman in her eighties from New York, with such an exquisite collection of clothes and jewellery, was doing down a side-street in Dublin.

But we had time. And I had coat hangers. And I knew she had too.

'How are we going to get the right women in here?' I asked. 'The modern-day Grace Kellys, Marlene Dietrichs, Audrey Hepburns, Molly Keeee –' I screeched to a halt mid-sentence. And I wanted to rewind it pronto like Chris Martin in 'The Scientist' video.

Car crash!

Verity had her bull hoof out and was scraping it along the floor.

'Molly *Kealy* Ringwald!' I said. 'That's her middle name. I have a book of fascinating trivia in my loo and that was in it . . .'

Rewind, rewind!

What on earth was the woman's beef with Molly Keats anyway? Maybe she just never liked her. Rebecca has always had an irrational dislike of Renée Zellweger. On another note, if ladies did come in here looking for a Molly Ringwald look, I might just go right ahead and cry. The eighties has always been my kryptonite. I once fainted when Rebecca called over to my house in a neon pink jumpsuit. True story. Broke my mother's good vase in the fall.

'Anyway,' I coughed, side-stepping the Molly Keats issue, 'how do we make sure we attract the right customers?'

'Well, I thought it was your job to find out,' she said matter-of-factly.

True.

'It's just there's not too many women like that left out there now. It's like a lost age, a lost femininity,' I said.

'Oh, they're still out there, Grace, under all the layers of high-street tat, amid the exhausting fog of living a life of too much haste. Too busy to get off the treadmill long enough to put on a fabulous frock and be good to themselves. Little uncut diamonds, all of them.'

'That's the kind of woman I'd like to dress!'

'You can't look at it like that, sweethawt.'

'What do you mean?'

'You can't wait for a woman like that to walk through the door demanding furs and diamonds. She won't. And the ones who do, you have to be damn careful of.'

Hmm, this was all a bit confusing. Did I make them sit down and do Jungian personality tests and problem-solving exercises when they walked into the shop? I could set up a little desk over there in the corner . . .

'You have to see the potential in every woman and allow her to dress in a way that she'll feel good about herself.'

'You mean kind of making her who she really is from the outside in?'

'Gawd, there's enough cheese on that for a sixteen-inch deep-filled Margarita!' Then she softened slightly, allowing a small grin to curl one corner of her mouth. 'But yes, exactly.'

Right.

'If invention is the mother of necessity,' she advised, 'then *reinvention* is the Goddamn kick-ass *queen* of all necessity.'

I liked it. Hadn't a clue how to formulate it into a business plan, mind you. But I liked it.

'Okay, so what now?' I asked, hoping to distil some more wisdom while she was pouring out the advice.

'That's what *you* need to figure out. Creative business – that's what you studied, right? Well, off you go! Internet it or something. I'm going to put on some scones and have a bath.' She hoisted herself from her armchair and headed for the kitchen. 'But I gotta tell ya,' she said, turning to me before she disappeared, 'any lady comes in here in pyjamas, like they do down in Spar, I'm getting my air rifle.'

Wow. Sometimes I couldn't tell if she was joking or not. And those times, I just nodded and smiled.

'Internet it.' Internet it? Okay. I took out my laptop and started 'Internetting'.

Oooh, 50 per cent off everything at Asos!

No: concentrate! I Googled 'How to make a lady who is very busy on the treadmill of life and wears unimaginative high-street clothing look like a lady who lived in the Hollywood Golden Era in a way that will help her reconnect with who she may have forgotten she really is because she is just so busy'.

That was not helpful. At all.

I tried again. 'Sexy ladies dressing for fun!'

Whoa!

Those images were frightening. Could anyone really be *that* bendy? Reminded me, though, that I needed to get myself the Hollywood. Then I went back and bought a pair of cute pumps with the most adorable little silver bows. (They were 50 per cent off!)

After that I YouTubed the Coldplay video again. It really was a good one.

I drummed my fingers on the keys, trying to think of something constructive, singing to myself about going back to the start.

That was it! I'd email my old college lecturer and ask her advice on business start-up models and hope to God she wouldn't remember it was me who'd handed in the *Elle* magazine spring-collection edition instead of an essay on consumer markets in Asia! (Easy, easy mistake.)

Genius!

Verity re-emerged a short while later, her cheeks all rosy from her bath and a plate of warm scones in her hand. 'Food for thought?' she said.

'Verity, do you really want me to get rid of this box of clothes? I don't understand – the stuff is incredible . . .'

'There's always one, you know,' she said, ignoring me entirely. 'Well, there may be many, but there's always *one.*'

Uh-oh. I had no idea what she was on about. Maybe her bath was too hot and now she had Hot Bath Syndrome. Happens to me, too. Makes you totally mad for a bit. I ordered nine sixteen-inch pizzas one night and made a den in my living room out of the boxes. Robbie was a cardboard front door away from taking me to St Vincent's.

'Would you like an ice-cream, Verity?' I knew the 'cooling tricks'.

'What? No, dear.' She sat in her chair and studied me closely. 'Do you think he's *the guy*?'

Oh.

She was talking about that. Liz with her diamond again.

'I don't know, Verity. He was the *only* guy for so long I sort of lost what I felt.'

I occupied my hands with the consignment, hoping to dilute the focus a bit with work. She remained silent, and I almost felt obliged to give her another answer. 'I think I just realized it wasn't like this any more.'

'Like what?'

'Like this,' I said, casting my eyes around the shop, the clothes, the magic. 'The thrill, the romance, the movie kiss . . .'

'You know what I found one of the most romantic things in the world?' she said.

'What?' I asked, lifting my head.

'Someone letting me warm my cold feet on theirs when I got into bed at the end of a long day.'

I flicked the zipper on a velvet jacket.

'Doesn't sound very movie romance, does it?' she said.

I shrugged, feeling exposed and out of sorts. 'Was he your *one*, then?' I said, unsure she was going to lift up the shutter enough to let me take a peek inside.

'He was,' she said, surprising me with her candour. 'There were many, like I've said, but then there's always *one*. David was my one. I had him. And then I lost him.'

'How? Like actually lost him? In a supermarket or something?'

She smiled at me, thinking I was joking. Which, obviously, I was. (But, seriously, Tanya lost me in Dundrum last year and got them to make an announcement on the Tannoy. I was mortified.)

'How did you lose him?' I said. 'And did you find him again?'

Suddenly there was a knock on the glass. We jumped. I turned to Verity and she nodded. I got up and headed for the door, still distracted by our conversation, agitated by the interruption. I let in an elegant woman in her mid-sixties. She smiled at Verity and eyed me suspiciously. 'I know this place is sort of a secret,' she said, in a hushed tone, 'but my friend was in here a while back and she said you, you know . . . *helped* her.'

Helped her? Helped her what? Zip up a tricky body-con?

Verity flicked her eyes to me, beckoned the woman to take the chair beside her and poured her a cup of tea.

'I'm just going to come right out with it.' The woman sighed, spooning sugar into her tea absently. 'My husband has admitted he's had an affair. He has promised me it's his first and I believe him. I left for a bit, but we both know we still want to be together. So we're going again. And we want it to be even better this time round.'

I gasped, shocked by her confession but more so by her frankness. 'How can you go back?' I said, the words out before I could stop them.

'Because I love him,' she said matter-of-factly. 'And I know he loves me. I have no intention of wasting the rest of my life as a proud, lonely, miserable old woman.'

My mouth opened again, this time nothing coming out but fresh air. I closed it again.

'What's that?' she asked, her eyes landing on the burgundy crushed-velvet jacket in my hands.

Verity rolled her eyes. 'Oh, we can do better than *that!*'

The woman stood up, came over to me and took it from my hands. 'May I?'

I nodded, not entirely sure what was happening. She held the jacket up to herself, spun up to the mirror and stopped dead as she caught her own reflection. 'This reminds me so much of Molly Keats's outfit in *The Wish Stealer.*'

Verity rolled her eyes again and sighed loudly. Honestly, even Rebecca didn't dislike Renée Zellweger that much.

'That was the first movie I went to see with my husband. Our first date? It was magical. I didn't catch one minute of the film, mind you. I was so consumed with sneaking sideways glances at him that I missed the whole thing!'

I smiled, despite myself.

'We rent it on our anniversary every year,' she continued, her eyes sparkling in the mirror. 'I suppose my secret wish is that he'll somehow fall in love with me all over again, like in the beginning, when we had eyes only for each other. Am I being silly?'

Verity and I said nothing. We could see she was having a moment as she gazed at her reflection.

'Well, I think I've just made your job a whole lot easier.' She smiled at Verity. 'I'll take this one.'

'Suit yourself.' She shrugged. 'I don't need that one back. You can have it for free. Good luck with everything. I mean that.'

Really? For *free*? But it was an original 1950s exquisitely made gold-silk-lined crushed-velvet jacket. How on earth were we supposed to make any money if she gave things away for free?

I watched the woman leave the shop with the jacket. I turned back to Verity, studying her as she sat in her armchair. I realized that this was what she'd been doing all along – only letting in women who really needed the clothes to help them in some way. Conducting her business like a stealth operator. She was the Vera Drake of vintage fashion – secretly using her unique skills to help desperate women out of trouble. That was why she wanted all this to *mean* something. Count for something. Like I had always done.

I smiled, promising myself I'd be the best Vera Drake assistant she could ever have hoped for. 'Hey, Verity,' I said, 'do you believe in wishes coming true?'

'Do I believe in what?' she said, staring at me like she'd just seen a ghost.

'Wishes, you know . . . Do you believe in them coming true?'

'Do *you*?' she said.

'Well, I know it might sound silly but me and Lisa went on a course to this place called the Wish Factory because I was feeling a bit lost and, well, to cut a long story short, I made a wish that I would get to work here with you, and well . . . it came true! Just when that woman was talking about her secret wish, it reminded me. Might sound daft . . .'

She sat staring at me for an uncomfortable length of time, as if she was in two minds about what to say. God, I hoped she wasn't thinking I was a lunatic and coming up with ways to fire me.

'Of course I believe in wishes coming true,' she said finally, her voice sounding distant. 'That's how I found him again. David. That's how I found him after I lost him. I wished for him.'

'You *wished* for him?' I said, sitting to attention.

'Yes. You asked if I believe in wishes coming true. No, not all of them. I don't believe you can go down to a Wish Factory or whatever it is and wish for something in exchange for money. I believe in Fate. Fate plays its hand like an expert card dealer every single day of your life. I believe it was Fate that brought you here. Fate that has you working here. You can't fire off a thousand wishes into the universe and hope for them all to be answered.

People who wished they hadn't missed that bus. Who wished they'd made that call. Who wished they'd win the lotto. That, my girl, is chance. They're different from the special wishes. And especially the Heart Wish.'

'The Heart Wish?' I said, my own heart beating rapidly.

'Yes. The Heart Wish. When you're truly honest with yourself, when all the layers of crap are stripped away, and your own heart is lying there as naked and true as the day you were born, *then* you wish for what you really want and send it out to the universe. People have been doing it for years. Not as easy as it sounds, though. You gotta go there to come back. I mean *really* go there.'

'Well, how exactly do you do that?' I said, completely agog.

She narrowed her eyes. 'Internet it.'

I was almost certain that was sarcasm. (But I was still going to Google 'Heart Wish' later just to be sure. I liked the sound of it.)

Then she pointed a bony finger at me. 'The Heart Wish is special. I don't want you telling everybody and anybody about the Heart Wish. Suddenly it's out there and mass-marketed like a cheap pair of PVC pants. Coveted by everyone because it's "trendy". It's too special. Trends come and go. It's real style that's timeless. Just like a Heart Wish. Plus I have a reputation to keep. I don't want anyone thinking I'm soft, you hear?'

Oh, I heard! I was still thinking about that air rifle she had mentioned earlier and I certainly wouldn't be taking any chances.

'One final warning, Grace.'

I gulped silently.

'The Heart Wish will only ever work on your guy. Your *one*. You can try it on a hundred others and it won't work. Heart Wishes are only granted by your *one*.' I nodded. I was enchanted, and so grateful that this woman, so wise and knowledgeable, who had lived her life behind a screen of circumspection, had opened the shutters a chink, just about wide enough for me to take a peek inside.

'Everyone has a *one*,' she said. 'For that woman it was her husband. Always had been, always will be. Clear as day. You can spend your whole life trying to fight it and you'll never win. Some find them early, some find them late. But, guaranteed, once you've found them, your world will never ever be the same again.'

'Tell me more about David,' I said, aware that I was pushing it, but wanting desperately to know more about the Heart Wish.

'He's dead,' she said. 'End of discussion.'

It was like someone had slammed the shutters closed again. And I knew then it was time to go home for the day.

I wrapped my scarf around me tightly as I walked home through the city streets. The light from the lampposts drenched everything in a gorgeous golden glow while a soft flurry of snow started to fall. It was like I was walking through my own personal greeting card. Everywhere was deserted and it seemed so peaceful. I sat on an empty bench on the canal, allowing the silence around me to still the buzz in my own head. My mind was in overdrive.

The love of Verity's life had been a man called David. And he was dead? I didn't care how old you were, that must be the worst kind of loneliness. To have someone and then to lose him.

Lisa. I just hoped Lisa was going to be okay. Poor Killian must be worried sick about her.

I wondered if that woman and her husband were going to work things out. Would he see her in that jacket? Would it bring it all back – the night the two of them were so consumed with their own love story they missed the one on the screen?

I thought about Rebecca and whether she was out there in Argentina hating Renée Zellweger's pants from *Bridget Jones* as much as Verity hated that lookalike hat of Molly Keats's from *The Whistling Wind*.

I looked up into the night as the snowflakes drifted through the air like tiny tufts of cotton wool. It was spellbinding and magical, and I wished I could float all the way up there and drift through it like a dream.

'I wished', eh? I thought of Verity and the Heart Wish.

Okay, then, why not? It was just me and the universe after all. What did I have to lose?

I closed my eyes tight and felt excitement tingle through me. I pictured my heart beating steadily in my chest and visualized cutting away all the doubts and worries, regrets and fears, like a scythe hacking through tangled undergrowth.

'Okay, then, Universe . . . Send him to me . . . Send me my Heart Wish.'

Oh, wow! It was *working*! I suddenly felt warmth start at my feet and travel up my –

No, wait a second, it wasn't travelling anywhere. I opened my eyes to see a dog with his leg cocked, pissing on my feet.

Wonderful, I thought, as I watched him pad down the canal in the snow. Not some celestial sign from the heavens after all, just another animal that insisted on peeing over my shoes.

## 32

Sunday morning. The one morning of the week I really missed having someone to curl into in bed. 'Tell me a story,' I used to mumble to Robbie, still drugged with sleep.

'Okay,' he'd start drowsily, tucking me into his chest. 'Remember that bloke I was telling you about in work with the wonky eye, got accused of staring at Ciara-behind-Reception's cleavage? Well, I said to them, "He has a wonky eye! It just has a tendency to sort of look downwards." So then they said . . .'

And that's how it would begin. The lazy Sunday.

I missed them. Sunday mornings now involved me fighting off my mother's pleas to go to Mass with her, followed by Buns and Prayers in the parish hall ('Sure, you've nothing better to do').

I slipped out of bed and padded to the window, peeking through the heavy curtains. Woo-hoo! It had stuck! Snow covered every inch of the world outside my window, like thick icing layered on top of a big, beautiful cake. I smiled, thinking of last night, thinking of the Heart Wish: maybe that had stuck too.

My phone beeped. Mum. Here we go, another 'Father Tom really does give a stunning sermon. Saw your old school mate Charlotte there last week with her husband and *three* children. I'm sure she feels she has a lot to thank God for.'

I opened the text. No Mass bribery today. Worse. Much worse.

Mum: **Buns and prayers on at same time, same place. What do you want to do for your birthday, Grace?**

Was it almost March? *Already?* My goodness, it was: March – and my birthday – were next week! Jesus, January and February were getting fierce short lately. I liked February. It was like the Danny DeVito of months: short but fun. And now March seemed like a very large serious Arnold Schwarzenegger-type month.

What did I want to do for my birthday? Set fire to my birth certificate and get hosed on martinis? Eat so many hash cakes that I didn't actually come round until I was thirty-one, by which time everyone would hopefully be over the 'Grace Turning Thirty' lark?

Even though I wasn't nearly as freaked out about it as the rest of my nearest and dearest, turning thirty still frightened me slightly. I mean, I still watched *Fraggle Rock* sometimes. Was that bad? Laughing along to silly old Uncle Travelling Matt on his misadventures. I'm sure some people might frown on that once you'd hit the big three-oh. And I was almost certain Lisa and I were going to have to stop having Hopscotch League matches with the kids out on my road too.

Being thirty was going to suck.

I texted her: **SNOOOOOOW!** Whenever it snows, she has to speak like Lisa Snowdon for the day. Or as much of the day as she can without getting fired or people thinking she has a full-on personality disorder.

**Awrigh! Ow u doin?** she texted back in her best Cockney-text speech.

**I'm good. You know, just me and Bette cuddling in the couch before I go to Mass with my mum. That's just the kind of rock and roll life I live now. Get over it.**

I started writing another straight away: **Have they told you yet when you're getting the** I paused before typing **results**, like it was Leaving Cert points and not her life we were talking about. I rang her instead.

'Another two weeks.'

I closed my eyes. It was torturous not knowing. She was being amazing. 'So what are you going to do today, then?' I said, as chirpily as I could, knowing she didn't really want to talk about it.

'Hang out with Killian, have a snowball fight and then tell him I might have cancer.'

Oh, God.

'You haven't spoken to him yet?'

'Grace, we're together six months and everything is going so well. I don't want to freak him out.'

'Lisa, he's crazy about you! He's going to want to be there for you. You have to tell him.'

'Yeah,' she said, her voice lifting slightly. 'Maybe you're right.'

'Of course I'm right! I'm the lady who hangs out with cats and goes to Mass with her mum! Now get dressed, go and see your gorgeous man, have a snowball fight and then tell him . . .'

'I/You might have cancer,' we mumbled together. We laughed, even though both our hearts were breaking. What else could we do?

We hung up. Another text beeped on my phone.

Tanya: **If you go off on another find-yourself retreat for your birthday I'm actually going to start legal proceedings to have you divorced from our family. Mum can't stop praying. Hope the job's going well. At least that's something. Smiley face**

Smiley face, my hole.

Another text alert.

'See how popular I am, Bette!' The cat narrowed her eyes at me from the bedroom door, then slunk off to find somewhere new to hide so she could jump out at me just when I'd managed to forget she existed. Oh, the suspense – this really was living the dream.

I checked the text. It was from my old college lecturer. **Hello, Grace, I'm delighted you're going into business. I've emailed you some pointers that I hope you will find helpful** I was pretty sure the first pointer was going to be 'Stop reading *Elle* magazine.' But still.

I whipped out my laptop to log on to my emails. 'I wouldn't mess with the Business Woman if I were you, Bette!' I called, as I waited for it to power up. (Trying to prove yourself to a cat, especially one that hated you, was very sad, I realized. Yet it was surprisingly satisfying.)

The email was super-informative. She said an organization called the Business Angels provided experienced mentors to start-up new businesses for no fee. How amazing was that? (Mind you, I had to give myself a stern talking-to about the angel side of it. My mentor would not come wearing a halo and wings, and I should just let that sink in now so I didn't feel let down when I met him or her.)

I sent off all my details, outlining where I was working and our plan for the future, with a PS that I'd been sick the day we'd read *Trump: The Art of the Deal* just in case they wanted to do a little pop quiz before assigning my angel. Hopefully, that would do it.

Wow. How productive was I for a Sunday morning? Who needed long lazy lie-ins and fabulous sex when you could email business-type people about your business-type thing for fabulous business-type advice?

Now that I was on my proactive buzz, I was going to post a notice on Facebook to see if anyone wanted to rent my spare room. There was only so much longer I could manage the mortgage on my own and there was only so much longer Jim Manahan could manage me crying in his office when we discussed interest rates.

I logged in, scrolling through my feed so I could live vicariously through other people's fabulously exciting lives before I went downstairs and had my bran flakes.

Five people were on holidays, lucky ducks. Oh, Sarah Moriarty from college had had a baby and needed seven stitches. Too much information, Sarah. I didn't need to know about the post-delivery state of your vagina. Just show me the child. Two new engagements. My stomach took a dive even though I was so happy for them, whoever they were, these 'friends' of mine. I thought one was a girl I'd met in a nightclub in Carlow four years previously. Random. I needed to do a cull on the friends front. But you couldn't really cull a newly engaged person, could you? That might look a bit psychotic from a single person about to turn thirty. People might talk. Anyway, I hoped they would be very happy together. She'd been slumped over a loo, crying her eyes out, when I'd met her, wailing that she'd just seen him snogging her cousin, so I was glad they'd patched things up.

All of a sudden I remembered that I still had 'In a relationship with Robbie Cotter' on my own status. What should I do? Change it? That seemed so harsh. I clicked on his name to see if he still had it on his.

'Single'.

I'm not sure why this came as such a surprise to me. But it did. Just seeing it. Right there in black and white. Well, blue: blue and white. Fuzzy spots danced before my eyes as the blood rushed from my head. I looked through his feed, searching the photos, feeling like a voyeur, a trespasser poking around a half-familiar world. He looked well. His hair was shorter and he was wearing clothes I'd never seen. He was the same Robbie. But different. He'd been tagged in various pictures of nights out. That same Jennifer Garner lookalike kept popping up in them and I found it hard to stomach.

But this was good: he was moving on. We both were. I smiled to myself, thinking of the Heart Wish last night. Perhaps things were happening just as they were meant to.

And then, amid all the declarations of sheer happiness and wonderment in all my 567 close 'friends'' lives, I posted a message reading: 'Room for rent in semi-detached Dublin 8 residence. Small and cramped with a window that only opens from the out-side. Must like cats (even evil ones). On the positive side, the jar of Party Rings in the kitchen is *always* full.'

I jumped off the bed, deciding that if any hard-up or not-the-full-shilling people wanted to take the glorified coffin room, I ought to give the house a proper spring clean. Lisa really had been clutching at straws when she'd told me the cobwebs looked just like the silver silk garlands she'd seen in Image Interiors and wasn't I the 'clever recessionista'? Also, I had to face it: the clogged-up bath plughole really wasn't creating the 'foot spa' effect whenever I took a shower.

The place was manky. It was after some serious love and atten-tion. Just like Erin Wasson when she wore that barely there dress to the Golden Globes. I threw on the only tracksuit I owned from the emergency section in my wardrobe (it was beside the trainers for my emergency run after I'd eaten too much naan bread). I tied a fabulous Liberty print silk scarf around my head in an attempt to de-vile the shiny green tracksuit (I'd dressed up as Steve Staunton one Hallowe'en; worked a treat with my red hair). And then I got to scrubbing the knickers off seven Maple Street. I hadn't really touched it since Robbie had left. It was sort of like some preserved crime scene of the last time we'd been together. Although he'd taken away most of his things, there was plenty of evidence of our seven-year relationship.

I cleared away little bits of memorabilia, like the B. A. Baracus duck on the edge of the bath from our *A-Team* themed soirée and the I Am Amazing mug he always made me drink my tea from if I felt down. It was hard. I felt like the widow who finally decides to throw out the suits still hanging in the wardrobe.

I rearranged the shoe-rack in my bedroom. I hadn't been able to touch it since he'd left. It reminded me too much of him. He'd built it for me last summer, to house all the shoes he'd ever given me. As part of my birthday present every year, he'd buy me a fabulous new pair.

*Fresh footsteps for all the fresh adventures.*

I stared at the ruby slippers that sat on their own rack at the top, presiding over all the others like a glistening crown, just like Dorothy's red shoes in *The Wizard of Oz*. He'd bought them as a moving-in present: 'Anytime you feel you need me, just click your heels and come home. I'll always be here. Except when I'm at work, or in the pub, or at a gig. Or over at my mum and dad's.'

I smiled sadly, stacking the shoes in order of every year I'd known him. And then I scrubbed the life out of the bathroom, the bedrooms, the hall, the sitting room, learning so much along the way! Like using floor bleach on wallpaper is not advisable. Or that cleaning the wallpaper in the first place is not really necessary, no matter how industrious and energetic you're feeling. In the middle of all this I called Mum to tell her I thought I'd sprained my elbow and did she think I'd need a cast, to which she said, 'No, you won't. It's called housework, Grace. Will you come over for evening Mass instead?' To which I said, 'Would you look at the dust on those skirting boards?' before 'accidentally' hanging up.

I also learned that Bette likes to pee under the stairs as well as in nice shoes. That diva was getting a litter tray first thing tomorrow. She could be the new Marlene Dietrich! (Marlene once wore a dress so tight for a performance at the Copacabana Palace Hotel that she requested a sand bucket in her room because she couldn't walk to the Ladies.)

Only one room left and I was done. 'The kitchen.' I could hear the *Psycho* knife music in my ears as I said it. Ah, yes, the room where it's a good idea to wash the tiles behind the stove rings after every stir-fry and not let it build up so much you've actually managed to create an extra layer of soundproofing on that wall.

Before I dealt with the toxic health warning on the other side of the kitchen, I organized all of Rebecca's postcards into a fabulous Inspiration Collage on the fridge that I just *knew* Dr Phil would pull his tall stool up beside and clap approvingly at. Every week Rebecca sent me another postcard from a different part of the world with a cute picture and more words of wisdom. Like **When life hands you lemons, make tequila!** all the way from Mexico, and **Even though I'm in Bolivia having an amazing time, this postcard is a damn good substitute for me.** I wasn't sure what the postcard of the wrinkly old naked lady with her boobs hanging down to her knees on a beach in Argentina meant. I hoped it wasn't something to do with me turning thirty.

I slapped on the Marigolds to tackle the tiles and took the large scrubbing brush (microphone) into my hand, pausing briefly to help Dusty Springfield finish off 'Wishin' And Hopin'' on my iPod when all of a sudden a man's face flashed in the kitchen window and I screamed so loudly I thought I was going to shatter it.

I'm not sure exactly how long I screamed, but long enough for Dusty to be well into 'I Only Wanna Be With You', by which time the man was banging on the window and Bette was standing at the door, back arched, fur on end, hissing like a rabid beast.

He gesticulated at me in a way that either said, 'It's okay, it's okay, I'm not going to kill you,' or 'I actually am going to kill you and then I'm going to bury you in the Dublin Mountains.' I couldn't decide at first but finally concluded it looked more like the former.

I went around to the patio door and unlocked it nervously. What on earth was some random man doing in my backyard, banging on my kitchen window?

Jesus!

I don't mean to be trivial about my possible impending death or anything, but my potential murderer was ridiculously handsome.

Phwoooooooaaaaaaaar! Yes, please, Mr Dublin Mountains! You know, if I did die, at least I'd die happy.

'Hi,' he said cautiously.

'Hi,' I said, half sexily, half afraid for my life.

God, he was gorgeous. Sort of like Patrick Bergin in *Sleeping with the Enemy*. Without the 'tache. And, hopefully, without all the characteristics of a nutter. Mind you, now I thought of it I really could have used some help rearranging the tins in my cupboard while I was tidying up the kitchen . . .

'I'm so sorry to have frightened the life out of you.'

I must have looked wild. Utterly wild. More like a rabid beast than Bette. I was wearing a green tracksuit with a silk scarf tied into a big bow on the top of my head and my face was still so paralysed with shock that I'm sure my eyebrows were probably tucked all the way up under it.

'I'm a friend of Rebecca's. I saw your post on Facebook and I wanted to come over straight away before the room was gone. I was ringing the doorbell, but I didn't think you could hear it over the loud music, so I thought I'd chance coming round to the back door . . . I'm so sorry,' he said again, with a slight, bemused smile.

'Oh, God, of course, yes. Yes. Don't worry,' I said, trying to lessen his embarrassment. 'Most men come through my back door . . .'

Holy sweet Jesus. Had I actually just said that? I clamped my hand over my mouth. I could feel my cheeks flame wildly. I'm sure it was *such* a sexy final touch to go with my shiny green tracksuit and headscarf. The thought of which made me redden further.

To recap: the handsome stranger had just seen me singing into a pot scrubber with the gusto of a Motown superstar before re-creating the-girl-is-scared-shitless scene from every Wes Craven movie ever made. And I was puce red. Puce red and sweating.

His fabulously chiselled face broke into a broad smile, like he was mocking me, and it made my tummy squirm. In a good way.

We both started laughing.

And there it was. The connection. I could feel it fizz between us. Like a lovely Berocca. We stood there grinning at each other coyly before I finally came to my senses and invited him in.

My phone beeped again. A text message from my newly appointed Business Angel saying he was available to meet up next week. Oh, my goodness. *What a day!* One that had started out with an offer of buns and prayers and was ending with my new business venture kick-starting in earnest. And, well, 'it' being sent to me.

Yes – *it*. You know, my Heart Wish – *it*! It was *him* – I just knew it. Who would have thought it could happen so quickly?

Fate. All wrapped up in a carefully spun wish. We never took our eyes off each other as I held open the door and he stepped in.

# 33

Well, what do you know? This whole Heart Wish thing was incredibly efficient, even quicker than Asos. Imagine! Even came with next-day delivery. Stephen 'Heart Wish' Kelleher moved in on the Monday morning. Thankfully, he didn't have any issues with sleeping in coffin rooms; he had been a massive fan of *The Munsters* as a kid, he told me. Oh, gosh, Stephen 'Heart Wish' Kelleher was a gas man altogether. (Actually, using his full title all the time was a bit tiresome: easier to call him Stephen.)

He also didn't seem to have any overt concerns with possessed cats. If there was one thing – apart from his outrageously fit body – that I already admired about Stephen, it was his naïvety.

Of all of the rooms to rent in all of the houses on Daft, or Facebook, or wherever, you had to click on mine, I thought, with a Humphrey Bogart raising of the eyebrow. Destiny. This was all so weird. How come all these wishes were suddenly coming true? Never happened before when I wanted to work for *Vogue*. Or have thirty-five-inch legs.

I stood at the bathroom door, leaning on the frame in my pseudo-nonchalant pose, as I watched him drag his stuff up the stairs. He didn't need any help: he could do it all himself.

Swoon.

'I'd say you've dragged a fair amount up your stairs to the bedroom, Stephen!'

Jesus! Was I speaking? What was I doing? I knew it wasn't safe to speak before my morning espresso.

'Erm . . . ha-ha.' He laughed feebly.

I needed to get a copy of *The Rules*. It had been so long since I'd flirted with anyone that my techniques were probably very early noughties. I needed to update them. Perhaps I could make out a chart-type thing with handy Venn diagrams and put it up on my bedroom wall as a reminder. Hmm. But what if Stephen needed to borrow something in my room, or to drag Bette screeching from under my bed when she had to go to the vet (when, as she rightly suspected I would, I eventually got around to having her put down), and he accidentally saw it? There is probably a rule against posting all the rules about the guy you'd like to date on your own bedroom wall in *The Rules*.

Meanwhile I had to get ready for work. All this hanging around looking like I'd just got out of bed when actually I'd set the alarm for six thirty to blow-dry my hair, painstakingly apply some 'natural-effect makeup' and lash some Sally Hansen on my pins was time-consuming.

'See you later, Stephen,' I said, trotting down the stairs. 'I'm off to work.' Oh, gosh, I loved saying that. I couldn't wait to tell Verity all about the Business Angel and the Heart Wish coming true.

'Erm, Grace, you're still in your pyjamas . . .'

'Ha-ha, that's gas,' I said, acting very chilled as I headed back upstairs to get dressed. I was breezy. I was cool.

*Jesus, where the hell was my espresso?*

As soon as I got to the shop and saw Verity, I knew something was wrong. She was standing in the middle of the floor, her house-coat buttoned askew, her hair wild, unbrushed and falling around her shoulders. I'd never seen her look so unkempt, so vulnerable. I saw her shoulders slumped as I'd never seen them before, her bent-over frame weighted with age. Her eyes shone at me from their hollow sockets.

Whatever was in her expression, I could see the young woman she had been. The woman with the world at her feet. Time really was merciless, the mind and spirit betrayed by the body that can never keep up.

Well, the world was literally at her feet right now. She stood among mounds and mounds of clothes, hats, scarves and shoes, like a weathered grey headstone in the middle of all the dug-up graves of her own past.

'What is it, Verity?' I said.

'I'm scared, Grace. I'm scared of saying goodbye.'

My throat swelled with the sympathy I suddenly felt for her. And for the valour in her honesty. What exactly was she talking about? The clothes?

'But, Verity, you won't have to. That's what the rental system will be designed for.'

'Yes, yes,' she said irritably. 'I know. It's just, well . . . I've never been good at goodbyes . . .'

I went to her, dropping to my knees to sift through the mounds, trying to organize them for her so she wouldn't feel so overwhelmed.

'That's how I ended up here, you know,' she said, the sadness deep in her dark blue eyes. 'Because I couldn't say goodbye.'

'How do you mean?' I said gently.

'David,' she said, her voice strained like she was confessing something. 'I couldn't say goodbye. He always said he wanted to be buried here in his home country, in Ireland. And I couldn't leave him. I couldn't go back to the States without him. I couldn't . . . say goodbye.' A single tear burrowed down the lines on her face, stalling at the end of her chin before falling to the floor.

'How long ago was that?'

'Twenty-six years,' she said, as though she had been dreaming the whole thing. 'Twenty-six long years that have done nothing to anaesthetize the pain. Time is a healer? For a broken wrist maybe. Never for a broken heart.'

I looked at the floor, both overcome with emotion and afraid to say anything in case it sounded trivial, stupid, patronizing in the face of her pain.

'That's why I named this place Best Wishes – it's after him. Because he was the best wish I ever made. The only one that would ever really work. Because he was my Heart Wish. I needed him back after the first time I'd been stupid enough to let him go.

'I'm sorry, Grace,' she said, shaking her head as if to shake off her mood. 'This is all just unearthing a lot of stuff from the past for me. I do want to do this. I do. I just haven't spoken to anyone about the Heart Wish in so long.'

She paused, bending down to pick up a black velvet pillbox hat. And instantly I could see it tugging at her memory, like a fish caught on the end of a line. 'I may seem old, ancient in fact, to someone who has their whole life ahead of them. But one day you will understand that even when you have lived through it all, there is never, ever enough time.'

I nodded, thinking I knew what she meant.

'Perhaps we should just get this done now, you know,' I said. 'Sort through it all so you don't have to do it by yourself? Maybe it won't be so bad. I know you'll need to be brave, but . . .'

'Grace, slow down. Slow down. You don't always have to chase around the place. Courage doesn't always have to roar. Sometimes it's the quiet voice at the end of the day saying, "I'll try again tomorrow."'

I sat for a moment, then slowly got up to leave, releasing her back to the world she loved most, even though it existed only in memories and souvenirs. I shut the door behind me softly.

Tomorrow was indeed another day. We could always try again tomorrow.

The next day I wasn't sure what I expected to find when I got to the shop, but it certainly wasn't Verity dressed like Amelia Earhart in head to toe 1930s aviator clothing!

'Tally-hooooo!' she hollered, as soon as I pushed through the door.

Oh, no.

Verity had lost it. What should I do? What did someone do in this situation? I was definitely not the best person to call on in a crisis. Lisa's 'Screw You Ian' tattoo on her foot was a permanent reminder of that. (So, this guy Ian had dumped her, she was upset, I got her drunk, and it was the next obvious step, really.

Now she always has to wear socks. Even with sandals in the summer.)

I wasn't sure Verity was the tattoo type. So that was good.

'Come on, Grace! Flight leaves at zero eight hundred hours!'

To where? Crazy Town?

'Verity, I get like this too when I haven't had my morning caffeine hit. Shall we all just take a second while I put the kettle on?'

'No, no, kid. Get involved! Get *involved*.'

Oh, God, this was embarrassing.

'Erm, okay.' I grimaced, teeth gritted. 'Er . . . hello, pilot, can I please have a lift to Spain? I'm going on my holidays, but I'm not a great flier . . . I get a little nervous . . .'

She looked at me as if I was the simpleton I felt I was. 'Grace, what are you doing?' she said.

'Eh . . . getting involved?'

'Right. Well, I meant try on some outfits, not pretend we're four-year-olds about to get on an imaginary plane to Spain.' She fixed her vintage leather aviator cap on her head. 'I'd forgotten I even owned this,' she said. 'Oh, the memories of Jimmy Stewart flying around the Grand Canyon!'

Hmm, I'd never seen that one. I smiled, relieved the sadness was beginning to ebb from her eyes.

The next few hours were fantastic fun. I must have tried on at least a hundred different outfits. Verity wanted to see them 'come to life' again so we could figure out what to do with each one and who exactly should be wearing them.

'I can't work out who you remind me of – Rita Hayworth, Debbie Reynolds, Ginger Rogers . . . ? Perhaps it's just the red hair but, you know, in that trouser suit you could be Katharine Hepburn standing right in front of me.' I flushed with pleasure.

She told me how it had been Katharine herself who'd bucked the trend and started women wearing trousers in America and Britain. In fact, Verity taught me a great deal as I changed in and out of every outfit, giving me the back-story of how the different styles had evolved and how Hollywood had had a direct influence on the fashion industry. Famous movies and their stars – Dorothy Lamour, Loretta Young, Liz Taylor, Vivien Leigh, Greta Garbo, Hedy Lamarr, Marilyn Monroe, Jayne Mansfield, Sophia Loren, Audrey Hepburn, Ingrid Bergman, Olivia de Havilland, Marlene Dietrich, Rita Hayworth, Lana Turner, everyone you could think of – and famous designers, MGM's Adrian, Paramount's Edith Head, Christian Dior, Givenchy, Balmain, she had stories about all of them. I felt slightly delirious as I listened, as if I had got into a time machine with her.

'Did you know the Hermès Kelly Bag was named after Grace Kelly was papped trying to conceal her pregnancy with one?' she said.

'Oh, yes!' I said, delighted finally to know something. I'd thought I knew my stuff but this woman was a complete encyclopedia when it came to vintage fashion. 'I was called after Grace Kelly so I know everything about her. She was one of my favourites.'

'Yes, she was special, all right,' she replied sadly. 'Another goodbye.'

I saw the same melancholy expression in her eyes as I'd seen the previous day. 'Verity, are you okay after yesterday? You've done amazingly here today.'

'What can you do, eh?' she said, snapping out of it. 'Bette always said that old age was no place for sissies and she was right! And stop being so gooey, you – I've always said that was the problem with the Irish: all so bloody sentimental.'

I smiled.

'And did you know,' she continued brightly, as if she hadn't momentarily tripped up on her own sadness, 'that Michael Kors says there is "a little Liz" in every collection he does after Elizabeth Taylor?'

I shook my head. There was so much I *didn't* know.

'Did you know that Eva Marie Saint single-handedly changed secretarial wear after the release of her movie *That Certain Feeling* in 1956?'

I shook my head again. I was devouring all this information. I felt like a kid at a party stuffing pink fairy buns with multi-coloured sprinkles into my face. I couldn't get enough.

'There was a thing in the thirties and forties called the Hollywood Star Machine, where teams of professionals working at the big film studios would assess the upcoming starlets to see how they could improve them and mould them into fabulous new ingénues.'

'Really?'

'Really. Rita Hayworth spent two years of her life undergoing painful electrolysis to move her hairline back two inches.'

'Amazing! Maybe that's what we should do.'

'Grace, neither of us is qualified – you can't go around zapping people willy-nilly.'

'No, no, I mean we could do our own little Star Machine in here, sort of like a little workshop when a new customer comes in and is unsure of what she wants. The same process, but for ordinary people.'

'I see. Well, you do know that people have been doing that for years? All the big studio designers – Head, Banton, Adrian, Rose, Orry-Kelly – used to answer letters from ordinary folk looking for advice on style and glamour. Many of them became celebrities in their own right, giving talks on radio and television. Edith Head used to give advice to all the ladies who still wanted to look stylish during wartime rationing, coming up with her Safety Pin blouse that had a safety-pin print and safety pins as substitutes for buttons. Perhaps that's something you could think about with all the women out there today who are trying to look fabulous in a recession.'

Good point. My head was swimming. I had so much work to do.

'But just remember the most important thing, Grace,' Verity said.

'What's that?' I asked. (Safety pins could be dangerous?)

'That aside from all the physical attributes we all want to

enhance – Hepburn and her famous shoulders, Marlene and her fabulous legs, Liz and her tiny waist – or all the things we want to detract from – Veronica Lake and her short frame, Vivien Leigh and her large hands (she hated them so much that she owned 150 pairs of gloves to keep them covered) – that there is something far, far more important than all this. Do you know what it is?'

'Erm . . . Good dry-cleaning?'

She rolled her eyes and flung one end of her silk scarf over her shoulder dramatically. 'When Elsie Pierce started writing about "feminine loveliness" all the way back in the thirties, even she said all of it was nothing without *charm*. It's a person's charm you've got to find, Grace. Start with that and you won't go wrong.'

Right. Charm. Got it.

Actually, I didn't have it at all. Charm? Would they wink at me? Tell me a joke? Do a little tap dance? What? Perhaps my Business Angel would know.

'Right, I'm exhausted after all that.' Verity exhaled, dragging herself up from her chair and switching on her old gramophone. 'It's time for a long hot bath and some Ella Fitzgerald.'

I turned and caught my reflection in the mirror. I was wearing a beautiful full-length fitted cream dress with a Chantilly lace overlay. It was stunning, but confusing; it could very well have been a wedding dress. I'd never tried one on in my entire life. Tanya had loved to play around in Mum's when we were kids but, strangely, it was the only dress in her whole wardrobe I had absolutely no interest in putting on.

'Suits you,' Verity said, as she left.

'I don't think so,' I said, shaking my head.

She smiled at me knowingly before disappearing through the alcove as 'Someone To Watch Over Me' floated past.

I felt the tag hanging down my back and fished it out. Christ, it was a *real* Givenchy! No wonder we were doing a rentals service.

My phone beeped and I picked it up dreamily – I was chilling

280

out, just hanging in my Givenchy dress listening to Ella Fitzgerald. The screen said 'Lisa's mum'. That was weird. I'd forgotten I even had her number. Last text I'd got from her was to tell me I'd be paying to have 'Screw You Ian' laser-removed.

**Grace, Lisa has collapsed. Not sure what's wrong. She's in A-and-E.**

I turned on my heel. 'Verity, I have to go!' I shouted behind me, racing out of the door.

## 34

Disaster. There was no way I'd be let in to see Lisa as I wasn't 'immediate family'. So said the guy on Reception when I explained who I was looking for. I could try when I got to the ward, but he doubted it. He didn't get it: Lisa *was* my family.

'Why are you in a wedding dress?' he said then, one eyebrow raised.

Wedding dress? *Yes!*

'Because . . . I'm getting married . . . and Lisa swallowed the rings by accident . . . and I just want to see if she's . . . passed them yet?'

He stared at me as if to say, 'Do I look like a simpleton?' Then he looked at his colleague and there was some more eyebrow action between them and finally he gave me an almost imperceptible wave. 'Floor four,' he said, 'and I hope they've given those rings a good rinse.'

I raced up to the fourth floor as quickly as I could in a full-length vintage lace gown, skidding on the polished floors around the corner and into her room.

'Grace!' Mrs Ferguson whispered, looking at me quizzically. 'She's sleeping.'

'Okay,' I whispered back, holding on to the stitch in my side.

Oh, God, poor Lisa! I looked at her asleep in the bed, tied up to a million tubes and monitors, so helpless. Tears stung the corners of my eyes.

'So, good news!' Mrs Ferguson said.

I swear to God, Lisa's mum had the oddest sense of humour sometimes – I was pretty sure 'good news' did not arise when the person we both loved was lying in a hospital bed.

'It's not cancer.'

Oh, that *was* good news! I burst into tears and collapsed back into a chair, which turned out to be a wheelchair. But there were no other chairs and I had to sit down. My heart was hammering and little dots were flitting past my eyes.

'A cyst has burst on her ovary. They're pretty certain there are more of them but the good news is they're benign. The bad news is they need to remove one of her ovaries before they turn precancerous and they're going to have to keep an eye on the second. But they think she's going to be okay.'

'Did they say . . . does this mean . . . ?'

'What, Grace?' she said kindly.

'That she'll only get half a period?'

I know – *I know*! Who the hell asks that kind of question? But I didn't know what else to say and I didn't want to be discussing Lisa's fertility with anyone else before I'd spoken properly to her.

'Em, so I tried calling Killian,' she continued, pretending she hadn't heard my question, which was very decent of her, 'but I didn't get any response. I left him a message so he should be here shortly.'

'Okay.'

'I'm going to pick up a few things for her and I'll get her dad to bring them when he comes in later.'

She left and I wheeled forward, taking Lisa's hand gently in mine.

'Hey,' she mumbled.

'I'm so sorry, I didn't mean to wake you,' I whispered, delighted all the same to see her awake.

'I was actually just pretending to be asleep till Mum left. She's been great but if she told me about Betty Morton's hip replacement or Orna O'Flanagan's twisted sinus duct one more time I was going to have to call Security.'

'Leese, I'm so glad you're okay.'

'Shit, what kind of drugs have they put me on?'

'Why?' I said. 'What's wrong?'

'Grace, I think I'm hallucinating. It's so weird. I can see you

283

right here in front of me . . . but you're in a wheelchair, wearing a wedding dress! This is some *strong* stuff!'

I laughed. 'Long story . . . So, good news, and some not so good news. How are you?' I wasn't sure she'd want to talk about it.

'I know, scary, huh? I mean, it's great it's not you-know-what, but the doctor has told me that becoming a mum could be difficult.'

I swallowed hard.

'I've spent half my life trying not to get pregnant.' She sighed. 'Turns out I should have popped one out a few years ago! Granted I'd be living in tenement housing with delinquent children while hounding "Screw You Ian" for child support but I'd be happy. And you'd come and visit.'

'Actually, I don't think I would. That sounds terrifying.'

She smiled, her eyes heavy with the weight of uncertainty. 'Funny thing is, I only really started to think about the possibility of kids over the last few months. Who knows? Maybe it was turning thirty, maybe it was meeting Killian, seeing him with his nieces and nephews. It just seems to come so naturally to him. Like he takes it all in his stride. And to do it all with someone like that, someone I feel this way about, I don't know, makes the whole idea far less terrifying . . .'

'Please say you've spoken to him about all this?' I said.

'I did, I did. And he was really good. Very supportive.' Her voice sounded distant, like she was processing it all over again as she said it. 'It's a lot to take on board all at once, though, isn't it? I think guys deal with things a little differently.'

'We're getting old, Grace!' She groaned, burying her head in her pillow. 'It's hard not to think about marriage and babies when it's all everyone seems to be talking about.'

I nodded, disguising my bafflement. It was strange to hear Lisa suddenly talking about all of this. How come I wasn't there yet? Was that weird? Was *I* weird? 'The Odd One'? The Lady Gaga or Tilda Swinton? The Lindsay Lohan of Disney? The 'anti' in antipasto? The eighth adopted sister that no one ever talked about in *Seven Brides for Seven Brothers*? (No, there was no eighth adopted sister. I was just getting all metaphor-y.)

'Lisa,' I said solemnly, holding her hands in mine, 'you are going to be a mum one day. I know you are. And you'll be a brilliant one.'

'Thank you,' she said, her eyes welling.

'And, hey,' I continued, 'when no one else wants to invite the crazy spinster with the cat over for dinner, you'll invite me and I can hang with you and play with your kids and eat meatloaf. Because that's what you have to learn to cook when you become a mum.'

'Really? Meatloaf? I think that's only in America.'

'See? *See?* I'd be a shit mum.'

'No, you wouldn't,' she said. 'We'll both be brilliant mums. One day.'

'Okay.' I sighed. 'But until then, can we please still play Who Can Roll Down the Steep Hill in Bushy Park the Quickest Without Rolling Off to the Side and Banging into a Tree?'

She smiled. 'When the hell did we grow up, Grace?'

We sat for hours while I told Lisa all about Peter André's search for love and Jessica Alba's dramatic weight loss, as I read the stash of magazines on her side locker. Her dad arrived and sat with us while we debated whether or not Kate Winslet played it too safe in monochrome. And as I found myself complimenting him on his fabulous Swarovski-crystal stud earrings, I wondered if Lisa was right about him being gay. To be fair, I'd seen Mario Balotelli sporting a similar pair, but I thought it was probably different for Premiership footballers. God, there were just so many rules.

A little later, Lisa's phone beeped beside her bed.

'Can you get it for me, Grace? I would but my arms are attached to drips and wires because I have to get my ovary removed.'

'Oooh, it's from Killian!' I said. 'He must be on his way!' I could feel her excitement rising as she waited for me to read it.

Oh, Jesus . . .

My stomach heaved. What the fuck was this? How could he send a message like this after everything that had happened, everything she was going through? I wanted to hurl her phone out of the window.

'What, Grace? What is it?' she said, her face falling. I wanted to wrap my arms around her and protect her from every bad bit of news this sodding world kept throwing at her. I was going to kill him. I was actually going to kill him.

'Grace, tell me,' she said sternly. 'Tell me!'

'He's not coming,' I said softly.

'Tell me what he said!'

I read the text aloud: 'Lisa, I'm so sorry to hear you're under the weather but I know everything is going to be okay. It's all a bit heavy seeing as we were only having a bit of fun, isn't it? The best of luck with it all and let me know how you get on.'

'I knew it,' she said, pounding the mattress with her fists. 'I knew it.'

The next few hours passed in slow motion. I crawled up on the bed beside her and held her as she cried bitterly in my arms, the weight of her disappointment crushing me entirely. The nurses would come in to check on her, she'd fall asleep, wake up, remember it, and start crying again. I texted her mum with the news when she was asleep. Turned out Mrs Ferguson was an adept texter and knew some eye-watering language. I bet she listened to the 'parental advisory' version of Kanye West albums!

Some time after eleven, I must have been half asleep but all of a sudden a hand was holding mine. It felt reassuring.

'Doctor?' I mumbled.

'Is that what you're calling me, these days? Good to know I've been promoted.' The hand tightened its grip.

'Robbie!' I said, suddenly wide awake and overwhelmed with relief. 'What? Why are you here? When . . . ?'

'Sssh,' he said, brushing my fringe from my eyes. 'Her mum called, told me everything, I just wanted to see she was okay. I'm not certain, but I'm pretty sure I may have punched Killian in the face.'

Of course Robbie was here. They had become the best of friends over the seven long years we'd been together. I bit my lip, trying to contain my delight. 'Well, you've saved me the job. Thank you.'

'I'm not sure my boss is too happy as it was right in the middle of a work thing, but these things have to be done.'

'You're going to have unbelievable rock 'n' roll street cred now.'

'Yeah, I think that might apply just to the artists themselves, not the lackeys who chase around after them like gobshites.'

'Did you give him a bleeder?'

'Been watching *The Fighter*, have we? A bit contemporary for you, no?' He smiled, shaking his wrist out. 'I actually think I may have sprained my hand but please don't tell anyone because I may be the coolest I've ever been right now.'

I laughed quietly. God, it was good to see him. And for everything to be normal, no awkwardness, no hurt, just a shared bond over someone we both cared for very much.

'Grace, can I ask you something?'

'What's that?'

'Why are you wearing a wedding dress?'

Well, not *entirely* normal. This was weird. I was sitting there in a wedding dress after everything that had happened! New York. The ring. *Us*.

'Is it some kind of shock therapy to get you over your fear of marriage?'

'I don't have a fear of marriage!'

He hung his head, staring at his hand as he flexed and stretched it in his lap. 'I'm sorry I brought it up,' he mumbled. 'She is going to be okay, isn't she?' he said, changing the subject and looking at her dolefully.

'She will,' I assured him. 'She's going to be just fine.'

We sat there in the half-darkness as the moonlight crept

through the slats of the blind and talked about the first few months of our lives without each other. I told him about Verity and the shop, and he told me all about the promotion he was up for in work and how much travel he'd be able to do if he got it.

'I'm proud of you, Grace,' he said softly, looking me straight in the eye.

'I'm proud of you too,' I whispered.

The bell for the midnight shift chimed at the nurses' station just outside the room and I stretched the pins and needles out of my legs.

'Hey, Red?' he said.

'Yeah?' I smiled: it had been a long while since I'd heard that.

'Happy birthday!'

## 35

'Scarlet for you, love! Did he ditch you at the altar?'

Huh? Me? Why was a flock of tracksuits trundling past me, shouting in my face? Ah, yes. I was walking along O'Connell Street in a wedding dress. Occupational hazard.

I burst into the shop, ready and armed with my big apology to Verity as to why I had high-tailed it yesterday, like Ginger Rogers in *It Had To Be You*. I didn't even wait for her to say anything before I poured out my story.

'Whoa!' she said.

Uh-oh. Was it air-rifle time?

'You apologize for the things you genuinely need to apologize for. Like spilling tea on my 1950s Balmain dinner jacket.'

She *knew* about that! Oh, God, let's just hope she didn't know about the jam on the 1940s silver pencil skirt.

'And for the jam on the 1940s silver pencil skirt.'

Damn.

'But you don't ever have to apologize in life for the things you don't have to be sorry for. Like looking after your friends.' The wistful look that I'd seen before crept across her face, and I knew she was thinking of someone in particular.

'Thanks, Verity,' I said.

'And what about this Killian loser? You want me to go rustle him up for Lisa?'

I bit my lip. It was hard not to smile, looking at this diminutive octogenarian in a floor-length navy blue evening gown, making fists with her hands.

'Actually, someone already has. But thank you.'

'Huh.' She tutted. 'No-good son-of-a-bitch sounds like my

third husband. Riding high when the times were good then running like a rabbi out of a pork shop when things got tough.'

'I know! Why is it that some guys just can't handle the riding and bolt when the pork gets tough?'

She blinked at me. 'You haven't had your morning coffee yet, have you?'

I shook my head.

'What else is up?'

I shrugged. Where to start? All of it, really. Lisa. Killian, the prick. That I was the eighth adopted sister in *Seven Brides for Seven Brothers*. That I'd sat in a wheelchair talking to Robbie for the entire night while wearing a wedding dress. I rubbed my eyes, suddenly exhausted.

Maybe it was because I was now officially thirty. Maybe this was what 'oldness' felt like. I was just going to go around yawning like someone in a Pharmaton ad for the rest of my life.

'Sit down there now and tell an old lady all about it,' she said kindly, offering me the gorgeous big leather armchair that only she ever sat in.

'I can't, Verity, as much as I'd love to. I have to change out of the wedding dress I met my ex in last night, then meet my Angel.'

She stared at me with about as much comprehension as a person watching an episode of *Geordie Shore*. 'We need to put *two* espresso shots in that coffee!'

After I'd changed, we sat and talked for a while over yesterday's scones and coffee so strong I practically had to chew it. I told Verity I couldn't be late because I had my first meeting with my appointed Business Angel after some 'Internetting'. She loved the idea of it but told me that sometimes, no matter how crazy and hectic life got, you had to quit chasing for five minutes and just sit down and breathe. And have a scone.

I found myself telling her about Robbie. About New York. About Tanya and the Wedding Cult. About seeing Robbie the night before and, by the way, he'd been the one to deal with

Killian. Once I'd started, I couldn't seem to stop. And she sat there and listened, soaking it all up like a sponge.

I double-checked the address for my Business Angel. It was weird that I hadn't noticed till now but it was on the same street as Best Wishes. I stood outside the door and looked down the cobbled street. Okay, so this was number three and the even numbers were on the other side. Down there was ten. Number eight. Number six. So number four was – oh, bugger!

I stepped back inside and shut the door, resisting the urge to lock it and becoming the biggest hypocrite of all time.

'Verity, I think the Business Angel is a stupid idea. It's just so silly. I mean a Business Angel? Really? It's so childish. And creepy.'

'Grace, you've just spent the morning telling me how amazing it's going to be, and you don't seem to be coming up with any fantastic brainwaves of your own about tying this all into a functioning business, one that I can approve of morally or emotionally. So you'd better get your sweet ass out there unless you think all I hired you to do was hang around trying on hats and smudging jam on my 1940s silver pencil skirts!'

I turned on my heel and bolted out of the door like a lit rocket.

So there I'd been, shiteing on about Fate and destiny and all things serendipity like that and now I'd got my comeuppance. (I had told Verity about Stephen 'Heart Wish' Kelleher and how excited I was. She'd frowned and told me it had been a bit quick. I told her that everything moved at a faster pace nowadays, that we had Wi-Fi and Internet shopping with next-day delivery and speed-dial buttons on phones, and she really did need to keep up with the times.)

Anyway, I was no longer a fan of Fate and 'hilarious coincidences' or any of that crap because there was absolutely nothing hilarious about knocking on number four, Cherry Tree Row. The door swung open and I inhaled sharply.

Good God, he was even better-looking in the flesh without a

net curtain covering half his face. Yes, that's right. Meet Creepy Staring Weirdo Net-curtain Pervert from over the road. My new Business Angel.

'Hi,' I said, trying to be breezy. Since I didn't so much speak as squeak, I didn't quite nail the breeziness. Must work on that.

He stared down at me, dark hazel eyes twinkling through thick black eyelashes, making me squirm.

'So, I'm Grace, your new recruit for the Business Angel scheme.' Why was I still speaking like an Animaniacs cartoon character?

'Do come in, please,' he said, in a gravelly voice that made mine sound comical in comparison.

I coughed and cleared my throat, attempting to bring it down a few octaves. 'By a hilarious coincidence, I actually work just over the road from you.' Oh, God, now my voice was too *low*. Like I was taking the piss out of him. Help me! Somebody help me!

'I, er . . . yes, I've seen you all right. Quite a few times, actually.'

I'll bet you have, you sleazy, incredibly handsome pervert! I should have come over in Verity's aviator gear – leather jacket, chaps, a helmet and goggles – to shield me from his creepiness. Although he'd probably see it as some sort of kinky S&M role play and start spanking me. And that would be a weird way to conduct business. It would definitely have caught my attention in a business lecture. Even if I'd been nose-deep in *Grazia*.

'So tell me, Grace,' he said, in a deep Laurence Olivier voice – if Laurence Olivier had been from Galway – 'what exactly is the business?'

God, he was so handsome, in a very old-fashioned sort of way. Big and burly with strong arms and hands, dressed in a tweed blazer and slacks, his thick black hair slicked back with a few silver strands peppering his temples. I could picture him now, sitting in a restaurant in Belgravia in the forties dressed in a smart suit and a dickie bow, sipping bourbon and smoking a packet of Pall Mall cigarettes.

'Is it a fancy-dress shop? Or are you an entertainer for children's parties?'

Was he mocking me? Was he a Galwegian-Laurence Olivier-lookalike asshole?

'It's a vintage clothes shop,' I said sharply.

'I'm sorry,' he said, dipping his eyebrows and giving me a smile. 'Forgive me. Clothes aren't really my thing. It's just I've seen you over there in a big pink . . .' He searched for the right word, like he had no idea how the ballgown should be classified.

'. . . dress? And then yesterday a wedding dress. And before that, well . . .'

He was talking about my skirt up over my head, with my Supergirl pants on show! I patted my dress down self-consciously, making doubly sure the back of it wasn't caught, another 'hilarious coincidence', in my knickers.

'You looked beautiful in all three, but I really don't know much about such things,' he said.

Hey, what was that? He wasn't *flirting* with me, was he? I suddenly went all coy and melty.

'So, please forgive me. Sit down and tell me all about the business and what you've planned for the future.'

'Wow, big question,' I said nervously. 'I don't know – a big house in the country, maybe, and just to be happy, you know. I'd like a few dogs also, rescue dogs preferably. But not ones with skin conditions.'

He looked up at me from under his heavy brows. 'Well, that sounds lovely, Grace, and thank you for sharing your dream, but it was plans for the future of the business that I was thinking of.'

'Of course.'

We sat at his desk, behind the infamous net curtain, and thrashed out loads of ideas about the business. George Madson, the artist formerly known as Creepy Staring Weirdo Net-curtain

Pervert, had his finger in a lot of pies but it seemed he was best known for running a successful business network and review magazine called *Connect* that was subscribed to by companies all over the world. I lied and told him I knew all about it and that I was a big fan. 'Number-one subscriber.'

'You'll have found the last edition interesting so? The feature all about young entrepreneurs taking over established businesses that have floundered in today's changing market?'

'Erm, well, George, to be honest, my postman is an alcoholic and often delivers *Grazia* to me instead. It's very frustrating.'

He smiled at me from across the desk, rubbing the stubble on his chin while taking me in. I looked away in case I went red. The way he looked at me, it was as though he was staring at me completely naked, and enjoying it.

You know, during our chat, I might have realized that he wasn't a sex pest *per se*, just incredibly sexy, and I might have got the two things a bit mixed up with everything else that was going on. With the stress and the pressure and all.

I cleared my throat, hoping it would also clear the sexual tension in the room. I had to remember not to take it personally. He was just a sexy person. He probably flirted with everyone and everything. He probably humped his own desk when there was no one else around. Actually, I hoped not because then he'd be too like my mum's friend Nora's annoying Jack Russell.

I smiled awkwardly as he leaned forward and leafed through my business plan.

'Okay, there are some great ideas here. And I hear what you're saying about Verity wanting to keep things "special". I really do, actually. People can all too often get greedy and end up losing sight of what was supposed to make it tick in the first place.'

*Swoon.*

'Perhaps we should think of introducing some corporate ethics here too, like a "Dress For Success" scheme for women who are trying to get back to work but don't have the means to buy presentable interview attire.'

*Swoon.*

Oooh, I loved it, and Verity would too. Oh, my: altruistic *and* sexy *and* successful! Must remember to put 'Have sex with George Madson' into the business plan.

*Joking.* (Maybe.)

'But obviously,' he continued, 'you want to make it a success-ful business too. And the key to doing that is understanding your customer and making sure we market you correctly.'

'We': I liked that. He was obviously taking me seriously and really wanted to help out with the shop. This was fantastic.

*Oooh.*

What was not fantastic was the framed family photo I'd just spotted on George's desk. I'm not saying it wasn't a fantastic picture – they all looked lovely in their matching polo necks – just that it wasn't fantastic he was taken, which meant I should stop slapping the table and laughing coquettishly every time he men-tioned 'evaluating the stock'. It was better this way: I needed to be professional and focused. Plus what would Stephen 'Heart Wish' Kelleher say, eh?

I smiled, thinking about my new room mate-cum-Heart Wish and the wild abandoned sex we were bound to be having soon. And, besides, George was also way too old for me: he must have been at least forty. I mean, come on! I was only . . . shiteballs. I was thirty, wasn't I?

Oh, God, I was actually thirty.

It had finally arrived. It was here.

My thirtieth birthday.

I felt myself wilt in the chair: Happy birthday, me.

'Good news, Verity!' I said, bursting through the door. 'Our Angel is an angel!'

She was standing behind the counter eclipsed by a gigantic bunch of flowers.

'You lied to me,' she said, peeping through the fronds of a splayed fern.

Uh-oh. She'd found out I never actually dated that guy from *Byker Grove*. (I'm not even sure why I said it, to be honest. She knew so much about actors that I'd wanted to look a bit cool and pretend I'd dated one. Even though it was a random *Byker Grove* actor. It was just that if I'd said Leonardo DiCaprio there was every chance she might not have bought it.)

'You never told me it was your birthday!' she said, shaking her head.

Phew! My pseudo-relationship with Andrew Hayden-Smith/ 'Ben', was still very much intact.

'I never lied! It never came up! Oooh, are they from Stephen?' I squealed, rushing to check the card.

*Gracie, to my oldest friend in the world (literally) – you are the best. I hope my ovaries haven't ruined your birthday. Love you loads, Lisa xxx*

Aw! How sweet was Lisa to think of me in the middle of the hell she was going through?

'To be honest, Verity, I was hoping to just pretend the whole thing wasn't happening. It's a biggie. I'm . . . *thirty*,' I said, with almost as much horror as if I'd just discovered I was part alien.

'Honey, *ninety* is a biggie. You ain't even scratched the surface. Now, pick yourself out something fabulous because we're going celebrating.'

'Are we going to Paris?' I shrieked.

She stopped in her tracks. 'No. We're going to the Merrion for afternoon tea. I hope you won't be disappointed,' she said, before shuffling off and muttering to herself, 'Honestly, I don't know another girl in the world who watches so many movies . . .'

Oops.

'I *love* the Merrion!' I said, trying to make up for my ridiculous Paris comment. Shit, that coffee must have been far too strong.

But I really did love the Merrion! Yay! And, hopefully, there was a new general manager in there by now who'd know nothing

of the time I'd tried to fleece a toiletries trolley when I was ham-
mered one Christmas. (As we've established, hotel toiletries are a
bit of a weakness.) And then I'd decided to crawl into the trolley
for Robbie to push home as it was 'going to be a nightmare trying
to get a taxi on Christmas Eve'.

Yay!

## 36

I looked around the Merrion and beamed proudly. Not only were we sitting at a terribly decadent mahogany table by the large fireplace, but I hadn't been asked to leave on account of any previous trolley misdemeanours. The little cakes and sandwiches stacked up on the tiered stand were just adorable. As was the tray of old bone-china teacups placed beside it. Everything looked amazing, like delicate hand-made props in the kitchen of an ornate dolls' house. Each pastry echoed a different painting in the hotel, with a mini landscape remodelled on a tiny slice of Madeira cake.

'Clever, isn't it?' Verity said, cutting the little cake painting in two and popping half into her mouth. 'I remember Picasso doing something similar with his paintings at one of his infamous dinner parties.'

I coughed and the piece of cucumber sandwich I'd been chewing went up my nose. Oh, no. Verity was starting to lose it like my granny had. She was missing vital words in her sentence structuring. Words like 'reading'. As in, 'I remember *reading* about Picasso doing something similar . . .'

I just hoped she wasn't going to try to convince me she was a spy too. Did all old ladies turn into spies?

'So, Grace, you were born thirty years ago today, named after none other than the Princess of Monaco,' she said, before I'd managed to clear the cucumber out of my nose.

I nodded. 'As much as I like her I'm grateful it wasn't after Ginger Rogers as my hair only turned red when I was seven and that really would have been too much to bear. Were kids as cruel in the eighteen-hundreds as they were in the eighties?'

She glared at me.

What? Did I get my maths wrong again? I was so shit at maths.

'So, your mother is as much of a romantic as you? A fan of the Hollywood Golden Era?'

'Oh, God, no. My mum hasn't a romantic bone in her body. She's a-romantic. I think she was born like that. Like she was born without tonsils.'

'I don't believe it. The woman who gave birth to you *isn't* a romantic? Well, how come she was watching Grace Kelly movies in the first place?'

'I dunno.' I shrugged. 'Maybe she saw one when she was at home mitching one day with "tonsillitis" before they realized she didn't have any and she had to go back to school.'

'I don't buy it,' she said, pouring her tea through the cute silver tea-strainer thingie, then replacing the thingie in the cute silver tea-strainer thingie holder. Gosh, I never realized there were so many appliances you had to use if you were going to have a properly posh cup of tea. It was exhausting. Perhaps I was just more of a builder at heart when it came to tea.

'Verity,' I sighed, 'you've never met my parents. They're . . . different. My family is different. It's not a conventional set-up at all.'

Perhaps it was the warm hazy comfort of my big chair by the fire. Perhaps I'd had enough of trying to hide from it in the face of everything else that had happened lately. Perhaps it was Verity, this lady in the winter of her life, who'd seen the seasons tick over a thousand times already and couldn't be fazed by any of it. Perhaps it was because she'd been so honest with me. Shared her secrets. Bared her soul. Unwritten the written rule and told me what her wish had been. Or should I say *who*?

But I sat and told her about my family. Things I'd only ever told Robbie, Lisa and Rebecca. Lisa had had her own experience of it, too, of course, in a different way. Because her dad's affair, if he'd had one, might have been with a man.

They always sounded so romantic, didn't they? All the big affairs back then? Carole Lombard and Clark Gable? Spencer Tracy and Katharine Hepburn? Elizabeth Taylor and Eddie

Fisher? But for every one of those scorching, magnificent affairs, there was a wife at home, heartbroken. For every Elizabeth Taylor, there was a Debbie Reynolds, who'd lost her childhood sweetheart.

'. . . and that was my mum,' I told Verity.

'Dad met Lynda at some business conference in London in the early nineties and their affair started some time after that. We only found out about it after she died a few years later, when Dad was so heartbroken, he couldn't get out of bed for weeks. Things hadn't been great up to then with him and Mum – fighting, tension in the house, Mum constantly agitated. I think she knew long before she actually found out.

'And, you know, I almost felt sorry for my dad. His hurt was so raw I could have almost touched it. Tanya and I did everything we could to try to cheer him up – putting on little plays for him at the end of his bed, making him his favourite cake. But there was just nothing any of us could do.

'I remember reading about Clark Gable when Carole Lombard had been killed in a plane crash, how he had simply fallen apart with the grief. How his *joie de vivre*, his spark, had left this world with her. And I remember thinking Dad was just like him. But not in the way a kid would normally idolize her father.'

'He was never the same.' Verity sighed. 'And I can imagine your father never has been either.'

I shook my head. 'It was like he had come alive only to die again, right in front of us. I don't know how Mum and Dad stayed together after that. Or why. Maybe it was for us, Tanya and me. But they did – for ever altered, for ever haunted by the ghost in our family that the rest of us had never known.'

Verity looked so lost in the story that it was like she'd crawled right inside it. Like she was among the thoughts in my own head.

'They both have that expression now, this quiet acceptance, that my dad married the wrong woman, and that my mum, heartbreakingly, still married the right man. None of us have ever spoken about it. It was just how it was.'

I picked up my teaspoon and stirred my tea, watching the golden liquid spin in loops.

Verity studied me as the firelight danced in her eyes. 'Perhaps your mum was a romantic,' she said. '*Is* one. It's just all choked up in a knot after how things turned out.'

'Maybe,' I said, shrugging. 'In a way I hope she's not. I don't think I could bear her disappointment.'

'And how do you and your sister get on with your father now?'

'Tanya spends her life convinced Peter's going to do the same thing to her and trying to control everything.'

'And you?'

'I just get on with it.'

'Really?'

'Yeah,' I said, picking at a mini pastry painting, not really having the stomach for it.

'Grace, no one's life is free from mistakes. Remember that. And part of getting older, reaching the milestones, clocking up the years, is accepting that and moving on. No one wants to end up like Norma Desmond in *Sunset Boulevard*.'

Her words fell around me gently, like a small snow flurry. And I felt them. Even though I was lost in a world of my own. In a place I had left a long time ago and never really revisited.

'I remember that day so clearly. I was about eleven and I came in from playing on the road to find Mum and Dad having a blazing row in the kitchen. They didn't hear me and I sat on the stairs, listening. Honestly, it was like a tennis match where they were lobbing insults, rather than balls, across the net, like they wanted to destroy each other. I don't think I ever heard my mother sound so distraught – before or since – and before I realized it I was in floods of tears. I ran to the TV room and shut the door, switched on the telly and turned up the volume to block out their voices.

'At first all I could see through the blur of tears were black and white shadows moving across the screen. Voices and music blocked out the other noise. And then I saw them, Audrey

Hepburn and Gregory Peck, in *Roman Holiday*. And I fell in love. It was magical. This princess who wanted to escape her own life for a while, pretend she didn't have to deal with her stifling duties, her responsibilities, she ran away. She fell in love. And all in the most beautiful clothes I had ever seen. And the way Gregory looked at her – I almost felt cheated for my mother. *That* was how a man was supposed to look at a woman.'

I smiled at Verity. 'After that first hit I was hooked on the glossy romance of it all. I could go on my own Roman holiday any time I wanted to get away from it all. I could disappear into someone else's life for ninety minutes of romance, love, fun, fashion. Someone else's drama. Someone else's story.'

I stopped suddenly, as if I'd been out of it and had just come to. Like when I needed to eat chocolate, or I'd been reading the *Vogue* September issue. Gosh, it had all got very serious, hadn't it? This was my birthday. I should be sitting here eating so much cake I might vomit over my shoes!

I thought I should feel sad after telling her all that. Exhausted. Drained. But I almost felt light and floaty, like I could drift all the way up to the beautiful crystal chandeliers above us.

'So tell me more about you, Verity. I'm bored with me,' I said, popping an entire Viennese whirl into my mouth.

'What about me?' She smiled. 'Did I mess up any children by getting married five times?'

I coughed crumbs out my mouth and we looked at each other, then started to laugh.

'You were *not* married five times!' I stuttered, crumbs still spraying from my mouth.

'Well, I beg to differ,' she purred.

Five husbands? Five? *Five?*

Who? When? Where?

'I never had any children,' she said, grinning at me, enjoying the fact that she had managed to astound me. 'Maybe it was just never meant to be.'

'I'm sorry,' I said softly.

'Don't be, kid,' she said. 'My life was full enough, believe me. I had enough blessings to fill a hundred lifetimes.'

I believed her. She clung to her past with such vigour that it must have been something pretty special.

'Though sometimes I think maybe it would have been nice to have a piece of David left here with me,' she said.

'It must be lonely,' I heard myself say, my words scattering around the fireplace like flecks of ash.

'It is. "A good innings", they call it, getting to my age. Trouble is, every time you finish one more lap, you've lost another team mate.' She smiled sadly. 'It can be lonely at the top.'

I stared at the flames in the grate, thinking about Mum and Dad, Tanya and Peter, Lisa, Rebecca and Tony. Robbie. Me. What was the score sheet going to be for any of us? And when our time was eventually up and someone blew the whistle, would we leave the pitch feeling we'd lost? Or that we'd won?

'So when do you think yourself and this Stephen fellow are going to get it on?' she said, perking up in her seat.

'My Heart Wish? I don't know. I thought you were the expert on that!'

'I never said so, Grace. I'm only an expert on my own. How on earth could I possibly know what *you* would wish for in your heart of hearts? Takes people long enough to figure out their own Heart Wish. You can never be an expert on someone else's. Unless, that is, they're a part of yours.'

Jesus. This was confusing. But it was all going to be fine, though perhaps I needed to hot things up a bit, get things going. Start dashing from room to room in my undies shouting, 'I left my clothes in here. Oh, God, sorry, I thought you were out!' How many times could you do that so it still looked authentic?

'Grace, I have a present for you,' Verity said suddenly, straightening herself in her chair and giving me a big smile. 'A birthday present.'

'Verity! Is it a pair of nineteen-forties sapphire earrings?' I said.

'Er, no, not exactly.'

Oooh. That was awkward. I was really going to have to stop jumping to mad conclusions.

'It's more of a story than anything material.'

So, not an *actual* present, then. Humph.

'Thank you . . . I love . . . stories,' I said, trying to hide my disappointment.

'I think you'll like this, actually. I wasn't sure when I was going to tell it to you. I needed to trust you first. I needed to know you were in this for all the right reasons before you got sidetracked by dazzle.'

Oh. My. God! Was Verity about to tell me that . . . she was . . . *my real gran*?

'It's about the shop,' she said.

Oh, right. Sorry, is there any chance we could just pretend I never mentioned that bit about her being my gran? And I know I'm going to have to cut down on *Golden Girls* reruns.

'Best Wishes is a little bit more special than it might actually appear on the surface. Like a lot of things really. But underneath it all is . . .'

'An ancient archaeological site?' I asked, in a small voice.

'Not exactly. Grace,' she said, steeling herself. 'I want to share my secret with you.'

I wished she'd spit it out before I said something else ridiculous! I inched forward to the edge of my seat, hanging on her every word.

'The shop is full of things from the past,' she declared.

Excuse me? That was it? That was the big secret? That was my birthday present? Erm, Verity, that was no secret. It was a *vintage* clothes store so I had pretty much put two and two together. That was a sum I could handle.

'That's not all,' she offered mischievously. 'The fact of the matter is . . . that the stock is from some very special people.'

If I inched any further on this seat I'd plop onto the floor.

'You see, Grace, before I came here, I worked as a dresser my whole career.'

'What do you mean, a dresser?'

'Well . . . for all the big movie stars.'

*What?* I replayed all the little casual mentions of big names over the last few weeks, telling myself there was no way on God's earth . . .

'Marlene, Bette, Joan, Ingrid, Grace, Audrey, Marilyn, Liz . . . all of them.'

I dropped the teacup and felt it crash to my lap as if in slow motion. 'Wh-what?' I stammered.

'That's right. I spent my life dressing them. At all the big studios. Paramount, MGM, Universal, Columbia. With all the big studio costume designers. For all the big movies and all the big award ceremonies. I even got to go to the Oscars in 1949 when costume design was first recognized by the Academy. I dressed Liz that night. My, she was so nervous. I kept telling her she'd feel a lot more comfortable if we loosened her corset a little, but she wouldn't hear of it. "Tighter!" she kept saying. "I want it tighter!" '

She smiled and I saw that expression again – the one that always danced across her face when she was lost in her memories. I sat paralysed with my jaw hanging and tea all over my lap. I couldn't move. I was completely overcome with shock.

'I travelled the world with them and became close to many of them. Their lives were exciting, charming, exhilarating, yet sometimes chaotic and troubled. They seemed to be served on a platter for people to devour. There were the wonderful times and there were the difficult times. And sometimes all you need is someone to share it with, someone to help shoulder the excitement and the disappointments. The good, the bad, the ugly. And always – *always* – the stylish and the glamorous.'

I collapsed back in my seat, winded by what she had said. Verity had been a Hollywood dresser? The lady who organized these legendary movie stars on set and beyond as they assembled the iconic looks that still inspired fashion to this very day? I could not believe it. I felt if I were to reach out and touch her I could physically grab hold of the past. A past I'd been so head over heels in love with and bewitched by almost my entire life.

I wanted to know everything. Stories about Liz Taylor. About Grace Kelly and her romance with Prince Rainier and her decision to give up her career at twenty-six. About Marilyn's tragic life. About their talent, their work, their appreciation for style and fashion. About everything. Where did you even begin?

But I knew it was too crass. They had been her friends and this had been Verity's *life*. If she had loved them as much as her smile suggested, she would protect and defend them fiercely. Like a gate-keeper to a sacred Wonderland.

I sighed heavily, thinking that maybe she'd let me in to have a walk in the gardens some time. Maybe. If she had the inclination to unlock the gate and I was lucky enough to be asked to step inside.

'Verity, that is extraordinary,' I said.

'You can see now why I never regretted not having my own children. They were my babies. All of them. They were my life. And when I married David, he came on board for the adventure. He was a tailor so we made a great team. He made suits for all the leading men – Clark Gable, Gary Cooper, Jimmy Stewart, Humphrey Bogart, Richard Burton, Tony Curtis – and we lived a very charmed life, Grace. We travelled, saw the world, attended the most splendid parties, went on fabulous group holidays, but sometimes it was the lazy Sunday barbecues over at Liz and Richard's with the gang that were the best days. We really made the best friends anyone could have wished for and were very, very lucky indeed. As they were to have us. We were a dynamic duo, David and I. That was for sure.'

This was like a dream, I thought, as the story continued to unfold.

'And that is what is so special about the shop, and why I'm so protective of it. Why the people who want to rent my things need to be borrowing them for very special reasons.'

'Why?' I said, still not getting it.

'Because they belong to them, Grace, that's why. Because they belong to my babies.'

'You. Are. Shitting. Me.' I refused to believe that this story could possibly get any better. I was too far gone to control my reaction.

'Oh, I am most certainly not "shitting" you, Grace. Over the years, they left me with dresses, bags, jewellery, hats, all sorts of things. Sometimes as a thank-you. Sometimes just because they knew how much I loved it all. Other times because a particular piece had made us die laughing, or sweat buckets of stress over. Like Marilyn with the hat that got caught in a train door just before she was about to shoot a scene in *Some Like It Hot*. Or the string of pearls Liz's little dog swallowed on the set of *Cat On A Hot Tin Roof*. I didn't exactly love my job that day, I can tell you, rooting through poop to get the costume finalized!'

I smiled in a stupor, drunk on the story.

'Anyway, after a few decades I had amassed a huge wealth of stock that I had no idea what to do with. David and I were thinking of opening a little boutique museum in our home off Hollywood Boulevard before he got sick.' Her eyes glazed over with sadness.

'And then, well, I brought him home. To Ireland. And, as I've said to you before, I could never say goodbye. I could never leave him here on his own and go back. We'd been everywhere together, been everything to each other, and I was nowhere if he wasn't with me.'

My eyes were stinging with uninvited tears. I was trying my best to be strong in the face of her bravery, but it was a battle I was slowly losing. Her loneliness choked me. I could see now why she pined for her old life. And I ached for her, for the wound in her world that had bled out everything she had ever loved.

Although I was never quite going to make it on that maths quiz show where you can win a holiday to Florida, even I could figure out that Verity was a lot older than I had originally thought. If she had been working with Dietrich and Garbo in the thirties, she had to be in her mid-nineties at least.

What a remarkable woman. What an extraordinary story. I

think it was quite possibly the best birthday present I had ever been given in my entire life.

'You know, I worked on that movie, Grace.'

'What movie?'

'*Your* movie. *Roman Holiday*.'

My eyes widened. Come to think of it, I couldn't be sure that I'd blinked or breathed in the last ten minutes. Perhaps I was dead. And if this was Heaven, it was awesome.

'You didn't?' I squeaked, finally finding my voice.

'Oh, I very much did. Hand-tied every one of Audrey's belts and ruffled and puffed out every one of her skirts.'

I stared at her, feeling my hand gravitate towards hers without my consent, until it was resting softly over it. She cupped it, and I thought I'd burst with gratitude.

'Thank you,' I whispered, feeling as though I'd just reached in and held hands with my own past but, for the first time, unafraid of it.

'You're welcome, kid. Happy birthday.'

Then she sat up even straighter and fixed me with a serious look. 'I just want you to do one very important thing for me. Just please, please, be careful what you wish for.'

I nodded dutifully.

'But then, in my wildest dreams, I could never have thought of wishing for everything I ended up having in my life.'

'And is that why the shop is called Best Wishes?' I asked.

'Yes. A tribute to my babies. But mostly to David. Because sometimes, Grace, the very best wishes can, and do, come true.'

## 37

Every time I walked into Lisa's hospital ward I got a fright. Sometimes it was the lady from the next bed in her nightie-type thing wandering about with the exposed back and bare arse. But mostly it was the freaky tribal man propped up in the bed beside her.

Not an actual man. That would be weird. And against hospital practice, I would imagine. But a big wooden figure Rebecca had sent from South America that was supposed to ward off disease or something. Lisa loved it. I thought it was the most frightening thing I'd ever seen and questioned whether or not it was actually a witch doctor used to ward off friends. (Rebecca was so upset she wasn't around for Lisa, but I talked her down, telling her everything was under control. She was at a payphone during a downpour after which she had to get her ear syringed again.) Anyway, our voodoo friend was called Ronaldo and he was staying.

Lisa really was looking so much perkier. Still sad, but with a 'Fuck Killian and my right ovary. I still have a left one. And maybe I'll have sex with a random stranger soon' glint in her eye.

'Can we please get "Screw You Killian" tattooed on your other foot?' I begged.

'No.'

'Oh, go on.'

'Maybe.'

Verity was so thoughtful, giving me a little get-well-soon present for Lisa as I was leaving to visit her: the most beautiful ruby clip-on earrings I'd ever seen in my life. When Lisa opened the card Verity had sent she smiled broadly. It showed a beautiful woman in a gorgeous dress, sunglasses on, headscarf flapping in the wind, waving from her pink Cadillac. *Being Fabulous Can Be Exhausting!'* it read.

'It really can, can't it?' I said, sighing dramatically.

Lisa thought I'd been on the gas-and-air again. But I hadn't. I wouldn't be so stupid as to go at it again after the last time. (Got called into hospital HQ and warned if I was caught again they would press charges. 'Press charges against having fun?' I said. 'No,' they said. 'Press charges for endangering patients' lives. Even though you're wearing incredibly fabulous Lana Turner emerald court shoes.' Actually, they didn't say that last bit, about the shoes. But they should have.)

I was just insanely giddy because Verity had given me another present. Apart from the amazing gift of trusting me with her story, she had given me – wait for it – *a pair of Grace Kelly's gloves*!

I could understand why Lisa thought I was as high as a kite. I kept petting her face with Grace Kelly's gloves and laughing like I'd just stepped off the set of *The Swan*. Grace Kelly's *actual* Hermès gloves.

Lisa was so excited when I'd told her Verity's secret about her special place. Rewind: that sounded creepy. When I told her Verity's story of why the shop was as extraordinary as it actually was. And she managed to be incredibly impressed even though she wasn't really into film at all and her favourite actor was Brendan Fraser.

I was still on Cloud Nine. In fact I wasn't sure I'd ever come down. It was enchanting up there, like my whole world had for ever more been sprinkled with magic.

'It's amazing, really, when you think of it, though,' Lisa said, 'that they were Grace Kelly's actual gloves.'

'I know!' I squeaked, staring at my splayed hands in the fabulous cream calfskin beauties. 'The nurses think I'm being extra careful about the MRSA virus. And, in fact, I don't think there's anything quite like a bit of Hermès when it comes to protecting yourself from superbugs.'

Lisa snapped a pair of blue plastic sanitary gloves on her hands from the cardboard box beside her bed. 'There! Almost the same effect!'

Then she leaned over and clipped on her sparkling ruby earrings from Verity. 'So remind me again: Grace Kelly was in *Raiders of the Lost Ark*, right?'

I crawled up on the bed beside her and Ronaldo and gave her a big hug. Although she was still attached to the drips and wires, she looked a million times brighter. The operation had gone well, thank God, and she was improving day by day. There had been no complications during the procedure and they were hopeful that the prognosis on her second ovary was good for now. Her relief was tinged with disappointment over Killian, but she was being incredibly brave and I was so proud of her.

'Lesbians!' Mary shouted, from the next bed.

Mary. The ninety-two-year-old with the bare bum beside Lisa in her convalescent ward. She'd seemed terribly sweet the first few times I'd met her, and I was wondering if perhaps she could be a friend for Verity (I could talk to her about a lot of things, but corns? I was lost on the subject of corns) until I discovered that the only thing that ever really came out of her mouth, apart from 'The jelly and ice-cream is lovely here. Have you tried it?' was 'Lesbians!' So I'd decided to leave it.

'Lesbians!' she roared again. She shouted it any time I plonked myself on the bed beside Lisa. Which was a lot.

'Oh, Mary,' I said, 'don't be so grumpy. Have you had your jelly and ice-cream yet today?'

'Oooh, yes. It's lovely here.' She softened and looked at me kindly. 'Have you tried it?'

'Go and put a respiratory mask on to shut her up, will you?' Lisa said, under her breath. 'Or pull over her curtain at least.'

A short while later, Mary fell asleep watching *Cash in the Attic*, like most people, so we got to catch up properly, without any more homophobic rants. I told Lisa all about the meeting with my new Business Angel and how he was going to help us get the business up and running with an expertly executed marketing strategy. And then I told her all about Stephen 'Heart Wish' Kelleher and the night I had wished for him down at the canal. She said that sounded a little bit like a fed-up prostitute but I assured her the canal had looked beautiful and serene and snowy on that particular night, none of the usual kerb-crawling going on. Which she said sounded far more romantic.

'So was this another technique you learned down at the Wish Factory then?' Lisa asked, intrigued.

'No. You can't exchange wishes for money.'

'That sounds like prostitution again.'

I laughed. 'It was actually Verity who explained it. You have to try it but you're still a bit high on morphine and hormones so you might end up wishing for an eight-foot female body-builder or something. We'll wait till the drugs have left your system.'

'Lesbians!' Mary muttered in her sleep.

'Well, at least it doesn't involve going back down to Kerry and looking at our vaginas in a hand mirror again. I think mine must be a bit angry with me now I've ripped out one of my ovaries.'

'I have a feeling that ovary has always been keeping you back!' It was time to introduce humour into the situation.

'Really? Like my Achilles heel?'

'Yep. I think your luck is about to change now, Missy. You just wait and see!'

'I hope so, Grace,' she said, sighing heavily. Maybe it had been a bit soon for humour. 'I just want things to be easier, you know. I'm ready to meet someone, I really am. I know we say that everyone is obsessed with marriage and what the hell is the rush, but I'm scared of getting left behind, Grace.'

I swallowed hard, digesting what she was saying. If Lisa, of all people, was beginning to think along these lines, I was going to be the one left behind.

Still, none of it made any sense in my head. I had finally arrived at thirty and nothing was different. The plus side was that I still passed the pencil test. I'd always been afraid the day I turned thirty my boobs would flop to my knees like a pair of Basset Hound ears. Not the case.

'How did you get on with Robbie the other night?' Lisa asked, as I was cupping my breasts, like prize melons at a fair. She was so used to my little ways and didn't give it a second glance. 'He's been amazing.'

'Really?' I asked, not doubting it for a second.

'Yeah, he's been in a couple of times and he even made me a chocolate fudge cake.'

My heart stung at the memory. When Lisa and I had been so gutted we couldn't get tickets to Slane to see Madonna, he'd baked us a chocolate fudge cake to cheer us up. And when Lisa found out her dad was possibly gay, he'd written 'Being A Fudger Is Cool' on the top of another cake in pink icing.

'He's so thoughtful,' I mumbled, almost to myself.

'Was it awkward at all? Seeing him?'

'I suppose,' I shrugged, 'especially seeing as I was in a wedding dress. But we got to chat and I think everything is cool now. It was good to clear the air.'

'Oh, God.' She was staring up at the ceiling. 'Poor Robbie.'

'Why?' I asked defensively.

'Jesus, Grace, because the first time he sees you after you finding the engagement ring he bought for you, you were in a bloody wedding dress!'

'But he was fine!' I said. 'Honestly, he was cool about it all!'

'Oh, for crying out loud!' she said. 'That's because he's too nice to punish you over it. Grace, the guy is still completely in love with you.'

'He's not.'

'He is! Are you blind?'

I recoiled from the words, not wanting to hear them. Not wanting to believe them. I wanted Robbie to be happy. I wanted him to move on with his life.

'Lisa, he's just not the one,' I said, the words slicing the air like razor blades. We sat there in the silence, listening to the rise and fall of Mary's snores.

'Why not?' she asked, a few minutes later, almost petulantly.

'Why not? Lisa – because he's just not! To be honest, and I know you don't want to be talking about Killian, but it was seeing you two together that made me realize that.'

'What?' she said.

'Just seeing you two together – the passion, the excitement, the thrill. You couldn't keep your hands off each other . . .'

'Grace, I cannot believe I'm hearing this.' Incredulity oozed from her words. 'We had just got together. New couples are always like that!'

'Yeah, but that's the opposite to marriage! Why would you want to get married knowing you're never going to have that again?'

'Because you have something so much better!' she said, sounding totally exasperated. 'You have trust and support and genuine *love*. That's what you have! And you had passion, you had a spark! God, you *had* fireworks! Everyone fed off it just being in your company.'

I felt myself wilt. I didn't want to be having this discussion with her, this argument. Here. Now.

'And do you know what the irony is in all of this?' she said. 'All I have ever been looking for – all I have ever wanted – is something even halfway close to what you had. Something that real, something that special. How fantastic does Killian look now? Bolted at the first sign of trouble. And where has Robbie been? By my side and yours.'

Before I even knew I was crying, I could feel the heat of the tears on my cheeks.

'Well, maybe you should stop looking at what everybody else has and figure out what you want for yourself,' I said angrily.

'Ha! Choice words!' she said. 'Looks like you should do the same.'

'*Fine!*' I shouted, getting off the bed.

'*Fine!*' she said, shouting louder.

'Lesbians!' Mary shouted, suddenly waking from her slumber.

'Shut up, Mary!' we called back.

Suddenly a nurse burst into the room, demanding to know what on earth all the noise was about and ordered me to leave immediately.

'Gladly!' I said, grabbing my coat and racing out of the door.

'Oh, and, Grace,' Lisa bellowed after me, 'you and Robbie are not your fucking parents – why don't you try giving him and you a bit more credit?'

I ran down the corridor as quickly as my legs would carry me and stabbed the lift button. I just needed to get the hell away from there. I bolted in and breathed deeply as the door slowly closed behind me, blocking it out. Blocking it all out.

## 38

I found that trying to make your Heart Wish fall in love with you could be hindered by bouts of wailing, like those of a dying engine, with mascara rolling down your face.

'Sweet Jesus!' he said, looking at me as if the freak from *The Exorcist* had just walked through the front door.

'Oh, God, Stephen!' I howled, pinning myself up against the wall in the hall. 'Did you ever just have one of those days?'

'Erm . . . I guess?' he said. 'Difficult customer?'

'I had a fight with my best friend! And she's just had her right ovary removed. *Stephen, I am going to hell!*'

*Right back to where you've just come from, you crazy* Exorcist *lady*, he must have been thinking, but he said, 'Would you like a whiskey instead?'

'I would, Stephen. I would,' I said, dragging myself into the sitting room and lumping myself onto the couch. Three whiskeys later I was feeling much better. I now had hiccups but the wailing had subsided and Stephen looked relieved.

'Come here, Stephen.' I patted the patch on the sofa beside me. 'Come on over.'

He inched forward with a 'What the fuck?' expression on his face that I chose to overlook. He perched on the edge of the couch and gave me a hesitant smile.

'Oh, Stephen,' I sighed, 'did you ever need a shoulder to cry on?'

'Um, yep. Sure. You know, everyone has crappy days. And I'm sure it was just a discussion that got out of hand with your friend. I'm sure it will all be okay . . .'

Oh, my God. How amazing was Stephen? Like *truly* amazing! He was the most fantastic guy I'd ever met, I thought, as a stray hiccup ricocheted through me. Tentatively I placed my head on his shoulder. 'Thanks, Stephen,' I whispered, in my best sexy Mae West voice. He might have been confused by the temporary American accent, but that wasn't important right now. We were bonding. I was bonding with my Heart Wish.

'Stephen, I have something to tell you.'

'Okay,' he said nervously. 'Is it about me leaving socks on the bathroom floor?'

'Oh, God, no, Stephen! I don't care about things like that! There are far more serious things happening in the world. People are getting their ovaries removed!'

I could feel his back stiffen with tension and thought that perhaps Stephen 'Heart Wish' Kelleher was a little squeamish. Bless.

'What is it, then?' he asked, bracing himself.

'Well, Stephen, the thing is –'

Just then the doorbell went. Arrrrgh! Saved by the bell – not! We were having a total Zack and Kelly moment just there, I thought, as I staggered towards the front door.

Screech!

Sorry, Ab-Norman.

'I need to do my washing and see my mammy,' he said, blinking through his milk-bottle lenses.

'Of course you do, Norman. Of course you do,' I said, leaving the door ajar for him and wobbling back up the hall. Wow, this whiskey was amazing! And I loved how extra handsome it made Stephen look. I needed to drink more of it, actually . . .

'Stephen, Stephen, Stephen . . .' I hiccuped, zigzagging back into the sitting room with the whiskey bottle in my hand, and plonking myself right on his lap. 'You haven't met Norman yet. He's Bette's son and he likes to do his washing here.'

He eyed the cat. 'Okay . . . I'm not sure what's going on here exactly but I just want to tell you guys that I'm not really into the whole drugs thing, so I might just pop out for a bit.'

'I'm not on drugs!' I shouted. 'Norman may very well be on

prescription medication but he is not, like, my dealer, if that's what you're getting at. Are you, Norman?'

I spun my head around to Norman, standing in the middle of the sitting room with his laundry basket, and he shook his head.

'Have you got some shit in there, man?' Stephen asked, nodding at the basket.

'No,' he answered obediently. 'Just some boxers. With some skid marks on them maybe. So a little bit. I'm sorry, Mammy,' he said to Bette.

'This has all got a little bit *Clockwork Orange* for me,' Stephen said, attempting to lift me off him.

'Oooh, Stephen, you love movies too!' I slurred, draping myself over his shoulders. 'Oh, God, how perfect is this! And you are just so sweet to not want me to be a drug addict.'

I cupped his face in my hands and thanked him from the bottom of my heart. I turned to Norman and held my hand out to him, taking both his hand and Stephen's in mine. 'On days like this, guys, I honestly don't know where I'd be without you both.'

Then I might have started singing 'Thank You For Being A Friend' from *The Golden Girls*, but I couldn't be sure. Things were starting to get a little blurry with all that whiskey swigging.

'Stephen. Steve. Can I call you Steve?'

'Erm,' he fumbled, eyeing the door, 'actually, no one ever calls me Steve . . .'

'Cool,' I answered. 'It can be our little thing.'

Aw. Steve was so cute. He sort of looked like he wanted to cry when he smiled.

'Steve, what I was about to tell you before our dear friend Norman came to clean his shitty boxers and see his mum was that, well, okay, I'm just going to come out with it . . .'

'Oh, God,' he muttered under his breath.

'Stephen. Steve, I wished for you. There.'

'I'm sorry?'

318

'Yep. That's correct. I wished for you and you arrived out of the blue in my garden as if from the heavens above . . .'

'Well, no, actually. I arrived on the thirty-one from Raheny . . .'

'Sssh, Steve,' I counselled, smudging my finger up to his lip. 'Doesn't matter. Thing is, I wished for you, and you came to me and you are my Heart Wish. Now, I know we're supposed to take these things slowly and it's all about the chase and all that, but I'm a little too old for that now, Stephen. Sorry, *Steve*. Actually, can I call you Stevie?'

'I'd prefer that you didn't.'

'Stevie, listen to me. I'm thirty. I've seen it all. I don't want to waste time with this nonsense so I suggest we just cut to the chase and get on with it.'

He stared at me with a look that was one of either extreme love or extreme terror. It was hard to tell when he kept going in and out of focus like that.

'And you know what the best thing about all of this is?' I asked him, offering the apotheosis of my entire proposition. 'I am going to shit the bed!'

'What?' He recoiled.

'No, no, I'm sorry. I'm a little drunk. I meant to say, I'm going to be shit easy to get into bed.'

I climbed off his lap and wasn't exactly sure if I'd heard a sigh of relief or one of pure lust but it prompted me to climb the stairs and wink back at him provocatively nonetheless.

'You know where I'm gonna be, big boy!' I purred, missing the top step and snotting myself on the landing. I stumbled into my bedroom and threw all the clothes on my bed onto the floor.

'I'm getting lucky tonight!' I said to myself, flinging a pair of jeans and a jumper into the corner of my room. Through my blurred vision I suddenly spotted the wedding dress I'd taken from Verity's shop to get dry-cleaned. It was hanging off my wardrobe door. It was the one I'd met Robbie in, and even through the numbing effect of the alcohol, I could feel the dull pain.

'Oh, God, Robbie,' I sobbed, collapsing in front of the dress. 'I'm so sorry for hurting you. I'm so, so sorry.' I raised my arms and hugged the dress to me as though it was him that I was clinging to, rocking it back and forth in my arms. 'I'm so, so sorry.'

I woke some hours later with my brain lashing against my skull, like a bag of angry cats. I looked down. I had somehow managed to climb back to front into the dress in my sleep. What the hell? I stood up and looked in the mirror.

Oh, Christ. Bride of Chucky. My hair was in clumps on the side of my head and my mascara like tyre marks across my face. I burped and nearly vomited on the taste of the whiskey.

Oh, sweet Jesus. An image flashed in my head. Stephen. *Stephen!*

It came flooding back to me. Oh, Jesus, I really was going to vomit! I was pretty sure I'd almost sexually assaulted him the night before. That was not how the Heart Wish was supposed to pan out! Had I no respect for it? Verity would be ever so cross with me.

Oh, poor Stephen! What must he think? I needed to apologize ASAP.

I marched to his bedroom door and knocked.

No answer.

He must hate me!

'Stephen, please,' I said, pushing the door open.

He was lying in his bed in the dark and shot up when I came in, raising his arms to his face to shield himself from the light spilling into his room.

'Please, no, Grace, no . . .'

Oh, God. He wasn't shielding himself from the sunlight: he was shielding himself from *me!*

'Stephen, let me explain. You must think I'm crazy but I just had this really shitty day yesterday and got far too drunk and . . .'

And then he screamed. He screamed so loudly I thought my brain was going to start bleeding out of my ears. His eyes had adjusted to the light and he was looking at me like I was a possessed serial killer, screaming just like I did when I realized I'd missed the last day of the January sales.

Well, that was a bit rude! I mean, I knew I was hung-over and all but I couldn't have looked *that* bad?

'You're wearing a – a – a –' he said, his eyes wide with terror.

Wearing a what? What was going on?

'*A wedding dress!*' he shrieked.

Oh, balls. I was, wasn't I? Right enough, it probably wasn't helping matters much.

'Please, please, just let me go,' he stammered, talking to me like I was Kathy Bates in *Misery*. 'I'm sure you're a lovely person, really. And I know you'll find a husband one day, the right guy. You can keep my deposit, I just want to go now!'

'Erm, okay, no probs,' I said, like I hadn't just barged into his bedroom in a wedding dress the morning after I'd told him we were meant to be together and then tried to make him have sex with me.

'Do you want tea? I'm going to throw the kettle on.'

With that he jumped out of bed, pulled on his jeans, ran straight past me, raced down the stairs and bolted straight out of the front door.

'Tea for one it is.' I sighed.

## 39

Okay, so the only mature thing to do when you've put on a wedding dress and tried to have sex with your housemate, and you don't have anyone to talk about it with, because one of your best friends is in Venezuela and the other one hates you, is to pretend it never happened.

Talking about it with Tanya wasn't an option. She'd turn into Britney's dad, taking over my estate and controlling my assets. It mightn't take her very long. She might, however, get my loo fixed, which would be great.

Bette didn't understand. I'd known she wouldn't. And she'd taken to sleeping on the end of Stephen's bed – *Stephen*, who'd been in the house barely a wet weekend – so it was pretty clear whose side she was on.

Pretend it never happened, and eat seven chocolate-chip muffins in three minutes (they were teeny tiny so it was fine, but I still felt a bit vomy).

'What's going on with you?' Verity said, as I came through the door.

'Oh, er . . . nothing. I'm just really hungry,' I said, wedging two more muffins into my gob. Then I caught a glimpse of my reflection in the full-length mirror. I had a beard. A chocolate goatee beard. And it did not look fabulous with my 1950s frou-frou skirt. I looked like Eddie Izzard.

'This came for you,' she said, smiling auspiciously, placing a cardboard box up on the counter.

'Oh, Verity,' I said, through muffiny mouthfuls, 'is it a restraining order? Do restraining orders come in boxes like that? Do you think it's a restraining order?'

'Well, why don't you have a look while I go and get you your coffee?' she said. She was used to these early-morning caffeine-deprived bouts of psychosis.

Okay, Grace. Calm. *Calm!* Restraining orders didn't normally come in brown-paper parcels tied up with string. Not in *The Sound of Music* I'd seen anyway. I wiped off my beard, picked up the curious parcel, sat down in the big leather armchair and took a deep breath.

I unwrapped the crisp brown paper carefully, thankful for no immediate official An Garda Siochana stamp anywhere.

A shoebox.

What was inside it? Who was it from?

I lifted the lid carefully. Oh, my God! I inhaled sharply, clamping my hands over my mouth. The most perfect pair of vintage crystal-embellished dainty court shoes I had seen in my entire life. I fished the card out of the envelope, my fingertips trembling.

Of course.

Of course they were from him.

*Grace,*

*I know I'm meant to be leaving you alone, and I will, I promise. But I couldn't let this milestone go without marking it. I know turning thirty held as much fear as it did promise for you, but you're going to be fine. More than fine: you're going to be great. I'm rooting for you. We had a great 20s, didn't we? Your 30s are going to be even better. Here's just a little something to start you off on your adventure. One step at a time; one foot in front of the other; you'll get there.*

*Love*
*Robbie*

The tears were racing down my face before I even knew Verity was back in the room. A beautiful pair of shoes to mark another birthday. I looked up at her in a stupor of confused emotion, holding the card to my chest, like a reprieve. Like confirmation that everything was going to be okay.

'It's from your Heart Wish?' Verity asked, raising an eyebrow.

'No, it's from my ex, Robbie.'

'He called in here earlier to drop it off,' she said, busying herself around the counter. 'Wanted to see where you were working as he knew how much this place had come to mean to you. Charming fellow. Caught me off guard. It was almost like a sandy-haired Gregory Peck had just stepped off set to see me, steal a wink, tip his hat and, before I knew it, he was gone again.'

'Do you think he looks like him?' I said, smiling through my tears, delighted she saw it too.

'Oh, my dear, I do. Almost stopped my heart right there.'

'Verity . . .' I was distracted by a large box in the corner of the room '. . . is that another birthday present for me?' I thought I could excuse the fact I sounded like Verruca Salt on the grounds that I was still in a stupor from Robbie's gift.

'That?' she spat. 'Euch, no. Just a box of trash that got sent here accidentally.'

'But it's addressed to you,' I said, studying the scrawled black label on the silver wrapping. 'With your exact address.'

'Ten out of ten, Miss Marple. Have another cup of coffee.'

'You haven't even opened it, Verity.'

'Oh, for heaven's sake,' she barked in frustration. 'That's because I know exactly who it's from and I'm not interested!'

Whoa! It wasn't unusual for Verity to be fiery, but I'd never heard her venomous before.

I stepped away from the box and wrung my hands together awkwardly. 'This button company got my order mixed up once,' I said, 'and they sent a box of buttons to my house every month for a year. At one point I had so many buttons, my living room was like a giant ball pool. But with buttons. And honestly I was so cross –'

'That box is not from a button factory. It's from a husband-stealer,' she said. 'She got the order mixed up too. Confused my husband for her lover. *I* got pretty cross about *that*.'

Holy shit!

'What? Verity . . . Jesus Christ . . . If she got the order mixed up, is there a . . . *husband* in that box?'

'No,' she said, shaking her head. 'Nathan Poulter is not in that box.'

Nathan Poulter? The famous Hollywood heartthrob from such movies as *What the Heart Desires* and *Mississippi Summer*? Why the hell would he be in that box? Was he friends with David Blaine?

'Sit down,' she said, and I scuttled to the other seat obediently.

'I'm so confused, Verity,' I said. 'My head is full of shoes . . . and buttons . . . and Nathan Poulter . . . and none of it is making any sense.'

She stared at me. Her lips pursed. Her mind was ticking over as she decided whether to steam ahead or retreat.

'Nathan Poulter was my husband.' She sighed. 'Husband number two, to be exact.'

I screamed. I screamed so loudly that Verity got an awful fright and I hurt my larynx. It took me an entire three minutes to stop screaming (so Verity told me later – I don't remember much).

'You were married to Nathan Poulter?' I asked, for the forty-third time. (Again, Verity was keeping count. I was still very much in shock and not entirely sure of my whereabouts, who was president or what my name was.)

She continued to heap the sugars into my coffee, lifting the cup to my lips and forcing me to drink.

'That's right. Before my best friend Molly Keats stole him.'

More screaming. And this time thrashing about.

More coffee. More sugar.

Throbbing larynx.

Some time later I was lying prostrate on the *chaise longue* with a packet of frozen peas on my face, fanning my head with a beautiful French cream-lace fan.

Verity chatted on, confident all the major shocks were now out in the open as I tried to assimilate them.

'Molly Keats? *The* Molly Keats?' I said again.

'Yes, *the* Molly Keats. The one you find so talented and beautiful and funny!' she said, her eyebrows knitting again at the mention of her name. (I hadn't known Verity long before I decided that her eyebrows deserved an award for best performance in a supporting role – I mean, she really worked them hard.)

Wow. No wonder Verity didn't like Molly. I was going to have to tell Rebecca she was being seriously irrational about Renée Zellweger. After all, Renée had never made a move on Tony or anything.

Wait, wait. Didn't Molly Keats and Nathan Poulter film *Mississippi Summer* together?

Verity clocked the penny dropping.

'Nathan got Mollycoddled right in the middle of that long, hot, sticky Mississippi summer!'

I couldn't believe it. I didn't know what to say. I felt like I'd been transported into a 1940s copy of *Heat* magazine.

'Verity, if he was your *second* husband, and David was your fifth, who were the first, third and fourth?'

'Oh, they were nothing special,' she said, waving a hand. 'Bert Rowlands, Jonathan Glover and a traffic warden called Stewart.'

I didn't scream this time because my larynx was too sore. Nor did I thrash about. But only because I was balancing peas on my head.

*Bert Rowlands?*

*Jonathan Glover?*

*And Stewart the traffic warden?*

Okay, so Stewart wasn't *as* impressive, but I didn't want to be mean and leave him out because, let's be honest, being a traffic warden is a very virtuous way to earn a crust.

326

But Bert and Jonathan? Two Oscar winners? Two of the Hollywood Golden Era's most famous leading men?

Jesus.

'Well, none of them mattered,' Verity said. 'It was lucky number five. David.' She said his name like it was caramel in her mouth. 'He was my first love. I let him go the first time round and wasted four good marriages, not to mention four good wedding dresses, trying to shake him off. I never did. Never will.'

Something stirred in my stomach. This was . . . I don't know what it was . . .

'Do you still speak? You and Molly?' I said, hoping that if she was about to throw something at my head, I'd be protected by the peas.

'What do you think?' she barked.

Erm . . . No . . . ?

'Why else do you think she sends me box after box of her precious film artefacts? Peace offerings! Ha!'

'Wait! That box is from her?' I squeaked, pulling the peas off my face and twisting towards the box in the corner.

'Yes,' she said, staring at it with as much distaste as if Molly herself was squatting with her dress around her knees and peeing in the corner of her shop.

'That was her stuff the last time, too, wasn't it? The hat and the jacket that lady took? They were her clothes from *The Wish Stealer*?'

'Bravo again, Marple. She knows about my shop. Knows what's in here. Thinks she's doing me a favour sending me all her *crap*. Hopes we can be friends again. Sheesh, you'd think she'd get the hint after fifty-five years. She was always a bit slow.'

I plopped my head back on the *chaise longue*, still unable to believe all of this. That I was lying here surrounded by *bona fide* Hollywood treasure. And now a box of Molly Keats's precious movie costumes.

My head swam as dresses floated across my eyes like shimmering holograms. I was like Mr Benn, leaving my normal life at seven Maple Street and disappearing into the enchanted world of Best Wishes every time the bell tinkled and I walked through the door.

All the secrets. All the history. All the magic. Like the only child in the world who knew the dolls got up and danced when no one was looking.

I sighed heavily. Poor Verity. I didn't like Molly any more either. (But how bad on a scale of one to ten would it be if I had a tiny root in that box later?)

'Nathan Poulter was not the love of my life, but that wasn't the point,' she said, suddenly downcast. 'We were friends, best friends.'

I instantly thought of Lisa and our awful row and my stomach churned. 'I'm sorry,' I said, truly meaning it.

'Not your fault, kid.' She smiled, resurfacing from her melancholic moment. 'That's life. And sometimes so is five marriages.' She chuckled. 'Some people even thought me and Lizzie were in some secret competition or somethin'! Well, she went and beat me in the end – eight marriages! Seven husbands, but eight marriages in total. How many husbands are you at now?' she said jokingly.

'Euch. Me and marriage. I dunno. Maybe it's not for me. Everyone else seems to think it is, but . . .' I searched for the words like I was ambling around in the dark trying to find the light switch. 'Anyway,' I said, wanting to change the subject, 'who's Lizzie?'

'Honestly, Grace,' she said, rolling her eyes in exasperation. 'You know many other Lizzies who went down the aisle eight times? *Elizabeth Taylor!*'

I kept forgetting. It was going to take me a while to get used to all of this. I really hoped Verity wouldn't judge me that the only famous person I'd ever met had been Phillip Schofield. On a train to Bristol. And I hadn't even met him. I'd just waved. And he'd never waved back.

I just could not believe Verity had been married to Nathan Poulter! And been friends with Molly Keats! It was too much. That would have been like me being friends with Kim Kardashian!

Actually, I take that back. I'm not sure why I said that. It would have been like me being friends with Kate Winslet.

Wow.

No wonder Verity didn't want to sell any of this stuff. But we couldn't bin Molly's things, could we? Could you imagine? It would be like me binning Kim Kardashian's Hervé Léger dresses!

Doh! I mean Kate Winslet's Oscar dresses. Obviously. (I'm going to have to stop watching *Kourtney and Kim Take New York*. It's beginning to have all sorts of adverse effects on me.)

What else was in that shop, I wondered. What other treasures?

I put the peas on my stomach, hoping to ease the knot of indigestion that had set in since I'd thought of Lisa. We weren't going to be like Molly and Verity, were we? To be honest, I hadn't got fifty-five years of stuff to box off to her. I still had all the buttons out in the shed. That might keep me going for a while . . .

'Verity, do you mind me asking how you met Molly?'

'Hey, kid. You don't be thinking of your friend Lisa. She's a special one. Not all friends are meddling fools who crock up a good friendship.'

My stomach lurched violently. Had I really fallen out with Lisa? *Lisa?*

'I met her on the set of *All the Pretty Things* and we hit it off immediately.' Her face broke into a smile – it got away from her before she could stop it, like a horse bolting from a stable. 'We were the best of friends, me and Molly. Thick as thieves. She was a New York girl like me, living her dreams out in LA. And that was what stung the most, Grace.'

'That someone from New York could be such an ass-wipe?' I asked.

She smiled, despite herself. 'That, and the fact that, apart from David, she had been my only other real partner in crime. And she let me down. Badly.'

I thought I was going to be sick. I didn't want to let Lisa down. Not after she'd already been let down so badly.

'We ran riot in Dublin in 'forty-nine,' she reminisced sadly.

'Staying in the penthouse in the Gresham for two months while she filmed *The Forgotten Princess* in Wicklow. But there it is, Grace. That's life. I'd been an only child and had always wished for a friend like Molly, one that was more like a sister. Turns out you got to be careful sometimes what you wish for. Ironic it was Molly who told me all about the Heart Wish. Even more ironic her biggest grossing movie of all time turned out to be *The Wish Stealer.*'

'Erm . . . is this a bad time, ladies?'

We both turned around to see George standing at the door, a little bemused. 'It's just I'd arranged with Grace to pop over to see the shop this morning, but I hope I haven't interrupted anything.'

I couldn't think straight. My head was full of last night and this morning and everything in between, and all I could do was throw my arms out and say, 'Do you like my outfit, George?'

He seemed to take me in from top to toe. 'Nice shoes,' he said.

The shoes. Oh, my God, the shoes. I'd almost forgotten about them in the middle of everything else.

Fuck the peas. I suddenly needed a brandy. It would make me gag at this hour, but that was what people did in these circumstances, didn't they? Neck it back like hard asses? Images swam around my head until I thought I really would throw up. Stephen, Lisa, Molly Keats, Nathan Poulter, Robbie and the shoes.

It was all nauseating.

Overwhelming.

The room was beginning to spin and I was sweating profusely. I grabbed the bag of peas, tore it open with my teeth and emptied them over myself in the hope I'd cool down.

Didn't work.

George and Verity were staring at me as if I was the crazy girl in *Play Misty for Me*. I thought about crying. I told myself under no circumstances could I start singing 'Misty'.

*What the hell was going on? Why was my life so bloody out of control and confusing and spinny?*

Verity, calm as a heroine in a movie out to charm her leading man, waltzed over to George and took the situation in hand. 'George, a pleasure to meet you. Verity is my name. I'm the proprietor. I've heard all about you. And I believe we're neighbours too?'

'Verity,' his voice was deep and gravelly, 'the pleasure is all mine.' He took her hand and kissed it, like a refined gentleman who'd just stepped in from the fifties. He was Laurence Olivier. And he was divine!

I clapped at the display, which was a little silly because Verity was only distracting him so I could grab a moment to pull myself together. But it all looked so dreamy – the tall, handsome man and the elegant old lady right on the set of this mish-mash old-movie world and all I could do was sigh and clap jubilantly.

Verity went out the back to prepare tea and I showed George around the shop. I told him the stock was worth a great deal as it was all designer, keeping the exact truth from him. He seemed very impressed with how we had arranged the layout and the look of the shop, and was very positive indeed about our approach 'going forward'. I felt a sudden glow of excitement about it all in his reflected praise.

'My daughter would just die in here,' he said, throwing me one of his crooked smiles.

'Oh, you have to bring her in once we get up and running!'

'She'd love that.'

He hovered over me, letting his smile linger just a few moments too long. I looked away self-consciously, knowing I'd already started to redden.

'You just have a little . . .' He raised his hand to my mouth and brushed a crumb off my lip with his thumb. My stomach flipped with the intimacy of it.

Verity waltzed back in with a tray of refreshments and I felt as if I'd been caught having sex on Grafton Street in the middle of the day. I took a step backwards and started coughing aggressively, just to make things all the more obvious, and flamed redder than the crimson silk dinner gown from 1943 that I was holding.

'Grace, put Rita's dress back and come and help me get the tea together,' she said, knowing I'd get a little thrill from it.

Rita Hayworth's dress? From which movie? I couldn't think! 'I'll be back to finish this later,' I whispered to the dress, as I hung it on the rail, then prayed that excitement hadn't made me say it louder than I'd thought.

George, cool as a cucumber, drifted towards Verity, his hands nonchalantly dug in his pockets, not taking his eyes off me for a second. He was a tall, broad man, and seemed even loftier as he sat down on the small wooden chair.

'Verity, your shop is exquisite. I'm very much looking forward to our working together over the next while.' He said this looking me directly in the eye. 'How long have you been here exactly?' he said, finally shifting his attention to her.

I didn't know where to look. He was definitely flirting with me, but he was *married*. Then again, flirting wasn't illegal, was it? Like I said before, he was just a sexy, flirty sort of person. I wasn't going to take it personally.

I kicked the peas under the *chaise longue* and smiled broadly. I had all of this completely under control.

## 40

A few nights later, I was meeting George at his friend's restaurant on South William Street. He wanted to go through a few things in more detail over a 'business dinner' and I didn't want to decline on the ground that he was a bit flirty for a married man. This was the real world. This was business. And I needed to be able to handle myself.

As soon as I walked through the stained-glass doors of the beautiful Michelin-starred restaurant, I stopped dead in the doorway to catch my breath. He looked just as I'd seen him when we'd first met. Like Laurence Olivier in plush, crisp surroundings, sipping bourbon. Minus the Pall Mall cigarettes.

I was patting myself down, trying to stop feeling so flustered, when he spotted me and waved. He stood to greet me and pulled my chair out. More of that old-school courtesy.

'You look beautiful,' he said, as I sat down.

'Right!' I said. 'Let's talk marketing!'

He smiled and took his seat. 'Okay, let's talk marketing,' he said, reining in the flirty charm, but still holding steadfast to his easy confidence.

And so we did. We discussed business strategies for hours and he was incredibly encouraging and receptive to my ideas. He wasn't there to sleaze on me. Hurrah! He was there because he believed in our business. It reassured me that I was right: he was just a guy who exuded sexiness no matter what he did. That was just who he was. End of.

Now that we had established that this really was a business dinner, I relaxed a bit more and we got to chatting about our lives and our mutual appreciation for Hollywood's Golden Era. It didn't surprise me one bit to discover he was a fan of the oldies.

Not when he looked like he'd walked straight off the set of *Rebecca* to join me in the decadent surroundings of this beautiful restaurant.

'How come you love them so much?' I asked, as I cracked the top of my crème brûlée.

'Well, my father and my uncle were censors for the film board in the UK so it was always in the family. We had library upon library of movies. My parents moved to Galway when I was a child and I missed my old boarding-school so much, and the uptight conservative old English ways,' he smiled as he poked fun at himself, 'that I would sneak out to the garage, which my father had converted into a screening room, and lose myself in one of the British classics like *Great Expectations*, *Hamlet* or *Oliver Twist*. Just to remind myself of my fabulously repressed homeland.'

'Gosh, you look good for your age,' I said, giving him a cheeky grin. 'And here was me thinking you were born in the late sixties. You're well preserved.'

'Well, I've always been a bit old-fashioned,' he said, grinning back at me. 'The oldies were far better than the films of my youth. Was never really one for the Flash Gordons or the Pink Panthers.'

'Oh, I loved Flash Gordon!' I said. 'He was so brave! Heading off to a world where peril and adventure awaited him!'

He shook his head and laughed at me. 'Well, you're special, I'll give you that.'

'Yes, well, sometimes more special needs than special forces.'

'I don't know about that. So what about you?' he asked, taking his tumbler in his hand and swirling his whiskey.

'Why do I love all the oldies?'

He nodded, eyeing me over the rim of his glass as he took a sip.

Because I couldn't bear the shouting and the screaming in my house. The slamming doors. My mother crying in her bedroom. I'd go into my room, lock my door and put on an old classic in which the drama was so romanticized it bore no resemblance to the real struggles that were going on at forty-five Cedar Wood

Park. Where love stories worked out. And if they didn't, it was okay because they weren't real.

Probably a bit too much to be sharing over a 'business dinner' while I milled through my crème brûlée.

So I carefully cut out a small slice of the truth and offered that to him instead. 'I dunno.' I shrugged. 'The romance of it all. The big grand gestures. The stylized kisses to the soaring music. The happy couple walking into the sunset at the end.'

'So you're a big romantic?' he said, raising an eyebrow.

'Not really,' I lied, steering him away from this particular line of enquiry, not wanting to encourage it. 'I guess I just love the style – the clothes, the old Hollywood glamour.'

'Well, you're in the right place job-wise, then,' he remarked, raising his glass for a toast.

I grabbed mine and raised it to his.

'To Best Wishes,' he said.

'To Best Wishes.'

We left the restaurant, walking out into the crisp March evening air. He placed my coat gently around my shoulders and I flinched under his easy familiarity.

'Well, thank you for dinner,' he said.

'No, thank *you* for dinner. It was great to go over the business plans for the business. And your friend's restaurant is wonderful. I hope it's a successful business venture for him. Has he been long in the restaurant business?'

Could I have stressed the word 'business' any more?

He raised his hat and placed it firmly on his head. Under the street light, with his trench coat on and his hat dipped to the side, he could have been a star straight out of a *film noir* poster.

'State of your man!' I heard a passer-by say, in a stage whisper. 'He must think he's Frank bleedin' Sinatra.'

George simply smiled. 'Verity is quite the saleswoman, isn't she?' he said, indicating the hat.

'Suits you.'

Suddenly he stepped closer, stopping mere inches away from me, his face hovering so close to mine I could feel his breath on my mouth. My heart seemed to stop as he bent down to kiss me. A gentle, soft, warm kiss on my lips. He drew away from me slowly, locking his eyes on mine as he smiled.

'Taxi!' he called, and whistled at one over my head. I was still glued to the spot, my heart stilled, my breath stalled in my chest.

'Safe home, Grace,' he whispered, as the cab pulled up beside us and he ushered me into it.

As I sat back, my heart started to beat again, pumping a growing anger around my body.

He was a married man. A *married* man! *Grace, what are you playing at?* I was never going to be a Lynda, my father's mistress, never going to come between a married couple. God, that was the last thing in the world I could ever do.

Maybe it had been his hat, the bourbon, the talk of old Hollywood movies. Maybe he'd got carried away. He'd phone tomorrow to apologize. I was sure of it.

## 41

*Last night I dreamed I went to Manderley again . . .*

I woke with a start, sweating, gasping for breath, blinking furiously in the darkness.

Oh, thank God. It had been a dream. *The* dream. Well, the nightmare to be more exact. Ever since George had kissed me a few nights before, I'd kept having the same nightmare. I was Joan Fontaine in *Rebecca* and George was Laurence Olivier. And Mrs Danvers was plotting to kill me because I'd kissed Maxim, and what about his poor wife Rebecca?

'But Rebecca's dead!' I'd shout, running from her in the misty shadows to the crescendo of the haunting Hitchcock soundtrack.

'She's not dead! She lives with him in a house in Blackrock and you are a horrible person!'

I threw back the duvet and screamed at the sight of Bette/Mrs Danvers staring at me from my bedroom door, her green eyes glowing in the darkness.

'Fuck sake, Bette. You could play every villain ever written, you know that?'

I pottered out to the bathroom, passing the shoe-rack. Robbie's new birthday shoes glinted from the top shelf. They caught me off-guard every time. Like the whole display was now somehow off-balance. I didn't know when I'd ever be able to wear any of them again. Maybe I should just flog the lot to the friendly shoe fetishist next door. God, I was losing it. I couldn't watch my neighbour clopping past me in Robbie's shoes for the rest of my life.

I splashed cold water on my face. It was only six thirty a.m. but Stephen had already left. Even though I'd crept into his room dressed like the Corpse Bride after I'd tried to make him have sex with me, I chose to believe that he was not purposely avoiding me, but was just very busy in work. Or had taken on an early-morning milk round to earn extra money. Yes, that was it: my Heart Wish was actually a secret milkman.

Had I put a spanner in the entire cosmic works of the Heart Wish thing by being a pervert in a wedding dress? I didn't have a clue. I was going to have to talk to Verity about it.

That night while I was in the middle of watching Elizabeth Taylor's original *Father of the Bride*, the milkman walked in the front door. I jumped off the couch to grab the remote and switch it off before he came into the room, skidded on the floor in my socks and snotted myself over the coffee-table.

No guy should ever walk in on a single girl watching a wedding movie. It was like a girl walking in on a guy watching porn. No one knew where to look.

And especially after our little episode the other night, or morning, I needed to be especially careful.

So much for that. Not only was the film still playing in the background, but I was lying on the ground with my legs splayed, looking like I was offering myself up for him to have his wicked way with me.

'Er, hi, Grace,' he said, walking into the room.

'Hey,' I said, as breezily as I could with my legs spreadeagled and wedding bells chiming in the background as Liz walked down the aisle.

'Grace, I have to tell you something . . .'

'You don't want to marry me?' I said, laughing nervously. Oh, God, I hoped he knew it was a joke.

'Em. No, not that.'

'Of course,' I said, pulling myself up to my feet. 'For the record that movie just happened to be on the telly. Oh, and I'm not sure I ever want to get married. And also, I hate sex.'

'Okay . . .'

'Actually, that last bit is a lie.'

'Okay.'

'I just don't want you to think I'm going to start dry-humping you any time soon.'

'Phew!'

Oi. Easy on the 'phews'! Was the prospect really that terrifying?

'I got you this!' he said, pulling a bottle of Prosecco from behind his back with a big red bow on it. 'A parting gift.'

I nearly started crying. 'Oh, Stephen. I'm so sorry. Are you that traumatized? I'm a disgrace. People are going to start putting "Dis" before my name. Dis-Grace.' Now I was hysterical.

'Hey, hey,' he said kindly, coming over and putting an arm around me. 'It's not that, honestly. In fact, I was quite flattered. I actually think you're lovely, if a little nuts. And you should never drink whiskey again. Ever.'

'Really?' I said, wiping my eyes.

'Really. Stick to the white spirits.'

'You really think I'm a nice person?'

'Of course. You're great! The only reason I'm leaving is because things have sorted themselves out with my old room-mate. We had this big row, but we've sorted it now so I'm going to move back in.'

'Well, that's good.' I smiled. 'I'm glad you worked it out. Well, perhaps you and I could go for a drink some time and get to know each other away from all the bridal wear and whiskey consumption.'

'That'd be nice, Grace. But I need to tell you . . .' He looked at me like my maths teacher used to when I couldn't figure out the simplest algebra equations.

'What?' I asked.

'Grace, I'm gay.'

Really? *Really?* Well, I'll be . . .! That was not good. According to Lisa, homosexuality was not great in a heterosexual relationship and should be avoided at all costs.

'The roommate was actually my boyfriend. We had this huge

row, yadda yadda yadda. God, he drives me nuts sometimes,' he mumbled.

'So that's why I didn't break you when I "accidentally" got locked out of the bathroom in my undies last week!'

'Bingo.'

'Phew! I was scared I'd turned thirty and just sort of withered or something.'

'God, no. Cracking body. If I was straight, you'd get it.'

'Yay!' I said, and he clapped, and we high-fived and all of a sudden I had absolutely no idea how I hadn't seen he was gay before now. We decided to open the bottle of Prosecco and continue our platonic love-in on the couch in front of Graham Norton.

'Now, is Graham Norton gay?' I said.

'I *think* so,' he said. 'I hope you work it out with your friend. Fighting sucks.'

'I know.' I sank into the couch. 'I miss her.'

'Text her!' he squealed, grabbing my phone off the coffee-table and throwing it onto my lap. 'Text her now and tell her you want to meet up.'

'Really?'

'Really.'

My stomach churned just with thinking of our row.

**Lisa** I typed feeling sick, **I don't want to fight. I miss you so much. I don't want to be like Verity and Molly Keats!**

She responded almost immediately: **No me neither. PS who's Molly Keats? Is she the new Catwoman?**

Yes! We were going to be okay.

Whoa. I hoped not. That would be a lot of Lycra for a ninety-two-year-old.

**Will you meet me for dinner next week?** I texted back.

**If you pay.**

**Go Dutch?**

**Deal. But I prefer Thai.**

'Job done?' Stephen beamed.

'Job done!' I nodded and we high-fived again. Honestly, I hadn't even had an inkling – how on earth?

'Hey, now that you're sorting stuff out, what the hell is the story with that grown man coming round to your house to wash his clothes? You seriously need to draw a line under that one.'

I smiled to myself, remembering the time Robbie had said to me I was the only one he knew nice enough to let him do it. 'Oh, he's not so bad,' I said, watching the bubbles fizz in my glass.

I looked at Stephen as he fanned his face with the *Irish Times* magazine like a *grande dame* in a panto. I cannot believe I asked the universe for a gay civil engineer as my Heart Wish. Had I wasted it now? Like the time I chose lucky number three at a fair and won a tub of cottage cheese while Rebecca and Lisa got a hundred quid each?

Not that Stephen was cottage cheese. He was far less lumpy and white. In fact, he was almost definitely wearing fake tan with skin so smooth even his elbows looked ironed.

'You must have thought I was a right nut job telling you I'd wished for you,' I said, burying my face in my hands.

'Yeah – what was *that* all about? I felt like a mail-order bride. *Male*-order bride,' he said, slapping his thigh in a self-congratulatory way and laughing heartily. Gay, straight, smooth elbows or not, he still had an engineer's sense of humour, God love him.

I told him about myself and Lisa going down to the Wish Factory and how it had led to Verity telling me all about the Heart Wish. How you had to mean it from the bottom of your heart and trust that the universe would answer it for you, if you were being truly honest with yourself. And how people had been doing it for years and years and years.

'Aw, that's adorable,' Stephen gushed. 'Maybe I wished for Jamie all those years back and I never even knew.'

'No, it's not like that. You have to make a conscious wish, send it out to the universe and receive it into your life.'

'Oh, right, and you know so much because you received a gay man already in a relationship?'

Hmm. He had a point. Had I got it all mixed up?

'Did anyone else happen to come into your life around then?' he said, intrigued by the whole idea.

'Em . . . no,' I answered, having searched my brain.

'No one at all?'

Well, there had been someone. But that didn't make sense.

George.

*George?*

'George?' Verity asked, the next day, from her perch in the large leather armchair. 'Are you sure?'

'Well, no, I'm not sure. I mean, he's married so it can't be right. I'm not very good at the Heart Wish thing, Verity. I mean, first it was a gay man and now a married one.'

'Oh, Lord, I can't tell you the amount of times I'd have to counsel a young actress in floods of tears at the end of a day's filming. I'd be untying her from her corset while she sobbed into her hanky after trying, and failing, to woo old Rock Hudson on set.'

'I'm not upset, Verity. I just want it to hurry up already!'

'Grace, you cannot tell the universe to hurry up,' she said, rolling her eyes at me. 'It's a process far greater than little old you. Just trust it.'

'Does the universe approve of adultery?' I said. I was referring to the note George had popped into the letterbox, which I was now holding in the air like a referee's red card. The universe was sending me off for kissing a married man!

Actually, perhaps I only deserved a yellow one, as a warning, because technically *he* had kissed *me*. I unfolded it, reading his words once more.

*Supergirl, I'm away on business for the next week or so but when I get back I'd love to take you for dinner again. There are many*

*things we need to discuss! A few business ideas you may find*
*useful.*

*Best, George*

Conveniently ambiguous. And 'Supergirl'? Because he'd seen me in those pants? Oh, God. I rubbed my temples vigorously.

'How did they all do it? All the movie stars with all their fabulous romances. How did they know who was their Heart Wish?'

'Grace, kid, it doesn't always have to be about the razzle-dazzle, you know. Take a step back and just let it be for a minute, will you? There is no way you can see the wood for the trees when you insist on hanging backwards from the branches with your eyes closed!'

What the hell did *that* mean?

'Irene Dunne was happily married to one man – a dentist – her entire life. No affairs, no parade of Hollywood romances, no drama. That was her lot, and she was happy. I had to go through four marriages to realize what I'd always known. Liz Taylor married the same husband twice. Marilyn Monroe married Arthur Miller, for crying out loud, and Katharine Hepburn was bisexual and had a secret affair with Spencer Tracy for twenty-five years. So who knows what's going to happen? It works differently for different people and you just have to go with what's right for *you*!'

'Well, what *is* right for me?'

'You're asking the wrong person, kid. Why not try asking her?' she muttered, pointing at the full-length mirror before disappearing through the alcove into the kitchen. I turned to it to see my own reflection blinking back at me.

Okay, fine. I'd try it!

'Hey, Grace,' I said awkwardly, giving myself a little wave. 'How are you doing today? Listen, I have a question for you: what's right for you? Me. You/me. Me/you?' I qualified pointing to myself and then to my reflection. 'You get me. I mean, I get

343

me. Oh, you!' I laughed at myself coyly, raising my hand to my mouth in a quaint, ladylike manner.

'What, in the name of all that is good and holy, is *fucking* going on here?'

Uh-oh.

Tanya.

## 42

'So, let me get this right. You tell me you're going to start this whole new life for yourself. This whole new career. Which actually boils down to you playing charades on your own and talking to yourself in a mirror?'

'I can see how it might look,' I said, fronting up to my sister, 'but in my defence, that is not *all* I do here.'

'Oh, thank God,' she said. 'I was afraid for a while there that you'd made some sort of regrettable decision when it came to your life.'

I inhaled purposefully, steeling myself for the certain rebuke that was coming my way. It had been a while. We'd stayed out of each other's way since our last 'discussion'.

'I've been calling and texting you for weeks now!' she said. 'Are we using smoke signals and carrier pigeons now that we've become a hippie?'

Oops. Perhaps I'd been doing more staying out of the way than she had.

'Come on, Tanya, don't be ridiculous. You know I hate birds ever since I saw how terrorized Tippi Hedren got in that Hitchcock movie.'

'Mum's been calling you too,' she said. 'We've been trying to do something for your birthday. I know turning thirty when your life isn't exactly sorted is not something people usually celebrate, but we thought we'd try to mark it at least.'

I staggered backwards and sank into Verity's chair, already too exhausted by this unyielding conversation to stand my ground and fight.

'Not again, Tanya,' I said. 'I thought we'd spoken about this.'

She looked away guiltily, tucking her hair behind her ears and taking a moment to straighten herself out. And I knew that this small gesture was as much of a capitulation as I was going to get.

'So this is where you've been hiding out? It looks nice,' she said, throwing her eyes around the shop, offering a temporary white flag. 'It's just I thought when you told me about the place, you might be doing more than standing behind the counter being a cashier.'

I shrugged, not feeling the need to justify myself any more than I had done. We had our plans, Verity and I, and I didn't want Tanya coming in and slowly popping each one, like a child with bubble wrap.

'Well, there you go,' I said. 'Why don't you try something on? That's always the best thing to do. It's hard to really judge something when you haven't seen it on, when you haven't stood in a man's shoes and tried them out.'

I turned to see Verity at the foot of the alcove, taking in the whole scene. She winked at me and I smiled back. *To Kill a Mockingbird*. The reference went over Tanya's head entirely.

'All our family has big feet, but I wouldn't be looking for man's shoes.'

'I'm Verity,' she said, smiling broadly and offering Tanya her hand.

'I'm Tanya, Grace's sister.'

'I know who you are.'

'Well, good. Nice that she hasn't forgotten all about me!'

'Was there anything in particular that caught your eye? These shoes, perhaps?' she said, brandishing a fabulous pair of black velvet peep-toes with a flash of emerald green lining.

'Oh, no, thank you. It's just, well . . . they're old? Why would you not want to buy something new?'

'Oh, I like new too, Tanya. But sometimes it's nice to appreciate something that has a bit of a story, don't you think? Something that may be a little older and perhaps a little more frayed around the edges, but has lived, breathed, been on an adventure that it doesn't need to apologize for.'

'Well, maybe . . . I mean, this is . . . nice,' she said softly, stroking the teal green silk dress draped on a hanger beside her.

'Try it on,' Verity said. 'Go on!'

Tanya trotted off obediently behind the dressing screen.

Right, that was it – I was taking Verity to the bank with me next time! She was such an unbelievable 'convincer' (an actual technical term – I'd just invented it), and maybe she could talk sense into Mr Manahan about all this 'variable mortgage rate' nonsense. Genius.

When Tanya came out in the dress, she caught me completely off-guard. The sight of her almost took my breath away. 'Tanya,' I said, 'you look . . .' I couldn't find the words. I hadn't seen my sister look this good in years. Since her wedding day, in fact. Why did she insist on always swaddling herself in blandness so her real potential, her innate specialness, couldn't be seen? If she couldn't see it, it wasn't there. If she couldn't see it, she could keep pretending this brisk person she'd become was all there was and nothing could get at her.

'Glorious!' Verity said, finding the word for me. 'I'm sure Ingrid wouldn't mind you borrowing it.'

'Who's Ingrid? The supplier?'

We nodded conspiratorially. Tanya looked just like Ingrid Bergman in that dress – her tall statuesque frame and high cheekbones, her blonde hair tied in a knot at the nape of her neck. She inched towards the full-length mirror nervously, holding her breath. And then she saw herself.

'It's . . . Oh, my . . . I didn't think . . .' she stammered, as if she'd just woken up from a coma.

Now she could see. *That* was her. *There* she was. *That* was Tanya. For the first time in ages, I saw the smile reach her eyes.

'Peter would love you in that.' I smiled, trying to keep her with us.

Too late. I saw her retreat. That flare, that hope, that smile receding before I could take my words back.

'Oh, for God's sake, Grace,' she said, 'where the hell would we be going? Why on earth would I wear this dress?'

Within seconds she was back in her own clothes, her own tight, restrictive, choking clothes, the fabulous teal silk dress discarded on the floor. I rushed to pick it up, not wanting Tanya to stomp her own frustration all over it.

'Nice to meet you, Verity,' she clipped. 'Grace, call Mum. We'll arrange that dinner.'

And with that she barrelled out of the door, but her presence haunted the room, like a silent spectre.

'I got that all wrong,' I said, defeated and deflated. 'It'll take more than a hot dress to melt that ice queen.'

'You didn't get it all wrong,' Verity said. 'You *read* it wrong, is all. You were on the wrong page. She wasn't there yet and you jumped ahead of her. Always dying to get to the happy ending. Always trying to race ahead so you can figure it all out. What have I told you about patience, Grace?'

She took the dress from me, looped it onto the padded hanger and hooked it back on the rail, smoothing it out methodically. 'We'll try again tomorrow,' she said to herself.

I knew the message she was sending me. I thought I was finally beginning to see what she meant.

## 43

It was definitely an occasion for the Shelbourne. I don't know why I felt so nervous; perhaps it was just excitement. I had never gone so long without seeing Lisa, except for that summer when my parents had had the cheek to send me to the Aran Islands to learn Irish. I still hadn't forgiven them. No one should be made to wear itchy wool cardigans that smelt of turf and live with a family that sang songs about the potato famine around the fire at night for fun. I even called child protection services from the village phone to report Mum and Dad, but they informed me that it was all 'legal'. Humph. The system needed a serious overhaul, if you asked me.

As I walked into the lobby of the fancy hotel, a porter greeted me, 'Good evening, madam.' That was why I loved it here. It made me feel like I'd just walked onto the set of *Breakfast at Tiffany's*. I wasn't wearing Audrey's exact dress, but one quite similar that Givenchy had 'knocked up for her'. I'd put up my hair in a similar chignon and had been smoking my theatre-length Cabriole for effect before I swung through the big revolving glass door into the hotel.

I raced into the bar, like a kid running to the tree on Christmas morning, bursting to see the presents Santa had left. And there it was, the most wonderful gift in the world – my best friend all wrapped up in a fabulous pink cocktail dress and her beautiful ruby earrings. She jumped up and scuttled over to me and we hugged the life out of each other for what seemed an age, squeezing out our apologies as we embraced.

We got a few wolf whistles and offers for threesomes, to which Lisa replied, 'Fuck off,' and flipped them the birdie. Which was a little embarrassing as one of the men was my dad's accountant. I think he was more embarrassed than I when he clicked who I was, giving me a mortified wave and exiting the bar swiftly.

'We may be getting old, Grace, but if we can still attract the attention of bored, middle-aged sex pests there's hope for us yet!'

'I think we need to drink to that.'

'No *thinking* about it.'

We sat at our table and clinked our martini glasses. 'To being amazingly popular with middle-aged sex-pests,' I said.

'To friendship,' she said.

'To friendship . . . How are you feeling?' I asked, taking her hand.

'Okay, you know. All this has made me stop and think about quite a few things. How I keep sacrificing what I want just so I can keep some bloke, who's a total knob, happy. It's time to figure out what *I* want.'

'Dr Phil?'

'Grace,' she said, eyes wide with sarcasm, 'it's the only thing on in the mornings. I cannot wait to get the hell back to work.'

We smiled, knowing she really meant it.

'Well, I kissed a married man so I'm going on *Jerry Springer*.'

'Wha –?' she said, hitting me with a spray of martini.

'Well, he kissed me, so hopefully I won't get too badly booed by the audience.' I told her all about George, the kiss, the 'Super-girl' note as she listened attentively, drinking it all in with her vodkatini.

'So what the hell does it all mean?' she said.

'Who on earth knows, Leese? I haven't a clue. I've been in my Robbie bubble so long I don't know the first thing about non-Robbie type people. I even tried to have sex with a gay man.'

'I'm sorry, Grace,' she said, lowering her eyes.

'Pretty pitiful, isn't it?'

'No, I'm sorry for what I said. I was out of line. It was none of my business. You know what's best for you and I had no right to lump all that Robbie stuff on you.'

'Hey,' I said, 'it's okay. You were only doing it because you care. And I've learned a lesson too with you and Killian. Don't try to replicate something else. Because you'll only end up with a cheap knock-off. You must be true to what you have. Because behind all the smoke and mirrors, behind the charades and the projected image, who knows exactly what it is you're trying to copy?'

I stalled as I heard the words trip off my tongue, stunned by how much they resonated once I'd said them out loud. I lifted my glass and took a drink, feeling the alcohol dull the sudden clarity I had found.

'Grace . . . ?'

'Yes,' I answered, turning to see a tall, handsome gentleman standing over my shoulder. I reddened at the thought he might have overheard any of our conversation.

'Holy fuck! George!'

He seemed a little taken aback. I couldn't blame him for that. I had, after all, just shouted, 'Holy fuck! George!' in the middle of a civilized swanky bar.

'Jesus Christ! George!' Lisa said, in a similarly loud outburst, and I cringed all over again. How many martinis had we had? Why was I slightly pissed with hot, puffy pink cheeks? Why did we keep shouting expletives in his face? *But, more importantly, what the hell was he doing there?*

'Hi. I was meeting some clients and spotted you as I was about to leave,' he said, with a small grin. His languid charm was unshakeable even though two martini-soaked baboons had cursed in his face. 'Good to see you,' he said, undressing me with his eyes, causing me to squirm unmercifully. *Hey!* I thought. *Don't undress me: I'm wearing Givenchy – I want to keep it on!*

Grace, think sober. Think *sober.*

'I'm very sober,' I said, in a quiet voice, which made him laugh. 'This is my friend, Lisa. She's not sober.'

'Hi, not-sober-Lisa,' he said, extending his hand.

'Hello, handsome married man.'

Sweet God, kill me. *Kill me!* I think I was actually slipping off my seat under the weight of my mortification.

He gave me a quizzical look. 'I'm not married.'

*What?*

'I'm sorry, could you repeat that, please?' I said, in a slow, measured manner, trying desperately not to shout, 'Holy fuck! George!' again.

'I'm not married,' he said.

'But . . . I thought . . .' I stuttered '. . . the family photo . . . You have a daughter . . . and you're kind of old . . .' Oops, I hadn't needed to say that bit. 'You're kind of old-*fashioned*,' I said, though I knew it was far too late and I needed a pint of water. Or for someone to shove a dishcloth in my mouth so I couldn't say anything else. A dishcloth soaked in water. Bingo. Multi-purpose.

'Okay, yes, I can understand where you got that from. I'm divorced, actually, but it's all amicable, which is good. Two children, a boy and a girl, both in their early twenties. But I'm very much single.' He looked me dead in the eye as he said this and my tummy flipped and Lisa clapped and I wished to God I had a water-soaked dishcloth in my gob. And one to cover my entire head as it was now purple with embarrassment.

'I don't want to interrupt the girls' night, ladies, so I'll leave you to your cocktails. Lisa, it was a pleasure to meet you. I hope we can do it again some time.'

'Good to see you,' I said, my head swimming with the haze of alcohol.

'Can I speak to you outside for a minute?' he said, placing his hand on the small of my back and almost swooping me off the stool under his arm.

'Sure,' I answered, as Lisa threw me an exaggerated comedy wink I hoped he hadn't seen.

Oh, God, he was so strong and dreamy, I thought, as we walked through the revolving door, his arm guiding me supportively as

I wobbled in my high heels. 'I'm sorry, I'm a little tipsy,' I apologized self-consciously, not daring to look up at him.

'Hey,' he said, lifting my chin gently, 'you're charming, you know that?'

'Yes,' I answered, trying my best to appear confident in front of this older man, when I felt about as formidable as putty.

'So you thought I was married? You must have had quite a shock when I kissed you.'

'Yes, I found it very . . . shocking.' Arrrgh! Why was I being so outrageously uncool?

'Would it be okay if I did it again?'

'I think so.'

'Oh, you think so?' He smiled cheekily, pulling me to him. His eyes lingered over mine as I looked back up at him, my stomach doing so many somersaults I was sure he could feel it as he pressed his body to mine. And then he kissed me, a divine, slow, deep kiss.

'Did you feel that shock?' he whispered teasingly in my ear.

Oh, I could feel it all right! Ding-dong!

'I'd love to get to know you better, Grace. Spend some more time together,' he said, pulling back to look at me again. 'I'm too old for waiting around, playing games. What do you say?'

I couldn't say anything. I was still lost in that kiss.

'Go back to your friend,' he said. 'I'll call you.'

I nodded, biting my lip, as he headed off into the night, looking back to give me a little wink before he disappeared around the corner. I turned back to the revolving door only to see Lisa's face smudged up against the glass, her eyes bulging.

I hoped that George hadn't seen my best mate doing that or he might very well have changed his mind in favour of someone 'a little more mature'. Just as she was about to signal a massive thumbs-up to me, someone stood into the revolving door, squashing her, and I burst out laughing as she was swept aside like a fly on a windscreen.

'That's what you get for being so nosy.' I giggled, pulling her to her feet.

'My God, that was amazing!' she said, wobbling drunkenly back to the bar. 'How do you feel? Oh, Jesus, we need more drink!'

We got back to the table to find a bottle of Champagne on ice waiting for us.

'From the gentleman who just left,' the waiter said, popping the cork and pouring two glasses.

'Holy fuck! George!' I squealed, sad that he was gone, but delighted he wasn't here to hear me shout that again.

## 44

*'What are you doing down there?'*

*'Where?'*

*'Down there?'*

*'Nothing.' I smiled. 'Just sitting on the roof.'*

*'But I told you this was all yours. I told you that you could have it all, remember? The moon and the stars and anything that you wished for. Do you remember?'*

*'I think so.'*

*'It's here. It's yours. Just give me your hand and I'll show you. You don't need to be scared of it because I've got you. I've got you.'*

*'Okay.'*

*I stood up on my tippy-toes to reach, stretching my hand out as far as I could, nervous because I was balancing on the edge of the world. I could feel the strain across my ribs. One more tiny stretch . . .*

*Suddenly my foot slipped from under me. And I was falling. Tumbling. Grabbing at nothing but darkness. I could see him overhead as I fell, his silhouette on our roof, shrinking further and further away under the backdrop of a million twinkling stars.*

I woke, gasping for breath, the darkness washing over my eyes as my heart clamoured to get out of its own skin.

It was a dream. That was all. Just a dream.

How long had I been asleep? Twenty minutes. That was all I'd planned for, just a quick nap before heading out for dinner in town. I was going to be late if I didn't get moving.

Right so. I shuffled over to my wardrobe, feeling the gravity of the world pull through my heels. What was up with me? I had the relaunch of the shop to plan! This was exciting!

*Wear yellow. If you feel sad, wear yellow – you know it cheers you up.*

'Stop it,' I whispered to myself, rubbing my eyes and stretching out the back of my neck. I switched on the lights, dispelling the ghosts. Of the house. The rooftop. Me.

I was just tired. We had the launch coming up and had worked so hard at it. Organizing all the stock. Getting our press pack together. Making and sending all the invitations. Verity had handwritten each one in navy blue calligraphy on beautiful cream Crane's Lettra card and tied all the envelopes with blue ribbons. She said she wanted to go to an after-party at Lillie's because she'd never been there. So that was what I'd been doing this afternoon. Organizing wristbands so everyone could get past the heavies at the door.

George had been amazing with it all. Actually, George had been pretty amazing full stop. I wasn't sure what label you'd put on it, but we were definitely seeing each other. We had been for about two months now.

And it was new. And strange. And lovely. Even though on the morning after our first night together I'd shut myself into his en-suite and cried in the bath for half an hour. That sounds awful, but it wasn't. I just needed to cry. I needed to mourn the end of something else. Properly.

That was the first time I'd been intimate with anyone since Robbie. I was scared it would be so different. And it was, of course. Perhaps George was trying to prove he was still young and virile, because he certainly proved himself over and over. The sex was exciting but I was still getting used to lying there and talking about 'it' afterwards. I wasn't sure if he wanted marks out of ten or not. I gave him a nine one night and he started laughing and told me I was hilarious.

I felt guilty that I thought of Robbie the first few times. But I suppose that was to be expected. I had shared a bed with him for seven years. It was only on the first night that I actually cried, but in the midst of all the passion and excitement, I could feel a pull of profound sorrow in my heart. And sitting in the bath that first morning, watching the water crash from the taps, I felt the last embers dying.

'Grace?' George had called, knocking on the bathroom door. 'You okay in there?'

'Yes,' I had heard myself say from somewhere far away, somewhere under water. 'Yes,' I said again, with more conviction, breaking the surface now.

'Okay,' he had said, pushing the door open. 'You're not going to tell me you're a devout Catholic girl, are you, and you're in there scrubbing away the sins of what just happened?'

I had laughed. 'Oh, sister, that nail brush really stings!'

'Because, you see, now you're only going to dirty yourself up again. And again . . .' He had sat on the edge of the bath and cleared away the suds so he could look at me. I watched his hands as they traced up and down my body in the water. '. . . and again . . .' He kept his eyes on mine as he played with me and my cheeks flushed with the intimacy.

'You're beautiful,' he had whispered, suddenly climbing into the bath in his jeans and T-shirt. He lifted me out of the water, pinning me against the cool marble tiles and kissing me so deeply I thought I would disintegrate like warm soap in his hands. I could feel the water at my feet slipping down the plughole, chasing further from me, until it had all disappeared.

But never mind about that. We were good. Everything was good. And tonight was a date night. Well, it was actually a serious 'business relaunch meeting' with George, but one that would undoubtedly end with him taking me over his kitchen table so, you know . . . multi-tasking. We all had busy lives. I really hoped they weren't going to take my master's away from me for sleeping with my Business Angel. You know what they say: every time a slutty post-grad gets her way, a Business Angel loses his wings! It was exciting, though: older boyfriend, proper job, sex on mahogany tables. I'd only ever really had sex on pine tables. I was growing up.

My hand danced over the dresses in my wardrobe, hovering

over the yellow pleated maxi. I pulled out a black one instead. More demure. More sophisticated for tonight.

I looked at my reflection in the full-length mirror. The dress was perfect for Chow. Halter-neck, low back and a skater skirt that puffed out to the knee. I'd heard amazing things about the food and it was meant to be sophisticated, but still quite laid back. And definitely trendy. I twisted my hair up into a high ballerina bun and clipped on Swarovski crystal drop earrings. Red lipstick with the black dress and red shoes . . .

I couldn't wear the red shoes. I couldn't wear any of Robbie's shoes.

*Fresh footsteps for fresh adventures . . . with an older man called George.*

It wasn't right.

I slipped into my black patent court shoes and I was ready.

'Are you off on a date with your boyfriend, love?' the taxi driver asked me, on our way to the restaurant. 'Lucky guy if you are!'

'Em . . .' Was he? I mean, was he my boyfriend? I suppose he sort of felt like that. And neither of us was doing anything wrong if he was. Perhaps it was time to really move on. Leave the past behind. Forget those dusty shoes on the shelf that continued to haunt me. Move forward.

'Yes,' I said, from the back seat. 'Yes, I am.'

Chow looked like an enchanted ice cave as it twinkled at me from a distance. A wall of glass stretched across the front, drenched in waterfalls of sparkling fairy-lights. If I'd known business meetings were going to be this decadent, I would have quit sitting at home learning Hitchcock movies off by heart and gone into business *years* earlier. I really had lucked out with my Business Angel, hadn't I? Suzanne from my entrepreneurs-in-business lectures had paired off with the owner of an egg mayonnaise packing plant in Offaly. She had Facebooked me saying she had developed a really bad gag reflex ever since and she was renouncing the world of business to become a yoga instructor.

George was fabulous, so wise and knowledgeable about the world, and definitely didn't smell of eggs. He could read market trends like I could read fashion trends so we made a pretty good team. No one, apart from Verity, Lisa and Rebecca, knew we were seeing each other. If my parents found out I was seeing a divorcé with grown-up children they'd start canvassing outside government buildings to have the Magdalene Laundries re-opened, like they'd threatened to do when I dated that guy who'd been given a suspended sentence for four years of 'habitually stealing Wham bars from the local Spar'.

Ah, yes, the crazy days of my misspent youth. What can I say? I'd been watching a lot of movies about Al Capone. I was quite enjoying being a gangster's moll.

I crossed the road to the restaurant and squinted from the doorway to see if I could catch sight of George. The place was jammed and I couldn't make him out among the throng at the front door. Just as I reached the maître d's desk, a roll of red carpet was unfurled before me, stopping just short of my black patent shoes. What the hell was this?

Then the lights were dimmed and iconic music from the Paramount film studios blared through the speakers while spotlights spun around the room wildly. I stumbled forward onto the carpet, shielding my eyes from the lights.

What the f– ?

Oh, no. Was I having that dream again? The one where hundreds of people get trapped on the roller-coaster at Universal Studios and I'm the only one who can rescue them?

Everyone in the room was staring at me and grinning inanely. I slapped myself across the face.

Ow!

Definitely wasn't asleep.

Now the grinners looked a little perturbed. Why was the girl on the red carpet, in the middle of all the lights and music, slapping herself?

Well, what the girl on the red carpet in the middle of the lights and music slapping herself would like to know was why there was a red carpet, lights and music in the first place!

Over my shoulder I could hear the beeping of a car horn outside the restaurant. I turned and watched everything around me start to unfurl like a slow-motion action shot.

Two waiters pulled open the giant glass doors at the entrance, like ushers at a big glass movie theatre, and a ginormous white stretch limo drew up at the end of the red carpet.

I screamed when I saw him.

George. In a tuxedo suit, standing out of the sun-roof with a stereo on his shoulder and a bunch of roses in his hand, U2's 'One Love' drifting from the speakers all the way back down the red carpet to where I was rooted in complete and utter bafflement. The restaurant staff and fellow diners clapped, like some weird gospel prayer tribute to the service industry.

George disembarked from his lookout post in the limo and started making his way up to me on the red carpet, handing the flowers and the stereo to one of the waiters. A wide grin stretched across his rugged, handsome face.

I narrowed my eyes. What was he at? And what in the name of all that was tasteful in the world, and like carbon footprints and stuff, was he doing in a fecking white stretch limo? Was this some crazy practical joke? Like the week before when he'd said, 'Surprise!' and handed me a cat wearing a big ribbon and told me it was one of the abandoned ones that had been run over from the shelter. It still had its leg in a cast. When I asked him why on earth I'd want another cat, having tried for months to abandon/run over the one I already had, he laughed nervously and said it was actually for his daughter.

And now here he was, sloping up the carpet towards me, grinning as if he knew something I didn't.

'Gracie,' he said, in his deep, gravelly voice, taking my hands in his.

Gracie? Was that my pet name now? It was a trial run if it was.

'Yes, Georgie?' I said.

He failed to detect the tease. 'Gracie and Georgie. That's you and me, Princess.'

I stared at him blankly before bursting out laughing.

'Princess, please,' he said.

*Princess?* Really? I preferred that. I'd tried to make Tanya call me Princess for around eight years. She just would not succumb to the pressure. I stopped trying last year.

'George, what are you doing?' I whispered. 'I'm mortified! Is this some local community movie-themed night or something? I wish you'd warned me. I would have worn my Betty Grable short white –'

'Gracie . . .' he said, cutting across me, standing up straight to fill his lungs, '. . . Gracie, I'm nervous. Just let me finish. Okay, here goes . . .'

Here goes *what*?

'. . . I know we haven't known each other all that long but I've fallen for you. I've fallen hard. My girl, the leading role in our very own love story. The main star on the red carpet of our movie. You said this was why you loved all the old films – the romance, the glamour. So now I'm just a boy, standing in front of a girl, asking her to love him – and marry him.'

*SAY MARRY MOTHER FUCKING WHO NOW?*

The limo . . . *Pretty Woman* . . . the stereo . . . *Say Anything* . . . *Notting Hill*. It was like a blurry pirate video edited together and jumping on the screen before my eyes. All I could think was 'Do not vomit on George – he must have paid a fortune for that tux.'

I watched him drop to one knee and look up at me, like one of those abandoned/half-run-over cats from the shelter. All fixed up in a bow and looking for a second chance.

I saw him in my head on his wedding day with his first wife. What he must have looked like. Happy and content, with a bad haircut (it was the eighties). It wasn't his fault she'd left him for some mega-wealthy property developer when times had got tough for him. He'd wanted things to work. He'd thought he'd be spending for ever with her when he asked her.

I saw Robbie at the ice rink in Central Park. The two of us sitting on our roof looking at the stars.

I saw the photo of my mum and dad on their wedding day on the mantelpiece at home. Coated in dust and obscured by incidental clutter, only Mum's left eye smiling out from a thirty-five-year-old memory.

I saw Robbie in tails waiting at the top of the altar for Jennifer Garner. Ben Affleck was going to be fuming. Would he marry her? The Jennifer Garner lookalike lady? Was he happy? Did he turn on the immersion for her? Bring her tea in bed? Make her laugh so much she had to sit down to catch her breath? Was he in love? A sob caught in the back of my throat. Was he grateful I'd walked away from our life together?

My hand felt like someone else's as I watched George take it in his.

'Gracie,' he said, his eyes boring into me solemnly. He was so gorgeous, I thought, as I watched the charade play out before me, like a doll, waiting for someone to move my arms and legs, be my voice, play the game for me.

From his top pocket he fished out a platinum band with a dazzling cushion-cut diamond solitaire, and as he hovered it over my ring finger I couldn't help but think that the platinum would look so odd with all my vintage gold jewellery.

'So, what do you say?' he asked.

I looked around me, wondering how on earth I'd found myself there. How life had conspired to spin its web without me knowing. But I did know. I was the spider's accomplice all along. Because I'd wished for it.

I'd wished for George.

I looked into his beautiful, earnest face, surprised to find I didn't feel the same panic I'd felt when I'd thought Robbie was about to propose. No all-encompassing fear. No desire to run away. Instead I felt numb.

I figured that was better. To be numb.

'Yes,' I heard myself whisper, as George picked up the doll and spun her round and round in his arms. Strangers clapped and took photographs. Champagne was popped, spilling all over the doll's dress. And all the while she thought of going home and sitting on the roof of the dolls' house and wondering how on earth platinum, of all things, was ever going to fit in with everything else.

## 45

*'You have to wish on it, you know, a shooting star.'*

*'Really?'*

*'Yes. But remember, you can't wish for something you already have.'*

*'What if I already have it but I don't know?'*

*'Oh, you'll know. Because you'll feel it. In there.'*

*He lay back and drew a heart around the stars with his finger.*

*I laughed, closing my eyes and making my wish.*

*I opened my eyes again to a blinding white light hurtling like a steam train through the black sky and straight for me.*

*'Make it stop!' I screamed. 'Make it stop!'*

*'But it's your wish?' I heard him say sadly, somewhere in the distance. 'You wished for it.'*

My eyes shot open and were immediately blinded by the 1.5-carat solitaire staring back at me.

Jesus!

Diamonds. The kryptonite of the hung-over.

I tried to look at it again as it fired lasers of fractured sunlight into my eyes. Nice one. Free laser surgery. I had had to squint to read the credits on *How Green Was My Valley* only last week.

I sat up, slowly deducing that I was in George's bed. In George's house. With a 1.5-carat diamond solitaire on my finger.

Well, there you go, I thought, staring down at it. I was like Joey in *War Horse* when they finally made him take the collar to plough.

I got dressed for work like a malfunctioning robot – zipping my dress on back-to-front and tying my hair into a pineapple ponytail on the top of my head.

I was Belinda Carlisle in a bad eighties video.

With a hangover and a 1.5-carat diamond solitaire.

I drank a glass of water at the kitchen sink and read the note George had left for me.

*Good morning, Princess! I've gone to the office but stay as long as you like. Mi casa es tu casa! Smiley face. PS thanks for saying yes, you've made me the happiest man on the planet.*

I vomited into the glass.
God, Champagne gave you a really bad hangover.

## 46

'Morning, Verity!'

'Morning, Grace.'

'How are you today?'

'Great. You?'

'Yeah, great. I think I have the wristbands for Lillie's sorted. Have you been easing yourself into some R 'n' B like I advised? Some Flo Rida? A bit of Waka Flocka Flame?'

'I like Drake,' she said, handing me an empty teacup while she got the teapot sorted.

'Yes, he's good, all right.'

She was looking at me oddly. Perhaps she was just being 'street'.

'Are you going to ask me if I've heard Far East Movement's new track or are you just going to get straight down to it and tell me you got engaged last night?'

She handed me a copy of the *Southside Herald*: a picture of myself and George inside Chow last night under the caption *'Aisle Be Better Second Time Round!'* staring back at me.

I vomited into my teacup.

I stood staring at the photograph. Black-and-white and grainy, the dots moving in front of my eyes like shifting sand. George looked so handsome and happy. And I looked like a missing person from a police report beside him.

Verity Chinese-chopped the back of my legs so I'd sit down and I plopped into the armchair, still staring at the page. What did it mean, 'Aisle Be Better Second Time Round'? I mean, yes, I knew he'd been married before. But what did they mean he'd be *better? And why, for Jesus' sake, was it on the front page of the* Southside Herald?

Verity prised open my jaw and wedged in a slice of Victoria sponge, like she was posting an awkward parcel through a stiff letterbox. 'Eat something.'

'Just like Alice in Wonderland, remember? Remember, Verity?'

I laughed, suddenly bordering on hysterical. 'You know, when we first met? Alice in Wonderland? Maybe this will shrink me and I'll be able to fit through a tiny magical door at the back of the garden and run away. Ha-ha!'

'Why complicate things?' she said. 'Just head out the front door now and run to your heart's content.'

I looked down at my hands as they bunched into fists on my lap. 'I was only joking,' I said softly. 'I won't be running any more. I'm growing up, Verity. That's why I said yes.'

'Okay,' she said, but with a quizzical tone. She studied me over the rim of her cup, like a meter reader clocking my vital stats.

Thirty-year-old tank. Seven-year relationship with previous supplier. Switched custom and has been with new supplier for a number of months. Going well. Electricity was what she wanted and, boy, does she have that now! Red light is flashing strong. Sure, didn't she have sex up against the fridge twice last night?

'The Heart Wish really does work, doesn't it?' I said, brightening my face with a smile.

'Yes,' she said gently. 'It really, really does.'

There was a loud bang at the front door. Verity and I whipped around to see Lisa burst into the shop like an extra from *Platoon*.

'The insurgents are coming! Hide!'

'Lisa, what the f–?'

Her eyes were wild and her hair was like a tumbleweed in a storm as she raced over to me. She pulled me to the ground and had covered me with a stack of dresses quicker than you could say, 'They're coming in along the eastern front.'

'What are you doing, you lunatic?' This new lease of life since hearing the news of her clean bill of health was getting out of hand. Only last week she'd told me she was going to adopt a donkey and have sex with someone from Galway. I said fine, but told her not to bandy the two things in the same sentence as I found it unnerving.

'Lisa, what are you doing?' I called, through mouthfuls of starched cotton. 'We'll find you your donkey, I promise! You just have to be patient. Apparently donkeys are even harder to get than orphans from Africa for pop stars.'

'You girls,' I heard Verity admonish us.

'Sssh,' Lisa warned. 'Goddammit, woman, do you want to stay alive? I'm trying to help you here.'

Oh.

Oh!

Oh, so *now* Lisa wanted to play *Golden Movie Hour*? *Now*? Not all the times I wanted to play it over the course of our friendship? All the times I'd put on a bonnet and borrowed her old crutches from when she'd snapped her Achilles tendon (in a highly competitive egg-and-spoon race in '92), and *pleaded* with her to let me play Hayley Mills in *Pollyanna* for just five sodding minutes? Oh, no, but now she was happy to play *Platoon* when it suited her?

'Your family are coming. They are not happy. I'm scared. I wish I was braver but I'm not. They terrify the tits off me. I'm hiding too.'

I heard one of the wardrobe doors suddenly open, hangers rustling frenziedly, then silence.

'You girls!' Verity sighed again.

My family were coming. *En masse?* This was not good. Last time this happened was when I tried to flush my school uniform down the toilet in the school gym in favour of an adorable over-the-knee white twirly swing number. The loos were blocked so badly the plumbing exploded all over the hockey pitch during the A team's inter-county finals. The school had promised a 'shit storm' that day, and well . . . you know . . . they delivered.

The bell above the door erupted. The barbarians were at the gates!

I inhaled sharply and performed some improvised 'last rites' on myself that went something like, 'You've been lovely in general.

You stole once in your life because you were dared to by Scott Perry: you fancied him and that was for love, and wasn't "try to fall in love with one and all" one of the Commandments? Plus, it was only a pack of incontinence pads from Arnotts and not, say, emeralds or a yacht or something. But you did give them to your granny as a present the following Christmas, which was a bit mean. And not very Christian. Especially when she wanted a pattern book for crocheting tea cosies. And one of her friends had wet herself the previous week when a game of bridge had gone on too long. But that's all, really, so now you must go and live like a princess in Heaven. Amen.'

'Engaged? *ENGAGED!*' The pitch of Tanya's battle cry said it all: it was going to get ugly out there.

'*We've never even met this man!*'

As she sat down in her armchair, I could hear Verity muttering about needing to strap herself in as it was going to be a bumpy ride. Ah, channelling Bette Davis in *All About Eve*. Bette was always good for a bit of melodrama. I was pretty sure I was getting hot under Bette Davis's actual collar that very minute, and I would have asked Verity to confirm it if I wasn't feeling a touch *All About Ever Getting Out of Here Alive*.

I heard a whimper from the wardrobe beside me.

Jesus, Lisa, hold it together, woman! It was one down, *all* down.

'Where is she?' Tanya ploughed on. I could feel her eyes scanning the room like an infrared camera.

'Where's who?' Verity said.

'This is so typical of her! Thinking her life is one big movie, all romance and daydreams and "finding herself". Engaged? *Engaged!*'

'There's more reality in a Disney film than her life right now,' Mum said, sighing.

'Careful now, don't say that,' Verity said. 'Bambi's mother got shot in a Disney movie.'

I bit my tongue. I wouldn't put it past that woman. Still hadn't quite figured out if she'd been serious about the air rifle.

'Who is this man?' Tanya said, badgering poor Verity. 'Do *you* know him? Did you set them up? Some other half-wit who dresses up in breeches and thinks he's Errol Flynn?'

'Well! I must say, you had me quite fooled, Tanya.' She chuckled back. 'You don't like the old movies as much as your sister? Come on, that performance *was* Sissy Spacek in *Carrie*.' She clapped feverishly. 'Bravo! Terrifying. Just terrifying.'

Oh. My. God. Was she mad? *Verity, get your gun!* She was going to have to join a witness-protection programme now and move to Laos. Just when I was getting really fond of her.

'*What?*' Tanya shrieked. She sounded like Bette when she dived from the top of the shelving unit onto my head.

'Calm down, love,' Mum said.

Yay! Mum was on my side!

'We might be able to get her into a programme in one of the Magdalene Laundries.'

No! Mum was *not* on my side!

Oh, for Christ's sake! When was that woman going to learn those horrendous institutions had been shut down years ago *and that we were not in the 1950s*! (Although whenever I brought this up I always seemed to be wearing my fifties polka-dot dress and 1955 pearl necklace and earrings.) I waited to hear if Dad had any pearls of wisdom to share now that the entire family had taken over Verity's shop. An exorcism from the local priest, perhaps? This was just the spur he needed to convert the attic into an electroshock therapy room.

Nothing.

No, as I suspected, Dad was 'staying out of things and waiting in the car'. I swear to God that was going to be the bloody epitaph on that man's gravestone: 'Here lies Tony Harte who, due to his own personal demons, preferred to stay out of things and wait in the car.'

'Can I help you?' I heard Verity ask, with far more patience than was owed in the face of two lunatics shiteing on about

370

defunct Catholic correctional institutions and hating me and stuff.

They ignored her.

'I spotted this *years* ago,' Tanya said. 'That's why I hid her copy of *Alice in Wonderland*. She was always chasing off into her own little dream world. Every day another Mad Hatter's Tea Party in a different dress with a different story.'

I swallowed hard under the fifteen layers of coats and dresses. It was either a lump or a stray button caught in my throat, but it hurt my heart either way. My favourite book. A beautiful limited-edition copy with stunning illustrations and gilt-edged pages. Dad had brought it back from one of his so-called business trips. She told me I'd left it on the top deck of the 34 bus because I'd been daydreaming again. Deep in my gut I could feel a sense of betrayal wrestle with a growing fury.

Those characters were my friends. The Cheshire Cat, the Caterpillar, the Mad Hatter, the White Rabbit. I didn't have any other friends in that house, did I? No one who'd help me pretend to be Alice when the noise got too loud and I didn't want to be Grace any more.

'Didn't make a blind bit of difference, though, did it? She only went and found the movie version in a car-boot sale and, well, that was that. The beginning of the end. The start of a whole new world of stories for her to run away to. She was obsessed with *Roman Holiday* for a whole year. One day it was Audrey, the next Judy, Ginger, Marilyn, Liz, Rita, Marlene. All up to the video player in her room to pretend to be someone better than little old Grace.'

I might be hiding in the trenches, but I couldn't escape the gunfire. Tears streamed down either side of my face. 'You used to do it too,' I whispered.

'Anyway –'

'What was that?' Mum said suddenly.

'What was what?' Verity said.

'That – that voice.'

'Ghosts,' she replied.

She wasn't wrong. A million ghosts of my past – every character in every story I'd ever loved, every actress I'd wanted to peel from the celluloid and layer on top of myself – suddenly haunted the room. And there I was, hiding under their very own costumes.

'No, there was a voice,' Tanya trumpeted, 'from under there!'

Uh-oh.

Her footsteps thundered towards me and all of a sudden my ankles were grasped and I was hauled backwards until I was ceremoniously delivered into the middle of the room. Thank Christ Tanya hadn't gone into midwifery. I'd seen more graceful deliveries on a farmyard. (Not an actual farmyard obviously, but I'd seen them on telly and that was good enough for me. TV was very educational that way.)

'What on earth are you fucking playing at?' Tanya shrieked, so loudly that I wondered if our vintage sunglasses might all have just simultaneously cracked.

'Honey,' Mum said, 'please tell me the *Southside Herald* got it wrong like the *National Enquirer* always does about aliens growing in people's eyeballs and things.'

I stared at Tanya. 'You used to do it too.'

They stood there glaring at me, their faces stuck mid-rant.

'Sorry?' Tanya said.

'You used to do it too. You used to wish for something more. You did it all the time. We both did it. We both went to that old wishing well in the little forest beyond the park and wished for all the things we wanted our lives to be.'

She stood there staring like she'd just seen them too. All the ghosts.

'Do you remember, Tanya? Do you?'

'Stop it, Grace,' she said, turning her back to me to collect her thoughts privately. 'Of course I remember,' she said quietly, after a moment or two.

'When was this, girls?' Mum asked gently.

We both stared at the floor. A hiatus in the battle. The troops too exhausted to fight on.

'When we thought Dad was going to leave you,' Tanya said, her voice fighting to stay level.

Mum shifted in her shoes, biting her lip and blinking rapidly. I wanted to protect her from what she was about to hear because she didn't deserve it. I looked at Tanya, slumped and resigned. She looked like a child again. One who needed comforting. Who needed to stop trying to be strong for once.

'We'd go down to the well and throw in our pocket money and wish for true love when we grew up,' Tanya said. 'For it not to fade and die. Or turn its back on us. Or break our spirit. Or make us cry in bed at night. Like it did to our mum.'

It was the quietest our family had been my whole life.

Perhaps Mum truly believed we never knew. But no one in our family ever spoke about it. It was like a ghost that walked every square foot of our house, each of us too afraid to admit it was there. Now, in this moment of stillness, I heard the deafening sound of years of repressed emotion cracking open and an unspoken vow of silence being broken.

'I'm . . . I'm sorry,' Mum whispered, catching her words before they shattered into sobs. She looked dazed. Lost. Like someone had discovered her life's work – the happy housewife with the lovely daughters – was a fake and she had been shamed and discredited. They accused me of living in a dream world, but my mother was the best actress I knew.

Tanya looked at me. We were both overwhelmingly frightened of what this might do to Mum. How would it play out now she couldn't hide behind her role? How did you put the pieces back together? Particularly since they'd been already broken to start with.

'Mum, this was never your fault,' I said, my heart breaking at the sight of her standing there utterly bereft and exposed. I ran to hold her. She felt so small in my arms, like the child I once was who had wished for love and happiness from a well.

'I'm so, so sorry,' she wept, as twenty years of disappointment drained into my arms. 'I thought I was being strong for both of you.'

'You were,' I said. 'You were.'

Tanya stared at us, her eyes wide and hollow with sadness. Mum stood back from me, wiping the tears from her cheeks with the back of her hands. 'I suppose I just always hoped I'd get him back. That things would go back to normal if I told him everything could be okay again. I never wanted him to leave, crazy as that sounds. I couldn't imagine my life without him even though I knew he was already long gone. He was all I ever wanted.'

Her voice cracked and she looked to the floor to steady herself again. 'He did it for you. He did it for both of you, you know,' she said, looking from me to Tanya. 'Staying. He thought he was doing the right thing for all of us.' She looked up at me, searching my face. 'What did you wish for, Grace?' she asked suddenly. 'What did you wish for down that well?'

I answered her with more honesty than I had previously in my whole life: 'For a man who would make me the best version of myself I could possibly be.'

'But you got that, Grace,' Tanya said suddenly, from across the room. 'You got your wish.'

God, she almost sounded resentful.

I kneaded my temples, my brain suddenly feeling like porridge. 'Tanya, stop going through my life like it's a bloody tax audit,' I said. 'Ticking bits off as right and wrong. You think you have it all sewn up, don't you?'

'What's that supposed to mean?' I heard the temper in her voice again.

'You're the one who doesn't have a clue,' I shouted back.

'Are you going to back that up with actual facts?' she roared. 'Or will you bottle it as usual and scarper off to find a giant hat to hide your giant head that's full of fear?'

All of a sudden two bullets were fired into the ceiling and we all turned to find Verity standing in the doorframe with an air rifle cocked in her arms.

Oh. My. God!

Well, that answered one question. (But raised another: was that thing legal?)

'Oooh, that was fun! The Duke promised me it wasn't loaded. Ha! I'm only glad I never pulled the trigger when I had it pointed at Nathan Poulter and Molly Keats. Seeing her run naked down our driveway into the lens of a waiting paparazzo was far more satisfying, I suppose. Anyway, I just wanted to break things up a bit. You were getting a bit rowdy. Continue.'

She sat back down in her armchair and folded her arms.

What the hell? There were two bullet holes in the ceiling!

'Guys,' a little voice said from inside the wardrobe.

Shit – Lisa!

'While we're taking a break, could I perhaps come out now? I'm still taking really strong tablets for my remaining ovary and they make me piss like a racehorse and I've been bursting for about half an hour now.'

'Come on out, Lisa.' Tanya sighed. 'You're not hiding anyone else in there, are you? Like your entire family or something?'

'Well, now that you mention it, I'm pretty sure my dad's been hiding in closets for a number of –'

'Grace,' Tanya turned to me, 'this isn't that game show, is it, where your family has to go through, like, seven major crises to win a trip to Crete or something?'

'What? *From Crisis to Crete*? God, no, Tanya – what do you think of me?'

'Well, I'm not sure how else you can explain getting engaged to some old-timer divorcé.'

'Oh, right, unless it was to win an all-expenses-paid trip to a Greek island?'

'Grow up.'

'Girls, please,' Mum said. 'What's going on here? What's with all the non-stop bickering? Enough!'

'Oh, I have grown up, Tanya,' I said, ignoring poor Mum. 'I'm all grown-up now, Tanya, so I can get married just like you. Isn't

375

that what you've wanted for me all along? To get married? Well? Isn't it? Congratulations! Your wish has been granted! But while we're at it, I don't see what the big bloody fuss is about, seeing as you seem to spend every waking hour resenting the fact you got married in the first place!'

I could see the words were hurting her and I hated myself for doing it but we were too far gone now. The wounds were already open and the blood flowing. What was one more cut when we were already swimming in it?

'What?' she said weakly, her voice faltering.

'You got exactly what you wished for too,' I said. 'Someone to love you through thick and thin, in good times and in bad. You got him. Peter's delivered everything you've asked of him. Although, God knows, you make it tough, testing him every day and pushing him to the limit, punishing him for a crime he's never committed, rebuking him, literally, for the sins of your father.'

The words hung in the fog of smoke and sulphur over the battlefield that Verity's lovely shop had become. I thought she would never speak again. I thought no one would ever speak again.

'Girls, please,' Mum said, breaking the impasse. 'Why should any of this affect the relationship between the two of you?'

We stood there awkwardly, eyeing each other self-consciously. I knotted my hands together, unsure where we went from there. Tanya looked at me sadly. 'I'm sorry if I've been hard on you, Grace,' she said, 'but I've always just wanted the best for you because you deserve it. And perhaps I did assume my life would end up the same as Mum and Dad's. It's like somewhere along the way – maybe when I saw how their marriage never really healed, just got kind of frozen – I decided it was stupid to expect so much from a relationship. Yes, that's what it was – best to just get on with it and keep your expectations down to earth. But, you're right, maybe I have got into a habit of lashing out at Peter, though he's never been anything but supportive. I haven't meant to. I really haven't.'

Her voice cracked and she caught a sob just before it escaped her. Mum went over and put an arm around her shoulders. 'You have a good marriage, Tanya. It's not a bit like me and your dad. What was wrong between us went too deep for us to know how to fix it. But Peter loves you and there's nothing wrong that you can't put right.'

Tanya looked at Mum and then at me. Suddenly she laughed. 'To think I came here to give you a piece of my mind. Well, you've certainly turned the tables, Grace. And you're right about one thing – even if I think you're mental for wanting to marry that divorced older man. I should let Peter see that I love him. And I do, in case you were wondering. I never really told him very much about our past and maybe it's time I was honest with him. I'm going to talk to him about this, all of it.'

I nodded, unsure I could speak without crumbling. 'Good,' I mouthed, giving her a reassuring smile.

'I know I've been very hard on you,' she said, looking at me earnestly. 'I just got so frustrated recently with you insisting on living in your little fantasy bubble. Because you didn't have to do it any more. You didn't have to live in a world of make-believe when you'd found something even better – the real thing.'

The tears spilled over now, racing down my cheeks and making dark splashes on my raw silk navy skirt.

'Girls, girls,' Mum soothed, collecting us both in her arms. 'My gorgeous, brave girls. It sounds to me like you've been fighting over the very same thing all along.'

'Right, Lisa,' Verity said abruptly. 'We're going to the kitchen to bake scones.'

'Okay!' she answered.

I'd almost forgotten they were there.

We watched them disappear to the kitchen and stood back to take each other in. We held hands in a circle, standing as equals, as women in our own right, not just mother and daughters. Linked by shared regrets, but also bonded by new hopes, new wishes.

'Girls, it's time to stop running,' Mum said. 'Grace, you've to stop running from your great fear of what real down-to-earth love holds in store for you. Tanya, you're to stop running from the messy uncontrollable reality of what love actually is. And I'm to stop running on the same spot and getting nowhere.'

'What do you mean, Mum?' I said.

'You know what I mean.'

I looked at her and I did know it. I knew it in my gut. After all these years, it was actually happening.

'I may not be in the first flush of my youth, but I still have a life worth living. And I've wasted too much of it wishing it were different. I'm the only one who can change that.'

'Oh, Mum,' I said, overcome by her bravery. 'You know we'll support you.'

'I do,' she said, smiling through her fear.

'God, we're a laugh-a-minute bunch, aren't we?' Tanya said, and we laughed as we clung to each other tightly.

'Grace, can you get us a stand-up slot in the International, do you think?' Tanya said.

We were off again.

'Grace,' Tanya said, smiling at me gently, 'one last thing.'

'What?'

'I only ever wanted you to marry Robbie because he has always, always been your leading man.'

## 47

'They're stuck!'

   'What's stuck?'

   'My shoes! My red shoes! They're stuck in the roof tiles!'

   'How did that happen?'

   'I don't know.' I laughed. 'I don't know.'

   'Hey? Remember what I told you? No matter where you're running to, you can always click those ruby slippers and come home.'

   'I remember.' I smiled. 'But it's not working now. I can't move them. They're stuck.'

   'Maybe that's because you're already home.'


I drifted out of sleep and into Thursday morning. The day before the relaunch. I had a million things to do, yet all I could do was lie there, trying desperately to grab hold of the last wisps of my dream before it eluded me entirely.

Thursday morning.

I still felt the same.

It was still just me on another Thursday morning. But everything had changed. Everything was different. Tanya had gone home to talk to Peter. I wasn't even sure where she was going to start, but she'd agreed that perhaps counselling was the way forward.

I was pretty sure my parents were going to separate after thirty-eight years of marriage.

And I was engaged to a man called George.

Everything looked different too – my face in the mirror as I applied my lipstick. Everything sounded different – Bette's paws on the wooden floor as she plodded past me. And felt different – the soft cashmere under my fingertips as I buttoned my cardigan.

It was as if everything had been spring-cleaned, a layer of grime removed. Everything looked, sounded and felt clearer.

And that made it all the more confusing.

I stepped back and stared proudly at our window display. If Audrey, Grace, Ingrid, Marlene and the girls had a choice of any tea party to come to in the whole wide world, I'd like to think they'd come to this one. Not just because their dear friend Verity was the hostess, but also because it was simply splendid! Vintage tea sets sat on cupboards and shelves around the shop, looped with splashes of fairy-lights, and pale pink roses were bunched into open teapots. Every kind of hat under the sun hung on cupboard and door knobs, chairs and handles.

Verity was afraid to have a movie-themed launch in case it was too conspicuous and unearthed too many secrets so we'd decided on a Mad Hatter's Tea Party instead. Because that was where it had started for us: Alice scrimmaging around at the door, desperately trying to escape her own world and burrow into Wonderland. The Caterpillar smoking her long, slim cigarettes and proffering advice to the lost, confused girl. (Verity wasn't best pleased when I called her a caterpillar and asked if she needed her chin lasered, but I told her it was only because she was wise and not because she had an old-lady beard.)

I asked her if she was sure she should've been encouraging my 'flighty escapism' after what had come out in the wash with my mum and sister. But Verity said that not *everything* had to come out in the wash. That sometimes stains and imperfections were a good thing. That was why she surrounded herself with vintage clothes, old things, old memories. Because sometimes that stubborn old stain was proof that you'd lived, proof that you'd been somewhere, done something. That you'd made certain choices. That you were present. That missing button on a blouse after a moment of pure passion with a lover. That wine stain from a friend's dinner party. The ink mark at the bottom of your handbag after you'd written your mother's birthday card.

I looked around the shop at the catalogue of adventure surrounding me. All these women living their lives, making their choices, loving the people they loved, fixing their hats, buttoning their coats, collecting their handbags along the way. I raked my fingers across the shoulders of a row of dresses and sighed, wondering if these women had sometimes felt the weight of the world on them too.

'I can't keep running away, Verity,' I said, 'for fear that things don't turn out the way I'd wished them to.'

'No, Grace, you can't. Oh, I've seen so many of my girls do exactly what you've been doing.'

'Really?' I said, wanting to wrap myself in their lives, layer every inch of their experience over mine. I unhooked a velvet cape from a padded silk hanger and slipped it over my shoulders.

'Maureen O'Hara's. Another feisty Irish soul like you. All you girls so full of spirit that you trip up over the size of your own hearts. Careful though, kid. Maureen got married "by accident" twice.'

'By accident? How does that happen?'

'Easily enough,' she replied, like it was akin to mixing up your order at a coffee counter.

I wouldn't accidentally be marrying George, I thought. Sure the wedding wouldn't be for months, years even. There was no way I'd be getting my skinny lattes mixed up with my tall, extra-strong, sweet husband.

*Husband!*

Jesus! I shrugged off the cape and hung it up again.

'You know, Grace, more important than all that – all your "flighty escapism" – you can't keep running away from *you*. It's like trying to lose your own shadow. You are who you are. Accept it. You can't tell a bee to stop being a bee.'

'No, I suppose you can't.'

'Just so long as you accept what you are – missing buttons, unstitched hem, faded pattern, stains and all! And then just be the very best darn outfit you can possibly be under the circumstances.'

Somehow her words seemed to connect to my memory of that well in the forest. Of what I had wished for – someone with whom I could be the very best version of me.

She pointed at my heart with the barrel of her Crosman .22 air rifle, which – speaking of Heart Wishes – I really wished she wouldn't. We had got talking as she was about to put it away and she had given me the full low-down on it. No wonder she was getting into the rappers: with her love of firearms, she had plenty in common with them. I was afraid to ask her if she was allowed to have it – 'out of her cold dead hands', and all that. She had probably been mates with Charlton Heston. As we chatted, she waved it around for emphasis. I didn't want to ruin things, but I was actually scared I was going to soil myself.

'And let me tell you,' she counselled further, 'you can get away with dressing many things up and not quite getting it right – the uncomfortable tug of an ill-fitting dress, your feet chafing in shoes a size too small – but dress your heart up the wrong way and it'll pinch every day of your life.'

The bell tinkled above the door and two customers entered the shop.

'Anyway,' she said, hiding the gun behind the wardrobe – thank you, Jesus! 'You have your Heart Wish tailored to perfection now, don't you?'

'Erm, yes,' I said. 'Even the peeps at Savile Row would be impressed.'

It was great that Verity had been listening to Drake recently: we could speak 'street' together now.

'Ladies, our relaunch isn't until tomorrow but please feel free to take a look around while you're here,' she said, then disappeared to the kitchen.

I studied the two women as they raked the hangers across the rails, admiring the dresses. Both were groomed and glamorous, swaddled from the toes up in designer garb from Brown Thomas.

'Let me know if I can be of any assistance,' I said, giddy at the thought of one trying on the Rita Hayworth golden ballgown they were fawning over.

'Oh, thank you, dear,' said the one with the chestnut bob. She was incredibly striking, polished and immaculately put together in a white blazer and tailored navy Capri pants, expensive jewellery dripping over her tanned skin. She was trying her best to hold out as a thirtysomething, yet the summers spent holidaying in the Marbella sunshine betrayed the truth.

'Could I try this one, please?' she asked, flourishing the ballgown in front of her.

'Of course!' I said, leading her to our new dressing room. This little parlour was my favourite spot in the entire shop, with its old-fashioned dressing-table, the mirror surrounded with lights and a cherry-red *chaise longue* behind a thick gold curtain.

'Would you like some shoes too? Perhaps these pewter peep-toe sandals?'

'Perfect!' she said, her large brown eyes widening with approval. 'You seem to know your stuff.'

Perhaps I was being paranoid, but I suddenly felt self-conscious. Like she was almost eyeing me too closely. She nodded to her friend and disappeared behind the curtain. I was just being silly. I didn't even know this woman.

I waited patiently outside the dressing room. I couldn't wait to do more of this when we were properly up and running – helping women dress for nights that would provide some of the best, most treasured memories of their lives. I wondered what her particular occasion was.

She waltzed out from behind the curtain, resplendent in the shimmering gold ballgown, like a movie star stepping out to greet her adoring fans.

'Is it for something special?' I asked, feeling a buzz in my stomach.

'Well, I suppose you could say that,' she answered, with a smile, as her friend let out a peal of laughter behind me.

Oh, goody! What was it? I wondered.

'I want someone to fall in love with me again,' she said conspiratorially. 'Do you think this dress will do the trick?'

Oh, wow – this was perfect!

'Yes, I absolutely do!' I said, wondering who the man was and why she thought he didn't love her any more. It made my stomach swim with sadness. Maybe their lives were just busy. Maybe he'd stopped looking at her. I doubt he'd stopped loving her. You didn't just stop loving someone. Anyway, he had to fall in love with her all over again in that dress. He simply had to! I felt a tingle up my spine.

Her friend appeared to agree. 'That has to do the trick,' she said, clapping excitedly.

How wonderful this was, I thought. What a tender, special moment in the making.

'It's for revenge,' she purred, the words dripping from her tongue like molten toffee.

Eh?

'It's for a gala ball. My ex-husband is organizing it. He'll be with his new girl but I know I can still ruffle his feathers. Some charity fundraiser for children from disadvantaged backgrounds,' she said dismissively, waving her hand.

George was going to that. How funny!

'Humph,' she said. 'How ironic! Since he can't seem to get enough of children these days.'

Weird. This did not sound like the lovely romantic moment I'd been imagining. Sounded more like *Fatal Attraction* to me. Which meant the woman standing in Rita's dress was a potential bunny-boiler. Umm, must remember where Verity had stashed the air rifle.

'Well, I'd hardly call the new one a child,' her friend said. 'I mean, she is *thirty*.'

'I suppose.' She sighed. 'Still, she has to be an immature fool to fall for his veiled charm. He doesn't love her, you know.'

She gazed at me coldly and my stomach sank even before my head had caught up.

'I know why he's doing it, why he's got engaged,' she said,

addressing her friend as if I wasn't there. 'For popularity. It's a PR stunt. Get some new girl who's as clean as a whistle and will make him look good in public. Try to cover over the cracks of the last disaster.'

I squirmed as they stood there eyeing me, like cornered quarry. They smiled at each other smugly, as if congratulating themselves on a successful day's hunting.

So this was the ex-wife, come to make a point. Whether she thought she was doing it as a favour to me, or whether she was simply doing it for her own satisfaction, I couldn't tell. All I knew was, I had to get away from them.

I nearly bolted right out of the shop. Then I decided – *no*, that wouldn't do at all – I wasn't going to go to ground. I wanted *them* gone. I would stay put, sit there with my own thoughts, and wait.

She changed out of the dress as I stood tall, facing them with as much dignity as I could muster.

'Can I take this, dear? Or has somebody got dibs on it?' she said.

'You can rent it. The stock isn't for sale,' I said, just about able to speak. My words tasted bitter in my mouth. It wasn't the only thing that wasn't for sale in this shop.

'Okay, I'll do that so.'

Holding the dress up to herself, she smiled and looked at her reflection in the mirror.

'George will just *die* when he sees this.'

## 48

After they'd left, I crawled to the front of the shop, gasping for air as I held on to the door for support. My head was swimming and I couldn't seem to focus properly. It was like everything had become pixellated. The sea of dots shimmered in front of my eyes and I felt dizzy and nauseous.

'Princess?'

I looked up, trying to make him out through the flurry of specks. I managed to zero in on him. He was leaning in his office doorway, smoking a cigarette, smiling at me like he'd just won the prize goat at the village fair. I looked up the road. He hadn't seen them, had he? I doubted it or he wouldn't be looking so pleased with himself.

He stubbed out his cigarette and made his slow approach, running his hands through his thick black hair as he stretched his arms languorously above his head. I didn't like his jumper, I thought. Green didn't suit him.

'Princess . . .' he purred, reaching out to touch my face.

'*No!*' I said, sidestepping him and making a sudden bolt for it.

I ran and ran, my silver court shoes pounding one in front of the other on the footpath, my lungs screaming at me to slow down, but I couldn't. I couldn't stop running until I got there.

'Grace? What on earth are you doing here?'

More dots spilled before my eyes, like my head was inside a 7-Up can.

'I've just run for half an hour in four-inch heels. I think I may have shin splints. And I . . . I think I'm also going to be sick.'

I wasn't sick, but I did do a sort of mini-faint and Robbie lifted me up from the porch and brought me in. Thank God he still worked from home on Thursday mornings. If I'd had to run all the way to his office, after running all the way to his flat, I'd have been in leg braces till October.

'I haven't run that fast since Brenda Howlett said she was going to chop off my pigtails and glue them to the school gates.'

'You were never the best at running,' he said.

'Oh, I was in my own way,' I said quietly.

We were sitting in a stagnant pool of exposed secrets. Everything said, everything unsaid.

I looked around Alan-the-perv's flat, relieved not to see any sex swings hanging out of the ceiling. Or johnnies lying on the floor. Or, worse still, pictures of the Jennifer Garner lookalike in frames that said 'Most Incredible Person Ever'.

Was he with her? I looked at his big kind hands and imagined him brushing a strand of silky chestnut hair from her eyes.

He'd had his own hair cut since the hospital. He looked sharp. Different. His eyes somehow older, wiser. Like he'd learned something since I'd seen him. It stung me that he was growing, changing without me. Drifting from me. But what had I expected?

In all the time I'd known him, he'd never looked more his own man. So far from the twenty-two-year-old I'd met all those years ago, with the cheeky grin and the floppy hair. His shoulders were strong, confident, like he'd borne the weight of something that had almost crushed him. Almost.

He looked at me with a pride in his eyes that I envied. He smiled softly, the corners of his mouth curling, and I held my hands firmly in a knot for fear I'd reach out and touch it.

'She became a hairdresser in the end, Brenda Howlett,' I said.

'She wasn't the one who gave you the diagonal haircut and dyed your fringe yellow, was she?'

'No, that was when I thought being accepted as a "model" by a hairdresser in Dundrum village was a precursor to getting scouted by Élite on the streets of Paris. It wasn't. Turns out getting your hair turned into a piece of modern architecture for "nearly free" by some seventeen-year-old with seventeen face piercings was not how Miranda Kerr got started.'

'You still looked well, you know.'

'My head looked like a Mondrian painting. People with red hair shouldn't have yellow fringes. And no one should have a blunt diagonal line at the back of their head.'

'I did like how you tried to justify it all by saying it was a bargain at five pounds. And if you'd gone out looking to get that done it'd have cost you at least seventy.'

'Silver lining and all that.'

He twiddled with his shoelace and I studied him surreptitiously. My stomach melted with the weight of the familiarity. I'd been looking at that man for so long it was like suddenly hearing a favourite song after a long time and finding you still remembered all the words.

'Grace –'

'Robbie –'

We started together.

'You go first,' I said.

'What are you doing here?' he said. 'Surely not to tell me Brenda Howlett became a hairdresser in the end?'

'Em . . . no . . .' I said, scrambling to connect my thoughts, trying to arrange them into neat piles of sense. Why *was* I there?

I stared at the floor, wishing the words would come. I looked up. He was gazing at me intensely, unapologetically. I felt my hand drifting to his and grasping on to it like a lifeline. He gripped back, curling his fingers around mine. 'I came to tell you that –'

'That you got engaged. I heard. Well, rather I *saw*. Congratulations.'

'Th-thank you.'

His fingers stumbled over my diamond solitaire and he dropped my hand.

'I read about the proposal. Not the films I thought you

liked . . .' He trailed off, dipping his head into his hands. 'But, hey, what would I know?'

*You would know. You would know!* my head screamed.

'Everyone loves *Pretty Woman*,' I said, cringing in my seat. How ironic. Bought and used by George like a prostitute.

'I wish you nothing but happiness, Grace. I hope he's good to you.'

I clenched my hands into fists, suddenly angry at the ring. As if it was some stranger who'd just insulted my friend. I wanted to tear it off and throw it away. If it meant I could have his hand back in mine. Just for a while. Just for one more minute.

'Oh, for God's sake, Robbie,' I burst out, frustration overwhelming me. 'Stop being so polite about it all. Do you not care?'

'Do I not *what*?' he said, with measured calm, flicking his eyes up to mine.

'Do you not care?' I said again. It was almost an accusation.

His eyes suddenly flared with a rage I had rarely seen. 'Who the hell do you think you are?' he said.

His anger shrivelled me.

'I just, it's like you don't –'

'Don't *what*, Grace? Jesus Christ! What do you want from me? Shall I stab myself in the heart and bleed to death before you? Believe me, I've already as good as done that. This was your choice, let me remind you. *Your* choice. And now you're back to open up the wound. Why? To see if you can still make me bleed? I never thought you would be so cruel.'

'Robbie, no –'

'I thought I'd almost died when you left,' he said, now quiet again. 'But I never wanted to blame you for it. That's why I've never been angry at you. How could I be angry at the person who made me happiest? Grace, I worshipped you. I held you in my heart as more precious to me than life itself.'

He lifted his eyes to mine: they were hollow with hurt. 'How can you ask if I care? Do I *care*? Every fucking day.'

When I saw his pain, which I had caused, something broke inside me that I knew would never mend. Ever.

'Robbie, please. I'm so sorry.' His words ripped into me as I wept at the sudden clarity of my feelings. I loved him. I'd never stopped loving him. And now it was too late. I was too late. He was right. Who did I think I was?

I had run away and, in doing so, misplaced him. Replaced him. Let go of his hand. Lost my grip.

Lost him.

I'd lost the one I'd loved the most. Not because I was brave and daring and wanted to strike out on my own and find myself. But because I was a coward. The one real thing in my life had frightened me so much I'd run away from it. It didn't belong in the world of dressing up and make-believe that I could decorate with shoes and bags and coats and hats.

And now I'd chased myself right back to where I'd started. To him. And I didn't need an outfit or movie theme or film quote to get me there. Without it all, I was just me.

But without him, I wasn't me at all.

'Why did you leave us?' he asked quietly. 'Did you not love me?'

'I left because I was afraid I'd break it. I didn't believe it could work, so I made sure it couldn't.'

He stared at me like it was the last time he was ever going to see me. 'Get out,' he said, getting up and brushing past me.

## 49

When I'd finally realized what I'd done, going home to our house was agonizing. Putting the key into the door, stepping into the hall, hanging my coat on the stand. It was like an operation without an anaesthetic.

After all these months, it was as if he had just walked out of the door. No, it was worse. Back then I'd been in pieces, but also in a haze of confusion and distraction. Now I had finally woken up to the horror of what had happened. What I had done.

His absence was like an open wound in the house. I craved his voice shouting from upstairs, the smell of his aftershave as he kissed me at the door, his shoes in the hall. I sank to the first step of the stairs, so utterly crushed by the weight of loss that I was unsure if I'd ever stand again.

Hours passed. From my perch at the bottom of the stairs I stared at the hall door, replaying over and over the day we'd entered our home together for the first time, like an old video cassette jammed on a loop.

Never mind. I already knew what happened at the end of the movie. No fairytale conclusion. A real red herring. Never saw it coming.

The doorbell rang. It sounded different, far away.

I opened the door and saw Norman standing there holding the most beautiful bunch of cream roses.

Yes, it was Norman, and he was familiar, but I no longer felt like 'Grace', the other protagonist in our surreal encounters over the washing-machine. It was as if I had been dropped into someone else's dream.

'I can't marry you, Norman,' I blurted. 'I know I thought once that perhaps if neither of us found someone we could get married and you could move in here and do your washing, but –'

'Erm, no . . . you're okay, thanks. I'm flattered. But I have a girlfriend.'

As he handed me the flowers, he nodded over to a beautiful blonde twentysomething sitting on the wall across the street in a matching Cheryl Cole T-shirt, swinging her legs and waving at me.

*Shut the fucking front door!*

Literally. Shut it! My eyes were bleeding! She had to have been kidnapped and brainwashed. I should never have given Norman my DVD of *Seven Brides for Seven Brothers*. It had given him ideas.

'Anyway, these were delivered to you earlier but you weren't in, so I'm just dropping them in to you now. We're off to see a show, me and Lara. Her friend Nadia is in a community production of *Fifty Shades of Grey*. I used to go out with Nadia, so it's a bit weird, kind of like the three of us having a virtual *ménage à trois* or something.'

*Aaaargh!* My eyes *and* my ears were bleeding now!

I must have been doing that face I do when I accidentally imagine Enda Kenny doing naked splits because he was looking at me funny.

'Are they from Robbie?' he said, blinking through his milk-bottle glasses.

'I'm sorry?' I said, blinking back.

'The flowers. Are they from Robbie?'

'Erm, no,' I said. I severely doubted Robbie had sent me cream roses and a card that read 'Congratulations, you coward, for deserting us' in the time since I'd left his flat.

'Aw, pity.' He sighed. 'Mammy really misses him, you know.'

And with that he was gone. Off to his *ménage à trois* with Lara and her actressy mate. Like some terrifying remake of *The Unbearable Lightness of Being*.

I stood inside the door and read the card that had come with the flowers.

*Grace, if this is what you really want – if George is every-*
*thing you really wished for – we support you. Love, Mam and*
*Tanya xx*

I dropped everything and watched the arrangement fall apart
as if in slow motion, leaves scattering, the bag bursting, the water
trickling over the wooden floor and disappearing down the cracks.

I sat on the roof until the sun relayed with the moon and the stars
came out. I plucked petal after petal from the roses I had rescued
and sent them dancing into the night breeze. *He loves me, he loves*
*me not.* That was a game I'd already lost.

Some time later Lisa joined me. I heard her footsteps on the
roof, but faintly, as if through a fog. I still felt lost. Adrift. She
simply sat down beside me and said nothing.

'What have I done?' I said, after an age of just staring at the
moon. 'Lisa, what have I done?'

We sipped the vodka Rebecca had ordered her to buy. One text
to both of them and they were already here wrapping themselves
around me, even though one was seven thousand miles away.
Swaddling me like a warm, familiar blanket, trying to reassure me.

'You're going to be okay,' Lisa said softly.

'I know,' I lied, certain I was never going to be okay again.
Sure, I'd be some form of 'fine', and that would just have to do.

She told me he wasn't seeing her any more, the Jennifer Garner lookalike. I should have felt better but I just felt worse. There
wasn't something else standing in his way. He just didn't want me
any more. It was over. I'd hurt him too much.

We sat there – two friends with two broken hearts and three
ovaries – holding hands firmly. Neither of us knew what was to
come. But we'd brave it together. That much we knew.

I stayed there on my own after Lisa had left. She'd promised to
come into the shop the next day to help us prepare for the launch
party. I didn't want to let down Verity just because my life was a
car crash.

Looking up at the stars I wondered how many wishes had been made on them the world over. Whispered secrets offered up to those twinkling night-time comrades.

And how many had come true?

Just then, one star slipped from its spot, diving through the inky well into for ever. And I hoped that someone somewhere had made a good wish on that bright, burning star. And that it would come true. Not that I was sure I believed in any of that any more.

What I did believe in was stupidity.

Loss. Reality. Pain.

But I suppose I would still have wished a million times over to undo all the mistakes I had made.

I pulled out my phone and hovered over the keyboard. I needed to do this. I needed to let Robbie go. I needed to say goodbye.

**Robbie, I am so sorry about this morning. You were right about everything. You deserve someone who isn't scared of love. I'm working on it, but I'm sorry I made you suffer. I honestly didn't mean it. You will always be in my heart. Bye, x**

I pressed send and sat there in a daze. That was it. Over.

I heard more footsteps. Firm quiet padding across the flat roof. Pad, pad, pad towards me across the tiles. Getting closer and closer and then stopping.

Bette.

She sat beside me, her tail resting on my hand, the closest thing to companionship in all our time here together. We stared out at the night sky in silent complicity.

Maybe she didn't hate me after all. Maybe she just hated me not being 'us'.

And I knew exactly how she felt.

## 50

The next morning I woke with dread in my heart. Tonight was the relaunch. I should have been excited but all I felt was sadness that another big thing was happening in my life without Robbie in it.

I dressed in yellow, hearing his voice in my head: *Wear yellow if you feel down. You know it'll cheer you up.* A beautiful pale yellow silk dress with an organza skirt to the knee puffed out over layers of fine net. A sweetheart neckline with small cap sleeves and a bow belt tied right in the centre.

It was perfect.

I stepped into the ruby court shoes he had given me when we'd moved in here together. Feeling taller, stronger, like I was wearing a tiny piece of him. Like it was the only way I was going to get through today.

Because, before anything else, I needed to sort out one rather large problem.

'George.'

'Princess!' he said, standing to greet me as I barrelled into his office. 'Princess, where have you been? I've been calling you! I'm putting it down to you being caught up in the launch –'

'And I'm putting it down to the fact that you proposed to me to win some sort of popularity contest with your business associates!'

'What are you talking about?' he stuttered, the blood draining from his face.

He looked old, I suddenly thought. Not handsome and distinguished and charming. Not weathered. Just old. And worn out from trying too hard. In that instant I knew exactly why he'd always reminded me of Laurence Olivier. Because he lived life like it owed him something. With an air of entitlement.

I stared at him as his hazel eyes darted across the floor. 'I met your ex-wife,' I said.

'What? When?' he said. And he looked even paler, if that was possible. 'She . . . she . . . she told you about Lucy?'

'No, she didn't. But I have a feeling you're about to.'

'Oh, God,' he said, exhaling loudly, slumping into his chair and burying his face in his hands. 'What a mess.'

'I take it Lucy was the other child she mentioned you were interested in?'

He looked at me over the bridge of his clenched fists, like a man on a ledge, balancing on the edge. Debating whether or not to jump.

'Lucy was a friend of my daughter's . . .' he started, then noticed the horror on my face.

'*Legal!* She was nineteen. I told you my wife left me after my business went under. Well, I wasn't completely honest about that. She left me after my affair with Lucy. When she found out about that she got together with a property developer we knew socially. I often thought there was something going on between them, so I'll never know if she was just waiting for the excuse to dump me. If she was, like a fool, I gave her a very good reason to.

'Anyway, your man was a bit of a shady operator and they went after the property end of the business, which was already in trouble, so it came crashing down. The whole thing was a nightmare, especially because our daughter was in bits about the whole thing. It was a miracle that nothing got into the papers. I suppose it didn't suit any of us for the real story to come out, and since I'm in the media game myself, I know how to handle things. I'm luckier than some, though – I have other businesses that are doing okay, though I don't think I'll be back hiring helicopters to pop to the shops for milk anytime soon,' he said, giving me a weak smile. Hoping that a crack at humour might ease the tension.

He looked away from me and out of the window. He sounded

exhausted, as if the confession had drained every last ounce of his energy.

'Grace, I'm not proud but I'm telling you this because I want you to know the full truth now . . .'

'Where did I come into things? Was it really about your image?'

'Initially, yes, it was about what you represented. You were just so lovely and when I met you everyone thought you were perfect. This fantastic girl with a bright future and a clean past.'

*Everyone?* Who was this 'everyone' he was talking about? It sounded like his wife wasn't far off the mark in her bitchy comments. I suddenly felt like the troubled starlet in the black-and-white movie. The nobody that the studio bosses thought they could mould and turn into a somebody. Stick a pretty dress on her and make her smile until her face hurts and no one will ever know her heart is pumping pure pain. God, he didn't know me at all. And I didn't want to be a clean slate for anyone. Because then I would have known nothing, learned nothing.

'We thought it would be good for my image to date you, sure. After I split up with Denise there were a few gossip-column pieces and I wanted to avoid any more of that. It's very easy to lose your credibility when you go down that road so I was kind of on the look-out for someone who might fit the bill to be a regular girlfriend. To avoid the drama. People do that all the time, you know, tailor what they're looking for,' he said.

Then why did it all still feel like it just didn't fit? I wondered.

'And then you came into my life. And everything that happened between us was real, I promise.' He was pleading now. 'Grace, I wouldn't have proposed if I hadn't fallen for you.'

He got up from his desk and walked towards me purposefully, taking my hands in his, cupping them together tightly and rubbing his fingers over mine. He stared into my eyes with as much sincerity as I believe he possessed.

'Please don't leave me,' he said, and I could hear the fear in his voice. 'Grace, the proposal was real. The movie stuff, I knew you'd love it.'

I flinched, feeling as though I was in a terrible late-night rom-com with a bad actor. And in the back of my head I could hear Robbie: *I wasn't going to ask you to be my wife in front of a thousand strangers . . . I knew you'd hate that.*

'I love you,' he said.

Maybe he was speaking the truth. It didn't really matter now anyway.

'George,' I said, retracting my hands and backing away, 'I'm sorry but it's over.'

He squeezed his eyes shut and bowed his head. 'I feel like an idiot,' he said. 'I know how it must sound to you but I was going to make a life for us.'

I stared at my shoes, trying to figure out how I'd got there in the first place.

'Please just say you'll forgive me,' he said. 'Or consider forgiving me after a while.'

I removed the ring and placed it on his desk, feeling like Charlie at the end of *Willy Wonka and the Chocolate Factory* when he gives back the everlasting gobstopper. I really hoped he wasn't going to tell me to keep it and suggest that we take a glass lift right to the top of his expanding magazine empire.

'You used me, George. That's a cruel thing to do to someone,' I said quietly.

'Doesn't everybody use someone, though?' he said. 'To make their own life better? Love is selfish at the end of the day. That's just how it is.'

'Well, that's not how I like to see it,' I said. 'Seems like you and I bought two tickets to the movies and ended up at completely different shows.'

He sighed and shook his head again. 'I'm sorry, Grace. I truly am. I played this all wrong.'

'It's not a game, George.'

'I know,' he said.

'You can make it up to me, though,' I said, and his eyes lit up with renewed hope. 'As a friend.'

'Okay,' he said. 'Okay. What can I do?'

'I want the Best Wishes relaunch on the front cover of your next magazine and featured in all the Business Angels' newsletters as an example of a fantastic start-up. Push all the relevant journalists to attend the launch. I want you to put all your PR muscle to good use, coming up with some cracking ideas to get the word out about Best Wishes. Better doing that than coming up with not-so-cracking ideas to get yourself a woman. I mean, honestly, George – what do you think it is? The fifties?' I smiled at him. Some day soon I was going to see the funny side of this. I knew real heartbreak, and this wasn't it. This was just a bit . . . well, a bit ridiculous, really. George looked so sheepish. And I knew he wasn't a bad man. Just weak. And a little selfish.

He nodded. 'I'd be happy to help, Grace. Far from doing you a favour, it's a completely legitimate story. You, Verity and the shop deserve it.'

'Thank you.' I headed for the door. 'George,' I said, turning to him before I left, 'I can't really be that angry with you.'

'Why's that?'

'Because I used you too.'

'How?' he asked, his eyes searching mine.

'To try to replace something that was completely irreplaceable to me.'

## 51

The bell tinkled over the door and Verity looked up from her armchair.

'Verity, I'm not getting married.'

'Me neither,' she answered. 'Well, not again anyway.'

I smiled. 'I'm sorry for bolting yesterday. There was something I really needed to do.'

'Well, I'm just glad you phoned. I was worried your shoes got caught in a drain again and you'd called the fire brigade and they'd taken for ever to get there.'

'Oh, no.' I sighed, sinking into the opposite seat. 'I wouldn't do that again after the last time. Got fined two hundred quid for wasting their time.'

'You okay?' she asked gently, after a moment or two.

'I'm fine. It wasn't to be. George wasn't my Heart Wish, Verity.'

'I think we all knew that.'

'You know the way some people just aren't good at maths, or languages or, like, fixing toilets?'

'Yes?'

'Well, I'm just not good at wishing. Or fixing toilets.'

'Sometimes it turns out you might actually be better than you think.'

'No, Verity, not me. I tried fixing the cistern again last week and I was standing on the seat part and my foot slipped down the loo and got trapped in the U-bend and I nearly called the fire brigade again but I didn't have the two hundred quid if they thought it wasn't enough of an emergency.'

She chuckled to herself and I laughed with her.

It was nice to laugh.

It eased the pain in my heart, if only for a few fleeting moments.

Just then the bell tinkled again and we looked up to see Lisa at the door brandishing party hats and Ajax.

'I wasn't sure what to bring to get the place ready,' she said, 'but if, in the event, we need bleach and party hats, we're covered.'

I couldn't help laughing.

'She's not getting married,' Verity said, nodding to me.

'She's right, I'm not,' I said, wafting my bare ring finger.

'Grace, that's not your ring finger. You just flipped me the finger.'

'Oh, right, sorry.' I tried again. 'I'm not marrying George.'

Her face brightened visibly. Wow. Did *nobody* like George? God, maybe it's like when I fancied Eamonn Holmes and everyone thought I was mad.

Lisa started giggling, then Verity joined her. Then we were all laughing, with tears rolling down our faces.

I wasn't sure at what point my tears had become those of grief and upset, but I kept up the façade with a pained grin.

'Oh, Grace.' Lisa sighed, wiping her eyes.

'Oh, Grace' is right, I thought, feeling my heart knot in my chest.

We got to work sorting out the shop and making sure all the clothes were in the right places before we added the finishing touches for the party.

'So is the point of tonight to tell people that old clothes aren't just for charity shops and you can look good even if you dress like someone from the Bronze Age?' Lisa joked, lifting two bronze earrings to her lobes and smiling at us sweetly. 'What do you think? Am I just like Alicia Silverstone yet?'

Actually she didn't look far off. 'A tiny bit further back, Leese,' I said.

'Seriously? She made *Clueless* in 1995! That was *yonks* ago.'

Verity and I laughed. We'd really have to give Lisa a proper lesson one of these days.

'Right, girls, I'm off for a bath,' Verity said, getting to her feet. 'This dame needs at least a two-hour soak for a big event.'

'Oooh! Are you going to have a milk bath like Elisabeth Shue in *Casablanca*?' Lisa piped up, thrilled she'd finally remembered something more fitting of the era.

'Taylor. In *Cleopatra*,' I corrected her.

'Exactly!' Lisa nodded.

'Not today, dear. I only have two litres of Avonmore out the back. Didn't have time to pop to the shops for any more earlier,' she said, disappearing into the alcove.

We looked to each other, neither of us sure if it was a joke or not.

Lisa helped me sort out the jewellery displays in all the cabinets around the shop and I worked in silence as she distracted me with her stories.

'Hey,' she said, turning to face me, 'how you doing after last night? After today?'

I shrugged. I should have felt closure. Sadness, sure, but some sort of finality on things. But I felt nothing except agitation, like I had wasps crawling under my skin.

'It is what it is,' I barked, not meaning to. Lisa was only trying to help. She'd taken a whole day off work to come and keep me company today. And I was grateful for it. Even if I felt like the worst company in the world right now.

'Grace?' She stalled, the words hovering in her mouth as she looked away from me.

'What?' I pressed. 'What is it?'

'Please don't be cross with me, but I met up with Robbie last night.'

Robbie? Why would she have met up with Robbie?

'I didn't know what to do,' she blurted. 'I didn't want to be disloyal to you but he was a mess. Said he'd had a text from you and his head was all over the place and . . .'

'Hey, Lisa,' I said, 'it's okay. I don't mind that you met him. He's been so good to you over the past few months. You did the right thing.'

'Yeah,' she muttered sheepishly. 'It's just maybe I shouldn't have told him what I told him . . .' She lifted her eyes to mine, biting her lip.

'Why? What did you tell him?'

'Sort of . . . everything.'

'Like . . . ?' I pressed.

'Everything that's gone on with your family. Your parents separating. That you were having a really tough time. I just wanted him to understand, for your sake. To know that you weren't trying to mess with his head.'

I sat there, feeding a string of pearls through my fingers, feeling the tears trace down my face.

'Leese, it's okay,' I said, my voice cracking. 'I'm glad he knows. I hope he knows I never meant to hurt him.'

We sat in silence, letting intermittent sighs fill the gaps.

'I wish there was something I could do,' she whispered, placing her hand softly over mine. 'I hate seeing you both like this.'

'I wish there was too,' I said, meaning it with all my heart.

'I'm glad I told him I thought you and George wouldn't last.' She smiled, puncturing the swell of sadness in the air.

'Did you? What did he say?'

'Said he thought George looked like, and I quote, "an old, smug prick".'

I laughed despite myself. 'Robbie's *always* quoting Shakespeare.'

We giggled. 'He was so concerned about you, Grace. I mean really concerned. He still cares so much about you. Maybe if you just . . .'

'That's just Robbie,' I said, shaking my head. 'He can't help being kind. It's just who he is. It doesn't mean . . .' I trailed off, my thoughts too tangled to translate into words.

I sat there, staring at all the glistening jewels staring straight back at me.

'Okay, well, I'd better go home and get ready for the party,' she said finally, getting to her feet. 'I have to leave some extra time to pick up a few litres of milk for my bath.'

'Just remember to get full fat,' Verity counselled, returning to the shop in a bathrobe and turban. 'Plumps out the skin lovely.'

'You gonna be okay?' Lisa asked quietly, squeezing my hand.

'You betcha,' I said. 'I'm in my castle here. Nothing can get me.'

I thought of all the fairytales I'd embellished over the years, and then thought that maybe this one would turn out to be true. I looked around the shop, our little enchanted kingdom, and smiled at Verity.

'Let's have tea, you and me,' Verity said, 'before the mayhem begins.'


It was seven o'clock. The large mahogany grandfather clock in the shop ticked loudly in the expectant silence. I felt like Marty McFly staring at the clock tower waiting for the lightning strike, caught in the time machine of a million worlds gone past, hoping it was about to change everything about Verity's and my future.

Tonight had to be a success. I didn't know how Best Wishes was going to survive as a viable business if the launch wasn't a triumph. Verity couldn't go on like this for ever, her shop floating like a ghost ship, lost on a sea of nostalgia and sentimentality. If she was serious about this – if she wanted the world to step aboard, to breathe life into her vessel – she had to pull into port and drop the gang-plank.

I looked over at her. I could sense her nerves. She had re-adjusted the Betty Grable hat at least ten times. She loved that hat: a beautiful black sculpted velour, with grosgrain ribbon and a sparkling rhinestone, that Betty had thrown over her head on the last day of a film shoot when the director shouted, 'That's a wrap.' It had flown through the air like a bridal bouquet and spun through the car park on the Paramount lot before landing right on top of Verity's head.

'How are you doing, Verity?' I asked.

'Fine, dear,' she lied, retying her perfectly knotted scarf. 'Nobody worth having at a party ever shows up on time.'

We'd done all we could do. Sent the invitations, decorated the shop, organized all the wristbands for the guests to the after-party in Lillie's. Verity was looking forward to Lillie's. It would bring back the days when she'd practically lived at the Cocoanut Grove, she said. Umm, I was afraid she was going to get quite a surprise.

Best Wishes had never looked more perfect, like an enchanted world waiting to be discovered. Rich fabrics lined the wardrobes, which were illuminated by whispers of fairy-lights looped around the solid brass rails. Verity's old costume reference journals were bookended by quaint little vintage teapots. Jewellery was draped over teacups, dangling from sugar bowls. Bracelets were lassoed around the necks of chilled Champagne bottles. And there were tiny assorted cupcakes stacked on beautiful bone-china cakestands.

It was bewitching. If they just came to the tea party, if they just stepped inside this captivating treasure trove, they'd see it. They'd see the real icing on the cake.

I smoothed my dress and straightened my bow belt for the fiftieth time.

'Grace, stand away from the door,' Verity cautioned. 'We don't want to put anyone off.'

She was right. My nose was pressed up against the glass, and to anyone outside I would have looked like a cute pig-girl in a fabulous yellow dress. Not to mention an incredibly over-anxious pig-girl. In a fabulous yellow dress.

I was so full of nerves I thought I was going to implode. But we had to look calm. Like we were in control. Like we were the gate-keepers to this fabulous magical world.

Suddenly the bell above the door tinkled into life and we were on.

Lights!

Camera!

*Action!*

'Final checks,' Verity said, applying a slick of Chanel rouge lipstick. 'Well?' she said, turning to face me. 'Are we ready for our close-up?'

## 52

Two hours later the shop was buzzing. From worrying about the place being empty, now I was worried that we'd have nowhere to fit everyone. Or that Verity would be so overwhelmed by the noise that she'd get out her air rifle and start firing into the ceiling again. Not really what the social diarists were used to at a launch party.

Journalists queued to speak to the star attraction, Verity, perched in her mahogany throne commanding the room, empress of all she surveyed. They were captivated by her – by her charm, her enthusiasm, her vivacity, her dynamism. Just one bite of her addictive, moreish originality, washed down with a swig of tea from her dainty china cups, and they were hooked.

Bloggers, writers, journalists, fashion reviewers peppered her with questions. Who was she and where had she been all their lives? What had brought her to Ireland? How had she assembled her collection? How had the shop gone undiscovered for so long? Why were we renting the clothes instead of selling them? Was it true that we were giving style tutorials? And that we were going to help job-hunting women who were struggling financially? And what was this about a *Meet Me at the Movies* night every month with old favourites playing on a projector reel at the back of the shop?

We had to thank George's influence for the sheer swell of journalists. There was no way we would have attracted that level of attention on our own. By twelve noon the only verified RSVP we had had was from a volunteer for the *Knitting and Stitching Bi-annual South Side Newsletter.*

'I think he's done right by us after all, you know,' Verity whispered, on her way to a mirror with a dazed fashion editor in a wide-brimmed slate blue felt hat; Verity had told her it would be perfect for her colouring and bone structure.

I spied him across the room, staring at me but making no attempt to come over. Though our engagement had been splashed in the papers, none of the journalists had noticed that we hadn't spoken all night. Too many other things to distract them. I raised my glass in salute and he raised his. He winked at me nervously and I smiled back. George definitely wasn't the worst. No. He was like a once promising actor who'd made some bad choices along the way. There was always the chance of a comeback, I supposed.

Tanya was in another corner, looking at her reflection in a mirror and lifting her hair off her shoulders as Peter looped a string of pearls around her neck. She was wearing the earrings he had given her for Christmas and the magnificent teal green dress she had tried on all those months ago.

I had texted her and Mum earlier to thank them for the roses and to say that I wouldn't be marrying George, but could they not say anything tonight because I wasn't ready to talk about it. The two of them had behaved impeccably. They hugged me when they arrived and said absolutely nothing about men or weddings or me not knowing what was good for me. They said how lovely the shop was looking and how delighted they were that I had found my spiritual home. They both used that expression – 'spiritual home'. It was a bit spooky and *Invasion of the Body Snatchers*-y, them being so nice about everything, and sounding like clones of each other with the lines they had worked out in advance, but I was really touched that they had made the effort.

Tanya smiled at Peter now, touching the necklace gently as he fastened the clasp around her neck. It was the smallest of gestures, but I felt it. Like the furthest ripple in the water after the stone has dropped in, I felt it. I felt it for them.

'Gracie, well done.'

My dad. Coming and saving me from the lump in my throat just in time.

'Thanks, Dad.' I smiled broadly.

'It's truly beautiful in here. We're all very proud of you, you know.' He put an arm around my shoulders clumsily.

'Thanks,' I said again. I didn't know what to say or do to ease his discomfort.

We looked out at the mêlée in front of us, allowing the laughter and chatter to peal through our own silence. All the time his arm remained in position, stiff and tentative.

'Grace,' he said, hesitantly, 'you're okay about . . . me and your mother?'

I steeled myself. Waiting for the words I'd been holding my breath for my whole life.

'I'm moving out of the house, Grace.'

I nodded. 'Okay, Dad. I think Mum needs her life back,' I said finally.

I heard his heavy sigh. It had become his personal soundtrack. I touched his other arm gently, turning in towards him slightly. 'And you do, too, Dad.'

His face collapsed. He had maintained the same stoic expression for years – one of silently accepting his lot. Suddenly it seemed the effort was too much. His eyes welled with regret and frustration, and the yearning to make himself understood.

'I never meant to love her,' he said, trying to catch his sob. But it was too late. The tears were falling. 'Lynda. I never meant to love her.'

My God. My father had finally come in from the car and was facing the music.

'Maybe you were meant to love her,' I said softly, squeezing his hand. 'I'm just sorry you lost her.'

I held his hand as we stood in silence, looking out at the happy throng. I wished the laughter and the chatter would soak it all up, every last drop of our sorrow and regret.

'I could say I can't imagine how that feels,' I said, 'but I do. In my own way. That loss. And it is devastating.'

'I'm so sorry, Grace,' he whispered, his words catching in his throat, 'I know this has always been your armour. The dressing up. The movies. The romance and glamour of everything you never had.'

But I did have it, I thought. I did. I'd just been doing it so long I stopped seeing what was real and what was make-believe.

'Dad, we've all been stuck in the past too long. We need to move forward. I'll help you. Let's set up a time together. Afternoon tea every Sunday?'

He couldn't answer me. So he squeezed my hand, and I squeezed his back.

And, with perfect timing, Lisa stumbled over to us. 'Grace! Grace!' she shrieked, cupping my face in her warm clammy hands. ''Smazing! 'S just amazing!' My dad slid away when it looked like she was going to give his face a good strong squeeze as well.

I smiled as she took another swig of Champagne from her teacup. My kind of tea party guest.

'Bec is coming home in two months and then we're all dressing up like Lindsay Lohan and going to Lillie's!' she said. 'But don't worry, I haven't told a soul that Lindsay's movie shit is in here, okay?'

'Okay,' I said. 'Thanks a million.'

She hadn't a notion. I think she may have read in *Starz* that Lindsay was playing Elizabeth Taylor in her biopic and that they were somehow, perhaps, more or less the same person. She also thought the green velvet original Hedy Lamarr cape she was wearing was from a *He-Man* movie remake she'd seen on the Science Fiction Channel.

Rebecca's latest postcard had arrived in the post just as I was leaving the house this morning. 'After all, tomorrow is another day!' Vivien Leigh's famous line from *Gone With The Wind*.

I had pinned it to the fridge next to the others and thought she might have read my mind.

'Grace, we're going to Lillie's!' Lisa said, sloshing her Champagne around her teacup. 'There's a really hot Website Man here who already has a wristband. I don't know his name. Will we just call him Website Man?'

'We will,' I said, trying not to laugh.

'Anyway, I told him about the ovary.'

'Oh,' I said. 'Really?'

'Yes, but he's totally fine with it! You know why?'

'Why?' I said.

'Because,' she said, in a stage whisper, 'he says that we might only have to use johnnies like *half* the time!'

At this rate she was never going to make it to Lillie's: she'd be tucked up by ten in her bed with a kebab, I was sure of it.

'Grace, text Bec and tell her I'm getting back in the saddle and raring to go. Go on. Go on! *Gwawn!*' she said.

Fine. I'd humour her. I fished out my phone from between the folds of my skirt. A text message. Funny I hadn't felt it vibrate.

*Jesus!* It was from Robbie.

I couldn't breathe. I had to get away from Lisa, from everyone. Luckily, she was too busy grinning at Website Man to pay me any attention.

'Sorry, Leese. Just have to run to the loo. Back in a sec,' I said, and dashed straight through the crowd and out the back.

My hands were shaking as I opened the message.

Hey Red, Hope the launch is going really well. I'm sure it's fantastic. I'm sorry about yesterday. You caught me off guard. Bad timing and all that – you know yourself. Heard there's some stuff going down with you. If you ever want to talk, you know where I am. X

I suddenly couldn't breathe. My heart was banging in my chest making it hard for my lungs to grab any air.

He had texted me. Robbie had texted me. What did that mean? *Jesus, what did that mean?*

Okay, breathe. Just breathe.

What now?

*What should I do now?*

I steadied my hands, inhaled purposefully, and then I texted him back.

I always want to talk to you Robbie Cotter. I want to talk to you for ever. Could we start again tonight? Will you meet me on our rooftop at midnight? I'll be the one in the yellow dress and the red court shoes. The ones you told me to wear when I just wanted to go home. XX

My hands shook as I pressed send and watched it fire off into the universe. I don't think I breathed until my phone beeped again with a reply.

And I'll be the one with my heart in my mouth, dying to see you. As always. XXX

## 53

How on earth was I going to get through the next few hours? I was fit to burst! I rejoined the party and smiled inanely at everybody, stealing glances at the grandfather clock, wishing the hours away until it was time to see him.

How was I going to shake Lisa? If she managed to make it past kebab-and-bed-by-ten, she was going to drag me to Lillie's. I might have to throw her onto Website Man before the party was over, then encourage her to go home and 'surf the net' instead. It had been a while. I thought it would do her the world of good. She'd just better use a johnny if she was trying to avoid any spam in her inbox, though.

I glided through the guests, smiling and nodding at everyone, feeling like I wanted to tell them all that they were amazing and I loved them. Even that tiny bald journalist whom I didn't know at all. Mum and Tanya eyed me quizzically before I moved on, never staying in one spot too long. I needed to distract myself or I would spontaneously combust. I felt light and giddy as I moved through the crowd, as if I knew something they didn't.

All of a sudden a tiny woman burst through the shop door and whistled for immediate silence. The party came to an abrupt halt. Oh, marvellous! What a wonderful distraction!

But, actually, *who the hell was she*?

Everyone stopped and turned to the diminutive little creature at the door in a red velvet floor-length formal dinner gown, feathered headpiece and long white gloves with a Cabriole theatre-length cigarette holder poised aloft in her dainty hand.

'Well, well, well,' she boomed, her strong voice belying her shrunken frame and wrinkled face. 'If Muhammad will not come to the mountain, then the mountain will just have to come to Muhammad.'

Oh, my God. It was her! It was *her*! I recognized the eyes, the irreverent curl of her smile. Underneath the mask of old age, it was her!

'Well, well, well,' Verity barked back, rising slowly from her perch. 'The mountain looks more like a tiny road bump to me. A painful little road bump that I can already feel is the shape of a certain Molly Keats!'

I *knew* it!

The crowd gasped as it took in the stand-off. Heads turning one way and then the other, like spectators at the OK Corral. A murmur rippled through the crowd.

'*Molly Keats!*'

'*That's Molly Keats!*'

'*What is Molly Keats doing here?*'

'*Did you hear Molly Keats was coming?*'

'Internet's a great thing,' Molly boomed, in her famous New York drawl.

Everyone hushed again as the face-off continued.

'Saw all about your relaunch. I'm assuming my invite got lost in the post? Although the post is pretty good since so much of the stuff I send you gets returned to me!'

Verity stared from across the room, her eyes narrow and angry. She was trying to tough it out, but I could tell she was shocked at the sight of her old friend landing on her doorstep out of the blue. Molly had outplayed her in some style.

'No wristband, no entry,' she said, waving a hand dismissively and turning towards the kitchen.

There was another collective gasp.

'Oh, Verity, you stubborn mule! You just gonna keep on ignoring me? I've flown more than five thousand miles to see you.'

'Well, that was pretty stupid of you without a wristband, wasn't it? And by the way,' she said, before disappearing through the alcove, 'I haven't remarried – in case you came all this way to do a spot of pilfering.'

'Humph,' Molly said, stubbing her cigarette out on a silver tray she produced from her handbag and folding her arms in exasperation. 'When I heard you were launching a shop with half my clothes in it I thought I at least deserved an invi– ?'

Oh, sweet Lord, the woman was about to give the entire game away!

'Ms Keats,' I swooped in. 'Wonderful of you to come. Big fans. Amazing body of work . . .' I babbled like I was sweetness and light personified, my new-found exuberance suddenly coming in very handy. 'Perhaps we can continue this conversation somewhere a little more private?' I steered her towards the back of the shop.

The journalists were clamouring for an interview with one of the last living legends of Hollywood's Golden Era, a woman who was believed to be a recluse. For all the gripes Verity had with Molly Keats, she would have to be grateful to her for one thing: we were going to be on the front page of newspapers across the world in the morning.

'Molly!'

'Molly!'

'Molly!'

They caterwauled behind me, gaining momentum and pushing forward as I tried to shepherd the tiny woman through the alcove and down to the kitchen.

'I've got this,' George said, smiling at me and stepping from the crowd to block their way. Our eyes locked momentarily before I turned and ducked through the archway.

'Thanks,' mine said.

'You're welcome,' his replied.

I stayed in the kitchen for the first few minutes of slander, name-calling, and even scone hurling. And then I realized that, fascinated as I was by old Hollywood, I really didn't need to hear all of that. So I left them to it. I sat on the floor in the back hallway for a while, thinking about Robbie and what I would say later. I couldn't really think in words – I just came back to this image of holding him tight and never letting go. Then I got up and went back to the party. Maybe I was growing up – choosing real life over Hollywood drama.

After a full hour Verity and Molly emerged, arms linked and brandishing a glass of sherry each. The room erupted when they walked in and stooped to take their bows.

More flashes went off.

I rolled my eyes and smiled to myself. I had watched a lot of cheesy melodrama in my time, but never had I seen such hammy overacting. They were as bad as each other.

'Verity, what's going on with you two?' I hissed, under my breath.

'We're going on a road trip, Grace. Molly and I are doing Route 66. Her nephew's gonna drive us. She says he's a bigger drama queen than the two of us put together and it'll be a right old hoot. Gonna visit some friends along the way. Just hope we don't get arrested like the last time we went on one. Our chauffeur then – the Duke – took some liquor from a gas station on the PC1. We were *borrowing* it, for crying out loud! Anyway, we've wanted to do this trip since for ever. Always swore we would, but then, well, stuff got in the way. But you know what?' she said, leaning in and raising an eyebrow. 'Life is too short to have regrets, kid. You fall down. So you get back up, dust the muck off your pretty little outfit and you just keep going, do you hear me?'

I nodded. 'Okay . . . but who's going to help me with the shop when you're gone?'

'Your mother. I've spent most of the evening speaking to her. You think she named you after Grace Kelly for nothing? You think she isn't an old romantic? She's even more up-in-the-clouds than you are, kid – she's just spent so long wishing she wasn't. Get her in here. Let her rediscover the person she's been trying to pretend she's not all these years.'

I looked at my beautiful mother, as ever cloaking her vulnerability with grace and class. She was laughing at her reflection as a stranger placed a fabulous crystal-embellished floppy felt hat on her head that dipped down over her eyes. Her laughter floated through the air and I wanted to bottle the sound and keep it with me for ever.

'I will,' I said. 'I promise.'

'We've done ourselves proud, kid,' she said, winking at me.

'We have, Verity,' I said, breathing the success of the night deep into my lungs, thinking how far I'd come since Eleanor Holt and Mrs Macnamara in her tube of turquoise taffeta.

'We've been on a journey, haven't we, you and me?' she said.

'You can say that again,' I said.

'Me clinging to my past. You getting lost in everyone else's. Neither of us going anywhere.'

'You were like Boo Radley,' I laughed, 'hiding out in your little cave.'

'Well, thank you, dear,' she said, rolling her eyes. 'Out of all the movie characters you say I remind you of, I think I'm most flattered with that one!'

'Verity, like Boo Radley, you came out of hiding just in time to save me.'

Her navy blue eyes suddenly danced with emotion as she grabbed my hand in hers. 'Well, I want to thank you for enticing me out.'

I smiled at her and we clung to each other as the room swarmed around us.

'I never thought it would lead me all the way out the door and down Route 66!' she said, laughing and wiping tears from her eyes with the back of her hand. 'But where are *you* going next, Grace?' she said, fixing me with her earnest gaze once more. 'Where's your road leading? You said you wanted passion, fireworks, excitement. Was it where you'd hoped it would be? Gary Cooper over there?' She nodded towards George, standing in the corner and talking to a pretty young journalist. 'Sure it's exciting, but Gary fell in love with every single one of his leading ladies. Those men are only ever meant to be a holiday. Somewhere you visit for a while to feel the heady exhilaration of a break. They're not where you go when you need to feel *home*.'

'I know,' I mumbled, almost to myself.

'I said there was a time I was just like you. Chasing rainbows with no discernible pot of gold. Trying to re-create something I already knew I'd found. Kid, don't waste four marriages rainbow-chasing wishes you thought you'd made.'

'Verity, the Heart Wish was true.'

'Grace, stop it now, you hear me?'

'No, no, Verity, it was Robbie. It was Robbie I wished for all those years ago. Someone to make me the best version of me I could be. It was him. I got him. I got my Heart Wish.'

'Oh, thank God! You've finally come to your senses! I was so afraid it was going to take you a couple more decades and a marriage to Gary Cooper!'

Her face broke into a smile. 'So . . . what now?'

'I've texted him.'

'Texted him what?' she said.

'To meet me on our rooftop at midnight. And he says he'll be there.' I broke into a smile.

'And what are you going to say when you see him?'

I took a deep breath, trying to steady all the emotions swirling inside. The excitement. The hope. The terror of messing up again. And, for the first time ever, the unparalleled determination.

'I'm going to say, "Robbie Cotter, you are the love of my life. No one understands me like you do. No one makes me laugh like you do. No one wants to make me love them as much as you. And no one has ever made me want to spend the rest of my life with them like you do. Will you marry me?"'

Verity shrieked so loudly I thought the glass chandelier was going to shatter all over the entire party.

'Sssh, Verity. You can't get too excited. I don't know what he'll say. I don't know if I'm too late. But I . . . I have to say it. I have to say what's in my heart. I have to finally be honest and then, well, whatever is meant to be will be.'

'Oh, my brave, brave girl.'

She took my hand and ushered me into the fitting room, pulling the heavy gold curtain behind her, leaving Molly outside to hold court with her mob of adoring fans.

She led me to the old dresser and I watched her in the mirror, framed by a constellation of soft light-bulbs, as she proceeded to dress me as she'd done all 'her girls' before me. A hat, gloves, the perfect scarf, the right jewellery. I was already wearing my perfect shoes, my ruby slippers. To get me *home*.

As she worked silently, she was dressing me for my biggest part yet. My own marriage proposal.

At the door of the shop, I took a last look back before I slipped away. All the people who'd been there for me and always would be. Mum, Dad, Tanya, Peter, Lisa, Verity. Verity and Molly huddled in the corner, heads together, nattering away like they'd never been apart. Molly looked up, caught my eye and winked, and I knew that Verity had been telling her all about my Heart Wish. I smiled, thinking how funny that the story of the Heart Wish had now come full circle. I smiled as I caught Lisa snogging the face off Website Man up against a rack of clothes and I only prayed she wasn't going to spill Champagne down that Grace Kelly/Edith Head dress. I watched Mum looping a shrug around Tanya's shoulders and sharing a laugh as they looked into the mirror.

And I felt hope. Hope and excitement for all of our futures.

The sounds of laughter and clinking glasses followed me into the cold night air, gradually fading as I got further from Best Wishes and closer to seven Maple Street. To where my heart was.

I looked up to the million stars drizzled across the night sky and I whispered softly, 'I wish he says yes.'

*The Beginning*

# Acknowledgements

'The path of the second novel never did run smooth, eh?'

For the book that nearly never was, my deepest and most sincere gratitude to my publishers at Penguin for their unreserved patience with me and *I Wished For You*. Thank you so much for withstanding the countless stop-starts when I'd flit off to do another acting job at a week's notice and unsettle all the deadlines once again. And thank you also for understanding that my 'other job' is just as important to me. The book possibly should have been called *I Wished You Were Completed A Year and A Half Ago Like You Were Supposed To Be*. But here it is, better late than never (I would say that, naturally).

So a big huge thank you . . .

To Michael McLoughlin at Penguin Ireland for this incredible second opportunity. I feel so lucky to get to do what I love doing. To Cliona Lewis and Patricia McVeigh for all their help along the way. And a special word of gratitude to Patricia Deevy for your encouragement throughout. Your guidance along the way has been so insightful, and has, hopefully, led me to being a better writer. I just hope that you guys have taken my photo off the dartboard in the office now that I've *finally* delivered the book!

To my editor, Rachel Pierce, for being as enthusiastic about this story as I was; for your insight and wisdom and unparalleled expertise. It is such a joy to work with you. To my copy-editor, Hazel Orme, whose care and meticulous attention to detail was so important in polishing the final book.

To Keith Taylor, Cat Hillerton and Lisa Simmonds in Penguin editorial and production.

To Brian Walker and the Penguin sales team in Ireland and Gemma Shaw and everyone in the UK sales team.

To my literary agent, Faith O'Grady, and everyone who looks after me at the Lisa Richards Agency. I'd be lost without your unstinting guidance, encouragement and, of course, your help in trying to juggle the madness.

To Joanne Byrne for all your help in all that you do!

And, finally, thank you so much to my wonderful family – Mum, Dad, Mark, Paul, Noeleen and my husband, Brian – for your constant support and belief in me. I love you all very much. And to my wonderful friends, ditto.

A special word of thanks to all the fabulous stars and designers of the Hollywood Golden Era for being my inspiration and such glamorous, wonderful muses.

And just one last thank you . . .

To each and every one of you who has bought the book and shared the adventure.

# *He just wanted a decent book to read ...*

Not too much to ask, is it? It was in 1935 when Allen Lane, Managing Director of Bodley Head Publishers, stood on a platform at Exeter railway station looking for something good to read on his journey back to London. His choice was limited to popular magazines and poor-quality paperbacks – the same choice faced every day by the vast majority of readers, few of whom could afford hardbacks. Lane's disappointment and subsequent anger at the range of books generally available led him to found a company – and change the world.

*'We believed in the existence in this country of a vast reading public for intelligent books at a low price, and staked everything on it'*
**Sir Allen Lane, 1902–1970, founder of Penguin Books**

The quality paperback had arrived – and not just in bookshops. Lane was adamant that his Penguins should appear in chain stores and tobacconists, and should cost no more than a packet of cigarettes.

Reading habits (and cigarette prices) have changed since 1935, but Penguin still believes in publishing the best books for everybody to enjoy. We still believe that good design costs no more than bad design, and we still believe that quality books published passionately and responsibly make the world a better place.

So wherever you see the little bird – whether it's on a piece of prize-winning literary fiction or a celebrity autobiography, political tour de force or historical masterpiece, a serial-killer thriller, reference book, world classic or a piece of pure escapism – you can bet that it represents the very best that the genre has to offer.

## Whatever you like to read – trust Penguin.